Second Down

False Start, Book One

Travis Starnes

Signup to get free previews of upcoming books before they're released at

http://tstarnes.com/preview-notification-newsletter/

Contents

Prologue   1

Chapter 1   6

Chapter 2   22

Chapter 3   33

Chapter 4   43

Chapter 5   51

Chapter 6   61

Chapter 7   69

Chapter 8   80

Chapter 9   90

Chapter 10   100

Chapter 11   113

Chapter 12   122

Chapter 13   133

Chapter 14   143

Chapter 15   157

Chapter 16   168

Chapter 17   179

Chapter 18   192

Chapter 19   203

Chapter 20   214

Chapter 21   224

Chapter 22   238

Chapter 23   248

Chapter 24   260

Chapter 25   271

Chapter 26   282

Chapter 27   291

Chapter 28   300

Chapter 29   309

Chapter 30   322

Chapter 31   338

Chapter 32   349

Chapter 33   363

Chapter 34   374

Chapter 35   387

Chapter 36   398

Chapter 37   409

Chapter 38   424

Chapter 39   434

Chapter 40   447

About the author   453

Also by

Prologue

2024

I opened my eyes to the sterile white ceiling of the hospital room, the same view I'd been staring at for weeks now. I almost cursed being awake, since awake meant pain. The doctors were doing what they could, but at this point, it was almost impossible to keep the pain management up.

Half the time, I was so doped up I was barely conscious, which was probably how everyone wanted me to be. I was so close to the end, regardless of what they said about fighting and how strong I was, I didn't want to waste these last few days or hours or however long I had sleeping. I'd sleep forever, soon enough.

I tried not to be bitter about it. I knew it could have been worse. I hadn't lingered for months and months, gone in and out of remission. Hell, I'd been able to skip chemo entirely. By the time I went in to see the doctor about the pains I'd been having, it was too late to do anything. The cancer had spread quickly, eating away at my body like termites through wood.

"Mr. Sims, are you certain you don't want to talk? It might ease your mind," the hospice priest said, just about scaring me out of my bones.

Hell, I'd forgotten he was there. He'd been talking to me as I'd drifted off again. I turned my head slightly, meeting his eyes. I could see he was trying to be kind. To offer sympathy. Part of me wanted to brush him off, but I could also feel it.

Today was the day. I knew it.

I wasn't sure I wanted my last day to be completely silent, with no one to talk to.

"You know," I started, my throat so dry it felt like sandpaper. "I was gonna be somebody once."

"Really?" he said, I think surprised that I'd actually spoken to him finally.

"Youngest varsity quarterback in Wheaton High history. Made starter as a sophomore. Took us to our first state semi-final in fifteen years."

"That's quite an accomplishment," the priest said, but in that humoring 'you peaked in high school' kind of way.

I let out a bitter chuckle that turned into a cough. "Yeah, well, fat lot of good it did me in the end."

"What happened?" he asked gently.

I closed my eyes, memories washing over me. The roar of the crowd, the weight of the football in my hands, and what happened next.

"Dad died. Just after the season ended. He was a sheriff in Midland in the nineties when they had that bad gang problem. Came up on some kids stealing a car, and boom, they just shot him as he got out of his car. The doctors said he went fast, didn't even have time to know what happened. Didn't feel a thing," I said before drifting for a moment. "Bullshit. I sure as hell felt it. After that ... nothing else seemed to matter."

I didn't talk for several minutes, just remembering. Remembering the funeral service, Mom breaking down, Joshua just standing there like a fucking robot. Everyone telling me how great a man he was, how I needed to be the man of the house now, how I had to help my mother.

"I dropped out," I finally said. "She had these headaches that would take her down for days. Migraines. Had to quit her job ... freshman year? I don't remember. She couldn't work. We went on government support and she got disability, but it wasn't enough, so I dropped out and went to work."

"That must have been incredibly difficult."

"Coach tried to talk me out of it. Said I had real potential, you know? That I could go pro if I stuck with it. That I should get my education, which would be really what would help my mom. But we needed the money then, not in eight years or however long it would have taken. Still. Pro. Can you imagine? Instead, I ended up in construction. Spent my life building things for other people while my own shit fell apart."

"That was only a small part of your life. Work isn't all we are. Surely there were happier times?"

"I don't know. Maybe. I mean, I had some laughs, but mostly, it was just … constant struggle. Work, bills, taking care of Mom. Never enough time or money. By the time things settled down, there weren't really any other chances. I was too old to go back to school and I couldn't afford it anyway. So I kept working. Just thinking if I could get a little more, you know? Just a little ahead, I could figure out something. But I never got ahead, and then the job that I'd poured my life into, trying to scrape a little out for myself, it caused this shit. Not that the company would pay my medical bills. Can't prove they gave me the cancer, so they get to make the next chump sick."

"What about friends? Or your family?"

"Do you see anyone here?" I said, trying very hard not to snap at him. "I moved from job to job too much and half the guys I worked with were illegals, so they didn't stay put long. And family? Mom … she was never the same after Dad died. The migraines got worse, and then the depression set in, and then Joshua … man, my little brother. He finished her off."

"I'm not sure I know what that means?"

"He was always a strange kid. Mean, angry all the time. I remember him being such a pain in the ass. But as he got older he got … you don't know who my brother is, do you?"

"I'm sorry. We are given very few personal details, I'm afraid."

"He was the West Texas Strangler."

"Really?"

That had gotten him. The gentle, well-practiced tone slipped in his shock. I didn't bother holding back a chuckle. The one thing I got for having a serial killer for a brother was I one-upped every story anyone else had. I'd used it to get free beers enough nights, that was for damned sure.

"Really. Don't get me wrong, it was a shock, for sure. Like I said, he'd always been strange, but we'd never thought he'd … you know?

3

I heard some people on the news say if Dad hadn't died Joshua would have kept it under control, that Dad's death was what put him over the edge. I know he did those interviews and convinced everyone it was his childhood, but I gotta tell you, he had it easy. Mom doted on him. And he wasn't the normal kid he likes to tell people he was, traumatized by the death of his 'brutal' father. He was a fucking psychopath from day one. After they caught him, it destroyed my mother. Her mind had always been fragile, but that … that was the final straw. She never recovered."

After staring for a moment, the priest started to open his mouth to say something, but I cut him off. I'd done this song and dance a few times. People just don't know what to say to that, so they fall back on platitudes.

"Don't," I said. "Don't try to tell me every family has problems or whatever else you're gonna say. He was crazy, and they pumped him full of shit, and he's gone. What's done is done, I figure …"

My words were cut off as I began another coughing fit. I gripped the bed rails, my body convulsing as it tore through me. Each hack felt like a grinder was scraping my insides raw. I couldn't catch my breath, couldn't stop the violent shaking.

A nurse rushed in just as it started to settle down. She fiddled with the machines, silencing their urgent beeping and checked my vitals, but there wasn't much she could do. I'd turned down the last of the meds and told the docs I didn't want to stay completely doped up all the time, a zombie waiting to die, so there was a limit to what she could give me.

All she could basically do was wait around and mark the time of my death. I saw her exchange a look with the priest. It was the kind of look that said everything without saying a word.

"Would you like to pray together, Blake?" the priest asked as the nurse left the room.

"I've never been the praying type. Don't see the point in starting now."

"Prayer doesn't have to be religious. It can be a wish, an offering to the universe. Sometimes, it's just a way to speak what's in your heart."

I almost said forget it, but … what did I have to lose? I'd held it in all these years. Sure, I'd been pretty bitter, but I hadn't blamed anyone, said it was anyone's fault. Shit happens. You keep living until you don't.

Maybe it was time I told the universe to fuck off. Or maybe ask for what should have been mine for once. I wasn't even sure what I was going to say when I opened my mouth.

"I wish my dad hadn't died. That's where it all went wrong, you know? If I could do it over ... man, I'd do everything differently."

I don't know if the words were supposed to make me feel better, but they didn't. The weight of them pressed down on me, heavier than any construction load I'd ever carried. All those years of struggle, of just trying to keep my head above water. And for what?

"It's never too late to forgive yourself, Blake," the priest said. "It's not your fault. You can still let go of that guilt you've been carrying."

Man, he could see right through me. I turned to look at him, wanting to say something. To argue, maybe. Or to agree. I'm not sure which. I opened my mouth, but I was having trouble getting the words to come out. The air was so hard to push.

"I don't ..." was all I could manage.

Blackness began to drift in from the edges of my vision. The priest, his eyes so kind, went blurry.

And then ... nothing.

Chapter 1

1994

I opened my eyes, trying to figure out what woke me. I finally realized the sound I was hearing was my alarm clock. I reached over and slapped around for it a few times until I hit the button to make it shut up.

Everything felt ... wrong. Out of place. Damn. That dream hit so hard. I blinked a few times, rapidly, trying to shake off the feeling of it. The dream had been so vivid, like one of those where you go through your whole day just to wake up and realize you hadn't done it yet, except this hadn't been 'just a day.' It had been a whole life.

I'd been so old at the end of it. And man, had my life sucked in the dream. Like, really sucked.

I sat up and swung my feet over the edge of the bed, feeling the carpet in my room and hoping to ground myself a little bit. It was just a dream, but it had been so real. More vivid than any dream I'd ever had. I could also remember so much of it. Normally I didn't remember my dreams for shit, so this was a weird feeling. It's like every day of a life I'd never lived was just stuck in my head.

I rubbed my face. Man, I hope this faded, 'cause it was messing with me. Looking over at the clock, reality kicked in and at least got my brain working again. It was eight forty-five, and I was supposed to meet the guys at the high school football field at nine-thirty. We lived just on the edge of town, which meant town was within walking distance, since the whole place was small, but it was mid-August and hot as hell.

Today was the first day of practice and tryouts for the high school football team, and I'd been so excited. High school football was a big deal in Texas, and a gateway to the NFL and everything I'd dreamed of. I'd been in Pee-Wee and played in middle school, but those were nothing compared to the next four years. I had a real chance to do something, and it all started today.

Another flash of memory almost hit me, but I pushed it down. It was so weird. I remembered last night, playing on my Game Boy, too excited to sleep. Just as clearly, I remembered being old, lying on a bed, and talking to a priest.

Man, I was screwed up.

I could hear Mom and Dad moving around downstairs and the smell of coffee, which meant Dad was up. Mom never drank it 'cause she said the caffeine gave her headaches.

I got dressed in comfortable clothes, knowing I was going to be running in the heat all day. I put a few things in my small gym bag and headed downstairs.

I was still trying to shake off the feelings caused by the dream. Josh and Mom were sitting at the breakfast table already, eating. For a kid who never did anything, Josh always got up early, which seemed weird to me. I'd sleep till two if I didn't have anything to do.

As I reached the bottom of the stairs and walked into the kitchen toward the breakfast nook, Dad walked in from the living room already wearing his uniform for work. I froze in place the moment I saw him, a wave of sadness crashing over me so suddenly and intensely that I had to grip the doorframe to steady myself.

"Whoa there, champ," Dad said, reaching out for me. "You okay? You look like you've seen a ghost."

I blinked once, and then twice, shaking off the feeling. "Yeah, I'm good. Just … didn't sleep great."

"Today's a big day, Blake. You need to be on your A-game for the tryouts."

"I know, I know. Excited, I guess. Couldn't really settle down last night."

He slapped me on the arm and gave me one of those smiles of his. Damn, that dream really messed me up. It was so intense.

I went to the cabinet, grabbed a bowl, and poured myself some cereal, using the moment with my back to everyone to collect myself. I was feeling kind of settled when I turned around and went to sit down. I couldn't help sneaking glances at Dad. He was right there, alive and well, sipping his coffee and leafing through the morning paper. Why was I feeling like this?

"Yeah, gotta be at your best to run around and bash your head into other idiots," Joshua said, looking up from where he was reading the back of the cereal box.

God, he was such a pain in my ass. He was almost three years younger than me and was starting middle school this year. He'd been annoying as a kid, but ever since he started hitting puberty, he'd become a raging asshole.

"Shut up. All you do is sit in your room and read comics like some kind of loser. You have no idea what it takes to play football."

"Yeah, it's real hard chasing a ball around. You're the fucking loser!" he said, screaming that last part, going from zero to sixty in a heartbeat like he always did.

I turned to Mom, expecting her to say something about Josh's language. But she just sighed and rubbed her temples.

"Blake, leave your brother alone," she said, sounding tired.

"What? He started it!" I protested. "Did you not hear what he just said?"

"I said knock it off, both of you. I've got a headache, and I don't want to hear it."

I clenched my jaw, frustration bubbling up inside me. Of course, Josh was getting away with it again. He always did. I was about to argue further when I caught sight of Josh's face.

There was something in his eyes, something cold and empty. For a split second, I saw him older, sitting in a courtroom wearing an orange jumpsuit. The him in my dream, as the judge listed off crimes too despicable to even think about.

It was just a dream, but the look in Josh's eyes … there was just *nothing there*.

I let it drop.

"Whatever," I muttered, shoving a spoonful of cereal into my mouth.

Dad set down his paper and picked up his coffee cup. "So, how're you feeling about tryouts, champ? Think you've got a shot at quarterback?"

He was playing mediator, like he always did when the rest of us started shouting. Maybe it was because of the stuff he saw at work, but he never let any of our petty stuff get to him. He was always the one to calm everyone down and get us back in our own corners.

I always admired that about him.

"Yeah, I'm pretty sure I'll get the starting spot for the freshman team. Unless I totally blow it, you know?"

"Good. I like that kind of confidence."

"I don't know if it's confidence," I said through a mouth full of cereal. "I just know the competition. There was this kid from Midland who was supposed to give me a run for my money, but I heard his family's moving to Houston. So that helps."

"What about JV or varsity?"

"Maybe JV, but I doubt it. And varsity?" I shook my head. "Kenneth Ward's still got that locked down. He's a senior this year, thank God. Otherwise, I'd be warming the bench till I graduated."

"Hey now, don't sell yourself short. You've got talent, Blake. If you work hard, who knows? You might surprise yourself."

I just kind of shrugged, but when I met his eyes, the wave of sadness hit me again. It was so strong I had to look away, pretending to be super interested in my cereal. How long was this dream going to screw with me?

"I'm going to go lay down. I put your lunch in the fridge. Make sure you grab it before you go," Mom said as she got up, set her dishes in the sink, and headed for their room.

She'd had it rough in my dream, too, although I didn't have the sadness when I looked at her, as I did when I looked at my dad. I could remember things about her from the dream, but for whatever reason, they didn't hit as hard.

"Thanks, Mom," I called after her.

Dad glanced at his watch. "Speaking of going, I've got to hit the road. I can drop you off at the school on my way to work if you want."

I nodded, grateful for the chance to spend a few more minutes with him. Plus, it was already hot as hell and I didn't want to make the ten-minute walk into town.

"Yeah, that'd be great."

As I stood up to clear my bowl, Josh muttered something under his breath. I chose to ignore it, not wanting to start another fight. But I couldn't shake the uneasy feeling in my gut as I looked at him.

"You coming, Blake?" Dad called from the front door.

"Yeah, just a sec!" I shouted back, grabbing my bag and lunch from the fridge.

As I headed out, I caught one last glimpse of Josh, hunched over his cereal bowl, but looking at me, a creepy assed smile on his face. The image from my dream flashed again … him in that orange jumpsuit. I shook my head, trying to clear it.

It was just a stupid dream, right?

They had a person out in front of the gym directing us where to go. We had temp lockers where we could drop our stuff, although they had no locks on them, so they warned everyone not to leave anything valuable in them.

I had left my wallet at home for that exact reason. I didn't know they'd let us put our stuff in the locker rooms, but even if they hadn't, I wasn't crazy about the idea of my wallet just sitting in my bag on the bleachers. Then I had this strange thought where I almost asked where we could leave our cell phones when I realized that was nuts. No one our age had cell phones! The per-minute costs on those things were crazy. Hell, I'd never even *seen* someone with a cell phone, except on TV.

And yet, I had a distinct image in my head of holding this … rectangular screen kind of like a big calculator, and I knew it was a cell phone, even though it was nothing like the cell phones I'd seen on TV.

Then it hit me. The image was from my dream, again.

I shook off the thought. So weird!

After dropping our stuff, we headed out to the field. They had two sets of bleachers, and they had the freshmen go to one side and everyone else go to the other. Most of the coaches went that way, while two followed us.

I recognized pretty much everyone on our side of the bleachers since the whole county only had one middle school and one elementary school, so we'd all been together since we were little, for the most part. We all played in the same pee-wee league and on the same middle school team.

I knew these guys better than I knew probably anyone else. There were a few exceptions. There were about four faces I didn't recognize and two faces that were missing, although both those kids I'd known were moving near the end of middle school. The new faces were probably people who moved into the area over the summer or whatever. We didn't get a lot of transfers in, but every couple of years, a new kid would show up. The four I was seeing were more than I remembered at one time, but middle school to high school was a big leap, so there was probably a reason.

Equally surprising was the coach who followed us, carrying a clipboard. Especially, since he was followed by Mr. Plummer, who owned the feed store in town, which serviced just about every farm and ranch in a seventy-five-mile radius.

"Alright, listen up!" the younger guy said. "I'm Coach Heidemann, and I'll be leading the freshman team this year. Helping me will be Coach Plummer, who I'm sure most of you know from the feed store. He's volunteering his time to help out this season. While you may know him as the guy who helped your grandma figure out her azaleas last year, when he's on this field, he's a coach! You will respect him as such, *is that clear?*"

We just kind of looked from him to Mr. Plummer.

"I said, is that clear!" Coach said again.

"Yes, Coach," we all responded.

Mr. ... or rather Coach Plummer chuckled in that genial way he always had about him and said, "Glad to be here, boys."

"Alright. Now, I know you're all itching to make JV or Varsity, but with very few exceptions, you'll be starting on the freshman team. This is where you learn the Wheaton way of football and how things work at the high school level. Now I know you were hot stuff in middle school or club ball. This, however, is *five-A football*. It's a whole different kind of ball than you're used to. It's gonna be harder, faster, and more aggressive than anything you've played before. The guys who excel in this program go on to D1 and D2 schools in college. We've even had a few make it all the way to the pros."

He paused to let that sink in. I think we all had dreams of getting recruited into a good program, which was the next step on the way to the big goal. The NFL.

"Now, don't think of being put on the freshman team as a sign that you're less important or not good enough. This is your training ground. We're bridging the gap between playing as kids and playing like men."

When he paused, Coach Plummer said, "Y'all are gonna learn a lot here. More than just football."

Coach Heidemann nodded. "The next two weeks are crucial. We'll see who's cut out for this and who's not. You'll be run hard and taught our system, and those of you who fit in will make the team."

I wasn't worried. I knew he was probably right, and this was going to be a whole new level of ball, but I knew I could keep up with anyone on these bleachers. Some of these guys, though, looked nervous. Especially the four new guys.

"Alright," Coach Heidemann clapped his hands together. "First things first - we warm up. Let's run!"

For the next three hours, we ran drills. It was the middle of August and it felt like we were practicing under a heat lamp as we ran, did footwork, and basic fundamentals. So far, everything was stuff I knew, although I hadn't really played much since the season ended the previous fall and hadn't done any drills since middle school ended.

I probably should have spent a little more time conditioning and a little less time goofing off all summer because we were only halfway through and I felt wrung out.

We all sat on the bleachers and pulled out our lunches. Thankfully, the school had Gatorades and water, so we at least had something cold to drink. I found a place with my friends from middle school and pulled out the sandwich Mom made me. I was starving.

"Did you see that new kid eat it during sprints?" Elijah, my best friend, snickered and elbowed Hunter.

"Yeah. Fucking hysterical. He was, like, two seconds from crying," Hunter laughed as they both looked down at the guy, who very clearly heard them.

Normally, I thought Elijah was hysterical, but for some reason, he was rubbing me the wrong way. They were just kind of being jackasses for no reason. The kid, Miguel I think he said his name was, didn't do anything. Yeah, he'd fallen down, but he wasn't the only one. Jake, who was part of our group, tripped on the tires and no one said anything to him. They were also being a lot louder than normal, I think so he would hear them.

"Guys, lay off," I said before I'd really even thought about it.

Elijah looked at me like I'd grown a second head, but then kind of shrugged and switched topics.

"Did you guys see Brenda? Man, her ti..."

I more or less stopped listening. For once, I was hungry and just wanted to eat. But also, everything he was doing, stuff I knew I would have contributed to before, was now annoying me, and I honestly just didn't want to deal with it.

I also started having the weirdest sense of déjà vu all of a sudden. I could almost remember the first passing drills, which weren't even starting until the afternoon session, and feeling sick as a dog. My passes sucked and I wasn't hitting anything. Again, it took me a second to realize I was remembering that stupid dream. It felt real though, and Gabriel was here.

He'd sat on the bench seventh and eighth grade, only playing when I needed a breather or we were up enough to let the B team go in. He wasn't a bad guy, he'd just never had ... it. And yet, in my dream, he completely out-threw me that day, while I struggled. I remembered, halfway through the session, running to a garbage can and throwing up.

He'd managed to get the starting slot, only to lose it to me during the second game when he threw five interceptions in the first quarter. I remember, or dream me remembered, how everything clicked after that and I'd gone on the next year to JV with a clear path to Varsity my Junior year. I also remembered always wondering what happened on the first day of tryouts that made me so sick and almost screwed everything up.

I don't know why, but just then something else hit me, but not from the dream this time. I remembered Joshua's eyes and how he'd looked at me this morning. That creepy-ass smile of his. I don't know what made me think of it, but I sniffed the sandwich, then I lifted up the bread and put my nose right next to the ham and sniffed again.

It was incredibly faint. So much so that I barely noticed it over the smell of the ham, sweaty guys, and fresh-cut grass. The smell of bleach. It was so faint I had to sniff twice to figure out what the smell was, but it was definitely there.

There was no way that was an accident. Not so little that I couldn't smell it without putting my nose right up to the meat. The little son-of-a-bitch poisoned my fucking sandwich. I would have been sick as hell, although it was so little maybe it wouldn't have put me in the hospital.

I was hit again by the dream memory of feeling sick and throwing up, ruining my first day of tryouts.

"What's wrong?" Jake asked, one of the other guys in my group of friends, seeing my face. "Bad mayo or something?"

I didn't say anything for a moment, shaken. "Uh, yeah. Think it might have turned. I'm gonna toss it and grab something from the vending machine."

He shrugged and went back to his sandwich as I got up and tossed my whole lunch in the trash, even the sealed bag of chips. I'd have to start making my own lunches from now on. I went into the locker room and pulled out a few loose bills I'd stuffed in the side pouch of my bag, in case I got hungry.

More than anything, though, I was having trouble shaking the dream.

The chips and candy bar from the machine weren't really enough to get me through the rest of practice, but I'd live. Besides, we were breaking out into groups in the afternoon, and I was passing to some of the wide receivers, which was so much better than footwork and fundamentals.

I was in my element and feeling confident.

I was up first and Elijah was up to run the first route. We'd done this a hundred times in middle school and even a bunch of times over the summer to get ready for this, although we hadn't gone hard enough to actually stay in shape.

"Alright, let's see what you've got, Sims!" Coach Heidemann called out.

I grabbed the ball and dropped back as Elijah took off, running fifteen yards out and cutting left hard. It wasn't a hard pass, and he was undefended, but I nailed him right in the numbers. We reset and went again, each time, one of the guys would run out a little further and bam, I'd hit him running.

Honestly, I was on fire. I couldn't miss, although the new kid, Miguel, the one who'd tripped earlier, fumbled two of my passes. I could hear Elijah and a few of the others laughing loudly at him, making comments, but I could see the guy was nervous.

"Hey, you okay?" I asked as he came running back and handed me the ball.

"Yeah, just ..."

"I get it. Just get your hands on it and pull it into your chest. You're leaving your hands out, which is way harder. Just pull it in and use your body to hold it in place."

"Yeah," he said. "I knew that. Stupid."

"Hey, no. I get it. It's kind of nerve-wracking, with everyone watching. You've got it this time," I said and then yelled at Coach, "Can we try that again?"

Coach gave an 'after you' gesture and we set up again.

"Hike," I said and Miguel took off.

He was fast; I'd give him that. He got down twenty-five yards and cut left, turning just as the ball was coming in. He got his hands around it and pulled it in, hard against his chest, completing the reception.

Slowly, he held the ball up in victory and I gave him a little nod. He had pretty good hands, he was just a little nervous. Elijah had shut up at least, which was something.

We kept running plays, with me and Gabriel switching off. I'd like to say I hit every pass, but at least I'd hit most of them. Gabriel did okay close in, but anything over twenty-five yards or so and his accuracy became questionable. With that, he'd be able to do some short dinks, but he was never going to make serious passing plays.

We switched it up, with multiple runners, where we were supposed to look at one, and then throw to the other, or look at two, and throw to a third. Then they put in some of the defensive guys, who'd been off working on their own, to try and block the passes.

That's when things got really interesting. I was killing it, cutting balls in just out of their reach, dropping them down where they couldn't be touched, something I'd learned last year. Even with defenders, the majority of my passes were finding a receiver.

After about an hour, Coach Heidemann blew his whistle. "Sims! Neiva! Over here, now!"

I jogged over, Gabriel falling in step beside me. Coach's expression was hard to read.

"What's up, Coach?" I asked, still riding high on getting to throw the ball again.

"Sims, what the hell was that out there?"

"Uh, passing drills?" I said, a little unsure of what he was getting at.

"That wasn't passing drills. That was playground nonsense. You're running around like a chicken with its head cut off, improvising instead of throwing to your assigned man."

I opened my mouth to say something, but then shut it again. Which might be the first time I ever shut up when being called out on my plays. In middle school, I'd been something of a loudmouth, always arguing with the coach.

I don't know why I shut up this time.

"Look, that might've flown in middle school, but this is high school ball. There's a right way and a wrong way to play, and what you were doing out there, that's the wrong way."

"I ... uhh ..."

"I'm not trying to chew you out, and I could see how much fun you were having out there, but this isn't about fun. This is about *learning the system*, and you're not doing that. Trust me, this come-to-Jesus moment happens every year to our freshman QB. That's why I brought Neiva over, too. You both need to hear this."

Gabriel looked like he was about to barf on his shoes.

"You've got some good natural ability, Sims, but if you want to progress, you need to learn how to play real football, not just backyard ball."

"Yes, sir," I said, but it happened again.

Deja vu. I'd had this conversation with Coach Heidemann in my dream, only a little later in the year. Then it hit me, Coach Heidemann was in my dream, as was Coach Plummer. Hell, all of the coaches were. I knew Coach Heidemann was hired last year so maybe I saw him at a game, but I thought they'd said this was Coach Plummer's first year helping the freshmen, so how was he in my dream?

So weird.

Coach pulled out two small binders from his bag. "I'm sending you both home with these. It's what we give all our freshman QBs. We're gonna start simple - reads and progressions."

He handed us each a binder. I flipped mine open, seeing diagrams and play breakdowns.

"Sims, this is what you need to focus on," Coach said, tapping the binder. "Understanding where to throw the ball and why. Each play has its own read and progression, and it's there for a reason. Neiva, I want you to look at this, but the first thing we need to do is work on your mechanics. I'll see about getting you both some time with Coach Easley when he starts working with the JV QBs on this stuff."

"Sounds good, Coach," Gabriel said.

"Alright, we're about done for the day, so both of you get out of my sight. I want you both ready to come out tomorrow and work. Really work. Got it?"

"Yes, Coach," we said in unison.

"Sims," he said as we both started to walk away. "I saw what you did for Hernandez out there. That's the kind of thing I like to see. I can teach you everything in that binder, but leadership, that's where it's at. You're the QB and I expect you to lead the team. I wanna see more of that out there, got it?"

"Yeah."

"Good man. Alright, get lost," he said, swatting me on the leg as I turned and jogged off the field.

I had managed to put it out of my head while I was playing, but on the way back to the locker room, it all hit me again. The sandwich, the speech, the faces I knew that I didn't actually know.

It was all so weird. And the dream still hadn't faded. It had been all day and I could remember every moment of it just as well as I could when I had woken up.

What the hell was going on?!

I was still in my head when I got to the locker room. The whole morning had been so weird; it was honestly hard to stay focused. I was amazed I'd done as well as I had during practice, but then I'd always been able to focus once I started playing football.

Coach had always told me that's what gave me my edge. Or was that, my coach would tell me that? It was honestly hard sometimes to keep my memories straight and the dream memories straight. I needed to get my head screwed back in place.

I was still thinking, going round and round about everything, when we got back into the locker room and started changing our shoes. The other stuff I could wear home, since there was no reason to use a locker room shower if you didn't have to, but I wasn't going to walk out on the asphalt in cleats. A good pair was hard to break in, and I didn't want to wear them out any faster than I needed to.

The locker room was divided just like … like it should have been, with guys who played together last year all kind of grouped together and the freshmen pushed off into one corner near the showers. When we'd been checked in this morning they'd directed us to this corner, making sure to tell us none of these spots were permanent. Teams had their lockers together, so we'd get our assigned locker once we got placed on a team. That was true for everyone, even those who knew what team they were going to be on already, like some of the seniors and basically all of the freshmen.

I was putting on my shoes, and going slow as hell as I was thinking about the locker I would have this year in my dream, since I was on the freshmen team then too. Then I saw Elijah walking up to Miguel, the guy who'd tripped during practice. He was cocky as hell, practically strutting, flanked by Mason and Hunter. I knew that walk, and the look on his face.

As he walked by the bench where Miguel had his stuff, his arm swept out, knocking Miguel's bag on the ground, upside down, all the stuff pouring out.

"Sorry," he said, not even bothering to hide his laugh.

"Watch it," Miguel said, going down to a knee to start scooping his stuff up.

"You watch it, fucking wetback. What are you even doing here."

Miguel shot up to his feet. "What the hell did you just say?"

"You heard me," Elijah sneered.

Miguel stepped over the bench and got right in Elijah's face. "I'm here to play football, jackass. Same as everyone else."

"What you're gonna be doing is riding the bench. You better not even be thinking about trying to take one of our spots."

He gestured at the rest of us, including me in his sweep. I am not even sure why I did it, but I half slid down the bench, away from them, as if to make it clear I wasn't part of any of this.

"I'll do any damn thing I please. If you think you're better, then you need to be better," Miguel said, and shoved Elijah hard.

Elijah stumbled back, more surprised than off balance, I think. He was pissed. He launched forward, slamming a forearm into Miguel's chest, pushing him hard against a locker, almost causing him to fall backward over the bench. A little to the right and that could have been a lot messier, since the bench was close enough to the locker that he definitely would have hit his head on it. The clang of Miguel hitting the locker was loud enough to get the attention of everyone else in the locker room, at least those with line of sight to our corner, to stop what they were doing and look over at us.

Miguel's fist was cocked back, ready to fly, when two of the other freshmen, I think their names were Jamal and Tyrell, came up from the side and grabbed him, pulling him back from Elijah. After a beat, Mason did the same thing to Elijah, although from the look on his face, I think he was hoping one of them would push him while he 'pulled Elijah back,' so he could get in on the fight.

Mason liked to fight and had been in the vice-principal's office a bunch of times in eighth grade.

"What the hell's going on back there?" one of the coaches yelled from the other end of the locker room where their offices were.

Miguel, not breaking eye contact with Elijah, responded without hesitation, "Nothing, Coach."

Mason moved closer, stepping into Miguel's space, crowding all three of them. "You better watch yourself. You and your *boys*."

We could all hear what he meant by 'boys' and Jamal clenched his fist. Instead of holding Miguel back, it looked like he wanted to throw down with Mason. Tyrell at least had better sense, pulling both of them back.

"They're not worth it," Tyrell said quietly as he pushed both of them away from the confrontation.

I just sat on the bench, sneakers half-laced, watching. Well, watching and remembering, as more memories hit me. These weren't dream memories though, they were my memories. In middle school, I would have been right with Elijah and Mason. Hell, I would have been leading them, making sure Miguel knew his place.

I'm not sure I would have put some of the overtones on it, but I definitely would have enjoyed the game of it. Jockeying for position, making sure my place was staked out in the social hierarchy. It would have been fun.

Then I had another memory, this one clearly from my dream, when I was older than I was now. Maybe in my twenties, but who knows? I saw myself on a construction site, looking tired and annoyed as a few of the older guys made comments they thought I couldn't hear about peaking in high school. Years of memories of being the butt of jokes.

I remember hating every minute of it. Yet, when it had been my turn, I hadn't thought about it twice. Had I been a dick?

"He won't last a week," Hunter said to Elijah, pulling him and Mason in the other direction now that it was clear the confrontation had died down.

"Blake, you coming?" Elijah asked as they got to the doorway, headed out to the parking lot.

"Yeah ... in a minute."

He shrugged and walked out with the other guys. I looked from them back to the guys left in the locker room, and Miguel caught my eye. I gave him a weak smile, hoping he saw it as a silent apology. He just shook his head and turned away from me, joining the other guys.

As I walked out, I felt a little sick. I'd always thought I was one of the good guys. Realizing I wasn't was a serious reality check.

Chapter 2

I was lying on my bed, listening to the ceiling fan go round and round, both tired but also not wanting to just lie here because I would have to deal with my own thoughts too much.

Today had been another brutal practice, so much so that one of the sophomores had gotten heat stroke and started vomiting by the stands. I had drunk a lot, more than most of the guys actually, and it had been hell on me. I couldn't figure out why none of the other guys were bringing much water with them and were just trying to push through, even though we were running all day without shade in the glaring sun.

It was another thing on the long list of things I had started noticing, and it was really bugging me. It had been two days since the dream and I still couldn't shake it. I hadn't had it again, but I could still remember every damn detail of it.

Every time I looked at my dad, I remembered the funeral I had gone to in the dream, and every time I looked at my brother, I remembered seeing him in court. Weirder than that, though, was that I was remembering some stuff that happened over the last two days from the dream, which meant I had dreamed it before it happened.

Like, I remembered that kid getting heat stroke, 'cause he puked partially on the track and Coach Wilson had gotten on him for it, and sure enough, as soon as he started, the coach was yelling for him to get off the track. The exact same words.

I also remembered all the hazing Elijah and the guys were doing to the new guys. If anything, the run-in between Miguel and Elijah on the first day had only made things worse, with him, Mason, and the rest taking every opportunity to get digs in on them or show them up. It was exactly as it was in my dream, except in my dream I had participated rather than been upset by it. It was like everything was playing out how I remembered it, except for me.

Today, Mason had been going off on Tyrell for practically the whole game, until he said something about Tyrell's mother and Tyrell almost threw a punch. He would have had Connor not grabbed him and pulled him back. I wanted to say something. To step in and defuse it, but I hadn't.

I had been friends with Elijah and the rest since all the way back to elementary school. We had all been in the same grade, and the same class, since we were little kids, and they had been my friends the whole time. We had had our birthday parties together, and we had hung out at each other's houses. We were our own little gang.

And I hated it.

Even a week ago, I had still been on board with all the dumbass shit we did. Hell, it had only been a month since we snuck out one night and took all the street cones they had around the holes they were fixing on Broad Street and carried them over to Main Street, using them to divert traffic into the oncoming lane, like the workers had done that one time they had repaved all of Main Street. I had laughed with the other guys when cars would follow the cones and then have to swerve to avoid the cars coming the other way, whose drivers had no sign or cones to warn them they would suddenly be head-on with another car.

It was obvious to me now how stupid and dangerous that was. Had there been an accident and they discovered we had done that, I could have gone to jail, but at the time, I had thought it was hilarious.

That was bad and obviously I was a jerk; but why, all of a sudden, did I realize how stupid it was when I knew for a fact it wouldn't have fazed me a few days ago? It seemed crazy that this dream would mess with me like this, especially days later.

And it left me in a dilemma as to what to do about Elijah and the rest of the guys, one that I hadn't decided what I was going to do about yet. All I knew was that I wasn't going to be able to keep standing off to the side and hope no one noticed me, but I wasn't going to be able to join in with them either.

That really only left me with one choice, but that one kind of sucked, too.

I was just starting to think about how I'd go about dealing with this when I heard something, pulling me out of my head. I knew it wasn't Joshua. He'd been in his room, next to mine, and I hadn't heard him come out, and the noise was coming from downstairs. It took a few more seconds to realize I was hearing my dad raising his voice, which was notable by itself.

My dad had never been one of those 'scream at the top of your lungs' kind of parents. Honestly, he never even gave us spankings. He usually went with the 'I'm really disappointed in you' thing, and sometimes stacked groundings on top of it.

Looking back at the moment, after my realization of what a shit I'd been, I wasn't sure if that was a good thing or not, but I guess it was just his personality. He was always the mediator, always the one telling everyone we'd figure it out.

Which made him yelling notable. More so because it was clear he was yelling at my mom. I got out of bed and crept to the top of the stairs, leaning against the wall out of sight and listening hard, since it sounded like they were in the kitchen, and the stairs led right to it.

"... to shout. I was just saying we need to address this before school starts," Dad was saying. "Joshua's grades tanked last year, and now he's been kicked out of the Y program. I'm not sure what we're going to do. You're having a tough time with sick days. You can't start taking off to pick him up every day. We need to deal with this behavior before it gets worse."

"It's probably just a phase, Tom. Besides, I'm not sure why we've singled Joshua out. Blake's had his own problems and you don't seem to have an issue with him, or did you forget the night the sheriff brought him home drunk this summer?"

"And we punished him for that. But this is different, Heather, and you know it. He scared that woman, and if what she said is true ..."

"It isn't. She just doesn't like him because he's shy. If he'd really told her that, she would have called the sheriff and she didn't. She just wanted to be able to kick him out without giving us our deposit back."

"Come on, Heather. If this was the first time, okay. But combined with the thing at school last year, it's not. And you know it."

"Why are you always on him but giving Blake and his hoodlum friends a pass. We've talked about this, Tom. I will not treat our children differently just because they act differently. I know you relate to Blake more 'cause he's into sports and Joshua's the sensitive and quiet type, but that doesn't make him worse."

"That's not fair."

"I think it is, and I won't stand for it. Joshua's fine. Yes, he's very imaginative and I'll admit he might not be as good with people as we'd like him to be, but he's still a kid."

"Which is the time he should have friends or be out playing. He's always in his room and when he does come out, he just wanders off by himself. I'm worried he's too cut off."

I could hear Dad wanting to say weird, but not saying it. He wasn't wrong. Joshua was weird. The things he said sometimes, or the way he looked at people, like he was plotting. And I remembered the thing at school last year. He brought a note with the names of some of the other kids in class on it, and some of the kids said he told them it was the order he'd 'take each of them out.'

The school had called Mom and Mom had blown it off like she always did. At the time, I just kind of ignored it except to make jokes about my creepy little brother, since word had reached the middle school, which was across the street from the elementary school and all the kids rode the same buses. There'd been jokes comparing him to that guy at UT back in the sixties and Carrie, but honestly it had helped my notoriety having the crazy brother, so I just rolled with it. Besides, he and I had never been exactly close.

Of course, that was then. After the dream and what he'd done in it, I'd started looking at him differently. Watching him. He was creepy. It put everything he'd done into a new context, and I honestly thought Dad wasn't going far enough.

Not that Mom would listen. Joshua was the baby of the family, and he'd always been special to her. Also, I hadn't made it easy. Like the realization I was having about Elijah and my friends, I was also having some thoughts about myself and how I'd been behaving at home, too. As much as I'd been a dick to other kids, teachers, and pretty much anyone else I could find that would get a laugh out of my friends, I'd been worse to my parents.

The visit from the sheriff was because we'd set fire to the nativity scene in front of First Baptist Church the previous Christmas for ... I actually couldn't remember why we'd done it. Probably, someone made a stupid joke or something. The Sheriff caught us and took us to my dad, to let him settle it instead of arresting us, out of professional courtesy to a fellow cop.

Mom had been pissed. She'd always been super religious, more so than Dad, who went to church on Sundays and special occasions but otherwise didn't have much to do with it. Mom had been outraged. She'd demanded I stop hanging out with Elijah and the other kids and made me talk to Pastor Green about how I was going to go to hell if I didn't shape up.

"Just ... leave him be. He's getting to that age, and will calm down eventually," Mom said. "I have a headache and need to go lie down."

I heard Mom leave, probably to go to their bedroom which was downstairs, and I could just picture Dad standing there, arms crossed with that look he got when people were being stubborn. His cop face.

I made my way back to my room as quietly as I could. I honestly didn't know if Mom was right or Dad was, although I suspected it was Dad. Either way, Josh wasn't my problem. I had enough to deal with without having to worry about him.

"Alright, let's see how it looks," Coach Heidemann said, waving us back onto the field.

Everyone was keyed up for today's practice, and we'd been running hard all day. Today was the last full day of practice, with team selections to be announced the following day and school starting on Monday. Everyone wanted to make the team, although Elijah had this idea that he was somehow going to be one of the few freshmen to ever get selected for junior varsity.

He'd been good all week, there was no doubt about it, but I knew we were all going to end up on the freshman team. Well, I didn't know, but I remember that being what happened in my dream life, as I thought about it. True, it was only a dream, but nearly everything was happening exactly as it had in the dream life, which was making me just accept that things would end up the same as they did in my dream life.

Sure, some things had happened differently, but there almost seemed to be a reason for that. Like, by this point in my dream life, I was more or less riding the bench and Gabriel was getting most of the downs, all because I got super sick that first day and screwed up. But I knew why that was different. In my dream life, I'd eaten the weird-tasting sandwich and here, I'd sniffed it and found that Josh had tampered with it ... and I'd only checked it *because* of the dream.

Also true was that things were different with me and the guys. And again, I think I had the dream to thank for that. Every time they started, I remembered how the older dream me was treated for those first several years, and I felt bad for him. While it's humbling for a dream to point out you used to be a horrible person, I was pretty sure without it, I would be right in there with them.

Hell, in my dream life, I *had* been right there with them, bullying the new guys practically off the team, except for Connor, who ended up turning on the other three and joining us.

But, in that life, even playing pretty much the same level of ball, none of us had made junior varsity, so it seemed like a reasonable bet that none of us would. I was still playing hard though, because I remembered blowing my chance to start at QB in the dream life. I didn't want to blow it again.

We ran out to the field and set up. Tyrell, who was trying out for center, was in front of me. He was actually beating out Mason, who had been my center all through middle school. Not only was he bigger than Mason, but a lot of Mason's bulk was ... soft. Tyrell was like a brick wall. He'd tackled me in some drills two days before, and even going easy, it had felt like being hit by a truck.

Mason had actually been moved to the defensive team, which pissed him off to no end.

We were doing a running play, which was Coach Heidemann's go-to move. I guess at the freshman level, most QBs didn't get enough time to really learn passing, so a lot of our playbook was running plays, with occasional short dinking passes. Coach Holloway did things a little differently. He liked more of a passing game and tended to use throwing plays a lot more. I think they planned it like this, a little passing in freshman, about half and half on JV, and then really breaking out on varsity, to give new QBs room to really learn the game.

It was another reason why I knew I wasn't getting off the freshman team. They had a guy who started where I was last year and was on JV now, going through the process.

And it worked.

Wheaton had six all-district and three all-state QBs in the last ten years, which was coincidentally when Coach Holloway came to Wheaton. That was saying something since Texas took football so seriously, so being all-state here would put you in contention for consideration nationwide. In the last seven years, every varsity QB from Wheaton had gotten an offer to play in college. Sure, not all had been Pac-10 schools, but they'd all been D1 schools at the very least.

So, I couldn't exactly knock his process.

I positioned myself behind Tyrell, looked left then right, to ensure everyone was set and ready, and said, "Set. Hut."

There were no audibles or anything, since we all knew the plays that were happening, which was going to make this much harder than it would be in a real game, where the defense couldn't just set up for the exact play we were going to do every time. There would be days where we did it for real, with Coach Heidemann running the offense and Coach Plummer running the defense. But today was not that day.

We were running an inside trap which, if everything went perfectly, Tyrell would push forward into Mason, their defensive right tackle, and Connor would cut right behind him pushing their defensive left tackle. In theory, that should open up a hole down the center that Hunter could blast through and pick up some yards.

It started off great. As soon as Tyrell snapped the ball, he pushed forward like a freight train, smashing into Mason, pushing him back several steps. At the same moment, Victor, our right offensive guard hit their left defensive tackle, kind of glancing off him, just to slow him down a second and then pushed through to the center lineman.

Connor had already crossed behind Tyrell, and then all but missed as the defensive lineman sidestepped, pushing Connor down as he did, causing Connor to faceplant. This left the lineman wide open as Hunter started to go through what should have been an opening. He did what every defensive tackle wanted to do. He planted Hunter so deep in the ground, all we needed was the tombstone to bury him.

The coach blew a whistle, already starting out to us.

"What the hell was that?!" he yelled. "This is a simple play and we're gonna run it a lot this year, but everyone has to do their job for this to work. Nielsen, you have got to hold your block. If you don't, the whole play falls apart. And Forde, you can't just lower your head and expect the hole to be there. These aren't training dummies and the defensive line is gonna try to stop us, so sometimes plays don't go as planned. You gotta read and adjust. You ran right into Hoffman like a damn present."

"Sorry, Coach," Connor said as Hunter pushed himself off the ground.

"Take a minute, regroup, and let's try that again," Coach said, heading back to the sidelines.

I had a memory of Coach Holloway yelling at us, again from the dream life. Coach Heidemann was always more composed than Coach Holloway, who would have ripped into us and had us doing laps for that kind of miss.

As soon as the coach was out of earshot, Hunter got right into Connor's face.

"Are you a fucking idiot? Learn to do your fucking job so I don't have to get my ass reamed over your stupidity.

I actually kind of liked Connor. He was built like an ox and I bet if they really went at it, Connor could drop him if he wanted to, but he didn't seem like the fighting type. He knew he'd messed up, I guess, because he didn't say anything.

29

Which only pissed off Hunter more.

"What are you even doing out here? Shouldn't you be back on the farm with all your other inbred family? You're a waste of goddamn space."

Connor might not be the fighting type, but Hunter kept going, jabbing his finger into Connor's chest.

"You're just a dumbass redneck who doesn't know shit. It's football, dumbass. You hit people. How hard can that be? You're just a fat farm kid who needs to go back to homeschooling. Go back to shoveling pig shit or whatever you people do in between sleeping with your sisters."

I saw Connor's fists clench at his sides, his jaw tightening. This was about to get ugly fast. I actually remember the fight between Hunter and Connor, although I hadn't known Connor's name in my dream life. I'd been way over on the bench, but I remember Connor taking a swing at Hunter and getting kicked out, banned from the team.

Was this that?

I wasn't on the bench this time though, and Hunter was the one instigating it instead of resetting and just running the play again.

"Back off, Hunter," I said, stepping between them and pushing Connor back a step. "It's practice. We're all here to learn."

"What the hell, Blake?" Hunter said, looking genuinely shocked. "You're defending them now?"

"We're all on the same team, Hunter. Everyone makes mistakes. I just want to play football and stop with all the drama."

"What has been with you lately?" Elijah said, coming up from the side. "You've been so goddamn soft lately."

"What's up with me is you've been on these guys all week, and they've been busting their asses just as hard as any of us."

"They're dragging us down, is what you mean. They're dead weight. A bunch of no-talent losers who're just going to slow us down when the season starts."

"They aren't making any more mistakes than anyone out here. It's been a week, guys. One week. And they've already picked up a lot. Just cut them some slack, Elijah."

"What's up with you, Blake? You're turning into a real pussy lately. When did you become so weak?"

"What's up with me is I'm done being a jackass. You've been on them all week and I'm done with it."

"You're done with it? What, you're going to choose these fucking rejects over your real friends?"

"I'm not choosing anyone, Elijah. I'm just not going to keep standing by while you're up in people's faces, trying to show everyone how tough you are. I'm just here to play football and we're all on the same team."

I hadn't really even said anything, but his face went beet red.

"What the fuck does that mean? You're too good for us? You always were fucking soft. If you're going to side with them, then maybe you should get off the team, too. It explains why you're playing like shit now, too. You should just drop out, go work fucking construction with the rest of the losers."

I didn't care what Elijah thought of me. Not anymore. But for some reason, that hit a nerve. Maybe it was because that's exactly what happened in my dream life, but I saw red.

"Say that again," I said, getting up in his face.

We'd never fought, but Elijah was a wide receiver, shorter and more wiry than me. I wasn't Connor's size, but I knew I could take him if I wanted to.

I was surprised, however, when Miguel and Tyrell moved up behind me, both glaring at Elijah. Miguel was also a wide receiver and about Elijah's size, but Tyrell was a house. He even made Connor look small. I saw Elijah's eyes flick to Tyrell for a second and then back to me. I could almost see him trying to figure out how to get out of this without losing face, because he clearly did not want to mess with Tyrell.

"Look at you," he sneered. "Trading us in for these losers. You're pathetic, Blake."

"What the hell is going on here?" Coach Heidemann yelled from the sidelines. "I said reset the play. Get your asses back in formation now!"

Elijah pushed me away from him, his eyes almost burning as he glared at me. "This isn't over."

He looked betrayed and was as angry as I'd ever seen him. As we reset for the next play, I could feel his glare boring into the back of my head.

31

This was going to make things harder.

Chapter 3

We managed to finish practice with no more incidents, although it was a rough finish. Everyone was icy toward each other, even the kids who were not directly part of the conflict. The vibes were just off, and the coach wasn't having it. We'd ended up having to run laps for the last ten minutes of practice, with a threat that we'd spend the entire next day running laps if we didn't get our heads out of our asses.

The locker room wasn't any better. We managed to stay in our space and didn't have any blowups, but I kept catching Elijah glaring at me every time I looked in his direction. The rest of the guys joined him, adding the occasional muttered threats to go along with the glares.

I got looks from the walk-on guys, too, although different ones, like they were trying to figure me out. I knew that so far, I'd been more or less standoffish, clearly friends with Elijah and the rest, while not participating with them in any of the mistreatment. I also hadn't stopped it, which meant until today, they had probably put me in the enemy category.

From the way they were looking at me, it was possible that estimation was changing, but they weren't ready to accept me with open arms either.

Not that I'd expected it.

I hadn't stood up to Hunter because I was hoping for some kind of favoritism or whatever from the new guys. I'd done it because I couldn't take seeing them treated like that, not with how I remembered feeling when people had treated me the same way. Even if that was only in a dream.

I just wished I'd given it a little more thought before I'd done it, because I was pretty sure I'd just burned a bridge with the guys that I wasn't going to be able to fix. Those guys had been my main group of friends since forever, and the way we'd acted, it had kind of alienated us from being friends with anyone else. Sure, we'd had hangers-on in middle school, since we'd been popular football players, but they all wanted something from us.

Now, at best, I was going to have a few guys that might be apathetic to me and a bunch of guys who were going to actively hate me for being a traitor, which I was positive is how Elijah was seeing me. Not that I would change my actions. I couldn't continue hanging with Elijah and the rest of them now that I could see how they really were.

But part of me wished I could. I didn't want my freshman year to suck, and that seemed like exactly how it was going to be.

I put the rest of my stuff away, grabbed my bag, and headed out of the locker room without looking at anyone. I was walking home again today, since I didn't have my license yet, Mom never felt like driving if she didn't have to for work, and Dad wouldn't be home from work for a few hours.

I had my head down, mostly just trying to ignore everyone, when a voice yelled out, "Blake!"

I looked up and barely readied myself before Brandy flung herself at me, her arms locking around my neck as she nearly knocked me off balance as she kissed me.

I stumbled back a step as she began to kiss me aggressively. Honestly, I was mostly trying to get my bearings. We'd been dating for seven months, but with how messed up this dream had my head, I hadn't even thought about her all week. I did vaguely remember she was supposed to be back from cheer camp today, but it had completely slipped my mind.

"Whoa," I breathed as she finally pulled back. "Hey there."

"I'm back! Did you miss me?"

"I, uh …" I said while my brain scrambled to catch up. "Yeah, of course. How was camp?"

"Oh my God, it was amazing!" Brandy bounced on her toes, her ponytail swinging. "But never mind that. I saw you out there today. When did you get so good?"

"You were watching practice?"

"Duh! As soon as I got back, I had to come see my man in action. Seriously, Blake. You were incredible. I watched all your games last year, and you were good but ... not this good."

I wasn't sure if I agreed with her or not. I think I was a little better because I was starting to take some of the stuff I remember being taught my freshman and especially sophomore years in the dream life and applying them. Considering how clumsy we'd looked as a unit, especially today, I wouldn't think anyone would call what we did 'amazing.'

"Thanks," I said, rubbing the back of my neck and taking a slight step back from her.

Brandy kept talking, but I wasn't really registering what she was saying. I started having a memory of this reunion, although slightly different, since she'd commiserated with my sitting on the bench and Gabriel starting instead.

I also started to remember something else from the dream life. A fight we had around Christmas because I found out she'd been cheating on me with Mason since the middle of the summer. Part of me wanted to be disgusted by the revelation, but for the dream me, it was the distant past, and I found myself torn between being heartbroken and apathetic, which was a really strange sensation.

I vaguely remembered that in the dream timeline, I had discovered Brandy's affair when someone, one of the girls on the cheer squad I think, told me she saw them kissing outside of the diner just before Christmas break. The revelation had led to Mason being ostracized from our group until he eventually broke up with her, at which point the guys let him back in. The whole situation had been a mess.

I tried to think about what happened to her in the dream life after that, but in that timeline, we hadn't kept in touch once she broke up with Mason. Other than seeing each other around school, we never really spoke. She had gotten involved with a basketball player by the end of the year, and I think she was kicked off the cheer team our sophomore year after a falling out with another cheerleader who was close to Mason.

The more I thought about it, the more certain I became that Brandy and Mason were already seeing each other before she went to cheer camp. Although I'd been pretty much accepting that the dream was somehow matching with my life, but part of me had written that off as just predicting what was going to happen.

My friends were jerks, so that wasn't any kind of premonition, just a realization that they really were and I had been too. Maybe that was maturing or whatever. Coaches yelling and pushing us? I mean, that's just football. Joshua being a creep? I mean, it wasn't a big leap, although serial killer seemed like the kind of wild escalation that dreams had.

I couldn't really think about my dad, 'cause when I did it made me incredibly sad. But looking at Brandy and feeling the revulsion toward her from the dream instead of what I felt when I saw her in June. This was different. This was changing my opinion of someone based on something I had no way of knowing was true or not.

But ... looking at her, I could feel a pit in my stomach. I just knew it was true.

"... and then Missy tried to do a backflip, but she totally wiped out! You should've seen Coach's face. I swear, I thought she was gonna ... Blake? Hello? Earth to Blake!"

"Sorry, what?" I said, suddenly snapping back to the here and now.

"Seriously? I've been talking for like, ever," she said, crossing her arms and cocking her head. "What's going on with you?"

"Nothing, I'm just ... tired. Practice was rough today."

"Aw, poor baby. Want me to kiss it better?"

She leaned in, but I took a step back.

"I just really need to go home, get a shower and lay down for a bit, if that's okay."

"Oh. Okay. Will you call me later?"

"Sure," I said, trying to give her a smile.

Brandy hesitated for a second, then quickly pecked me on the cheek before turning to leave.

"Elijah. Mason. I'm back," she said past me as the other guys came out of the locker room.

I couldn't help myself and looked back. Maybe it was my imagination, or the image of her kissing Mason in my dream memories, but I could swear she was giving him a look, and he was returning it.

36

I just shouldered my bag. The whole situation gave me a lot to think about as I started the long walk home.

Connor hit the ground, slipping and letting his defender through, which caused the pocket to start to collapse around me even as the rest of the line tried to adjust to stop more from getting through. I'd been in the middle of my read and no one was open yet, there was no way I was making it through the rest of them before I got hit.

I spun to my right, just twisting away from Victor's outstretched arms and made it around the chaos, continuing right and pushing as hard as I could as everyone started to angle for me.

It was a race to pick up as much yardage as I could before they got to me. There were too many people between me and the end zone and I was forced to step out of bounds after about twenty yards. Close enough to the goal line that I was a little annoyed I didn't make it the last few yards, but still a good run.

"That's it!" Coach Heidemann blew the whistle, signaling the end of practice.

I tossed the ball to Coach Plummer and jogged back to join everyone else.

"Nice hustle, Simms," he said as I caught up to them. "Alright, everybody in! Good work today, everyone. Rosters will be posted shortly, so stick around. Alright, hit the locker rooms. Simms, hold back a minute."

I watched everyone else walking toward the locker room and tried to think what I might have done to get me singled out from everyone else.

"That was some run, Blake. You've got a lot of talent and I can really see you going far with our program, but I want you to think about how you want to do that. The quarterback is the leader of the team, and that means you set the standard for how the rest of your guys play. If you buck the rules, they're all gonna do it."

"I'm not sure what I did wrong, Coach."

"You ran out of the pocket instead of dumping the ball or hitting one of your check downs. I know it worked out for you this time, but we play tight in the pocket for a reason. I know you've probably watched a few of the college guys and even one or two of the pros who get a lot of credit for how mobile they are, but I want you to think about how those players are in the minority and why you don't see it in high school much. More often than not, it ends in a sack and lost yardage. You gotta stay in the pocket longer, go through your reads, and either pass the ball or hand it off. It's about making the smart play, not the flashy one."

"What if I get through my reads quickly and see they're all covered?"

"If you're getting through your reads that fast, it means you're not doing it correctly."

I bit my tongue, memories from my dream life flooding back. I remembered watching how the game evolved and changed in the mid-2000s, focusing more on spacing and quick reads, how unbelievably fast everyone moved. Even in the community flag football I'd played in that other life, the game had been much quicker, with shotgun spreads and more passing than running.

Of course, there were a lot of changes that led to that, more than just a QB that liked to run, and I couldn't exactly make an argument based on some half-remembered dream of a life I hadn't actually lived.

"Yes, Coach," I said instead.

"Just think about it. Like I said, you did good, and sometimes it will be necessary, but I want you to succeed. I'm seeing a lot of raw talent already, and I think you can do great things. But that requires you to be a team player."

"I understand."

"Good. Alright, get going," he said, whacking me lightly on the side of the leg with his clipboard.

As I jogged towards the locker room, I couldn't help but think about how the game would change in the coming years. Players would get faster, more athletic. If I remembered correctly, we weren't that far off from some of those future quarterbacks' early years in college.

Not that I should be making plans based on a stupid dream, but it wouldn't hurt to get faster, focus on my conditioning, just in case.

There was a crowd already gathered near the corkboard outside the coaches' offices when I got into the locker room. The coaches were still in the offices, huddled up and talking, but Hunter was coming out carrying several pages that he began to put up on the board with thumbtacks.

He looked back and gave this look to Elijah just as someone shouted, "Roster's up!"

I don't know why I was nervous, since I knew I made it. Even without what happened in the dream life, I was sure I'd made the freshman team. Coach Heidemann's speech all but confirmed it for me. You didn't lecture a player about making sure they stayed within the system if you planned to cut them ten minutes later.

I waited as guys pushed to the front, tracing down the list of names for each team, looking for theirs. Most of us already knew more or less what team we were going to be on, and there wasn't much need to check the rosters of the other teams, although I did notice Elijah going to the JV list first, like he was certain that was where he was going to find his name listed.

"This is bullshit," Tyrell said, particularly loudly, as he pushed his way back from the list and went to his temporary locker, slamming the door shut hard enough that it just rebounded back open, instead of closing.

That was surprising. Tyrell hadn't made many mistakes and he was huge. I couldn't imagine not wanting someone like him on the field. Connor was much quieter as he made his way to join Tyrell, sitting on the bench, staring at his feet. His body language made it plainly obvious that he hadn't made it either.

Even that was surprising. Yes, he'd had a few problems over the last week, but he'd also had some solid blocks, enough that I would have thought the coaches would give him a chance to train up into the position.

I mean, that was the whole point of the freshman team, wasn't it?

I felt bad for them.

As the crowd emptied out, I made my way up to the list to at least confirm that I'd made it and get back on the field for the team meetings. I was surprised that I couldn't find my name either, enough so that I went down the list a second time, just to be sure I didn't miss it. I then checked JV, which I wouldn't have thought I'd made it on, but still made more sense than not being listed at all.

I didn't find my name there either. I even checked varsity just to be sure before going back and looking at the freshman list again. No matter how many times I checked it, I kept getting the same answer.

I wasn't on the list. I hadn't made a team.

I was still kind of reeling when Coach Holloway came out of the offices and said, "Alright, gentlemen, gather 'round!"

While everyone else moved to stand around the coach, I stayed by the board, shell-shocked as much as anything else.

"First off, I want to thank each and every one of you for the effort you've put in this week. The dedication and hard work you've shown is truly impressive. Now, for those who didn't see their names on that list, this isn't the end of the road. Far from it. This is just the beginning of your journey. You have a whole year ahead of you. A year to train, to improve, to come back stronger than ever. Any of the coaches you worked with this week will be happy to sit down with you, give you some pointers on where to focus your efforts."

He looked around at everyone, clearly not wanting to single any one person out, but I couldn't help but feel he was looking directly at me as he said that.

"Now, for those who did make the cut," he continued. "I want to see you out on the field in five minutes. We'll have a quick assembly as a group, then break into individual team meetings. We'll go over expectations, both on and off the field, and what you can look forward to this year."

Very few kids got cut. With three teams that could have a full roster, there were a lot of open spots. The locker room emptied as all the kids who were on the lists ran out, whooping and hollering.

I limply sat down on a bench. There were almost fifteen of us left behind, looking like we'd been hit by a bus. I was surprised that, in addition to myself, all four of the walk-on freshmen had been cut.

It was all just ... unbelievable. I couldn't wrap my mind around the fact that I hadn't made the team. How was this possible? I'd been given way more snaps than Gabriel, and he'd made it while I hadn't? It didn't make any sense.

A wave of self-loathing washed over me. It had to be that stupid dream. I'd let myself get caught up in all this dream life nonsense, convinced I was destined to make the team and even lead JV next year. Now here I was, cut before the season even started.

It was so damned disappointing, all I wanted to do was go home and never see the field house again, but at the same time I didn't want to leave because that would mean it was real. That it was final. Jamal, Tyrell, Connor, and Miguel seemed to be feeling the same way because they all just kind of sat slumped on benches, with the same hang-dog expression I had.

I was so lost in my thoughts I barely registered Coach Heidemann coming back into the locker room until he spoke.

"What the hell are you five still doing in here? You should be out on the field with everyone else!"

I looked up at him, more confused than anything else. "We were cut, Coach. We shouldn't be on the field."

"Cut? What are you talking about?"

I stood up and walked over to the roster sheet, pointing at it. "We're not on the list, Coach."

"What?" he said, joining me at the board, looking down the freshman players' list. "This doesn't make any sense. Wait here."

As he left, I turned to the other four guys and said, "That was weird, right?"

"Yeah," Miguel said, the rest of them exchanging glances.

We all kind of just ... waited there as the minutes ticked by. I was feeling some serious emotional whiplash, from absolute certainty after talking to Coach Heidemann, to absolute dejection, and now just confusion.

Finally, Coach Heidemann returned with Coach Holloway and Coach Easley in tow. They huddled around the list, muttering to each other before taking it off the wall and disappearing into the coaches' offices.

"What the hell is going on?" Jamal said, clearly not able to take it anymore.

"I have no idea," I replied, right before being hit by a massive memory from the dream.

In it, I'd been with Elijah, Hunter, and the rest, creating a fake list that we put up in front of the real one, to convince a bunch of the guys trying out, that we didn't like, that they didn't make the team. Could it be the same guys? In that other life, two of the kids we'd pranked had quit even after being told they'd actually made the team. The other two hadn't made it the following year after more hazing and bullying.

I instantly got angry, realizing exactly what had happened. Hunter had put the list up and looked at Elijah. The assholes. The anger turned to shame as I remembered participating and laughing along with them as we did the same thing in my dream life. I'd thought it was so funny, the sad looks on the faces of the guys who'd been so sure they were going to make the team.

Before I could say anything to the others, reassure them it was a stupid prank, the coaches came out of their offices.

"There's been a mix-up. This isn't the correct list. All five of you made the freshman team," Coach Holloway said.

Tyrell let out a whoop of joy, and Coach Heidemann chuckled. "Go ahead and get out on the field with everyone else."

The coaches headed back out to the field and we followed behind them, a little slower.

I slowed down until I was walking next to Jamal and extended my hand. "I'm glad you guys made it."

He grasped it firmly and said, "You too, man."

I knew it was only a dream, but not having a part in making that list at least helped ease the guilt of having taken part in the prank in my dream life. Not completely, but a little bit.

Chapter 4

I was lying on my bed; the playbook Coach Heidemann had given me open on my chest. In middle school, we'd just kind of learned plays and run them. There hadn't been all this homework. I'd forgotten how much work it was at this level.

The thought almost made me laugh out loud. The thing I'd 'forgotten' hadn't actually happened to me. It had only been a week since the dream, and already I was starting to think of things from it as my past, as much as just a dream.

The past week had been wild. The first week of practice had been a major moment in my dream, the start of the career I'd never had, and it really stuck with dream me. Now that I'd lived it for real, everything I remembered from that week in the dream had happened. Not just happened but had been identical.

The only things that had been different were how I'd done that first day. Instead of getting sick and screwing up, I'd played much closer to how I'd always thought I should, and that had rippled out into me getting a lot more play time through the week, which in turn had me pegged as a starter for the freshman team. That and all the stuff with Elijah and the rest.

But again, that had been a conscious choice. They'd done exactly what I'd remembered them doing in the dream. The difference was that in the dream I'd gone along with it as opposed to being annoyed by it and standing up to them. That had, again, rippled out into other things being different.

But everything not connected to those two things had been identical in every way, down to the order things happened in and what people said.

Not that I believed in that crap, but was it like ... prophecy? Was my dream showing me the future?

It wasn't just this week. I could remember everything from that life. Not just remember it, I could feel it. I was almost certain that, if I tried, I could do some half-decent welding from those last few years before I got sick, when I'd finished that welding program and jumped careers.

But if I was seeing the future, how did things end up differently? Wouldn't the dream take into account the changes and show me what actually happened, and not the slightly different version?

Honestly, it was making my head hurt just trying to think about it. But I couldn't stop. So much was the same, and I'd made decisions based on that, like not eating the sandwich, that had actually worked out in my favor.

Should I be taking this more seriously? Should I be actively trying to make decisions based on the dream to change things for myself?

Maybe not with everything, but some things. Like Brandy. That was already heavy on my mind. True, it was probably not great to break up with someone based on a dream, but I'd seen how she looked at Mason. In my gut, I knew I wasn't imagining it.

Brandy wasn't the worst part of my dream, or the part that had been occupying my thoughts the most. Every time I saw my dad, I relived his death in my dream. The phone call that shattered my world, the chaos that followed, Mom breaking down completely, and Josh becoming more ... Josh.

I remembered the funeral and how awful that had been, dropping out of school early the next year when Mom started having her episodes and couldn't work anymore. Arguments were made that Josh really started his descent into what he became with Dad's death. It destroyed all of our lives.

Was my dream telling me Dad was going to die? Was it real? Was this why I'd had the dream, to do something to save Dad? I had a pit in my stomach every time I thought about him being gone, but it was more than just me. It was everyone.

Should I try to stop something I wasn't even sure would happen? But that wasn't really even the question. The real question was, could I afford not to?

So much else had come true. If I tried to pretend this wouldn't and then it did ... I wouldn't ever be able to forgive myself.

I started to think through what I knew about the night my dad died. The details were fuzzy because nearly all of my memories were wrapped up in a haze of depression that kind of obscured everything.

I don't remember it clearly, but I know he'd gone to work that day pretty much like any other day, driving the fifty miles down to Midland for his shift. Dad had come across a group of people, kids the paper called them, stealing a car. I seemed to remember something about it being an initiation for new members of a gang. He'd tried to arrest them, and one of the kids pulled a gun. They said he was killed at the scene.

There was something else. The gang was based in Midland, but there were stories about the kid who did it living right here in Wheaton. People talked about how weird it was, that Dad and his killer were both from the same small town but never met until that night, fifty miles away.

But what could I do about it?

Telling Dad, or really anyone else, wouldn't work. "Hey, I had this dream where you were shot next year, and I think it's true." They'd never believe me. Hell, *I* barely believed it.

I also couldn't just wait until the day of the shooting and run in to save the day. For one, I didn't know exactly where it happened in the city. For another, I could just as likely get shot as save Dad. Of course, if I couldn't think of anything, that would still be an option, but I needed better options.

I lay there the rest of the night, thinking through everything I could remember. Over and over.

By the time I fell asleep, I still hadn't thought of anything.

I slouched in my seat as I tried to focus on the teacher's voice. The classroom felt stuffy, even with the windows cracked open to let in the late August breeze. It seemed like hardly anyone was paying attention. Half the people in the class were on the team with me. The rest were people I had only ever seen in passing. Stoners and idiots. The one thing we all had in common was that we were terrible students.

Which was why we were all sitting in remedial math.

"Good morning, everyone!" the teacher, who seemed on the young end for a teacher, maybe not even thirty yet, said after the bell rang. "Welcome to pre-algebra. I am Ms. White, and I will be working with you this year. Now, I know math is not everyone's favorite subject, but I promise, by the end of this year, you will all have a solid foundation in the basics you need to tackle more advanced concepts."

She set a stack of papers for us to take on my desk to pass back, which was a first for me. I had not sat at the front of a class since I was in third grade but had picked it on purpose as part of my promise to myself not to end up like I did in the dream.

In that other life, I had sat at the back of class and blown it off. I had always thought I would end up being a famous NFL player. What did I need with algebra? It was how I ended up in this class in the first place. I had barely paid attention last year and skated by with a C minus.

Of course, sitting in the front of the class was not going to be what fixed that. I had been a terrible student, basically forever, and it was not like the stuff I remembered from my dream life would bail me out. There was not much math in construction. If I was going to get out of this class and into on-level classes, I needed to do more than just want to do better.

Which was why, when the bell rang and everyone else escaped from the room as fast as they could, I grabbed my backpack and stopped next to Ms. White, who was erasing the whiteboard, her back to the room.

"Ms. White? Can I talk to you for a minute?"

"What can I do for you …?"

"Blake," I supplied. "I've been thinking a lot about this class, and I would like to discuss the possibility of moving out of remedial math."

"Getting into on-level classes? Blake, you are here because this is where your grades placed you. This class is for students who struggle with more advanced material," she said in a somewhat dismissive voice.

"I know my past grades weren't great, but I really want to do better."

"Blake, I appreciate you wanting to do better, but the last thing I want is to move a student into a class they are not ready for. Most of your friends are in this class. Don't you all call it math for jocks? No one is pushing you to be valedictorian. Just do your best and they will let you have your play time. I've been teaching long enough to recognize patterns, Blake. This class is typically the right place for students like you."

"That is not what I want. I mean, I get that it probably looks like that, that you have had a lot of 'students like me,' but just because I play football, doesn't mean I'm the same as the rest of your students. I'm really trying to improve this year. I know I can handle on-level work if I apply myself … and maybe get a little help."

She studied me for a moment. "You are not the first student to try and charm me into helping them get better grades, you know."

"That's not what I'm doing," I insisted. "Look, I know I'm never going to be a math whiz. But I can be an okay student. I just … I wasn't trying before. I want to change that."

"That is commendable. But talk is cheap. I need to see real effort."

"If I show it in my work, will you believe me then? Will you help me work towards moving up?"

"Show me you can do the work first, then we'll talk."

"Deal."

My morning didn't stay as positive as it had after that first reaction. I found my English teacher, Ms. Mace, to be alright. She had been as skeptical as Ms. White had been at my sudden interest in moving up to on-level classes, but she had listened. If anything, she had been more receptive than Ms. White had been, although she also made it clear I needed to put my words into practice if anything was going to happen.

But Mr. Walsh, the science teacher, that guy was a piece of work.

I had gone at him the same way I had Ms. Mace and Ms. White, that I knew I was in remedial classes for a reason, but I'd realized over the summer that I did not need to be there, and I wanted to do the work to get back on level.

He cut me off before I even got started. He gave the same spiel of, "If you want to get into on-level classes, you have to show you are capable first," but then he added that he thought it unlikely.

In the most condescending way possible, he had made it clear what he thought of athletes and where they belonged in school. Which was a weird counter to how he taught his class, which was pretty good. He engaged with the students who were there for reasons other than sports. Patient, empathetic, giving easier, toned-down explanations that still got the message across.

Apparently, he just hated athletes … or, as he put it, 'jocks.' It was like he was in an eighties teen sitcom.

The lunch lady slopped the lunch on my tray, some kind of meat and noodle thing. I wrinkled my nose. This was what I imagined prison food would taste like. Then I had another flash of stories from when I was older about how school lunches had "gone downhill" after lunches went through a "getting healthy phase," with regulations limiting cheap, unhealthy ingredients. That might have been all well and good, but then school budgets had been slashed while the limits stayed in place, which ended with schools walking a narrow path of virtually inedible food.

So maybe I did not have it so bad.

I stopped as I got out of line, looking across the rows of tables and kids. If this had been middle school, I would have known exactly where to sit. This being the first day of a new school, I did not know the lay of the land. I looked over the faces, kids who were definitely freshmen and kids who looked like adults compared to them.

Except, I realized that I did know where everyone was sitting. I knew which were the band kids, which were the theater kids, which were the nerds. I was still getting used to this "accept the dream" plan I had made, so it took a minute to remember where all the groups were sitting.

Including the athletes.

A table for basketball kids, a table for baseball, and so on, all sitting pretty close together since there was crossover between them.

I made my way over to where the football players sat, remembering they kind of divided it into a table for freshmen, a table for JV, and a table for varsity. Except not all the freshman team was at one table like I remembered. Elijah and the rest were sitting with the bulk of the freshman team, but the walk-ons were one table over, separate, even though there was room for them with the other freshmen.

I could feel Elijah's eyes boring into me, waiting to see what I would do. Although we had had that blow-up on Friday and had not spoken about it since, it was not the first time we had had a big argument. Maybe one of the biggest, but it was not unfixable yet.

It was getting there, however.

If I went to sit with Elijah and did something to show them that I was still "one of the guys," they would probably get over it. If I snubbed them, it would be a nail in the coffin.

It was not even a question, though. I'd made my decision already. I turned and headed for the walk-ons' table.

"Hey, guys, mind if I join you?"

They looked up at me, clearly surprised. Connor's eyebrows shot up so high they nearly disappeared into his hair.

"Uh, sure," Miguel said hesitantly, looking over at the others, everyone trying to decide if everyone else thought it was okay with no one saying anything.

I could feel the eyes on me as I sat down. Even people not involved in it, mostly other football players, were watching the drama.

"You know you're making enemies over there, right?" Connor asked.

I shrugged. "Yeah, but they weren't really my friends anyway, so it doesn't matter."

I had barely sat down, though, when I saw Miguel, who was facing the table where Elijah and the rest were sitting, get a look in his eye. Apprehension and worry; for a second, I thought it was Elijah, and things might get physical.

Then Brandy said, "Blake? What the hell are you doing?"

I swung around and looked up at her. She looked at me, then at the other guys, and then back to me.

"I'm sitting with these guys. They're new on the team."

"You don't need to do that. I'm sure they're fine," she said, giving them a look like they were something she wanted to clean off her shoes. "Come on, let's go sit with Elijah and everyone else."

"Nah, I'm good here. Actually, let me introduce you ..."

"I don't need to know their names," Brandy interrupted.

The guys shifted uncomfortably, with everyone trying to look anywhere but at us.

"Look, it's clear they are never going to be important. No offense," she added, glancing at the freshmen. "But seriously, Blake, you need to go patch things up with Mason and the rest."

"I have no plans on patching anything up," I said. "I've just realized they're jerks, and I have no interest in hanging out with them."

"You can't be serious."

"Dead serious," I replied. "You don't have to sit with us if you don't want to."

For a moment, Brandy hesitated. I could see the wheels turning in her head as she weighed her options.

As she stalked off towards Elijah's table, I turned back to the guys. They all looked various shades of uncomfortable.

"Sorry about that," I said, smiling. "So, uh, how has your first day been so far?"

Chapter 5

The rest of my first day went well, even though I did not have a single class that did not have one of Elijah's group in it. Notably, Miguel and the rest of that group were not in the remedial classes. Only a handful of the other freshman players were in all the remedial classes, which I think showed again how bad of an influence they had been on me. It also meant that once I was out, I wouldn't have any required classes with them anymore. I would still see them in conditioning, which is what football players had instead of PE, and if I kept taking shop class, I would see them in those classes, too.

But I could at least limit how much I saw them. Thankfully, my history teacher was Coach Wilson, the special teams coach. There was no remedial social studies class, but there were AP classes. I was not sure if "doing better" was the same thing as trying for AP, but I told him I might be interested in working for that. He was ... indifferent about it. Like most of the coaches, they wanted us to do well enough to be eligible to play, but beyond that, they believed that football should be our priority.

Still, he wasn't going to stand in my way, and if worse came to worst, I could stay in the regular history classes. Beyond that, I had woodshop, for which I had already submitted a course change. One of the big things I could remember from my dream was how important computers were going to be.

They were just picking up steam now, and I remembered the big Windows release next year, where people lined up at midnight to buy a copy of it. Then there were the smartphones, the iPhones, the tablets. In ten years, computers would rule the world. In fifteen, you would have to know computers to get any job that was not straight manual labor, and even some of those would need computers.

Since I had decided to just go with the dream and all the stuff that was coming true, I was going all the way. So I was dropping woodshop for typing. I knew there were computer science classes and I think some kind of business computer classes, but I did not know what kind of grades or other classes they required, and we only had a week to change classes before everything was locked down. Besides, I assumed typing would be helpful in all those other courses.

It was a good first step.

"Blake! Wait up!"

I looked up to see Brandy jogging towards me from the track where the cheerleaders were gathered after their practice finished.

"Hey," I said, slowing my pace just enough for her to fall into step beside me.

"Oh my God, you will not believe what happened at practice today," Brandy launched into her story without preamble. "So, Tiffany was trying this lift she learned at the camp she went to, right? But like, no one else knew it and she did not explain it well, and she nearly dropped poor Melissa on her head. Coach was *furious* ..."

I kind of tuned her out, just making the appropriate noises of interest when required. Instead, I thought about seeing all the little signs every time she had been near Mason throughout the day. When she had gone back to their table at lunch, she had sat next to him. When I had come out to the field and everyone was gathering up, she was off to the side, talking to him, her hand on his arm. They had practically bounced apart when they noticed me watching them. It was like watching a car crash in slow motion, knowing exactly how it would end but being powerless to stop it. Worse, I was not sure I wanted to stop it.

"... and then Jessica said we should try a pyramid, but after the whole Tiffany disaster, I was like, no way ..." she was saying, as she reached down to grab my hand.

Something she had done a bunch of times before. I don't know why, but I pulled away, shoving my hand into my pocket. She noticed and faltered mid-step.

"Blake? Is everything okay?"

"Yeah," I muttered. "Everything is fine."

"What is your problem?" she demanded, stopping in her tracks.

I stopped to face her. "I do not have a problem."

"Yes, you do. You have been acting so weird lately. You don't talk to Elijah, you don't sit with us at lunch, and now you are hanging around with all those losers. What happened to you?"

"Nothing happened to me. I just realized I'm done with all the drama. And Miguel, Connor, and the rest are not losers. They are just trying to get by, same as everyone else."

"Please," she scoffed, rolling her eyes. "They are a bunch of nobodies. You think they are going to help you get anywhere? If you keep this up, you are going to be just like them. You are throwing away everything. Don't you care about being popular? About being respected?"

"Respect from who? Elijah? Mason? They are just a bunch of users, Brandy. They only care about you as long as you are doing what they want. The minute you're not useful, they are gone."

"What are you talking about? They're your real friends. You guys have been together forever."

"Real friends?" I snorted. "They are not my real friends. I used to think that way, yeah. But I was wrong. I was a jerk. I am not going to keep being that guy. I have had enough of all the games."

"I liked you when you were that guy. This new version of you? I don't know who you are anymore. If you keep going down this path, you are going to end up being a loser, too. Just another nobody who never makes it anywhere."

"Is that why you are messing around with Mason? Because you think he is going somewhere?"

Brandy's face went blank, her voice going up just a little too high. "What are you talking about? I'm not doing anything."

"Yeah, you are. I have seen you two together. It is pretty obvious something is up. My guess? It started sometime after the last school year. Maybe early in the summer, before you left for camp."

"You're paranoid. You don't know what you are talking about. Mason and I are just friends."

I sighed. I didn't want to have a fight about this. I just didn't want to have to deal with her anymore.

"You don't have to pretend, Brandy. It doesn't matter anyway. I'm breaking up with you, whether there is something going on or not."

She did not say anything for a second. Just stared at me open-mouthed, like she had never even considered this as a possibility.

"What?" she finally managed.

"Come on, Brandy. You had to have seen this coming. You have got Mason now. Does it even really matter?"

I guess she decided that surprise was not working, because she switched tactics on me.

"Please, Blake," she pleaded, stepping closer, reaching for my hand. "Think about this. You do not have to do this. I can talk to Elijah, fix things. You can be a part of everything again. Just ... do not do this."

I shook my head, stepping back. "I have already made up my mind. I can't go back, Brandy. Not to that."

With that tactic failing, she flipped her personality again. Which just went to show none of it was real anyway.

"Fine. You want the truth? Yeah, I have been seeing Mason. And you know what? He is better than you in every way. Stronger, tougher, everything you are not."

"Good," I replied. "I hope you two are happy together."

I turned and started to walk away, but she was not done.

"Blake, you are making the biggest mistake of your life," she called after me. "You think this doesn't matter? I will make sure everyone knows what a loser you have turned into. I can ruin you at school. You will be nothing."

I didn't even look back. I just kept walking, heading toward the road, leaving her standing there, yelling after me. Whatever she had to say next did not matter to me. I was done with all of it.

It turned out, the hardest part of wanting to be better in school was not trying to convince teachers to help me. It was doing all the extra work they were assigning. I had never been a homework person, either in my dream life or in middle school, so getting into it now was a serious challenge. Even four days into school, I was finding it was not just learning the extra material; it was learning how to learn.

I had to go to the library and check out some books on study strategy, which was extra annoying since I remembered from my dream life a time when I could just open a browser and type questions into a search engine. One thing was clear. This was not going to be easy. Or fast.

And then I had all the studying to do for football. That was, at least, closer to what I remembered from my dream, although then I did not really do much of it until after my freshman season was over and I got over the stigma of my bad performance at tryouts.

I was also going harder at it than I had in my dream life. In it, I still treated football like a game. And it was, but it was also more than that, and I did not realize it until dream me was an adult and I spent more time learning about football. There was so much strategy to the game that I did not realize, or at least connect with, as a kid in the dream life. We weren't really exposed to it in middle school, and I had the impression they only touched on it a little bit with freshmen, leaving most of it for junior varsity.

The only reason I was getting more of it was I had shown active interest and requested to learn more about it. Coach, I guess, figured that if I was wanting to learn about it, then it was worth it.

And I did. If I was going to make a serious go at the NFL, I could not just be a good high school player. I had to be great, and athleticism would only take me so far. Taking it seriously, becoming a student of the game, that was what was going to take me to the next level.

A knock on my bedroom door broke my concentration.

"Come in," I called out, not looking up from my work.

"Hey, champ. You have been holed up in here a lot lately. Everything okay?"

I swiveled my chair around. As I did every time I saw him since that night a week ago, I took a moment before I said anything to just take him in. Alive and well.

"Yeah, I'm good," I said, gesturing to the pile of books and papers on my desk. "Just realizing how much harder high school is. I didn't exactly kill it in middle school, you know?"

"Since when are you this focused on schoolwork? What did you tell me once? Who needs to know algebra to play in the NFL?"

That sounded like me. Damn, I was an idiot when I was a kid. Or last year. Or whatever.

"Yeah, I might not have been thinking clearly. I mean, there is no guarantee football will take me anywhere, right? And even if I do good enough to get a scholarship, I should take advantage of it and get a degree while I break records on the field. But, I need to get out of math for jocks if I want to do that, and maybe get good grades while I do it."

"I will admit this is every father's dream conversation, but I have to ask, what brought this on?"

"I guess I just realized how many opportunities I was missing out on. I want to start taking life more seriously – both football and everything else. Life is more about up here," I said, pointing at my head, then pointing at my arms, "than here."

"That is good advice," he said, smiling.

He would think so. It is something he would say when I was younger and trying to power my way through problems rather than reasoning my way through them.

Dad's smile widened as he leaned against my doorframe. "Well, I'm happy you decided to take school more seriously, but you have been locked in your room all week. Don't forget, you're still a kid. You should have some fun too. Maybe you could spend some time with your friends? Elijah and the rest of the guys?"

"Actually ... I'm not really hanging out with them anymore."

"No?"

"They are … not good guys, Dad. They are bullies and jerks. Always picking on others to make themselves feel big. They think it's funny to make other people's lives more difficult."

"Really?" he said, but not in a surprised way. More like he was confirming that was what I said. "You really are turning over a new leaf."

"Wait? You think they are jerks, too?"

"I do, and I always thought they were a bad influence on you. I have dealt with a lot of kids like that, and even more who wanted to be their friends and ended up in trouble. So yeah, I'm glad to see you've figured it out before they could take you down with them."

"If you knew, then why did you let me be friends with them?"

"Because I have seen how parents demanding their kids get better friends goes, especially teenagers. More often than not, they end up holding them tighter, instead of listening. The whole 'parents do not understand' thing. All I could do was wait, try to teach you the right things, and hope you would learn the right lessons."

I don't know if it was just because I realized what those guys really were like or because I had those memories from being an adult in my dream life, but I knew he was right. If he had told me they were no good, I would have just been annoyed and hung out with them anyway.

"Huh. I guess it finally worked."

"I guess so," Dad said.

"I did meet some new guys, though. They joined the team but were not with us in middle school. They seem like good guys."

"Good. I am proud of you, son." He crossed the room and gave my shoulder a firm pat. "Keep it up."

As he turned to leave, I called out, "Hey, Dad?"

He paused in the doorway. "Yeah?"

"Thanks. For … you know. Everything."

"It's what I'm here for."

Friday, I finished practice and walked out of the field house. I had gone extra hard today, and Coach was impressed enough that he let me and most of the offensive guys go ten minutes early.

Well, that was what he said. As good as we were doing, the defense was really struggling, missing blocks, misjudging plays, and fumbling over themselves. Mason, in particular, had drawn a lot of his anger. I don't know if he was distracted or what, but he seemed to not be absorbing what Coach Plummer was telling him. It was all I could do to keep from smirking every time he got yelled at since Coach would have had my butt for laughing.

I had to settle for enjoying him getting what he deserved.

Since Aiden and Mason were still on the field, Elijah and the rest were waiting for them, so I hurried to get changed and out of the locker room before they came in. Since I'd dissed them, they hadn't done anything against me directly, but they'd given me enough dirty looks and muttered curses that I knew it was coming eventually. Better to avoid them if I could.

They were just coming off the field as I left the field house. To make matters worse, the cheerleaders had just finished up, and Brandy came running across the field to where Mason was standing with Elijah and the rest and jumped up into his arms, wrapping her legs around his waist. He spun in a circle as the two laughed, completely wrapped up in each other.

I turned away and ignored them. It wasn't that I wanted her back, or really even cared that they were together. She'd made her decision, and I'd rather it were out in the open than thinking there was something between us while she was cheating on me behind my back.

The fact that they all stood around laughing with them just added to it. The Blake from my dream, the one who'd lived a whole other life, he'd wasted so much time with people who didn't actually care about him. People who'd drop him the second something better came along. And they had, as soon as dream me lost everything and was no longer of use to them, they'd dropped me.

As I walked along the end of the school building, heading for the parking lot and my route home, I saw a girl who was ... hard to miss. She was incredibly tall, even sitting down, with broad shoulders and a stocky build, shoulder-length black hair. It wasn't just her stature that drew my attention.

It was, as seemed to always be the case lately, a memory from my dream life. It took me a moment to place her though. She wasn't someone my dream self had thought about in decades. But then it clicked, and I felt another familiar sensation that was happening a lot lately.

Shame. Or at least, dream shame.

She was a new student who'd transferred in our freshman year ... this year. In my dream life, I, along with Elijah and the rest of the guys, had been unbelievably cruel to her.

The memories came flooding back, each one worse than the last. The cruel nicknames. The rumors we'd spread about her. The time someone, Aiden maybe, had stolen her backpack and thrown it in the dumpster where they tossed all the trash from the cafeteria. Half-eaten food and the like.

I'd forgotten all about her. Or maybe I'd made myself forget, not wanting to face how terrible I'd been.

I also remembered the worst of it, which I wasn't even involved with. Elijah and Jake had played a cruel prank during homecoming of our sophomore year. For weeks, they'd been slipping her notes from a "secret admirer." The final note they'd slipped into her purse said he'd left a gift in her locker. When she opened her locker, they'd rigged it to spring open, covering her in rotten food and garbage. It ruined her dress and crushed her spirit.

She'd dropped out of school after that, or at least she'd transferred out. Her family moved away and I never knew what became of her.

I don't know why, but I found myself veering off course, heading towards where she sat. Part of me was wondering what she was doing here. It was late, and most after-school activities were done for the day. What was she doing out here alone?

"Hey, um, is everything okay?" I asked when I got near her, although still far enough away to keep from being weird or spooking her.

"Go away," she said, without looking up from her book.

"I was just checking to see ..."

"I don't care. Just go away."

"Okay, sorry to bother you. Have a nice afternoon."

"Uh-huh," she mumbled, still not looking up.

I kind of awkwardly spun around and walked away from her. I didn't blame her for being closed off. I didn't know if the bullying had started yet, but if it had, she wouldn't be interested in being 'tricked' into any more friends. I think that's why I went to talk to her. Another attempt to fix wrongs I'd never done.

I looked back at her and caught her, finally, looking up from her book, watching me walk away. The moment our eyes met, she quickly looked away, back to her book.

Maybe I'd give her another shot later.

Chapter 6

Monday, we were playing our first full scrimmage in pads and everything, trying to get as close to a real game as possible playing against our defensive linemen. Our first game was on Thursday, which didn't give us much time to get ready. The time between our first practice and our first game was really short! Just a week into the school year. It was pretty stressful, and probably one of the big reasons why they liked putting all the freshmen on the freshman team. There just wasn't time for us to get ready before the season started.

We'd already run three plays and had picked up some yardage, which was getting the defense yelled at again.

"Okay, let's try that again," Coach Heidemann said, blowing his whistle.

We were pulled to the sidelines in between each play so the coaches could go through what we did right or wrong each time before giving us the next play. Although Coach Heidemann had us and Coach Plummer had the defense, I think they knew what the other was planning.

I jogged up to the line of scrimmage and got behind Tyrell, looking down either side of the line to make sure everyone was set. We were on the game clock, just like we would be in an actual game, so I couldn't take too long. Thankfully, everyone was where they needed to be.

"Set! Hut!" I barked, and Tyrell snapped the ball clean.

I dropped back and looked down the field. Elijah was my first read, out wide, sprinting down the sideline. He was fast, and for a second, I thought he might break free. But just as quickly, Gary, the other cornerback, came up fast behind him, staying glued to

Elijah. There was no way I could make the connection there, not without the ball getting knocked away.

I shifted to my next read, checking the pocket out of my peripheral vision and seeing Connor was holding his block, but barely. I'd probably only get one more read before the pocket collapsed.

I found Miguel, who'd managed to break free from his coverage and was making a move down the middle of the field. I cocked my arm back and fired a bullet his way. I knew I was going to hit him in stride as soon as the ball left my hand. He reached his hands out and got the ball, pulling it in, when Aidan came tearing in out of nowhere, smashing into Miguel from behind like a freight train. Miguel's head whipped back, and it looked like he was going to fold in half backward.

The ball bounced free, tumbling across the grass as Miguel crumpled to the ground. Aidan picked it up and started running with it all the way to the end zone, raising his arms in the air like a victor, while the rest of us, minus Elijah and the rest of the jerks, gathered around Miguel as one of the trainers came over.

Thankfully, as soon as the trainer got there, Miguel stirred and rolled over on his side. Mr. Romero, the trainer, still made him come off the field and helped him to the training room after making sure he could move on his own and hadn't actually broken his back.

I don't think Aidan and the rest realized how much everyone else, not just me and the other walk-on guys, but all of the freshman team, glared at them as they came back, whooping and hollering in victory over Aidan's touchdown. Coach blew his whistle, and we all headed back to the sidelines.

"If you would have thrown to me, we would have made the completion," Elijah said, catching up to me. "Open your damn eyes."

"Shut up, Elijah. Your teammate's injured. This isn't the time for that."

"This is practice, jackass. This is exactly what we're here for."

I stopped and turned on him just as we reached the sideline, poking a finger at him as I said, "I didn't throw it to you because Gary was on your ass, and you were too slow to break away from him. And what really matters is that Aidan hit one of his own guys with a cheap shot. Or did you guys forget whose damn team you're on?"

"I'm about to forget ..."

"Enough, both of you!" Coach Heidemann yelled. "Get your asses over here."

When we joined the rest of the offensive line, he said, "Hits like that can happen, and they will in a real game. What matters is you hold on to the ball until the whistle blows. That's the priority, protect the ball and keep possession! It's also important to protect your team. You other guys not in the play, you have to call out when your guy can't see a player coming at them. And if you are the one getting the ball, you have to keep your head on a swivel. Always be aware of what's happening around you! Don't let yourself get blindsided like that. Likewise, Blake, you gotta keep an eye on the whole field, not just your receivers. See what's developing and don't throw into something like that."

"Sorry, Coach," I said.

"It's okay. Aidan did a good job tracking the throw and diverting from his man and to where the ball would be. We have to anticipate what the other guys are going to do and adjust as needed. Let's keep going with a running play this time, twenty-two iso left, behind Nielsen."

Jamal nodded, looking to Connor, who he'd be following through the hole, hoping to break through their line and into open ground.

We lined up again and I called the play. Tyrell snapped the ball back into my hands. I stepped back like I was going to throw, and then dropped the ball down, putting it into Jamal's stomach as he ran past me, wrapping his arms over the ball.

He took off like a bullet, following behind Connor, who smashed into one of the defensive backs, opening a small gap for Jamal, who blasted through it. Unfortunately, the defense knew exactly where we were going to be, and they'd shifted right, our left, to have stronger defense on that side. Jamal was fast, but there wasn't nearly enough room for him to break through.

Worse, Mason was the back closest to him, putting his head down and launching himself at Jamal. Just like Aidan had in the last play, he put everything into it. Way too much, in fact. The two of them collided with a sickening crunch, Mason's arms wrapping around Jamal's waist as he drove him to the ground, almost like he was trying to put him through the ground.

Jamal's legs flew out from under him, his body twisting as he tried to break free. But Mason held tight, his helmet smashing into Jamal's and causing it to bounce hard against the ground.

Like Miguel, he didn't get up right away, probably from having his head rattled around too much inside the helmet. Coach blew his whistle, and everyone pulled up as the trainer ran out to check on Jamal, who thankfully started moving and was half up by the time a trainer got to him.

I jogged over to Jamal as he dusted himself off. "You okay, man?"

"Yeah, just got the wind knocked out of me," he said, although he was favoring his side a bit, and I knew it was probably worse than he was letting on.

I saw Mason and the other guys headed to Coach Plummer, and I decided I'd had enough of their bullshit. Instead of going with the rest of the offensive line to Coach Heidemann, I veered off, intercepting Mason. Jake saw me coming and gave a warning shout as I got to them.

"What the hell, man?" I said, getting in his way, intercepting him.

"What's your problem, Sims?"

"My problem? You and Aidan keep smashing into people like you're trying to take them out before the game even starts. That's my problem."

Mason took a step closer, almost chest-to-chest with me. "That's football, genius. Maybe your little buddies should toughen up."

"You're hitting them harder than you hit anyone else. You think I can't see that?"

He laughed, leaning his head back a bit, making a show out of it. "You're imagining things. Maybe if you weren't such a little ..."

I shoved him, hard enough that he had to take a step to catch himself. "You think this is funny? What if Miguel or Jamal can't play on Thursday because of you?"

Mason's face twisted in rage and he shoved me back, harder than I had pushed him. "You don't tell me how to play, Sims. Just because you're the quarterback doesn't mean you're leading shit."

My hands clenched into fists, and for a second, I thought I might just swing at him. I knew I shouldn't, since, at the moment, I was outnumbered and fighting could get me kicked off the team, but the jackasses were just so ... infuriating. Thankfully, before I could do anything, Coach Heidemann grabbed my shoulder and pulled me back.

"Both of you, cut it out!" he said, stepping in between us.

"Coach, they're going after us, harder than they're hitting anyone else. It's not right. If Miguel or Jamal gets hurt ..."

"This is football, Blake. Hits happen. You don't want to get hit, don't play."

"Yeah, but ..."

"I told him the same thing," Mason said smugly.

That was the wrong move, since it redirected his attention. "No, Blake's also right. There's hitting and then there's punishing your opponents. This is scrimmage and they're on your team. You need to control yourselves ... not just to keep them from getting hurt, but to keep you from getting hurt too. Now, you guys go to Coach Plummer, Blake, you come with me. We don't have time for this nonsense."

Mason and Aidan headed off while I headed toward the rest of the offensive line that was waiting to get the next play. I could feel Mason's eyes on me as I went though, and Elijah and the rest glaring at me as I headed towards them.

I was pissed, but I was also annoyed with myself. The last thing I needed was another escalation.

Thankfully, it didn't actually come to anything. At least, not at this practice.

The coaches kept a better eye on them for the rest of practice and I think Mason and Aidan knew they were being watched because they were on their best behavior after that. Once they weren't so focused on just hurting people who annoyed them, we even started making some progress on tightening up our plays, which maybe meant we wouldn't be a complete mess on Thursday.

I got home and took a shower as always, since I'd rather take a shower at home than at the field house if I didn't have to. When I got downstairs, I found Dad sitting in his chair, leaning back with his legs stretched out, one hand wrapped around a beer.

"Where's Mom?"

"Book club, I think," he said, looking up at me a second before turning back toward the TV, which was playing Monday Night Football.

Instead of a football game, it had some talking heads on it, going over all the preseason stuff, since the actual season wouldn't start until next weekend. Josh would be up in his room. He didn't ever participate in family stuff and couldn't care less about sports.

"Preseason stuff mostly, tonight. Not as exciting, but it'll do," he said, looking over at me as I sat in Mom's chair, which was next to his, separated by a little end-table thing.

"Think Nebraska's got a shot this year?" I asked as they started talking about college ball this year.

I'm not sure why I said that. Maybe to show off. I was usually a Texas Tech fan with Dad, or at least because of Dad. He'd gone to school there and was a Red Raider until the day he died, even the years when their program struggled. Like any kid, I mostly supported them 'cause Dad did.

This year, though, I was pretty sure I knew something he didn't. I remembered, from my dream, that Nebraska was going to have a season for the ages with their Black Death defense.

"I don't know. These guys are all pretty sure that Paterno is going to take it. They have him at the top of the coaches' poll."

"I'm pretty confident. They've got a solid offensive line and Ed Stewart is a beast. Trust me. It's going to be Nebraska."

Part of me wanted to say, 'I bet you,' but it felt a little unfair to do that to my dad, since I was pretty sure I knew the outcome. My dream had done me good so far, and I felt really confident it would continue.

Maybe it wasn't because I was a good guy, though. Even if I'd decided to take my dreams seriously, I couldn't help but be skeptical. Maybe I held back because I didn't really believe in it after all.

He chuckled. "You do sound awful sure for someone who wasn't around for all those heartbreaks Nebraska fans have gone through. But, hey, being sure of yourself ... confident, that's a good trait to have. Even if it does make you a traitor."

"Hey," I protested, but we both laughed. "We can still both agree the Cowboys will kill it again this year, right?"

"I hope so. They were so damn good last year; they've just got to keep that momentum going. Aikman's still strong, and if Smith stays healthy, we might see another ring, but you never know."

Again, assuming my dream was true, I did know. It would even be the Cowboys and Buffalo in the rare repeat Super Bowl, with the Cowboys taking it a second year in a row, although by not as much.

It wouldn't do to say anything, though. Even if I explained my dream to Dad, I would either seem childish or insane. Either way, he wouldn't believe me. Hell, *I* barely believed me.

We kind of wound down for a moment, both watching the guys on the TV talk about the coming season and just kind of existing together.

After about ten minutes, as it went to another commercial break, Dad asked, "So, how's the team shaping up this year? Got a lot of talent?"

"It's hard to say," I said, picking at the arm of the chair. "We've got some good guys, but Elijah and the others are kind of making it tough. There's a lot of tension. It's messing with the team chemistry. I've been trying to get them to back off, or at least realize we're all on the same team, but man ... they just want to beat their chests and let everyone know they're the most important guys on the team."

Dad set his beer down on the little table between us and looked at me. "That's not your job to fix, Blake. You just focus on your position, on doing your part. Let the coaches handle the rest. They'll take care of the troublemakers."

He made it sound simple, like all I had to do was keep my head down and things would work themselves out, but the coaches hadn't done much so far. I didn't hold out a lot of hope they'd rein them in.

"I guess. But I don't think the coaches really see what's going on. They're not paying enough attention to what Elijah and the others are doing."

"They will. Guys like Elijah, all the stuff they do eventually catches up with them. But they'll try to take you with them, so it's better that you keep your distance."

"Yeah."

Dad looked at me for a long moment, his expression thoughtful, before saying, "I'm proud of you, you know? Sticking with football, even with all the drama. That takes guts. Just remember, you can't control everything. Focus on what you can, be the leader they need on the field. The rest will come."

"Yeah, I'll try," I said, giving him a forced smile.

I turned back to the TV, thinking we'd lapse back into silence, but instead, he said, "Speaking of ... I was thinking about grilling out next Monday. Labor Day and all. Thought maybe you could invite some of the new guys on the team you mentioned over, make it a thing. What do you think?"

It caught me off guard, maybe because we very much weren't speaking about anything like that, unless he made some connection I didn't follow. I was becoming friendly with those guys, but we weren't really friends yet. At least not, 'hey, come over for a BBQ,' friends.

"I'll think about it."

"Good," he said, giving me a smile before picking up his beer and turning back to the TV.

I was hit with a sudden wave of ... something. Happiness and contentment for something I lost a long time ago that I hadn't lost yet. Hell, Dad and I didn't really spend time like this before. I was always off with Elijah when I didn't have to be somewhere, and I never really hung out with Dad. Something dream me always regretted. The way he looked at me, it felt kind of like everything would be okay.

I wanted to hold on to this moment!

Chapter 7

Everyone was nervous and amped up as we suited up in the locker room. Our field house was behind one of the goal lines in an older-style building, but we could already hear the noise of the crowd outside.

We were all freshmen, being the freshman team, so even though most of us had been playing for years, there was a big difference between middle school ball and high school, as far as attendance went. In Texas, football was king, and high school games could pull huge crowds. The varsity games emptied most of the town on Friday or Saturday nights as everyone piled into the stadium. Even for away games, we'd form these long convoys of parents, friends, family, and just fans, following the school team to whatever town we were playing against. My dad and I had been to a lot of varsity games over the years and had even been in some of those long convoys to away games.

Things weren't quite that serious for the freshman team, but the stadium still filled up a lot more than I, or anyone else on the team, had ever experienced.

I'd be lying if I said I wasn't nervous.

I was also supposed to be a leader on the team, and I wasn't the only one nervous. Miguel looked like he was going to puke.

"Hey." I nudged him. "You got this."

"First game, you know? What if I mess up?"

"Then you mess up. But you won't. Just like practice, right?"

"Right." Miguel managed a small smile. "Thanks, Blake."

I slapped him on the arm again and tried to give him a 'this is no big deal' kind of smile.

That was made harder by Elijah sitting a few spaces down by the other section of lockers mad-dogging me the whole time.

We hadn't had any more shenanigans at practice after Monday because the coaches had been calling out hard hits more, but Elijah and the rest had been becoming more … passive-aggressive.

For a second, it looked like he was going to come over and say something, start something, but the coach came out of his office.

"Listen up, gentlemen. Monterey's going to come at us hard. This is our first game and everyone on the other side of the field is a freshman too, so they're going to be looking to prove something. They have a good program, but not something we can't beat. Play smart, trust each other, and remember, it's not just about individual glory. We win as a team. Let's get going."

I was still feeling the nerves as we jogged out of the field house. Our cheerleaders were lined up in the end zone closest to the field house, holding a massive paper banner in black and gold with a mustang painted on it. I'd seen this done in the football games I'd gone to as a spectator, but I'd assumed that was only something they did for varsity games. I didn't remember them doing it for my freshman games from my dreams, but I hadn't played in the first one and had been in kind of a funk, so I wasn't really paying attention. I was pretty sure this was only because it was our first game, and they wouldn't do it for any of the others because I *would* have noticed that from my dream, but it still felt good to have it.

The Monterey High players were already on their sideline, having come out first as the visitors, but I ignored them. When we saw the banner, we all started yelling and took off for the paper banner. I'd come out first and I put some extra speed into my run, mostly because I wanted to be the first one through. Tearing through that banner and running through the line of cheerleaders for the first time was exhilarating.

As I jogged to our sidelines, I looked up into the stands. Dad said he was coming, and even told me where he was planning to sit, but I still had a moment of worry. I guess I'd spent too long in my dream life, because every time I looked for him, I expected him to be gone.

He was there though, sitting up front at the fifty-yard line, wearing a Mustangs cap I didn't even know he had. He'd switched shifts with one of the other deputies so he could be here for my first game. When he spotted me looking, he raised his hand in a wave, grinning broadly. I waved back, grinning just as big.

"Sims!" Coach Heidemann called. "You're up for the coin toss."

I jogged toward midfield, where the officials waited with the opposing team's quarterback. Coach said we didn't do team captains on the freshman team, and that he'd be rotating players through the coin toss throughout the season.

Sadly, my first time didn't go well, as it landed on tails, which was the other team's pick, giving them the first possession.

Monterey's kick returner caught the ball at their two-yard line and took off like he had something to prove, managing to slip through the coverage until one of our guys wrapped him up at the thirty-five. Not a great start for us.

Their offense was good, or at least good against our defense, managing to move the ball in steady chunks. They ran a few short plays, grinding out yardage. Finally, on third and long, Julius broke through their line and sacked their quarterback, forcing them to punt.

I pulled my helmet on as we ran onto the field, feeling the nerves as I was about to take my first snap in a high school game. I could remember, and even kind of feel, all of those snaps I took in my dream, for the two years I played, but that was kind of fuzzy. This was the real thing so I pushed the nerves down and tried to focus as I got into the huddle.

We lined up and I got behind Tyrell just like at practice.

"Red Forty-three! Hut! Hut!"

The ball snapped into my hands, and I spun, thrusting it into Hunter's gut. He secured it and charged forward, blasting through the hole that Tyrell and Connor opened up. One of their linebackers filled the gap, but Hunter lowered his shoulder and powered through the hit, stumbling but keeping his feet. He churned forward, fighting for every inch before their safety dragged him down after a solid eight-yard gain.

Not quite enough for a first down, but forward momentum. Coach Heidemann had made it clear he preferred a running game for the freshman team, as it was less likely to cause turnovers and would pick up yards. He said he would get me some passing plays, but even those would focus on short passes to pick up yardage instead of big plays.

"Nice run!" I slapped Hunter on the helmet as we jogged back to the huddle.

He shrugged me off. I just shook my head. They couldn't drop it, even when it was in their best interest for everyone to get along.

Monterey's defense toughened up after that, and we ended up having to punt a few plays later. The rest of the first quarter was a back-and-forth battle, both of us trading possessions as we each tried to find our rhythm.

Late in the quarter, Monterey started to put a drive together. They mixed runs and short passes, playing almost exactly the playbook that Coach Heidemann liked, marching down the field despite our defense's best efforts. As the clock ticked down, they punched it in from the two-yard line, their fullback diving over the top for the score. The extra point sailed through the uprights, and just like that, we were down 7 to 0.

I tried not to let it get to me as we headed to the sidelines for the break between quarters.

"Plenty of time left," I said to my guys, who were looking a little grim. "We'll get 'em back."

Coach Heidemann seemed to agree. "Good effort out there, boys. We're right in this. Blake, I want to open it up a bit this quarter. Their safeties are cheating up."

Early in the second, we finally got a break. It was second down and I was back behind Tyrell, ready to get the snap.

"Blue eightyyy!" I called. "Blue eighty! Hut! Hut! Hut!"

The ball slapped into my hands and I took a step back, faking a handoff to Hunter as best I could, watching as the Monterey defense bit on it hard, expecting another run. Instead, I pulled the ball back and stepped up into the pocket, looking downfield.

Miguel was my first read, and he was sprinting downfield, several steps ahead of his man. I planted my feet and let it fly. The ball spiraled clean, and for a second, time seemed to slow. Miguel reached out just as the safety closed in and *bam*, he caught it, pulled it in, and broke away for the end zone. The crowd roared as he crossed the goal line.

Touchdown.

We lined up for the extra point, and Dominic's kick sailed through the uprights. The score was tied. It was an amazing feeling.

The rest of the first half settled into another grind - run, pass, punt, with neither team able to break through. The defenses were keyed up now, flying to the ball on every play. By the time the clock hit zeros and the teams jogged to the locker rooms, the score was still stuck at seven apiece.

I do not know if it was the grinding nature of the game or what, but everyone was tense when we got back to the field house for halftime. Monterey had put up a fight in the first half, and we all knew this was far from over. I grabbed a towel, wiping the sweat off my face, and watched as Elijah, Hunter, and the rest came in through the door, having apparently hung back for a second.

I knew what was coming. Elijah had been glancing at me all through the second quarter, eyeing me like he had been since everything fell apart between us, and I knew in my gut that they hung back to talk about whatever was pissing him off.

"You really gonna act like that out there, Sims?" Elijah snapped, stepping in front of me before I could even sit down.

"Act like what?"

"Like you're out there playing for your new best friends. Passing to Miguel? Seriously? You've got me wide open half the time and you don't even look my way."

"You're not wide open. I'm making the right reads, Elijah. I'm not forcing throws just to make you happy."

"Bullshit. You're blowing it for us, man. This team could win if you'd stop playing favorites."

I could feel the eyes of the other guys on us now. The room was going quiet. I knew four new guys were on my side and Elijah and his four were against me whatever I said, but there were nine other guys on the team besides us, and they didn't need this shit. I wasn't going to back down from him, though.

"Elijah, I'm doing my job," I said, keeping my voice level. "I'm hitting the open guy. You want the ball? Get open."

"I was open!" he shouted, stepping closer, his chest puffed out like he was trying to intimidate me. "You just didn't see me because you're too busy sucking up to the new kids."

73

"You were covered, Elijah. Every time. I'm not gonna force it. I'm playing to win, not to make you feel good."

"That's bullshit!" he all but yelled.

For a second, I thought he was going to swing at me, the way his fists clenched. The whole room seemed to freeze, everyone waiting to see what would happen next. Before he could do anything, the locker room door slammed open, and Coach Heidemann came in. Elijah took a step back and I was pretty sure the coach didn't see what he was up to.

"Alright, everyone gather round!"

Elijah gave me one last glare, but moved away. I watched him for a second, then turned toward Coach like the rest of the guys, shoving the tension down for now. We had a second half to worry about, and I wasn't about to let Elijah throw me off my game.

As we jogged back out to the field, I saw that the crowd had thinned out a little. It was a Thursday, so maybe people had work or school the next day. Dad was still sitting in the same place, and I gave him another wave.

The kickoff return got to the twenty-five-yard line. I was pumped, ready to get things moving again. We'd been shut down for most of the first half, and I didn't want that to continue. I wanted us to start this year off strong with a win, and we were fairly evenly matched.

This was doable.

I snapped the ball and turned, pivoting to hand it off to Hunter, and then everything went to shit. The ball slipped right through his hands, bouncing off his hip pad. My stomach dropped as I watched it hit the grass. It didn't bounce far and it was within Hunter's reach, but he paused a full second before starting to dive for it, by which point a Monterey linebacker got there first, landing on it at our thirty-yard line.

I'd felt his hands on it before I let it go. It was pressed right up against his stomach. It should have been impossible for him to drop the ball. When I looked at Hunter, though, it was instantly apparent what had happened. He hadn't fumbled at all. He'd let the ball go on purpose. He gave me a little smirk as we ran off the field, confirming my suspicion.

Our defense managed to hold them to a three-and-out, giving us another shot. This time, we lined up in the I-formation.

Again I took the snap, this time for a passing play, but as I dropped back, before I could even set my feet, a defender blasted through untouched on my right side and slammed into me, taking my feet off the ground. I managed to keep my hands on the ball, but just barely. Jake had completely whiffed his block.

I hit the ground hard, losing us eight yards. From my spot on the turf, I saw Jake look to Elijah, who gave him a satisfied grin. Everything fell into place. They were doing it on purpose. Throwing the game and trying to make me look bad doing it.

Monterey's offense took advantage of the short field on their next possession. Their running back broke through the line and sprinted forty yards for a touchdown. Just like that, we were down 14 to 7.

Coach Heidemann pulled me aside as we prepped for our next series.

"What's going on out there, Sims? You're better than this."

"Coach, they're doing it on purpose. Hunter, Jake, Elijah, they're trying to make me look bad."

He wasn't having it. "You're the leader. Act like it. Figure it out."

I could only nod. I knew how it sounded as soon as I said it. Like I was passing the blame. Whining. The coaches couldn't see what I could. Couldn't feel Hunter drop the ball on purpose.

We got the kickoff and picked up some field position, setting up for another passing play. I was watching Jake this time and saw Elijah signal to him. I was still making my reads, but I was keeping an eye on Jake too, and saw him release his man early again. I was ready this time.

As the defender charged in, I spun away, tucking the ball and taking off toward the sideline.

Two Monterey players converged on me, but I cut back inside, splitting between them. Connor laid a beautiful block downfield, and suddenly, I had daylight. I'd always been quick on my feet, but since the dream I'd been working out, getting stronger and focusing on speed drills, even at home, to try to pick that up some. It wasn't enough to make me magically better in such a short time, but it didn't hurt either.

I could feel the other team's players on my heels, but I just put everything into it veering slightly to keep some distance between me and their safety, who was trying to track me down. Just as he was preparing to dive for me, I leaped for the sidelines, holding my hands just over the goal line.

Touchdown. We were tied up again.

I'd gotten lucky on that run, and I knew it. They pulled back a little after that, making the odds of that happening again a little less, even if it meant they couldn't press the pocket as hard.

The game became a slog, partly because my old friends were still trying to help us lose. It became more of a fight between me and them, than between us and Monterey. Every time Elijah's group tried to sabotage a play, I found a way around it. When Hunter "missed" another handoff, I kept the ball and hit Miguel on a quick slant. When Jake let his man through again, I rolled out and threw a lateral to Jamal.

The only time we played better was the four minutes I got sat and Coach put Gabriel in, to give him some field time. Elijah's sabotage suddenly stopped and they looked a lot better, picking up some yardage before Gabriel threw a bad pass that got intercepted.

While the interception was enough to keep me from sitting out on the rest of the game, it did help to sell the idea that I was the problem and causing a lot of the mistakes that were happening on the field.

The sabotage did its job, though. With two minutes left, they started their final drive from their thirty. Our defense fought hard, but Monterey kept grinding out yards. Finally, with six seconds left, they lined up and made a field goal from twenty-five yards that left the score 17 to 14.

Elijah had made his game clear. They were trying to get me pulled as the starter. It didn't seem to matter that Gabriel wasn't as good. They only cared about hurting me.

I worked myself up into being pissed about it by the time I got back into the field house. I saw Elijah, who'd come in ahead of me, with the rest of my former friends, and started toward him.

I was going to make sure he knew just what happened if he screwed the game for us again.

"Elijah!" I shouted. "We need to talk. Now."

Before I could reach him, a hand grabbed my shoulder. Hard. I could see most of the other guys with Elijah, but Mason was missing, so I turned around, ready to deal with him, only to freeze.

It wasn't Mason. It was Coach Heidemann.

"Come with me to the office."

He didn't wait for me, just let go and started walking, expecting me to follow. I glanced back at Elijah and saw him smirking, clearly happy I was about to get my butt chewed out for the game. It ate me up, seeing him so pleased his plan was working, and that he didn't give a shit what it did to the rest of the team.

Once in the office, Coach Heidemann closed the door and gestured for me to sit down.

"That was a tough loss out there. I saw how hard you were working to make plays happen in the second half, but Blake, you need to stick to the playbook if you're going to lead this team effectively."

"I tried, Coach, but Elijah and a few others were tanking plays they were involved in on purpose, trying to make me look bad."

"That's a pretty big accusation. I'm assuming you have some kind of proof they were doing it on purpose?"

He knew I didn't. That was how these things worked. It wasn't like they were going to write me a note saying 'we're going to make the team lose because we hate you.'

"No."

"Then let's deal with what facts we do have. Now, just as I noticed how hard you were working to make plays, I did notice some of your teammates were having problems on the field. We'll work on it during practice, but remember, you're running the offense. If there are specific issues during a game, you need to communicate them to us coaches. Not just decide what plays you want to do or bailing on the plays we give you. As you get more experience, we'll get you running audibles, but even those aren't just picked out of thin air. Audibles are still specific plays, planned and practiced ahead of time."

"But I did tell you, Coach."

"No, you told me Elijah and Hunter were playing bad on purpose, which again isn't something you can back up. But it also doesn't matter. You're the leader of the team. You're going to have guys that will cause you problems, and you'll have to deal with it. I know that's not fair, but leading a team isn't easy, and it's not always fair."

That annoyed me a little bit. I mean, I got it. Yeah, I was a kid, but I also had these memories from the dream, a whole life of being shown again and again life wasn't fair. It still sucked being confronted with it like this.

"We're not blind to what's happening out there," he said. "But unless someone's in danger or is seriously hurt, we prefer you guys to work it out yourselves. We're not babysitters, Blake."

I opened my mouth to protest, but he held up a hand. "Listen, you're only here for four years, and if you're lucky, another four in college. Then you're out in the real world, where people will try to sabotage you, get ahead of you, and there won't be an adult to run to for help. Now is when you start learning how to get your team where it needs to be, even if they're making it difficult. If there are players not doing their job, come to me with a plan. Not just telling me who's doing what, but a plan. We'll shift plays around and do what we can to get everyone working together."

I sighed. I was trying to keep my frustration in check, but it wasn't easy. They got to be jerks, doing whatever they wanted while I was getting talked to about leadership.

It was kind of bullshit.

"I get what you're saying, Coach."

"No, I don't think you do. Look, I see something special in you, Blake. You've got real potential, not just as a player, but as a leader. The way you help the new guys, how you adapt under pressure. But dealing with difficult people? That's part of leadership, too."

"This isn't exactly the inspiring pep talk I was hoping for after losing our first game."

"Because you don't need one. You played well today, adapting for what wasn't working. But being a good quarterback isn't just about completing passes or knowing the playbook. It's about getting everyone to work together, even when they're making it hard."

I had another strange moment of déjà vu. I remembered a similar conversation from my dream life, in my sophomore year. Before everything fell apart, of course. It was a different coach and this was a lot more blunt. But the general message was about the same.

"You're probably right, I just wish …" I said, my voice trailing off.

"That everyone would play nice and do their jobs?" Coach chuckled. "Welcome to leadership, kid. Now, don't think this means we're letting today slide. Tomorrow's practice is going to suck for you guys."

"Let me guess, lots of running?"

"Oh yeah. By the time we're done breaking down everything that went wrong today, you'll all be wishing you were somewhere else."

"Great," I laughed, standing up. "Can't wait."

"One more thing, Blake. We're just starting here. Show me you can run this offense the right way, and we'll talk about giving you more freedom to call the shots. It'll put you in a good position for next year."

I nodded and headed for the door. Now, I just had to find a way to work with Elijah that didn't involve punching him in his stupid face.

Chapter 8

While the game and conversation the night before were occupying a lot of my thoughts, it wasn't the only thing I had to focus on. Football was a priority, but now, so was school, and I'd been busting my ass to get the year started off on the right foot.

So Friday morning, I was sitting in the front row of my math class, trying very hard to follow everything Ms. White was putting up on the board and wishing I was a better student in my dream life. Remembering it had done a lot to get me ahead in football and deal with personal life problems, but it wasn't doing me any good in class.

So I struggled, trying to understand what I was seeing and hoping at least some of it would stick. I was focused enough that the bell ringing made me jump a little bit.

As with every time the bell rang, everyone started shoving stuff into backpacks and getting out of the classroom as fast as they could. Changing classes was a good point to stop and talk to friends for a few minutes before heading to the next class, so the faster we got out, the more time we had to talk.

I didn't move quite as fast, trying to copy the last few problems she'd worked out in my notebook so I could refer back to the steps when I was doing the homework.

I wasn't the last one out, but I was close.

Even with that, as I headed for the door, Ms. White said, "Blake, could you wait a moment, please?"

I diverted and stopped at her desk, waiting until the last two kids walked out, hoping this wasn't a bad 'talk to me.'

She smiled and held up a paper. "I have your quiz from Wednesday. I wanted to discuss it with you."

"How did I do?"

"You did very well, Blake. Take a look."

She handed it to me, and I looked through it. It was only one page front and back, I guess since it was our first quiz, and only one of the questions had an x on it. The rest all had check marks. On the front, the number ninety-two was circled.

An A. I couldn't help but feel a rush of pride.

"You told me you'd show me you meant business, and I've been watching you. You've been focused and paying attention every day, but this shows me that you really are taking this seriously. So, I'd like to give you some additional work to help accelerate your progress. I think with some extra effort, we can get you on level by the end of the year, but I want to make sure you feel you can handle it with your other obligations."

"I think I can handle it. I want to do whatever it takes to graduate right so I can get into a good program."

"That's an unusual sentiment for a freshman. A senior ... yes, but most freshmen see four years from now as an eternity away."

I just shrugged. "I guess I'm not most freshmen."

"First, I have to ask, how are you managing your time? Between football, schoolwork, and these new responsibilities, it's a lot for anyone to handle."

"To be honest, it's been a struggle. I feel like I'm constantly running from one thing to the next, trying to keep up. But I know if I can stay organized and focused, I'll find a way to make it work."

"Have you considered setting up a schedule? Mapping out your time can help you prioritize and stay on track. And don't be afraid to ask for help, maybe even a study partner."

"Yeah. Maybe," I said.

I wasn't sure where I'd find a good study partner. No one on the team, that was for sure. And it wasn't like I had time for socializing outside of football, not and get all the homework done.

"Well, think about it. If you can't, you're welcome to come by during lunch if you need help. Or if mornings work better, I'm here thirty minutes before first bell, since I know afternoons are out with football practice."

"Thanks."

"And I expect all of the additional work to be completed by Friday each week. No exceptions."

"I understand. But what if I can't catch up fast enough? With football and everything else."

"I think you can. Your progress has been excellent. If you maintain this focus, there's absolutely no reason you won't reach your goals."

I nodded, hoping she was right. It was the 'everything else' that was really worrying me.

She must have seen something on my face, because she asked, "Is there a problem with that?"

"No, it's just ... not all my teachers are as willing to give me a chance. Especially Mr. Walsh."

"Oh?"

"Yeah. He seems to have this thing against athletes. Like on Tuesday, I gave the right answer about different levels of classification of organisms, domains, kingdoms, phylum, etc, and he just dismissed it. Acted like I must have been guessing and got lucky because, you know, football player equals dumb jock."

I don't know why, but something about her expression made it seem like she knew what I was talking about. She pressed her lips together for a moment and her eyebrows dipped.

But she only said, "I see."

"I mean, I get it. Some guys live up to the stereotype. But I'm trying to prove I'm different."

"I'll speak with your other teachers. See if we can coordinate to help you get completely back on level and to see if there is some additional support available. But Blake, the ball's in your court. You'll have to prove you're serious."

"I will. I promise."

"Good." She gestured toward the door. "Now, get to class before you're late."

I hurried out, just happy someone had listened to me, and hoped she'd have better luck with Mr. Walsh than I had.

My legs ached as I walked up our driveway, still feeling the burn from Coach's "special conditioning" after yesterday's game combined with the walk home. He'd really torn into us, angry at how some of the guys had played the game. It annoyed me a little bit that, while everyone knew he was calling out Elijah, Hunter, and Jake specifically, he didn't actually say any of their names. It was more of an admonishment for how mistakes were made in general, as if everyone had dropped the handoffs or missed their blocks.

Then he'd run us like crazy, until some of the guys puked. I remembered a phrase from a documentary I'd seen in the dream life about prison camps in World War Two. Something about collective punishment.

It was bullshit then, and it was bullshit now.

At least the rest of the day's classes had gone well. Surprisingly well, actually. My afternoon teachers, at least those whose classes I'd had a chance to get back on level in, had pulled me aside to give me similar assignments to work on, just like Ms. White had, which suggested she had indeed talked to them.

It was a lot of additional work and I was going to be extremely busy with normal homework, the additional work, and studying plays. But, it *was* what I'd asked for.

The screen door banged against the house in the September breeze as I reached for the handle. Before I could touch it, the crash of splintering wood inside stopped me cold.

"Where is it?" Joshua's voice carried through the front door. "You took it! You always take my stuff!"

I yanked the door open to find our kitchen transformed into a war zone. One of the dining chairs lay in pieces near the fridge, its wooden slats scattered across the linoleum. Joshua stood by the kitchen counter, his face bright red, fists clenched at his sides.

"Sweetie, I promise I haven't seen your binder," she said, using that placating tone she always used with him, like she was talking to a toddler instead of a thirteen-year-old. "Let's look for it together ..."

"Shut up!" Joshua's arm swept across the counter, sending the toaster and a stack of mail flying. The toaster hit the floor with a metallic crunch, pieces of plastic skittering across the tile. "You're lying! You always lie!"

Mom took a step toward him, hands raised. "Josh, baby, please ..."

The moment I saw Joshua's muscles tense, like he was about to raise his arm and swing at her, I dropped my backpack and moved, grabbing him from behind, pinning his arms to his sides before he could reach her.

"Let me go!" He thrashed against my grip, trying to twist free. "This is your fault, too! You're always trying to make me look bad!"

"Stop it," I said, tightening my hold as he struggled. "You need to calm down."

"Blake, let him go. He's just upset."

"He was about to attack you," I said, nodding toward the destroyed chair. "Look what he's already done."

"Don't be ridiculous. Joshua would never hurt any of us. He's just frustrated."

"You're such a kiss-ass." Joshua's elbow slammed back into my ribs, but I held on. "Always playing the perfect son, like you're better than me. Like when you told Dad I was the one who dented his car. You're not better than me. You're nothing. Pathetic."

"You did dent his car. You know damn well you rode your bike into it."

"Blake, language," Mom scolded, like that was the biggest problem here.

"I hate you! I hate both of you! Let me go or I'll-"

The threat died as I pulled on his arms tighter, putting pressure on the joints, causing him to cry out in pain. Mom took a step toward him when he yelled out, reaching out her arm, which is when I saw them. Three angry red scratches running down her forearm, fresh enough that tiny beads of blood still dotted the skin.

"What happened to your arm?" I asked, nodding at her arm while I pulled him back a step so his wild kicks wouldn't hit her.

Pulling her shirt sleeve down to cover the scratches, she angrily said, "Blake Andrew Sims, you let your brother go this instant!"

I grimaced, but she was really mad now. She only used my middle name when I was in serious trouble. It didn't matter that I was keeping him from attacking her. She was always unreasonable, but when she got like this, she was almost as bad as he was.

I spun around and released Josh, shoving him away from both of us. He stumbled but caught himself, looking back between us with cold calculation that sent chills down my spine. I shifted my weight, ready for whatever he was going to do.

Thankfully, he stopped tensing and took another step back, although the look in his eyes didn't diminish at all.

"You'll regret this. Both of you. I'll make sure of it."

With that, he spun around and stormed toward his room, stomping with each step to let us know just how angry he was.

"What were you thinking?" Mom rounded on me the moment Joshua was gone. "He's just a child! You could have hurt him grabbing him like that."

"A child!" I said, gesturing at the destroyed chair. "Look what he did to the kitchen! And those scratches ..."

"You're only making things worse. You're his big brother. You're supposed to set an example, not escalate situations."

"He was going to hit you."

"Don't be ridiculous." She waved her hand dismissively. "Joshua would never do that. This is just normal pre-teen hormones. You weren't exactly easy to deal with at his age either, you know."

"Yeah, I was a jerk in middle school, but this is different. This isn't normal behavior. He needs help, real help. We should get him into therapy before ..."

"Therapy?" Mom scoffed. "Don't be dramatic. He'll grow out of it, just like you did. He's my son, Blake. I think I know him."

"Mom, please listen ..."

"That's enough," she said, rubbing her fingers into her temples. "I have a headache coming on. Just go. Get out of my sight."

I opened my mouth to argue but stopped myself. It was pointless. She'd keep making excuses for him until something terrible happened. Just like in my dream. I grabbed my bag and went upstairs as she headed for her room, ignoring all of the broken stuff on the kitchen floor.

I'd go back down in a bit and clean it up. I just didn't want to deal with her anymore tonight. Every excuse she made, every violent outburst she ignored, was just teaching Joshua he could get away with anything.

And doing nothing to stop him from becoming ... the thing he became.

I managed to get all of my extra assignments done early, which left me most of the week to focus on my regular homework and practice, which seemed like the go-to move. Ms. White was good with the schedule I showed her and agreed to give me new assignments on Fridays, but that she'd keep the date to turn work in on Fridays as well. She pointed out that I should always build in flexibility for weekends in case something happened and I wasn't able to get to it, although she said I should still try to be done on Sundays. That putting things off until the last moment would just end up with problems.

She had a point.

It also meant that, after a pretty busy weekend where I spent basically all Sunday doing homework, things would be easier for a few days, as long as I stayed on my homework.

I was still thinking this through as I headed to lunch, when I rounded a corner and saw trouble. Well, I saw Elijah, which was the same thing. This time, instead of directing his dickishness at me, he and Mason had some kid pressed against the wall, leaning into him, saying something I couldn't hear.

They were a little old for the 'beating up a kid for his lunch money' routine, although I wouldn't put it past them. Whatever they were doing, it certainly wasn't good. I'd half turned around before they could see me and started the other way when I stopped.

I was drained, bone-tired from everything, but I couldn't just walk past this. Ignoring it meant letting them win, letting them become more like the versions of themselves I remembered. Besides, I thought I knew this kid from somewhere, couldn't place him, but the recognition was nagging in the back of my mind.

What was clear was that he looked terrified.

"Listen here, wetb..." Elijah was saying when I doubled back.

"Back off, Elijah."

Elijah looked over his shoulder, glowering when he realized it was me. "Well, if it isn't Saint Blake, here to save another loser. I'm gettin' real tired of you showin' up wherever I am."

"What's your problem? What'd this kid do to you?"

"That's between us." Elijah jabbed a finger toward the freshman's chest before turning and getting up in my face. "Mind your own business for once."

"Well," I said, my voice steady, looking him hard in the eyes. "Now it's between us."

Without a word, he shoved the kid against the lockers hard enough that the kid slipped and slumped to the floor. Mason ignored the kid on the ground and moved to get on the other side of me, their threat very clear, as he clenched his fist.

"What's going on here?" a voice came from down the hallway as Mason started to lift his fists.

All three of us turned to see a teacher looking our way. Mason dropped his hands immediately, glancing back at Elijah, who threw me a cold look, lips curling into a sneer.

"Next time, Sims," he muttered under his breath as he backed off, slapping Mason on the shoulder.

As the two walked off, I reached down and helped the kid up, watching Elijah and Mason disappear down the hallway.

I held onto him for a second as he steadied himself, before letting go.

"Thanks," he said quietly, picking his backpack up and putting it on his back again.

"You okay? Those guys can be real jerks."

"Yeah, I'm good."

He shifted his weight, clearly wanting to bolt but trying to be polite.

"I'm Blake. Blake Sims."

"Eduardo Guzman."

The name hit me like a punch to the gut. Memories flooded in, not the vague half-remembered thoughts like I'd been getting, but sharp and clear like photographs. Eduardo's face, older and harder with the baby fat mostly gone, sitting at the defense table at the trial. He would be the kid who, in another version of my life, took everything from me.

I must have stood there, staring at him with an open mouth, for a long time, because he shifted uncomfortably and asked, "You okay?"

"Uhh, yeah. I'm good."

I managed a tight smile and turned, walking away from him, leaving him standing there, probably confused and dumbfounded by the entire confrontation.

"Hey ... thanks again," he called after me as I walked off.

I didn't turn around, just lifted a hand in a quick wave.

I found myself heading toward the cafeteria without really thinking about it, my feet moving on autopilot. But the closer I got, the more my stomach twisted, making the idea of eating feel impossible. I peeled off and sank down onto one of the benches outside, the rough wood biting into my palms as I sat, staring at the cracked pavement. The memory of Eduardo's older face in court replayed on a loop in my mind, his hollow eyes, the way he flinched at every mention of what he'd done.

Part of me wanted to get up, march back in there, find Eduardo, and break his hands so he would never be able to pick up a gun. Never be able to do what he did. Was going to do. The rage was hot, a fire that burned in my gut. But I clenched my fists until my knuckles ached, forcing myself to breathe, to think.

Eduardo hadn't done anything. Not yet. He was just a scared freshman, backed into a wall and being picked on. And if I went off on him now, I would just be another bully, adding to the pile. I closed my eyes, the courtroom scene playing out in my head again. Eduardo crying as he apologized, the raw edge in his voice when he said he wished he could take it all back. I could still hear it, how genuine it had sounded, how broken.

And then another memory. News a year and a half later, after mom fell apart and they decided it was cheaper to emancipate me than put a seventeen-year-old in the system, of Eduardo hanging himself in his cell. They'd called it a suicide brought on by depression. I hadn't cared at the time. I was at the lowest point of my life. My father was gone, my mother was gone, and my brother had been separated from me, put into the system, since he was a few years younger. Okay, Josh being separated didn't bother me. Even in that life, we'd never had a good relationship, but I was a young man without a family, all alone.

So I hadn't really cared about the news.

But I could remember some of it now, if I focused on things I didn't pay attention to at the time. He'd been destroyed by what he'd done, just like my dad. I concentrated hard, trying to remember more. Something about a family member, a cousin maybe. They'd begged for mercy from the court. He'd been bullied and had been convinced a gang would protect him. In a way, looking at it objectively, it wasn't hard to see how things could spiral out of control. How he'd be talked into something like that.

I rubbed a hand over my face. Hurting Eduardo wouldn't change a damn thing. It might even make things worse. He was already getting bullied. If I pushed too hard, I'd just shove him into doing the very thing I didn't want him to do.

My dad would still be out there, a cop on duty, walking into that scene one day like it was inevitable. Unless I did something. Unless I found a way to change Eduardo's path so that he never got to that point.

There was an obvious answer. And a terrible one. It was quite literally the last thing I'd want to do, but it was also clearly the only way to save my dad.

I had to become friends with Eduardo.

I sighed and leaned back against the bench, staring up at the clear September sky.

Jesus. Friends with the kid who might kill my dad.

What the hell?

Chapter 9

My stomach finally pushed me to get off the bench and head inside. I was still struggling with the idea that I needed to become friends with the guy who would maybe, if my dream was right, kill my father in a year and a half. It was the right call, really the only call, considering there was no way I could explain my reasoning. At least not without getting locked up.

I tried to put it in the back of my mind for now, until I figured out how to go about being friends with some random kid I'd never met before today. I'd done him a favor, getting Elijah off him, so maybe he'd be receptive to something more.

I was feeling kind of hollow as I got in line and got my food, keeping my head down and trying to process it all. I finally looked up to avoid two guys talking in the aisle way between the tables and caught sight of the girl I'd seen the other day, sitting outside the school. The Chinese girl whose name I still didn't remember.

She was sitting by herself again, just like she had the other day. I started to walk past her and had a thought. IF I was going to befriend Eduardo and fix the things that happened in my dream, then I shouldn't stop there. I had to try and fix all of it. All the shit I was going to do in the dream, during those two years of high school before it all fell apart. When I thought I was God's gift to the world. When I was as big of an asshole as Elijah.

I looked past her to where my friends were sitting. Connor and Miguel were looking my way, confused. They were probably wondering why I was so late to lunch and then just stopped in the middle of the cafeteria. I shook my head and waved them off before turning back to her table, putting my tray on the table in front of her and sitting on the hard, attached plastic seat.

She froze mid-bite, her sandwich hovering inches from her mouth.

"What are you doing?" she asked, somewhere between angry and annoyed.

"I saw you the other day, sitting in front of the school by yourself. And then I saw you here, by yourself again, eating your lunch, so I figured I'd join you."

"Why?"

"Because no one should have to be by themselves all the time."

She set down her sandwich and crossed her arms.

"I'm fine by myself. Why aren't you sitting with your football friends?"

"Maybe I don't want to sit with them right now. I'd rather be here."

Her chair scraped against the floor as she stood up abruptly, her hands flat on the table. "I don't know what your plan is, but I'm not going to sit here and let you and your friends play any more jokes on me."

"What?" I looked up at her, genuinely confused. "What jokes? What are you talking about?"

"Those guys over there," she said, pointing towards Elijah's table. "They took my physics textbook last week. Then yesterday, someone put an unpeeled banana in my backpack and then smashed it, getting it all over my work.

And now they've started calling me ..." She stopped, her face flushing. "Never mind. I've had enough."

"Wait, who did what?" I turned to look where she was pointing. Elijah and his crew were huddled together, laughing about something.

"Them. Your friends," she practically spat the word.

I couldn't help but notice Brandy was sitting with them, Mason's arm around her. Not the point at that moment, but it irked me a little every time I saw them. There was a point, pre-dream, where I thought she really liked me.

"Those guys aren't my friends." I shook my head. "They actually hate my guts right now because I won't play along with their BS anymore."

"You're all on the team together."

"So what? Just because we're on the same team doesn't mean I'm friends with them. People can be part of something and still not agree with each other. I had no idea that they've been messing with you, and I definitely don't condone it."

She lowered herself back into her seat but kept her arms crossed. "Right. Sure. That's exactly what someone like you would want me to believe."

"Someone like me?"

"Popular kids. One of them." She gestured vaguely toward Elijah's table again. "You know what, this is my table and I don't want you sitting here."

"I'm not …" I started to protest but stopped myself.

She was pissed and not going to listen to me. Just pressing her wasn't going to change her mind.

"Fine. If you really want me to leave you alone, I will," I said, picking up my tray and stepping away from the table. A step away, I stopped and looked back at her and said, "For what it's worth, I wasn't trying to trick you. I just noticed that you sit by yourself a lot. Thought maybe you could use a friend."

Without waiting for a response, I turned and headed for the table with Miguel, Connor, and the others. I could feel her eyes on my back as I walked away, but I didn't look back. Some things couldn't be fixed in one conversation. Sometimes, you had to give people space to figure things out for themselves.

She'd at least looked up to talk to me this time. That was progress, right?

I decided not to go to the JV game on Saturday because I wanted to get a head start on the extra assignments I'd been given for the following week, but I did manage to talk my dad into going to see the first varsity game of the season on Friday.

Kenneth Ward was as good as advertised, with a hell of an arm on him. He threw some pretty serious passes and really seemed to be able to read the defense. I could see a lot of what Coach Heidemann had been talking about in practice as Kenneth adjusted the plays based on the pressure they were getting from the other team.

The only thing that I thought was a problem was how much they ran, given how well he threw the ball. Coach Holloway seemed to really like just trying to punch the ball through with sheer brute strength. When they did let him pass, it was short dinky things designed to pick up a few safe yards. They moved the ball steadily, to be sure, but it took all of the excitement out of the game and kept the score low.

They still managed to bring in the victory with a 14 to 7 score. I was sure they were going to win some games that way, but I wasn't sure that kind of play calling was going to get them to state.

Which was a waste, considering how good Kenneth was.

That was still on my mind when I got to practice Monday afternoon. Looking through the playbook Coach Heidemann had given me, it was clear that was the kind of play style the entire school was running. There was good reason for it, I was sure. It would be easier to learn and a safer play style, but I wanted to get us to state by the time I was a senior. A gutsy thing to think, I knew, but ever since the dream, I wasn't just going through life just hoping for the best.

I wanted to get into a good D1 school, and from there to the NFL, and I wasn't going to do that just making short dinky passes and running the ball.

How I was going to get the coaches to do something a little more exciting, though, was beyond me.

I wasn't the only one with something on my mind. I showed up at the practice field a little early, since I wasn't screwing around as much as Elijah or a bunch of the other guys were before they got suited up for practice. I was surprised to see Miguel, Connor, and the rest of my new friends already out there. I would have been happy to see they'd stepped up their work ethic, too, except they looked worried about something, and had clearly been talking about it.

"Hey," I said, joining their circle. "What's up?"

"We're going to have another shit week," Miguel said. "Connor overheard them at lunch when he walked by their table."

"Yeah?" I said, looking at Connor.

"Not a lot, but enough that it was clear they aren't going to give up on it."

"They also couldn't stop trying to burn holes through you with how they were looking at you either," Jamal said.

"They're jerks. We can't let them get in our heads."

"It's more than that. They're gonna try something again during the game," Tyrell said. "Mark my words."

Miguel nodded. "They'd rather see us lose than let you succeed."

"That's what I don't get," Connor said. "Why trash our whole season just to get back at Blake?"

"Because they're idiots," Jamal replied.

"You need to do something," Connor insisted, turning to me.

"Like what?"

"Coach Heidemann's always pulling you aside to talk. He listens to you."

"I already tried that after the game," I said. "He didn't believe they were throwing plays on purpose."

"We still have to do something," Miguel said. "If Coach won't believe they're doing it on purpose, maybe you're going to have to talk to him about changing plays when things start looking sketchy. Like, in a way that isn't accusing them of something."

"You want me to ask for permission to call plays?"

"Audibles, at least. Coach is always saying you're supposed to be our leader, so that wouldn't come off as you just showboating or anything. You'd be doing your job as our captain."

"Besides," Tyrell added, "hate to say it, but they're kind of your responsibility."

"How do you figure that?"

"They were your friends. I'm not saying you're like them. We all know you're different from them, but ..."

"But they're still my problem," I finished.

I'm not sure I loved the idea, or that it was fair, but I'd talked the guys into sitting separate from them, and more or less position ourselves against them. I'd made them my responsibility, so it shouldn't be a surprise that they'd expect me to deal with it.

"Yeah," I said finally. "Alright. I'll talk to Coach."

"Now?" Jamal asked.

I spotted Coach Heidemann walking toward the field, clipboard in hand. "No time like the present."

I jogged over to Coach Heidemann before he reached the field. "Coach, got a minute?"

He checked his watch. "Make it quick, Blake. Practice starts in ten."

"It's about the offense." I fell into step beside him. "I've been thinking about last week's game-"

"Blake," Coach cut in, shaking his head. "We're not revisiting this."

"No, sir, that's not what I was going to say." I moved in front of him, making him stop. "I'm not accusing anyone of anything. But during the game, there were times I could tell things weren't lined up right. Players weren't where they needed to be, weren't looking for the pass. By the time I saw it, it was too late to do anything about it."

"Okay."

"I know we haven't covered audibles yet, but I'd like to start learning them. That way, if I see something's going to be a problem, I can adjust before the snap."

"Actually, that was always part of the plan. That's one of the reasons we have a freshman team, to transition from how the game is played in middle school to how it's played at this level. It's something you and the rest of the team need to master here before moving up to JV and varsity."

"Could we start this week? Have something ready for Thursday's game?"

"A week? That's not nearly enough time."

"I can do the work. I know it's not a lot of time, but I'm willing to do what it takes."

"It's not just about you. Audibles aren't just about you making calls. The entire offense has to recognize them, process them, and adjust their assignments accordingly."

"I get that. We don't need anything complicated. Just basic stuff to start - maybe changing the direction of a run or switching from a pass to a handoff. Then we can add more as the season goes on."

Coach tapped his clipboard against his leg, thinking. "I don't know ..."

"You told me I needed to be a leader for this team. That's what I'm trying to do here. Give me the tools to help us succeed."

He studied me for a long moment. "Alright. We'll work on some basic calls these next few practices. See how it goes. But if the team's not ready by Friday, we stick to the original playbook. Deal?"

"Deal. Thanks, Coach."

"Don't thank me yet. Now get suited up. Practice starts in five, and we've got a lot of work to do."

Well, that worked better than I thought it would. Now I just had to not screw it up.

The practice on Monday and Tuesday actually went well, enough that I was starting to feel that Coach Heidemann was going to agree to let us try using audibles at Thursday's game, but it was still a lot of work. And not just for me.

On Wednesday, Miguel caught up with me in the hallway as I was on the way to lunch, slugging my shoulder by way of greeting.

"You know you've screwed us, right?"

His tone was light and he was smiling, so whatever he was going to say, I knew he was just messing with me.

"What'd I do this time?"

"This," he said, holding up the playbook. "Football's supposed to be fun, not more homework. You've got us studying like it's finals week."

"Hey, you guys were the ones who wanted me to talk to Coach about dealing with Elijah's crew. This was the solution. Can't complain now."

"I guess. It's just ... there are so many signals and plays to remember and Coach keeps running us every time we screw up."

"I know. I'm right there running with you. Or did you forget? Besides, if you want to show them you deserve to end up on varsity next year, this is how we're going to do it."

He rolled his eyes, muttering something under his breath about 'torture' and 'studying,' but didn't say anything else. I was about to tease him again about his work ethic as we walked into the cafeteria, when I looked over and saw the Chinese girl sitting by herself again, and our eyes locked. She gave me a nasty look, as if daring me to bother her again and I looked away.

"That went well," Miguel snickered.

"Shut up," I muttered, getting in the lunch line.

We grabbed our trays loaded with mystery meat and overcooked vegetables. Edible, but just barely.

"You crashed and burned, dude. It happens."

"I told you, it's not like that."

"Sure, buddy," he said, laughing.

I just shook my head. It wasn't like I was going to be able to explain to them that I was trying to make up for past wrongs in a dream I had a month ago that I thought was prophetic. Even thinking that sentence made me wonder if I was crazy.

We were almost at our table when I noticed someone else sitting by themselves. Eduardo. I'd vowed that I'd make friends with him and try to keep him from joining the gang. Now seemed as good of a time as ever.

"Hey, I'll join you guys in a bit," I said, slowing my pace.

Miguel followed my gaze and laughed. "What, are you like the patron saint of loners now? Making it your mission to save every kid eating alone?"

"Maybe I am. Worked out pretty well with you guys, didn't it?"

"Whatever, Mother Teresa." Miguel shook his head and walked away.

He kept going, joining the others at our table as I turned and headed to where Eduardo was sitting.

I placed my tray down across from Eduardo, making him jump slightly. He looked up, like a startled animal ready to bolt. He was probably worried that it was Elijah or Mason, but calmed down after a second, although instead of his expression turning to one of recognition, it became one of confusion.

He looked down at his plate, and then back up at me, like he was debating something.

"Hey. Sorry for being a jerk the other day. I was in a rush, and it was ... just a rough morning."

"Ohh," he said, seeming to relax. "It's cool. You actually helped me out with those guys, so ..."

"Yeah, well, they're jerks. They hate me as much as anyone. What's their problem with you anyway?"

"No idea. I've got wood shop with Mason, but I barely talk to him, or any of the rest of them. Maybe it's just because I'm new?"

"You just moved here?"

"Yeah. My dad relocated us from Midland, even though he still works there, which means he has to drive two hours each way. He thought this would be a 'better environment,'" he said, shooting a pointed look at Elijah's table, where Mason was currently shoving Jake's head down toward his food.

Something in Eduardo's tone made me suspect there was more to the story, but I didn't push. I remembered what happened to him in that other life ... the gang violence, and the path he'd gone down. Maybe his dad had seen the warning signs early, tried to prevent it by moving his family away. But from what I was seeing, the move might have just made things worse. Being isolated, alone, and picked on seemed like a good recipe for someone turning to a gang for friends.

"I get the long commute. My dad works in Midland, too," I said instead. "He's a deputy there."

"My dad actually works for the city too. He's a groundskeeper. Long hours, but at least it's steady work."

From there, we talked about our dads' commutes, what it was like for him living in Midland, our families and the classes we were taking, and basically just got to know each other through the rest of lunch. He was actually a nice guy once he got over being so terrified. He was funny and self-deprecating, and for most of the conversation I actually forgot what he did in my dream. Getting to know him, learning about his cousin who had leukemia and his best friend in Midland who moved away two years ago, it was hard to reconcile the person in front of me with the one I remembered from my dream, sitting at the defense table, staring blankly ahead while the medical examiner talked about my dad's injuries.

I wasn't sure if that was making this easier, or harder, but at least I was able to push it aside and just focus on being friendly. What was very clear was that Eduardo needed friends. He was very clearly lonely and stressed from being a target for ridicule.

As lunch wrapped up, I started to gather up my trash, I said, "Hey, tomorrow you should come sit with us."

I nodded to the table where Miguel, Connor and the rest were still sitting, not in any hurry to get to their next class.

Eduardo hesitated. "I don't know, man. Football players ..."

"Miguel and those guys aren't like Elijah and Mason," I said, cutting him off. "They're good people. You'd like them."

"Maybe."

"Plus," I added, "having friends watching your back makes guys like that think twice about starting trouble."

Eduardo considered this, then nodded slowly. "Yeah, that would be good."

"Cool. See you tomorrow then?"

"Yeah, see you."

Walking to class, I actually felt like I'd accomplished something. True, football was going better than in my dream, but it was still mostly on track for the same result, since I knew I'd end up on at least the JV team next year with the way the coach was talking.

This ... this was the first huge change I'd made to my life compared to the dream. It was just one conversation, so I wasn't counting it as a victory or anything, but it was solid progress.

Chapter 10

Tomorrow was game day, and Coach had okayed us to use a few audibles in the game. I hoped it wouldn't be needed, and Elijah wouldn't be an idiot and try to sabotage the team again, but I knew that was wishful thinking. I knew Elijah from our past and from our future in the dream, and he'd always been petty and overly concerned with being humiliated and made to feel less than he thought he should be.

Elijah didn't think about the future and never thought about the consequences of his actions. He only thought about getting the respect he thought he was owed. It's why he kept ending up in trouble in high school and why he'd ended up in prison, just before he was ready to head off to college, for getting into a fight and breaking some guy's back to the point of paralyzing him. He'd done three years for assault and ruined his chances of ever playing ball again. All because the guy had disrespected him.

I wanted this life to be different than my dream one, with my family whole and happy and with me in the NFL, and I wasn't going to let someone like him get in the way of that. But I also couldn't be like Elijah. Stupid and short-sighted. I couldn't let him take me down with him.

I got to the locker room and started putting my stuff in the locker, and was about to get changed for practice when Coach Heidemann walked up to me and said, "Blake, come with me."

The way he said it, this wasn't a friendly visit. Not angry exactly, but serious in a way that had me wondering what I'd done wrong. Worse, we weren't headed to his office. He led me out of the field house and over to the school, toward the offices, which was … bad. He didn't say anything else as we walked, keeping a brisk pace through the halls while students rushed past us heading home.

We walked past the secretary without another word between us and into the vice principal's office.

"Have a seat and stay quiet," he said, moving to lean against the far wall.

The chair squeaked as I sat down. I'd been in here a lot of times ... in my dream life. Everything about the office was exactly as I remembered from my dream life, the potted plant by the window, the framed diplomas, even the little ceramic apple paperweight. Back then, I'd been in this office plenty of times, usually for pulling stupid pranks, bullying other students. Mrs. Ford had watched me like a hawk those first two years, before I dropped out.

But this time was different. I hadn't done any of that stuff. No sneaking around to stuff the mascot head with shaving cream. No beating up kids for standing up to me or stealing their shit because I thought everyone else would find it funny. No targeting the quiet kids just because I could. I'd been keeping my head down, focusing on football and actually trying in my classes.

So why was I here?

Coach was making it very clear from his body language that he wasn't going to tell me, arms crossed, staring at the desk, looking annoyed. I avoided looking at him, to keep him from glaring at me, looking at the floor tiles instead, counting the speckles. Anything to keep myself from fidgeting.

When the door finally opened and Vice Principal Ford stepped in, it was almost a relief. A brief one as Mr. Walsh walked in behind her. I don't know what his problem with athletes was, but he had one and he'd decided I was the focus of it.

"Thank you for coming, Mr. Sims," she said, circling around her desk and sitting in her chair while Mr. Walsh stopped to stand next to it.

"Mr. Sims, do you remember signing the student handbook on the first day of school?" Mrs. Ford asked.

I wasn't sure what I'd expected her to say, but that wasn't it.

"Yes, Ma'am."

"And do you remember that pledge including a commitment to academic integrity, which included not cheating on any schoolwork, tests, or quizzes?"

"I haven't cheated on anything."

"He absolutely …" Mr. Walsh said, before I could say anything. Mrs. Ford held up her hand, cutting him off.

"I didn't ask if you cheated. I asked if you remembered that part of the handbook that you signed, saying you agreed to it."

"Yes, Ma'am," I said.

"Good. There has been an allegation that you cheated on your recent quiz in science."

"That's a lie," I said, the words coming out before I could stop them. "I know Mr. Walsh doesn't like me, but …"

"Teaching students doesn't have anything to do with liking them or not, and none of our instructors would allow personal feelings to dictate how they give their instruction. And I did not say Mr. Walsh was the one who originated the allegations."

I looked to Mr. Walsh, who still looked a little furious at being cut off like he had been, although he was glaring at me and not Mrs. Ford. It suggested he blamed me for it, like I'd done anything. That wasn't my only problem, although one I'd have to deal with eventually.

It wasn't hard to figure out where the accusation came from, if it didn't come from Mr. Walsh. Elijah hadn't had any luck getting me kicked off the team by throwing last week's game, and had caught a fair amount of blame from it, so he'd switched to another tactic. He'd been smart to pick Mr. Walsh, although why Mr. Walsh would listen to another football player didn't make sense to me. Maybe he just saw a chance to deal a blow to one of us to feed whatever his hatred for us was, and he didn't care where the source started.

"Ma'am. There are some students who … they're upset with me because I wouldn't go along with some things they wanted to do. Are you really going to take this seriously without knowing the full story? Can I at least know who accused me?"

"No, that's against school policy," Mrs. Ford said. "And if it was just an accusation from another student, you wouldn't be in here. Mr. Walsh has expressed doubts about the grades you've been earning in your class. He believes it would be … unlikely for you to achieve such results without outside assistance."

"With all due respect, that's garbage," I said.

"What's garbage is you trying to get us to believe you would get the grades you've been getting without cheating. I've been teaching at this school for fifteen years. Never in my experience has an athlete in remedial classes received a perfect score on their first quiz and all of their assignments without outside assistance."

"Mr. Walsh ..." Mrs. Ford started.

"I know this school worships football," he continued, "but I will not accept cheating in my classroom."

"Gail," Coach Heidemann said, looking from Mr. Walsh to her.

"Alan, please," Mrs. Ford said. "This is about a specific allegation, not your personal opinions about student-athletes."

"And it's not true," I said. "I've been studying hard every day. Ask Mrs. Mace and Ms. White; they've both been giving me extra work to help me get on level and out of remedial classes. They can tell you I've been doing the work. They've seen my progress."

"Preposterous," Mr. Walsh scoffed. "I know what people like you ..."

"That's enough," Mrs. Ford cut him off sharply. "I'll speak with your other teachers, Blake. I hope you're being truthful with me."

"I am," I said. "I made a promise to Ms. White that I'd do whatever it takes to graduate. Not just graduate, but do well enough to get into college without relying on a sports scholarship. Even though I want to play football in college, I don't want to rely on football."

Mrs. Ford studied me for a long moment, clearly sizing me up. I looked back at her levelly, trying to show her I meant it.

"I hope that's true. You can go with Coach Heidemann now."

"Let's go, Blake," Coach said quietly.

My stomach churned as we walked out. This wasn't over - not by a long shot. Mr. Walsh had decided I was everything he hated about student-athletes and Elijah was stepping things up. I didn't say anything though. I kept my mouth shut until we were back in the hallway.

"Don't worry about this," Coach said. "I know you've been putting in the work. The other teachers will back that up."

"It was Elijah. He told them I was cheating. He hates me now and he's trying to get me in trouble since he couldn't get me kicked off the team. This is what I was talking about after last week's game."

"Focus on yourself," Coach said. "Don't worry about what other people are doing. If you're doing your best, it doesn't matter what other people do."

I didn't know if he was just trying to get me to shut up or what, but he really couldn't be naive enough to believe that. I wasn't.

This situation with Elijah was going to come to a head, whether I wanted it to or not. The question was when - and how bad it would be when it did.

Thursday night we were back on the field for our second game, and I was feeling a little more ready for this one. While I felt good having the audibles in case we needed them, I was still a little concerned with what Elijah was going to do. He'd been in on all the practices this week, of course, and knew that we'd been working on them, so he'd naturally have a plan for getting around that, too.

I felt stupid not thinking about it until Wednesday's practice, mostly spurred on by his reporting me for cheating, which was an annoying reminder that he wasn't done trying to get to me. I'd pulled the guys together after practice and we'd hung around the field, talking about how to deal with that. We had come up with the idea of a mid-play audible. It only worked on running plays, but if Jake blew his assignment again or Hunter was going to drop the ball, it gave me a chance to still make something happen. It relied on Miguel, mostly, keeping his situational awareness and knowing that I might still pass to him even though he was running a fake route, since he was the only one of us eligible to receive the ball on a pass.

It should be fine, as it would look like a fake to the refs and the other team, although Coach Heidemann would definitely know the difference and probably be pissed. So I made it clear we wouldn't do it until they started screwing around. If they played it straight, we'd play it straight. We practiced it for over an hour on Wednesday for Miguel to get the feeling, since he also had some blocking assignments should the run get that far, and he couldn't screw that up if Elijah's guys were playing it straight.

It was a risky move, and one we'd save just in case we needed it, but if we were going to lose the ball anyway, and maybe fumble it if a handoff went bad, it was worth a shot. Or at least, I wanted to be able to show up Elijah and make it very clear what they were doing.

Elijah and his group always did their warm-ups away from my friends, so I wasn't that worried about them overhearing me, but I still kept my voice down as we stretched.

"We've got this," I said. "We're not going to let them screw us like last week. I know it's not really fair to you, Miguel, but you've got to be ready for it if they start messing around again."

"I can handle it."

"You really think they'll try something?" Jamal asked. "Coach made it pretty clear in the pregame that he wanted everyone to stay on their assignments this time and not have any of the same mistakes from last week."

"Yeah, I'm pretty sure. Elijah isn't done making his moves to get at us. He's a jackass, but he's persistent. Just stick to what we worked on and do your best."

Except for a few dirty looks and a sneer or two from Elijah and his crowd, things were pretty calm during the pregame, and the coin toss. It wasn't the best return we could have hoped for, getting stopped at the fifteen-yard line, but we got to have the first drive of the game, so I would take it.

I didn't get any looks from Elijah and the rest, and there weren't any of those meaningful little glances, so I took a shot that they were going to start off playing everything straight.

Or at least, I hoped they were.

As it was the coaches' go-to, we started with a running play. I slapped the ball into Hunter's belly after the snap and, thankfully, he pulled it in tight, not dropping it. He managed to find the hole and got seven yards. Not bad for a first-down run.

"Nice work," I said as we huddled again. "Let's keep it rolling. Wing-T 31 on one."

Another clean play. Five more yards. First down.

We marched methodically down the field, mixing runs and short passes. Even Jake and Elijah executed their assignments properly. By the time we reached the red zone, we had a good rhythm going.

Back in the huddle, Coach had us run another running play, again to Hunter. Again, Hunter hit the hole hard behind his blockers and powered into the end zone for the touchdown. Compared to last week's team, these guys had a really weak defense and were letting a lot more plays through than I would have thought we'd get.

Getting on the scoreboard on our first possession was certainly unexpected.

For the next little bit, neither team managed to get much movement, and we kept switching possession of the ball. We had made it almost to the end of the first quarter without any shenanigans from Elijah and the rest, and I had started to think maybe they had decided to play it straight and actually try to win football games.

Maybe that was naive of me.

As we were lining up for the second down, I caught a look between Elijah and Jake and I just knew in the pit of my stomach that they were going to try something. The call that Coach had made was a running play with a handoff to Jamal, which made sense that would be when they would try something, since the runner usually got the blame if something went bad.

I got set up to take the snap, keeping my attention on Jake, trying to read his body language and figure out when he was going to do it. I knew it had to be Jake because Elijah would be running a fake route to draw off the defenders and get into a blocking position should Jamal break through, so Jake was the only one of their group in a position to screw up the play.

"Red 42! Hut! Hut!" I said, calling an audible that would shift our line over, assuming the defense was trying to line up on our weak side.

It was one of the few I had tried, and I could see Coach on the sideline reacting, trying to figure out what the hell I was doing because if Jake didn't try and throw it, it would kind of screw us on the actual run.

I was right, though. As soon as the ball snapped into my hands, Jake stepped aside, practically inviting the linebacker through, right where Jamal would be when I let the ball go. I kept the ball in my hands instead of putting it into his stomach, backing up two steps. Jamal figured out what I was doing and moved to block the linebacker Jake let through, giving me a second to find Miguel who was just cutting his route. I prayed he was paying attention as I let the ball fly.

The pass wasn't pretty, but it got there. Miguel hauled it in before getting knocked down at the thirty-five. First down.

"Time out!" Coach Heidemann yelled, a bunch of the guys holding up the T-sign.

The ref blew his whistle and I hustled over to the sidelines, already knowing what was coming. Coach's expression said it all.

"What exactly was that, Sims?" he said, grabbing my jersey and pulling me over next to him. "Because it sure wasn't the play I called."

"Jake missed his block, Coach. Jamal was going to get crushed in the backfield."

"But you called that audible that wouldn't have made the run fail either way. And changing to a pass was never part of that audible anyway. That was you freelancing mid-play."

"I knew Jake was going to miss his block before the play started, and I wanted to pull the pressure off of Miguel by shifting the line so they would have to react. It worked."

"I don't care if it worked; I'm not going to have some cowboy shit out there when I call a play. What do you mean you knew Jake was going to miss his block before the play started?"

"You know what I mean, Coach," I said.

He had made it clear he didn't want to hear me making any more direct accusations, so I left it at that.

"Blake, goddamn it ..."

"I'm not accusing anyone of anything, Coach, but I was right. Watch them, 'cause this isn't going to be the only one of these. It's going to cost us the game."

"Just get back out there and run the plays I call. We clear?"

"Yes, sir."

They played the remainder of the first quarter straight, not trying to screw anything up or throw the game. Elijah was too clever by half. He hadn't given up, though. I knew he'd try again. They knew Coach was watching them, and didn't want to be so obvious that they got caught.

Not that them playing it straight was a magic bullet that was going to make us win. The other team was still there and while their defense wasn't the best, their offense was really good. We ended the half tied at 7 to 7.

During halftime, Coach ran through adjustments, focusing mainly on our defensive coverage to try and stop the progress they were making on offense. If Elijah had been really smart, he would have just focused on what Coach was saying, but he couldn't control himself. He kept looking at me and then exchanging glances with his buddies, giving little smirks.

He might as well have announced what he was going to do.

The other team got the kickoff to start the second half and managed to get to our thirty before turning the ball over on a poorly thrown pass that Gary Konrad managed to snag and pull in before being tackled himself.

As we lined up for our first drive of the second half, the defense was showing blitz. I took the snap, dropped back, and looked to my reads. Miguel was covered pretty tight, so I went to Elijah, who managed to break free from his defender. He was wide open, a perfect opportunity. I released the ball, hitting him right in the hands.

And he dropped it. Just ... let it fall.

The ball bounced harmlessly on the grass as Elijah jogged back to the huddle wearing that same smirk I'd seen at halftime.

"My bad," he said as he walked into the huddle. "Lights got in my eyes."

That was some bullshit. I hope that meant he was done with his tricks for a bit and would play the next down straight. We'd done a passing play, and the rotation Coach Heidemann had for us meant a running play this time.

"I-Right 21 on one," I said, and we broke heading for the line.

The ball snapped into my hands and I stepped back, slapping it into Jamal's stomach. Almost as soon as I did, Jake simply stepped aside, leaving a massive hole in our protection again. An Aldine linebacker burst through untouched, hitting Jamal only a few steps into his run. It was brutal.

The ball popped loose as Jamal crumpled to the ground. A lineman scooped it up and took off, trying to break through into open field. I managed to chase him down and drag him out of bounds before he could score, but that hardly mattered now. Worse, Jamal wasn't getting up.

He was curled on his side, gripping his leg, his face contorted in pain. I ran back to him immediately.

"Don't move," I said, waving frantically to our sideline. "Help's coming."

Our trainer jogged out with Coach Heidemann close behind. They knelt beside Jamal, asking him questions and examining his leg while I stood nearby, fury building in my chest. Elijah and Jake were standing off to the side, fucking laughing. They turned so that Coach wouldn't see them, but I saw them. They'd gotten a teammate hurt, and they thought it was fucking funny.

"You think this is funny?" I said, getting into Elijah's face.

"What ... no ..." he stammered, looking past my shoulder.

"Blake!" Coach Heidemann said behind me. "Back off."

"They mi..."

"Get off the field and make room for the defense," he said, cutting me off.

It pissed me off. He had to see it, but he wasn't doing anything about it. It was bullshit.

When they finally helped Jamal up, he couldn't put any weight on his right leg. They had to practically carry him off the field.

When Coach made it to the sidelines, I went to stand beside him.

"You saw that, right? Jake didn't even try to block. And Elijah's dropped pass? They're doing it again."

Coach's expression darkened as he watched Jamal being helped to the bench.

"We'll deal with this later," he said.

Our defense managed to stop the drive, but they were already deep enough on our side of the field that they made the field goal easy, bringing the score to 10 to 7.

For what felt like forever after that, neither team could break through. Every time we'd start getting momentum, something would go wrong. Elijah let another perfect pass slip through his fingers. Jake "missed" his block again, forcing me to throw the ball away. Hunter even got in on it, running straight into our own lineman instead of through the hole that opened up.

Even with their sabotage attempts, we actually moved the ball pretty well. Miguel and the guys who were actually trying made some good plays. We just couldn't quite get into scoring range.

The clock kept ticking down in the fourth, and we were still trailing. Four minutes left, three minutes, two minutes. Still nothing.

With just under a minute remaining, we got the ball back at our own thirty. This was it, our last chance. There wasn't time for us to get a chance at another drive.

We set up, and the defense was playing back, expecting us to pass. I didn't call an audible to change it. I wanted the yardage, and I knew we could make it. As soon as the ball hit my hands, I saw Miguel breaking toward the sideline. The safety bit on Elijah's underneath route, leaving Miguel one-on-one with the cornerback.

Miguel put a beautiful move on him, cutting inside then breaking deep. I let the ball fly, putting everything I had into it.

The pass arced high through the air, Miguel tracking it perfectly, catching it in full stride. He bolted down the sideline with only the safety trying to track him down.

The guy was fast, though, diving as Miguel got close to the goal line, catching his ankles at the two-yard line. Miguel went down hard but held onto the ball. The home crowd exploded.

Coach called a timeout to stop the clock.

As we huddled up on the sideline, the scoreboard showed five seconds left.

"Good pass, Blake," he said, slapping me on the back as I got to the sideline.

"Coach, we can make the drive. Let's not tie it."

"That's the plan. I-Right 21. I don't want any screw-ups this time," he said, looking hard at Jake, who would cost us the game if he missed his block like he had been.

Jake nodded, withering under his glare. I could only hope it would work.

We broke the huddle and lined up. The defense was stacked tight, expecting a run. I got under Tyrell, trying to stay calm.

"Red 80! Set! Hut!"

The ball snapped into my hands. I turned and handed it to Hunter. The line surged forward, opening a small hole. Hunter hit it hard. For a moment, I thought he was going to score. Then the ball popped loose, seemingly in slow motion. It bounced once, twice.

A defender dove on it.

The referee blew his whistle. Game over.

I dropped to one knee, watching the other team celebrate. We'd lost 10 to 7, and I knew exactly why. There hadn't been another hand on the ball. Hunter had dropped it.

"Forde!" Coach Heidemann yelled as we all made our way off the field. "What the hell was that?"

Hunter opened his mouth, but Coach didn't let him speak.

"No, don't give me excuses. I watched you all game. That wasn't your only screw-up tonight."

I slowed my steps, turning to watch. Hunter blinked rapidly, his usual cockiness replaced by something closer to fear. Coach's face had turned red, veins showing in his neck as he pointed at Hunter's chest.

"You think I don't see what's happening? You think I'm blind?"

I couldn't help the small smile that crept onto my face. Finally. Someone else was seeing it, too.

Coach caught my expression and his anger shifted targets. "Something funny, Sims?"

"No, sir."

"Then get your ass to the locker room. Now."

I turned to go but spotted Elijah hanging back near the bench. The smart move would have been to keep walking, but I was tired of playing it smart. I changed course, heading straight for him.

"Looks like your little plan's falling apart," I said.

111

"I don't know what you're talking about."

"Coach isn't stupid. He's figuring out what you guys are doing. Keep it up, and you'll all be watching the games from the bleachers."

"Fuck you," Elijah spat. "I don't know what got up your ass, but I'm tired of you thinking you're better than us."

"All I'm doing is actually playing football instead of acting like a child."

"You're dead, Sims. You hear me? Fucking dead."

I laughed, which only made his face redder.

As I walked away, Elijah shouted after me, "This isn't over! You better watch your back!"

I didn't turn around. He could threaten all he wanted; I had more important things to worry about. Like how we were going to win any games when half our team was actively trying to lose.

Chapter 11

Coach ran us ragged again on Friday, I guess he thought that if he put us through enough pain, everyone would get on the same game plan.

The only thing that gave me any hope that things would change was that he paid specific attention to Elijah and his crew. The optimistic part of me thought that might mean Coach had finally seen what they were doing and was taking it seriously.

Or, Coach could just be pissed about Elijah's missed catches and Hunter's fumble. My warning to Elijah after the game hadn't just been for show. They'd tried to do it in a way that made me look bad, but they'd only really managed to make themselves look bad, especially in the second game. If they'd convinced more people to join them on their little crusade, maybe things would have been different, but they hadn't.

If anything, the rest of the team was getting pissed at them for screwing up. They may not realize it was on purpose, but everyone could see where the mistakes were being made.

My only real concern was that Elijah would give up on this ploy but think up some new way to get to me. It was obvious to me that the best thing he could do was to get the rest of the team to turn against me, and if I could think of that, so could he.

Still, if Coach Heidemann was recognizing what they were doing, it would make things a little better when Elijah finally decided to pivot and do something else because I wouldn't have to waste time convincing him it was something Elijah would do.

We also weren't the only team struggling. While varsity was 2 and 0, JV had our same record, except their games hadn't been as close as ours had. They'd lost their second game on Friday by fourteen points, which is not what the coaches wanted to see.

113

Their punishment, come Monday, was going to be a lot worse than the running Coach Heidemann put us through.

I also hadn't heard anything else about the cheating accusation. On Friday, Mr. Walsh was still giving me looks and being a little hostile to me, but he didn't say anything else, so I hoped the Vice-Principal had squashed that.

Again, since I knew in my heart Elijah was behind it, I knew he wouldn't stop just 'cause this attempt didn't work. I'd have to be on my toes, ready for him to try again, that was for sure.

Late Saturday afternoon, I'd finished a lot of the assignments I'd been given on Friday and had gone down to the kitchen for a snack when I found Mom at the kitchen table, her head in her hands, looking miserable. She normally worked at the hair salon on Saturdays, and then stopped at the grocery store for stuff to make dinner on the way home, but she'd called out today because of her headaches.

I knew there was some kind of condition Mom had suffered from years later, if the dream was to be believed, and it seemed obvious the headaches were connected, but I couldn't remember any details about it. By the time she'd actually gotten sick in my dream, we had absolutely no contact. When I'd gone to her funeral, we hadn't spoken in almost a decade, and I was still pissed enough at her that I'd done just enough to get her buried and ignored everything else. I hadn't even cleaned out her apartment. I'd just left it abandoned with the rest of her probate, letting the state deal with it.

I know she'd been to the doctor about her headaches several times, and they'd always just told her it was stress and they couldn't find any physical symptoms. I knew that was bullshit, but how do you tell someone they'll die in twenty years from an ailment you can't name and convince them to start looking into what it might be.

They might not see yet that Josh was crazy, but that definitely would have them looking at me like I was.

I was still trying to think of a way to help her, but the best I could do for today was to offer to go to the grocery store for her. She was surprised by the offer and actually smiled at me as she accepted; something she hadn't done in a long while.

So Saturday afternoon, when a lot of kids would be at activities or out with friends, I was at the grocery store, digging through onions and trying to decipher Mom's scribbles on the grocery list.

I actually wish I could have done more than this, but even with the stuff I knew from the dream, I didn't know how to cook for shit. In my dream life, I'd basically lived off of cereal, instant ramen packages, and hamburger helper. I wasn't sure offering to make sub-par food for her would have been that much help.

I'd just found an onion for the meatloaf she was planning to make and looked up to figure out where the celery was when I practically ran into Eduardo, both of us looking shocked to see the other one in the grocery store.

Unlike myself, however, Eduardo was with an older woman who looked amazingly like him, and who I could only assume was his mother.

"Eduardo?" I said, partly as a greeting and partly surprised.

I was trying to keep my voice friendly and casual. We'd managed to make it through an entire meal more or less cordially, but he hadn't agreed to sit with us yet. Yesterday, he'd been by himself again, and I'd needed to talk to Miguel and the others about the game, so I hadn't been able to sit with him. But I hadn't given up on befriending him yet either.

"Uhh, Hi. This is ... uhh, my mom," he said, shifting the basket in his hands and pointing to the woman next to him."

"Elena Guzman," she said, extending her hand with a warm smile.

"Blake Sims, ma'am. I'm a friend of Eduardo's from school."

"A friend? Eduardo, you didn't tell me you were making new friends! How do you two know each other?"

"Just from school."

"Ohh, do you have classes together?"

"Ohh God, no. I'm kind of the poster boy for a dumb jock. Eduardo's too smart to be in classes with me."

Eduardo gave a kind of nervous laugh and said, "I have wood-shop with some of his teammates though. Blake is the quarterback of the freshman football team."

"Football! That's wonderful. Young men need good activities to keep them busy, don't you think? And team sports teach such important lessons about working together."

'Not the way we are doing it currently', I thought. What I said was, "Uhh, I guess."

I'd reached the problem with my not having become friends with Eduardo yet. I wasn't really sure what to say here. We'd only had one conversation, and it had mostly revolved around how much we both hated Elijah.

"So, have you lived here long? We only moved this summer, which has made it hard for Eduardo to make new friends."

Eduardo looked at his mother with a mortified expression, which I got. Parents could be embarrassing, telling someone all the stuff they wanted to keep secret.

"From Midland, right? He said his dad is traveling back for work every day, which I told him was funny because my dad also works as a policeman in Midland and commutes every day."

"An officer! How nice. And you're here shopping for your family? Are you going to cook for them?"

I laughed. "Oh, I'm just the delivery boy today. Mom's got a headache, so I offered to help out a little. My cooking would make the cafeteria food seem gourmet. This is about the limit of my skills, finding vegetables that Mom can turn into actual food."

"Well, it's good that you're learning. Eduardo helps me in the kitchen sometimes. It's important for young men to know these things."

"Mom," Eduardo muttered, his cheeks reddening.

I cleared my throat, giving Eduardo a friendly nudge. "So, what have you been up to lately?"

"Nothing much, really." Eduardo shrugged.

"Eduardo's been very focused on his schoolwork," Mrs. Guzman said, giving her son an encouraging pat on the shoulder. "He's already at the top of most of his classes."

"Mom, please ..." Eduardo mumbled.

"That's actually really cool," I said. "I wish I was doing better. It's never been my thing, but I'm working on changing that."

"It's not that hard if you stay on top of your work."

"Says the boy who got perfect scores on his first two quizzes," Mrs. Guzman beamed. "You should have more pride in yourself, Eduardo."

He just shrugged again.

"I have an excellent idea. You should come over for dinner next week. It would be wonderful for Eduardo to have a friend visit. Maybe Tuesday?"

"Mom, I'm sure Blake's busy with football and everything ..." Eduardo started to say.

"I'd love to," I cut in, seeing an opportunity I couldn't pass up. "If you're sure it wouldn't be too much trouble?"

"No trouble at all! We'll look forward to having you," Mrs. Guzman said warmly. "Tuesday at six?"

"That'd be great. Thank you for inviting me." I smiled at both of them. "I should probably finish getting everything on Mom's list before she starts wondering if I got lost. See you at school Monday, Eduardo."

Eduardo nodded, still looking nervous. I was pushing it, but if his mom was willing to help me build the friendship I needed with him, I was going to let her.

Sunday, I spent the entire morning working on homework because I wanted to be done by the time the game came on. Dad had Sundays off, and he would always watch the game in the afternoon. When I was in middle school, I'd sometimes join him, but usually, used the opportunity to get out of the house and hang out with Elijah and the rest of the guys.

"Hang out" was the wrong word. It was more like "cause trouble".

Ever since the dream, though, and the feelings that came along with it, I made sure to be home instead and hadn't missed watching a game with him since the preseason started. Even if I managed to stop what happened to him and he lived a full life, I'd eventually lose him, just like every child eventually loses their parents. Most people just live busy lives, having fun when they were younger and losing touch with them when they got older. Having felt that loss in my dream, I didn't want my memories of him to be passing.

So, I'd vowed to myself that I wasn't going to have those regrets. I decided I was going to be on the couch, watching the game with him every chance I could. Something we could do together. Memories we would always share.

Of course, those memories weren't always perfect because Dad had decided he wanted to watch the Bengals get absolutely bloodied by the Patriots. It was an embarrassing showing, and it made for a kind of boring game. Especially since I really didn't care much for the Pats.

When halftime started, I'd had enough. "Hey, I think Notre Dame's playing today. Can we see if that's on, at least while we're at halftime?"

"Fine," he said with an exaggerated sigh.

This might not have been the first time I tried to convince him to change the channel.

I started digging through the stack of stuff on the coffee table, trying to find the remote when he said, "You're going to have to get up and change it. I haven't seen the remote all afternoon."

"Really? Mom had it last night during her shows."

"Yeah, I know. I used it before bed, too, but when I sat down to watch TV this afternoon, I couldn't find it anywhere."

I pushed myself off the couch and started to look in all the usual spots, the coffee table cluttered with newspapers, the shelf beneath the TV, even under the sofa cushions, but I couldn't find it either.

"When's the last place you remember having it?" I asked.

"Right here on the armrest." Dad tapped the leather surface. "But you know how things disappear in this house."

"Mom sometimes sits on the couch and puts it on the back, maybe it fell back there," I said, pushing it forward enough to see behind it.

And there it was. Well, mostly. The remote lay in pieces, its black plastic casing cracked, and the circuit board exposed.

"Found it," I said, holding up the mangled remains.

The back was missing, and so were the batteries. A large piece of the plastic where the back cover would have snapped into it still had the broken-off tab from the cover.

It would never go on again, even if the rest of it wasn't completely trashed.

"What in the world happened to it?"

I didn't have to guess. I knew exactly what had happened to it.

"You know exactly what happened."

"What?" he asked, honestly confused.

"It was Josh. He broke it. Probably threw it against the wall, and it dropped behind the couch after it broke. Maybe he broke it and threw it back there, who knows? But he did it."

"You don't know Josh did this."

"Yes, I do. I heard him watching TV down here this morning before church." I paused, tossing the broken remote onto the coffee table. "But even if I hadn't, we both know it's true."

"Blake ..."

"No, listen. I didn't break it. You didn't break it. And if Mom broke it, she would have said something or, at the very least, would have got it out from behind the couch. But more than that, we both know Josh is getting worse. His anger is completely out of control."

"Leave it alone."

"No! I can't. Did you know he cut Mom the other day?"

"She said it was an accident."

"It wasn't. I walked in right after it happened. I'm scared, Dad. He's getting seriously dangerous and it will only go downhill from here. What if next time it's worse? What if he seriously hurts her? Or someone else?"

I was once again screwed by the fact that there was no way I could explain my dream, or how it wasn't completely crazy that I believed it. All I knew was that Josh was going to get worse, and it was going to go way beyond hurting Mom or breaking remotes.

"Blake ..."

"We need to get him help before it's too late. Before he does something we can't take back."

"It's not that simple."

"Why not?"

Instead of answering, Dad pointed at the TV, which we'd never changed the channel on. "Look, the Pats are back on …"

"Don't change the subject." I stepped between him and the TV, turning it off. "This is important."

"This isn't your responsibility. Stay out of it."

"How is it not my responsibility? I'm part of this family, too. You're a cop. You know what the right thing to do is."

"Blake …"

"Should I just call the sheriff's office next time? Report the assault?"

"No." The word came out a lot angrier than I'd expected.

"Then what? Because this is crazy," I said, throwing up my hands. "Are we supposed to just keep pretending everything's fine until someone ends up in the hospital?"

Dad slumped his head back against the headrest of his chair, his voice sounding completely exhausted. "I promised your mother I wouldn't do anything that would put Josh in the system."

"What system? Like juvenile detention?"

"Mental health facilities. Psychiatric wards."

"But he needs help!"

"You never knew your Aunt Tabitha, did you?"

The sudden shift threw me. "Mom's sister? I thought she died when Mom was a teenager. Suicide."

"That's true, but it's not the whole story. She was in an institution and had serious mental problems. Back in the sixties, they called it manic-depression, but it went deeper than that."

"Ohh," I said, unsure of what to say about that.

"Your mother adored her big sister, looked up to her. When the doctors couldn't help, when Tabitha … your mother blamed the system. She's terrified of losing Josh the same way."

"It's different now. They know more about-"

"You don't know that. Part of my job is taking people to the mental health facility in Midland. Those places … They're soul-crushing. Patients surrounded by others struggling just as much or worse. Half the staff cares more about protecting the hospital from lawsuits than helping anyone."

"Then we find someone private. A doctor who won't put him in a place like that."

"It's not that simple, son. You're young. You don't understand how these things work."

I wanted to tell him I did understand. That I remembered being in my thirties and forties, remembered what it was like navigating the healthcare system, remembered the weight of adult responsibilities. But I couldn't.

"If we don't do something, we'll lose him anyway. His anger's getting worse."

"I'm handling it."

"Are you? Because it doesn't look like it from where I'm sitting."

"Focus on your own problems. Let your mother and me deal with your brother."

"What if it gets to a point where I can't just ignore it? What if next time he doesn't just cut Mom? What if ..."

"Enough! This conversation is over."

"No, it's not! You can't just ..."

"Blake," he said in a voice that made it clear he was done with this conversation. "Drop it."

I stared at him, this man I loved so much, this man I'd lost once already in another life. The unfairness of it all hit me like a physical blow. Here I was, trying to prevent one tragedy, while watching another one build right in front of me.

"Just ... think about it. It's going to get out of control," I said, holding up my hand when he started to yell again. "I'm not saying anything. I just want you to think about it."

He just made a noise and turned back to the TV when I turned it back on. I just hoped he'd listen to me before it was too late.

Chapter 12

Monday, things were peaceful for most of the day. Sure, there were dirty looks from Elijah, but that had become almost standard by now. The only thing missing was Jamal. He'd been in a splint on Friday after that bad hit he took at the game, but he'd said his parents were taking him to Midland this morning to the hospital to get it looked at further. Apparently, the doctor was worried about ligament damage, and they'd need to run additional tests with the equipment they had there.

I hoped that wasn't it. A break he could recover from. Yeah, he'd maybe miss this year, but he'd still have three more years to play and develop, which was enough to get recruited into a college program. Tearing a ligament or tendon would mean surgeries and maybe the end of his football career, which would make it a lot harder to get into a good school.

That was the reality for a lot of people who lived here. Unless you owned oil leases, which were mostly owned by big companies these days, there wasn't a lot of money in West Texas, and college was expensive. A lot of guys needed that full ride, or even a partial one, to get their college degree.

I know I did. There was no way Dad could afford to send me to anything other than community college or a trade school on his salary. So yeah, a break was the best-case scenario for Jamal. I couldn't help feeling guilty about it. I'd decided to break from Elijah and started this feud, and Jamal got caught in the middle of it. It really wasn't fair, and it was kind of my fault.

We got our answer about his testing that afternoon just after we got to the locker room and suited up. There was a commotion by the doors and we were all surprised to see Jamal hobbling in, getting greeted by the team. He was on crutches and in a cast, which at least suggested it wasn't as bad as we all feared. That and he looked in high spirits.

I'm not sure I'd make it to the next practice or look quite as cheerful if I'd ruined my football career.

"How bad is it, man?" Miguel asked when he got over to us.

"Hairline fracture. They said I probably strained the tendons, but they couldn't find any evidence of tearing or ripping," Jamal said, easing himself onto the bench. "Doc says it should heal up alright, but I've got to take it easy for a while to let the bone and tendons mend."

"Man, that is good news," Tyrell said, slapping him on the back. "Damn, we were all so worried."

"Yeah, me too," Jamal said, laughing.

"So, how long do they say you need to be in that thing?" I asked.

"Month and a half, maybe two." Jamal shrugged.

He was taking it well, but I could see he was still a little disappointed. Two months and the season would be over for him.

"So, your season's done."

"Yeah, pretty much."

"Damn, that sucks," Connor said.

We all got a little quiet at that. We felt bad for our friend, and it always hurt to lose someone like him from the team.

"Maybe next time you'll learn to keep your head on a swivel, Washington," Elijah said, laughing as he, Aidan, and Hunter walked past. "Or maybe you should take up dance. Put on some tap shoes. It's what you people are better at."

"What the fuck is that supposed to mean?" I said, hopping up and getting in his stupid face.

"It means your girlfriend should be doing anything but playing football. He sucks, you suck, and none of you should be on the team. Or isn't that clear enough, faggot."

I could feel my face getting red and the edges of my vision blurring a bit. Everything I had in me wanted to choke the life out of him.

"Shut the fuck up, or he won't be the only one in a cast!"

Elijah stepped right up to me, his chest bumping against mine. "Try it, Sims. I dare you."

"Elijah," Aidan said warningly, nodding toward the entrances to the locker room where Coach Wilson had just walked in.

Elijah's eyes narrowed.

"Your time's coming," he said quietly before backing away toward his locker.

"Come on," Miguel said, tugging at my arm. "He's not worth it."

I let Miguel pull me back to our side of the room but kept watching Elijah.

"Man, I thought it was us redheads who were supposed to be the hotheads, Blake," Connor said with a smile. "Should we start collecting for your bail now, ya think?"

The other three looked at me, I guess afraid of what my reaction would be. I really didn't think of myself as a hothead, but goddamn, Elijah got under my skin.

"Like any of you could afford to bail me out," I said with a small laugh to let them know it was okay.

The moment passed and the tension went out of everyone.

"I'm just saying, maybe we should get you some anger management classes before you do something stupid," Connor said, grinning.

"Speaking of doing stupid things," Tyrell chimed in, turning to Jamal, "I know you hate conditioning, but there are easier ways to get out of it. Hell, if you wanted out that bad, you could've asked me, I would have hurt you just enough to miss a few classes without missing the season."

"Yeah, but this way, I get to skip for months. Work smarter, not harder."

"You know that's against Tyrell's religious beliefs," Miguel said, which earned him a playful slug from Tyrell. "Plus, you get a sweet new accessory. Very fashion-forward."

"Oh, yeah. All the ladies love a man in need of help. Going to do wonders for my social life," Jamal said, pulling a black Sharpie from his pocket. "Speaking of which, y'all need to sign this thing. Make it look proper."

He held out the marker, and Miguel grabbed it first, scribbling something in Spanish that made Jamal raise his eyebrows.

"Man, I hope that's not dirty," Jamal said. "You know my dad knows Spanish, right?"

"Well, I guess you'll have to wait till you get home to find out," Miguel said, grinning.

Jamal's parents were very religious and had a tendency to go a little overboard when it came to being 'proper.'

The marker made its way around our little group, each guy adding their signature and maybe a few words. I didn't join in right away, still a little out of sorts from the run-in with Elijah.

"Five minutes!" Coach Romero called out, sticking his head into the locker room.

The guys gave Jamal a few slaps on the back and said a few more things, and then hurried to get into their gear.

"I'm sorry," I said, quiet enough for the rest of them not to hear.

Jamal looked up from examining Connor's terrible attempt at drawing a football, a little confused, and said, "For what?"

"This is my fault. Jake and them, they're out to get me, and you got caught in the middle because I was trying to get one over on them."

"Man, that's the stupidest thing I've heard today. Did you forget how this started? They had their sights set on me and the other guys from the jump. You stepped in and killed your friendship with them to protect us."

"I shouldn't have been friends with them in the first place."

"Probably not, but standing up to them put a target on your back. You did that for us. You got nothing to apologize for."

"Still ..."

"Look," Jamal cut me off, "they might've done this one way or another. Me and the guys, we appreciate what you did. Standing up for us wasn't the easy choice. You want to feel guilty or whatever, that's on you, but don't do it on my account."

"Okay. Well, I'm still sorry your leg got broken."

"Yeah, it sucks," Jamal said, holding out the Sharpie. "Now sign my damn cast so we can get to practice."

I took the marker, considering what to write. Finally, I scrawled: 'Get better soon. We need our running back back.'

"Real original."

"Stick with the classics," I said.

As we headed out to the field, walking slow enough so that he didn't have to push himself, I glared back at Elijah and the rest, who were always the last ones out of the locker room, I guess to try and show how important they were.

Jamal might be right, but this was now between me and Elijah, and I was going to get even with him for it.

Practice itself was brutal. Coach had run us hard on Friday after the loss, but it seemed like after having the weekend to think about how the game went, he was even more pissed, and he took it out on us on the practice field.

At one point, I even saw Coach Plummer go to talk to him, and Coach Heidemann yelled something, sending him back to running the defensive players through the tires. I'd been busting my ass with up-downs at that moment and the rush of blood in my ears made it impossible to hear what he said, but whatever it was, it was serious because Coach Plumber was pissed.

Coach ran us ragged until people were throwing up in trash cans. Strangely, Elijah and the other four kept throwing me dirty looks like it was my fault, and not theirs for literally throwing the game. I think part of it was that the rest of the team that was not part of their little clique was pissed at Hunter, and Elijah by proxy.

Instead of their little plan of getting the whole team against me, their plan had backfired, and they'd gotten the team against them instead.

Jamal, the lucky son-of-a-bitch, got to sit on the bleachers, reading playbooks and watching us get our asses run off. I walked back into the locker room with him, since it was hard to carry a play binder and use crutches at the same time, making us the last two in off the field.

"Blake! In my office!" Coach yelled as soon as we came into the field house.

Jamal looked at me like I was on death row heading to the chair, taking the binder and tossing it to Miguel to put in his locker. I gave him a shrug and headed to the coach's office.

As I followed Coach Heidemann into the office, he dropped the clipboard on his desk, letting out an exasperated puff of air.

"Close the door and sit."

I did as he instructed and sat across from his desk while he circled around and dropped into his chair. I was trying to figure out what I'd done wrong. Not that I needed to do anything wrong myself for this to be my fault. He'd named me captain of the team, which meant what happened on the field was my responsibility.

Yes, I'd warned him about Elijah and his crew and told him this was going to happen, and he'd mostly ignored me, but that didn't absolve me of the responsibility for the loss. I'd gone with the running play he'd called, even though we really only had Hunter to run it. I hadn't called an audible, I hadn't changed it up. When I put the ball into Hunter's hands, that was ultimately on me.

I sat across from him and waited for the yelling to start.

Instead, he scrubbed his hands over his face and said, "What are we going to do about this team, Blake?"

I blinked. "What?"

He leaned forward, putting his elbows on his desk and said, "You busted your butt on Thursday. I can see that, as could everyone on the field. You got us close to winning, but the team ... we're not there. We're not a unit. It's costing us games."

"I know."

"You're my captain, Blake. I want to hear your take. How do we fix it?"

He had to know what I was going to say. I mean, I'd already said it several times, and been shot down. Not just shot down. He'd made it very clear he didn't want to hear my thoughts on the subject, so I wasn't sure how to answer.

But ... he was asking.

"You're not gonna like what I have to say."

"Try me anyway."

"Some guys on the team ..." I took a moment, choosing my words carefully. "They're better than what they've been showing us on the field. They are hurting the team."

"What do you mean by that?"

"They're making mistakes on purpose. You had to have seen it, and I've pointed it out to you. Not just bad playing. It's ... deliberate."

Coach Heidemann pinched the bridge of his nose. "Blake, I can't just cut players because they're not getting along."

"I'm not asking you to cut them," I said. "Just bench the ones causing problems until they learn to play like a team."

"Our backups aren't as strong."

"Not normally, no, but they're better than the starters who are throwing plays on purpose. If we pick the right plays, focus on what works with who we have, we can win games. The guys we have might not be as talented, but they'll actually *try*."

"There are spots where we don't have enough backups. With Jamal out, I can't bench Hunter."

With him saying that, it was clear he accepted who the troublemakers were.

"Then don't. Keep Hunter, bench the rest. Coach, we're O and two. What we're doing now isn't working."

"Blake ..."

"You asked me for my thoughts, and these are my thoughts. Besides, if you don't do something now, what message does that send? That it's okay to let stuff off the field affect how we play? That throwing games is an option when you're mad?" I leaned forward. "Is that really what you want the team thinking?"

"Why is this happening? Really happening?"

"Most of the team isn't the problem. That's why you don't see this on defense as much. I've known Elijah and his crew most of my life. Until this year, I was just like them."

"And?"

"They need to feel important. They do it by pushing others down. The new guys, the ones who didn't play peewee or middle school with us, they were perfect targets. A chance to show everyone else who's boss."

"Okay, but you said they were trying to make you look bad by messing up plays. If you used to be their friend and were like them, how are you not one of my problem players?"

"Because I stepped in. I couldn't stand by and watch Miguel and the others get bullied. They saw it as a betrayal. Now, most of their anger's focused on me instead. It's stupid, but that's what's happening."

Coach went quiet, staring at his desk. The clock on the wall ticked away seconds that felt like hours.

Finally, he looked up. "Give me a list. Players you think need benching. I'll ... consider it."

The reckoning from my meeting with Coach Heidemann came the next day. We'd just made it out on the field when, instead of splitting into defense and offense to start warm-ups, Coach Heidemann called us up onto the bleachers.

Everyone was joking and having a good time, happy to have a small break before the coach started working us again. They didn't know what I knew. What Coach was going to say.

I couldn't help but steal a glance at Elijah. He was having a grand ol' time, talking to Hunter and Mason, picking on Wayne Lowry, his backup wide receiver. They'd stopped teasing Miguel and the other walk-ons and had been forced to find new targets for their mocking. I'd like to think they'd backed off of my friends because of the resistance we'd put up, but I knew that was foolish.

They were still coming for us, but when they did, it wasn't going to be teasing and banter. It was going to be serious. More so once Coach finished what he was about to say. Elijah was going to know I was behind it.

Hell, even if I hadn't been behind it, he would have assumed I was and accused me of it anyway.

"Listen up," Coach said, holding his clipboard. "After our first two games, we need to make some changes. We've come close, but we're not finishing strong. Our offense isn't where it needs to be to get past that last hurdle, so we're going to shuffle around some of the positions to see if we can't fix that."

Elijah elbowed Gabriel, our backup QB who'd unfortunately been hanging around with Elijah and the rest of them lately. I could just imagine what Elijah was whispering in his ear, that I was taking his opportunity. That he'd be better suited to lead the team than me.

That was too bad. I actually liked Gabriel, even if he couldn't throw a ball for shit. He'd started giving me the cold shoulder any time I tried to talk to him now. I wanted to tell him he was making a mistake, that Elijah wasn't his friend. He only wanted to turn people against me. He was using Gabriel.

Elijah said one last thing to Gabriel and turned to look up at me, a smirk on his face, like he knew something. I could just imagine what he thought he knew.

He was going to be sorely disappointed.

"Since Jamal is out for the season, Bennett McCune, I'm going to put you in at halfback," Coach said.

Bennett looked stunned and maybe just a little terrified. He normally played fullback, so halfback was a little different position, but we didn't have a backup for that, so Coach had to pull from somewhere, and it wasn't like he was going to replace Hunter, who Bennett was normally the backup for. Actually, he should have seen it coming, since he was the next most obvious person to fill the spot.

"I know it's not your usual position, but you've got the speed for it. I'm going to want you to put in extra hours with Jamal this week, learn the position inside and out. Think you can handle that?"

"Yes, Sir," Bennett said, trying to hide his smile and failing.

Sitting on the bench all year on the freshman team would guarantee riding the bench in JV, so this was his shot to show Coach Holloway that he had what it took to be moved to varsity, if not next year, then his junior year.

Which was what mattered. None of the scouts were offering scholarships to guys on JV.

"Next up, Clarke Reeves, I'm moving you to starting at offensive tackle. Jake, you're moving to second string."

Jake's mouth dropped open and he looked like someone had knocked the wind out of him. He looked to Elijah, like Elijah was going to do something to help him. Or maybe just wondering how things had gone so wrong. I knew those guys. Jake was a follower through and through. Elijah would have convinced him that what they were doing would get him what he wanted.

Instead, he got the opposite. Jake was too dumb to actually blame Elijah for it, so he had to settle for shocked and pleading. Elijah just gave him a 'just wait' hand signal, like this was just a temporary setback.

He also shot me a look, not smug this time, but ... calculating, maybe. He was trying to read me, to see if I was smirking or somehow indicating that I'd just made that happen.

I didn't move or make any expression at all, keeping my eyes focused on Coach.

"Last change," Coach said. "Wayne, you'll be moving to first string for wide receiver and Elijah, I'm moving you to second string."

Elijah's head whipped around as he glared at me. He didn't even bother trying to play it cool this time. I just kept my attention on Coach. It wasn't a surprise who Coach would put in for Elijah. Since the team was only freshman, we had a lot less depth than varsity or junior varsity, so most positions only had one backup player, and some had none at all.

This was where I had the most concerns. Bennett was fast enough to play Jamal's position and Clark was big enough to play Jake's, but Wayne had not wowed anyone in practice. He was fast and had good hands, but a lot of the time his head was not in the game and he made a fair number of mistakes in practice.

I'd convinced Coach that switching out Elijah was the only way we were going to win games, so if Wayne went and screwed it up, Coach would blame me for it and probably never trust my judgment again.

"For now, those are our main changes. Nothing's set in stone. We'll see how practice goes this week and decide if these changes stick for Thursday's game. After that, we'll reevaluate based on performance. Alright, go get warmed up."

As everyone started standing up, Elijah shoved his way toward me, probably wanting to threaten me again, since even he wasn't dumb enough to start throwing punches out here in the open. I knew that was what he was going to do and didn't want to deal with it, so as soon as Coach released us, I was already moving.

"Wayne, Bennett, hold up a second," I called out, deliberately turning my back on Elijah. "Listen, we need to make this work, and this is your shot, so I'd like it if we could ..."

"You think you're real smart, don't you?" Elijah cut in from behind me.

"... stay after practice the next few days and put in some extra work, to make sure you get the playtime on Thursday," I said, continuing as if he hadn't even spoken.

I did, however, turn slightly so he was in my peripheral vision. I could see him clenching his fist and I was ready to jump out of the way if he lost control. Wayne didn't seem to notice, but Bennett did, turning with a concerned look at Elijah and taking his own small step back so he was out of the way should something go down.

"Alternates!" Coach bellowed from the field. "Get over here and start your warm-ups!"

Elijah hesitated. For a second, I thought I'd misjudged him and he was going to take a swing anyway.

"Now, Garner!" Coach shouted.

With a final murderous look at me, Elijah stalked off toward the practice field.

I waved Miguel and Hunter over. Hunter glanced between me and Elijah, clearly torn. Elijah was glaring at him now, too, but Hunter must have done the math. He knew he was one screw-up away from joining Elijah on second string.

"Okay. Let's get to work."

Chapter 13

I managed to avoid Elijah for the rest of the day. After practice, I made sure to walk in when Coach did, grab my stuff, and get the hell out of there. It wasn't that I was afraid of Elijah and his bunch; I just didn't want to deal with his bullshit. I was going to be extra careful, because I knew he'd blame me for being benched, instead of taking responsibility for his own actions.

Hell, I'd tried to tell him that was what was going to happen if he kept playing those games, but Elijah was the kind of guy who could never see his own faults. He always had to blame someone else for his mistakes. I'd run into that type a bunch of times in my dream life, and they'd always ended up on the wrong side of everything eventually, causing themselves more harm than anyone else ever could.

I also went out of my way to avoid him all day on Tuesday, not even bothering to go to the locker room. Instead, I left everything with Jamal on the bleachers so he could watch my stuff, and so I could just leave when practice was over instead of getting trapped in the field house with him.

There was a moment he almost cornered me at lunch, but I managed to do an end run around the table filled with theater kids, who were partially blocking the aisle, slowing him down. It was kind of like playing football, in a way.

That night, I was supposed to be at Eduardo's house. I'd looked up the address he'd given me in the key map and he was way across the whole city. Admittedly, Wheaton wasn't a big place, but I didn't particularly want to walk that far, so I convinced Dad, who had the night shift, to drop me off on his way to work. Thankfully, they were having a pretty early dinner, so the time from when I was dropped off wasn't that bad. I had Dad drop me at the edge of his neighborhood and took my sweet time walking the rest of the way.

Their house was nice. Wheaton was not a big town, but it did have a 'good' side and a 'bad' side. The good side was east of Main Street, where the city park, schools, and government buildings were located. Good didn't necessarily mean rich. People like Coach Plummer lived just outside of town on what were essentially small, non-working ranches. It wasn't even particularly more dangerous. I guess the only difference was the streets were a little nicer and the houses a little bigger, and we were further from the cattle ranches to the east of town, which could stink to high heaven if the wind was just right. Or wrong.

To people outside of Wheaton, they probably wouldn't even notice the difference.

I'd dressed to be presentable enough, out of respect for his parents, and smoothed my shirt as I arrived at their front door and pressed the doorbell.

The door opened to reveal a man who had to be Eduardo's father. They shared the same serious eyes. His work boots and paint-spotted jeans suggested he'd just gotten home himself.

"You must be Blake," he said, extending his hand. "Come in, come in."

I shook his hand, noting the firm grip. "Thank you for having me over, Mr. Guzman."

Eduardo appeared behind his father, looking as uncertain as he did every time I talked to him. The guy had a major inferiority complex, which probably explained why it had been so easy for him to fall in with a gang.

"Hey," he said.

"Hey, man," I replied, following them inside.

The house smelled amazing, something with peppers and spices that made my mouth water.

"Elena, Eduardo's friend is here!" Mr. Guzman called toward the kitchen.

"Welcome, Blake!" Eduardo's mom's voice carried from the other room. "Food will be ready in about ten minutes. Go ahead and wait in the living room!"

Mr. Guzman led us into a cozy space dominated by a comfortable-looking couch, a recliner facing the TV, and family photos on the wall. Eduardo and I sat down on the couch while his father settled into what was clearly his usual chair.

"So, Blake," Mr. Guzman said, "how do you know Eduardo?"

"We started having lunch together at school. Eduardo's a good guy to talk to."

"Blake helped me out when some guys were giving me trouble."

Mr. Guzman's eyebrows rose. "That right?"

"I'd like to say I was just trying to do the right thing, but honestly, I really hate those guys. They're bullies who think they own the school."

"Well, you still helped my son. That makes you good in my book."

I smiled and kind of half nodded. A part of me felt bad that I was consciously doing a lot of this because of what happened in my dream. Even with my new outlook on my life, post-dream, I'm not sure I would have gone out of my way so much to be Eduardo's friend if it wasn't for my attempts to stop what happened in my dream from coming true.

I looked around the room trying not to feel quite so awkward when a large photo on the wall caught my attention. Eduardo's family was standing in front of a beautiful old stone house with some really impressive mountains in the background.

"Where's that?"

"Mexico," Eduardo's father said, looking pleased. "We visited Eduardo's abuela last summer in Guanajuato. Beautiful city."

"That's so cool," I said, turning to Eduardo. "How did you like it? I've never been to Mexico. Must have been pretty different than here."

"It was pretty nice. My grandparents live in this old house they've had forever; everyone knows them. They're like celebrities in their town. My abuela makes the best food. You would've loved it."

"I bet. What kind of stuff did you do while you were there?"

"Mostly spent time with my grandparents. My abuelo has this garden out back with these crazy-looking flowers, and he taught me how to prune them. My dad made me help fix the roof, though. That part wasn't as fun."

"It did you good," his father said, getting a grunt out of Eduardo.

Before he could say anything, though, there was the sound of running feet, followed by the appearance of a young kid, maybe about elementary age, practically bouncing with energy.

"Alex," Eduardo's dad said, "come meet Eduardo's friend Blake. He's the quarterback for Wheaton High."

"Uh, only on the freshman team," I said, feeling a little self-conscious, but Alex's eyes had already gone wide with excitement.

"You play football? Real football?"

He plopped down on the floor between us, staring up at me with unrestrained enthusiasm.

"Americano," Mr. Guzman corrected automatically.

Alex waved his hand dismissively. "That's what I meant, Papá. I wanted to play but the coach said I was too small for peewee. So now I'm stuck with soccer."

"Fútbol is the better sport, anyway," Mr. Guzman said firmly.

Alex groaned.

"I know, but it's not the same." He turned back to me and eagerly asked, "What's it like playing quarterback? Is it hard?"

"It can be. You've got to learn the playbook and figure out what everyone on the field is supposed to do. Plus, you're kind of in charge out there, so if something goes wrong, everyone looks at you."

Alex started launching into more questions when Eduardo's mom called from the kitchen. "Dinner's ready!"

I silently thanked her for the rescue from Alex's barrage of questions about playing football. Mr. Guzman pushed against the armrests of his chair, wincing slightly as he stood.

The kitchen table was already set, steam rising from bowls of rice and some kind of stew that filled the air with an amazing aroma of peppers and spices.

"This is pozole," Mrs. Guzman said, placing a final bowl on the table. "I hope you like spicy food."

"I love spicy food," I said, though honestly, I wasn't sure what counted as spicy to them, versus what counted as spicy to me.

"We'll see about that," she teased, spooning some into my bowl. "Some people think they like spicy until they try real Mexican cooking."

I picked up my spoon and took a careful bite. It was rich, complex, and yes, definitely spicy, but not overwhelming. The meat was tender and it had an interesting texture I'd never experienced before.

"This is incredible. I've never had anything like it."

She beamed at me. "Finally, someone who appreciates good food! These two," she gestured at Eduardo and his father, "don't even comment anymore."

"Because you already know how good your cooking is, Mamá," Eduardo said.

"Such a good boy," she said, grabbing his chin and squeezing a little before letting go. "So, Blake, do you have any siblings?"

"Yeah, I have a brother. He's a little older than Alex."

"Oh? Does he play sports, too?"

"No, he's not really into sports." I quickly redirected the conversation. "They mentioned you work in Midlands, Mr. Guzman. My dad makes that same drive every day, too."

"The drive can be rough some days. Eduardo said that he's a deputy?"

"Yes. He's been there about four years. He was in Abilene before that, but his boss got the job in Midlands, so Dad followed him."

The rest of the meal was split, half the time with me trying to draw Eduardo, who was painfully shy, into the conversation and half with Alex, who was about as opposite as his brother as a person could be, peppering me with questions.

As Mrs. Guzman started collecting the plates, I stood up to help, grabbing mine and Eduardo's dishes.

"No, no," she protested. "You're our guest."

"Please, I insist," I said, following her to the sink with the plates.

She gave me a look not unlike the one she kept giving Alex when he wouldn't mind her to stop asking about football during dinner, but let me follow her, finally taking the plates out of my hands and stacking them in the sink. When she turned on the faucet, I guess to rinse them, water suddenly sprayed everywhere, shooting up from where the spout met the base. Mrs. Guzman jumped back with a yelp.

"Esta cosa estúpida!" she said as she frantically tried to turn off the water.

Mr. Guzman pushed himself up from his chair, giving that same little groan again, and came over to join us, pulling open the cabinet beneath the sink.

As he bent down to look underneath, he let out a sharp grunt of pain, his hand flying to his lower back.

"Hector!" Mrs. Guzman said, nudging me aside and helping him to stand back up. "Your back! Go. Go. Sit back down. You know what the doctor said."

"I'm fine," he insisted through clenched teeth, but let her guide him back to his chair.

While they were doing that, I dropped to my knees and looked in the open cabinet under the sink. The problem was obvious; the coupling connecting the faucet to the water line had come loose.

"Do you have an adjustable wrench?" I asked.

"No, no," Mr. Guzman said firmly. "We can't let you ..."

"I help fix stuff at home all the time. It's just a loose connection. Five minutes, tops."

"We'll call a plumber," he insisted.

Mrs. Guzman tutted at him and disappeared, reappearing with a toolbox. "Here you go, Blake."

"Elena ..." Mr. Guzman started.

"Eddie," I said, using the nickname Alex had used for his brother a few times. "Come give me a hand."

Eduardo hesitated for a second, clearly unsure what was happening, but joined me at the sink.

I pointed to a section of the piping and said, "See this coupling here? It's just worked itself loose. Hand me that wrench, the bigger one."

I walked him through what I was doing, explaining how to check if fittings were properly aligned before tightening them. It was something that broke in a lot of sinks, especially in older, poorly maintained homes. I'd lived in a lot of shitty apartments in my dream life and had to fix this problem a bunch of times.

Finally, a place where something from my dream life actually helped me in this one. In a few minutes I had it fixed. Standing up, I turned on the faucet. The water flowed normally, no leaks.

"¡Gracias a Dios!" Mrs. Guzman clasped her hands together. "That's been broken for weeks. With Hector's back ..."

"What happened?"

"An accident at work last month," Mr. Guzman said. "It's nothing."

"It's not nothing," his wife said. I'd clearly touched on a subject they'd fought about before. "He can barely bend over and is always in pain. He's stubborn though. There's so much that needs fixing around here, which is just making his back worse."

The words came out before I could stop them.

"I could help. I'm pretty good with basic repairs. I'm sure Eduardo doesn't mind helping me with them. Actually, I could tackle some projects on Saturday."

"Oh, we couldn't ..." Mr. Guzman began.

"That would be wonderful!" Mrs. Guzman exclaimed.

"Wait, what?" Eduardo said.

"Come on, it'll be fun. Better than studying all weekend, right?" I said, slapping him on the shoulder.

Now that I started thinking about it, this was a great idea, even if it did eat up some of my weekend. I'd been slowly eating lunch a little more with Eduardo, but I'd also had to do almost all the talking. He'd been so reluctant to engage and he hadn't agreed to sit with the other guys yet. If this was going to work and I was going to keep him out of the gang, I needed him to build a set of friends here in Wheaton, and that would only work once I got him to open up to me.

Eduardo looked uncertain. "I guess ..."

"Great," I said, slapping him on the shoulder a second time, grinning from ear to ear like I'd just won a prize.

"It's settled then," Mrs. Guzman said, beaming. "I'll make lunch for you boys."

Mr. Guzman opened his mouth to protest again, but his wife gave him a glare not even the bravest of men would have challenged.

He swallowed whatever he'd been about to say and instead said, "You're very kind to offer."

"It's no problem at all," I assured him. "Really."

As well as things were going with Eduardo, things were going badly with Elijah and his bunch. I'd managed to avoid him most of Wednesday too, even though he'd become more aggressive in trying to corner me.

He'd almost done it at lunch, but Brandy had pulled Mason away to go do something and I had Miguel and Tyrell with me. Elijah was a coward at heart and only did his bullying when he outnumbered his victims. I guess it was hard to intimidate someone when you had to watch that person's friends just in case they tried to kick your ass.

I'd known I wouldn't be able to avoid them forever, but I'd hoped for a few more days at least. It was foolish, but I hoped that he would calm down after a few days.

Unfortunately, they managed to corner me in the hallway just before I got to the door that led out of the school to the field house. I could have turned around and walked the other way, I guess, but it was an empty hallway behind me, and I didn't particularly feel like running away. Avoiding them, sure, but I wasn't going to run from him.

He must have been waiting there for a while because he looked bored when I turned the corner, although that boredom shifted to almost glee when he saw it was me and that I was alone. He was feeling brave because he had Mason with him. I was both taller and outweighed Elijah, but no one other than Tyrell outweighed Mason.

"Hey, traitor!"

"Fuck off," I said, trying to walk around them.

Mason put himself in front of me, like he was blocking for Elijah. I took a step back, mostly to keep them out of my peripheral.

"I don't know how you managed to convince Coach to bench me, but you're going to regret that shit."

"No one had to convince Coach to do anything. I tried to tell you your little game was going to come back and bite you in the ass, and here we are. How many passes did you think you could drop before he benched your ass? If you played the game, tried to win it instead of playing at whatever pissing contest you've invented between us, you'd still be first string."

"Bullshit. Coach sees me in practice. He knows I'm better than Wayne."

"He also sees you during the games, and how you, Jake, and Hunter keep blowing plays. You can't be so stupid to think this isn't your fault."

Of course, I knew that wasn't true. Elijah was exactly stupid enough to think he had nothing to do with this. To him, everything he did was perfect, and anything that went against him was some kind of conspiracy. He was just dumb enough to think he had everything figured out.

"You've had this coming," Elijah said, "ever since you turned your back on your real friends."

"Real friends? You guys were never real friends. The only person you've ever cared about is you, Elijah. I just grew up enough to realize it. Maybe you should think about that, too, Mason. He'll only have your back as long as there's something in it for him, and as long as you're okay being his little buddy."

I think for a second, I thought that might have penetrated Mason's thick skull. But it didn't last. Mason wasn't bright enough to think for himself. Hell, the fact that I'd made him think even for a second seemed to piss him off. Like I'd forced him into an unnatural position.

We'd started to draw a crowd, mostly other players also on their way to the field house. I couldn't pay much attention to them. Elijah had started to move to my right as Mason took a step toward me. I could see him thinking about taking a swing at me long before he lifted his hand.

I'd never been much of a fighter, either when I was younger or in my dream life, but I had ended up in a few. Working in construction, as I had in the dream life, and spending your nights in bars with the guys from work, eventually, everyone did. Someone would get drunk enough to say something that couldn't be looked past or you'd get someone like Elijah on the crew, guys who peaked in high school but still wanted to act like the big man on campus, trying to prove something.

The two things I knew for sure were that I didn't want to face Mason in a straight-up fight, and I didn't want to fight two guys at once.

So I took Mason out before he could swing, stepping in toward him and driving my knee up hard, catching him right in the nuts with as much power as I could muster.

He doubled over almost instantly as I took a step back and turned enough to face Elijah. The step back hadn't been part of any plan or anything, but Elijah had started his swing right as I was doing it, so his fist sailed in front of my face, whiffing entirely.

I'd just cocked my own fist back, ready to return the favor, when someone said, "What's going on here?"

I didn't see who the teacher was, but it was obvious that's who'd said it because the crowd immediately started to scatter like roaches when the lights came on.

I wasn't going to stick around, bolting out the door past Mason, who was now down on one knee, toward the field house. There were enough people that it would be impossible for the teacher to figure out who was actually involved.

Say what you want about Elijah, but he wasn't going to rat me out. Besides the fact that they were just as culpable as I was, it would have made him look weak in everyone else's eyes.

And that was the thing he was truly afraid of.

Chapter 14

I managed to make it out of practice without any more confrontations again, although I was getting a little annoyed that to do so basically required me to skip going into the locker room after practice. Since I sometimes stayed with Miguel and Tyrell, and now I was staying after with Wayne and Bennett, it was hard to know when I was going to be done and headed either to the locker room or starting my walk home.

Had Elijah been a patient person, he would have just waited and watched for me to leave, but he wasn't. The longest he lasted was four minutes, at which point he went into the locker room.

He had always been short-sighted, although this time, it worked out in my favor.

I made the walk home, already shifting from practice mode back to school mode. It wasn't that bad, since the study Coach had me doing on plays and learning to read the offense was kind of similar. I still missed the days of middle school ball, where it was a lot less structured and more just fun, instead of high pressure.

Actually, thinking of how I played the game those two years in my dream life, it had been about the same. I was having a good time, showing off and trying to be the big man, instead of doing the work it would take to win games.

It was a startling revelation, really, and one that shattered some of the notions I'd had, during and after the dream. In it, I'd been convinced, both before Dad died and after, that I'd been on track to make varsity, state wins, a college scholarship, and the NFL.

It was clear to me now that I hadn't actually been on track for any of those things, because I wasn't taking the game seriously enough. Maybe I would have taken things more seriously once I made varsity, but it would have been a big transition, considering how Coach Heidemann kept saying this was just easing me into it.

Well, at least I was doing the work now. The same was true of my schoolwork, which was intensifying as we got further into the year. Especially now that I'd given up my Saturdays, which I had been spending almost all day studying, to help Eduardo's family.

It was a good thing, both because I was convinced it was what was going to help Dad, and because it was a nice thing to do for his parents. But it meant I was having to compensate, staying up later so I could get everything done ... with the exception of Wednesday nights. I wanted to be well-rested for game day Thursdays.

Mom and Dad were both working when I got home. This was a little unusual since Mom was usually busiest on weekends when people had time for hair appointments, but it happened sometimes.

I took the stairs two at a time, ready to dump my gear and collapse for five minutes before taking a quick shower and getting to work. Instead, as I pushed my door open, I froze.

Josh was standing with his back to me near my desk, rifling through the drawers. A bunch of stuff that had been inside the drawers was scattered on the floor around him, like he didn't plan on even trying to hide that he'd been in there.

"What the hell are you doing in my room?"

He didn't answer. He just turned halfway, as he put something in his pocket, before turning back and closing the desk drawer.

"Josh," I said again, stepping fully into the room. "What are you doing in here?"

"Nothing," he said trying to walk past me, not looking me in the eye.

I sidestepped, planting myself between him and the exit. "Like hell you were! What's in your pocket?"

"Nothing. Get out of my way."

"Not until you show me what you took."

"I didn't take anything!" he said, his voice going higher pitched than normal as he tried to go around me again.

I reached for his arm, but he still made to push past me, trying to jerk his arm free. I tightened my grip, pulling him to a stop. "Cut the crap, Josh. If you didn't take anything, why were you digging through my desk?"

"Let go of me!"

"Not until you tell me what you're hiding."

I reached for his pocket. He tried to stop me with his free hand, but I swatted it away and pinned him against the wall. He squirmed, shoving at me, but I found something with a familiar shape to it. I held him still while pulling a small, scuffed medal out of his pocket that I'd won during my first season of peewee.

It had been years ago and was probably silly to still have it, since I'd been six at the time, but it had a special place in my heart and I'd held onto it. To say I was furious was an understatement.

"This isn't yours!" I demanded, shaking it in his face. "Why the hell would you take this?"

"It's just a stupid medal! No one cares about it but you."

"If you don't care, then why'd you take it?"

"I was just messing around," he muttered.

"Bullshit."

He looked furious and for a moment I thought he was going to swing at me. I relaxed my grip on him, just in case, so I could either block it or step out of the way, but he only jerked his arm free.

"You can't tell me what to do."

"Steal my shit again, and I can break your damn face."

"You want to?" he asked, something cold and hollow in his voice.

We both heard the door downstairs open and then shut, signaling mom coming home from work. He gave me an evil grin and took a step toward the door and for a moment I thought he might make a run for it, maybe to mom for protection. He didn't.

Instead, he said, "Let me do it for you."

Before I could react, he turned and slammed his face into the edge of the doorjamb. There was a sickening sound as blood splattered across the wood, bright and shocking against the white paint.

He staggered sideways from the blow, even if it was self-inflicted, clutching his nose, and gave me the coldest look I'd ever seen.

I was so stunned I didn't even move. Not until he started screaming.

"Mom! Mom!" he yelled as he took off into the hall and then thundered down the stairs.

I raced after him. He'd set me up perfectly. I'd say I should have seen it coming, but how could I have guessed he'd break his own nose just to get at me. I made it downstairs just as Mom rushed into the kitchen to see what all the noise was about.

"Oh my God, Joshua!" She rushed to him, tilting his face to examine his bloody nose. "What happened?"

"Blake punched me in the face!" Joshua's voice cracked with fake tears.

Mom spun on me.

"How dare you hit your brother?! What is wrong with you?"

"I didn't hit him! He's lying. He did it to himself!"

"What? Why would he hurt himself?"

"Because I caught him stealing from my room! He was going through my desk, took my peewee football medal."

"Your what? Why would Joshua want some old medal?"

"I don't know why he wanted it, but he took it!" I pulled the medal from my pocket. "Here, I caught him with it!"

"He's lying!" Joshua sobbed, keeping his hand pressed to his nose. "I didn't touch that stupid thing. He's always bullying me, Mom. He hates me and now he's making up stories!"

"I saw him do it! He slammed his own face into the doorframe!"

Mom pressed her lips together. "That's ridiculous, Blake. You must think I'm stupid to believe something like that."

"But ..."

"No. I've had enough of your lies. You're grounded for two weeks. And if you ever lay a hand on your brother again, it'll be much worse. Do you understand me?"

"This isn't fair!" My voice rose with frustration. "He's manipulating you!"

"Go to your room. Now."

I stared at them both. Mom had grabbed a paper towel and was pressing Josh's nose firmly as she tilted his head back. He was eating it up, playing the victim, but when she looked away from me for a second to get more paper towels, Joshua's eyes met mine with that same cold emptiness. The same evil smile.

I spun around and stormed up the stairs, slamming my bedroom door behind me.

Thursday was the farthest away game we'd played yet. L.D. Bell High School was clear on the other side of Dallas, a good four hours away from Wheaton. To manage it, we got an early release at lunch. The game itself was scheduled for five pm, which meant we'd get back to Wheaton around midnight. It was a crazy long day, but that was one of the downsides for a rural division that was as spread out as ours.

We got to eat lunch at school and they would feed us pizza on the bus on the way home, but it was still going to be a really long day. If this was a varsity game, half the town would follow the convoy to the away game, but the Freshman and JV teams were lucky to get some of our parents, let alone people not related to the players.

We also didn't rate the charter bus the varsity team would get for far away games. Just the standard school bus.

Elijah and his buddies staked out a spot at the back as soon as they were on, like they were still in middle school and it actually mattered. Wayne, Clark, and Bennett had been jelling with my other friends over the last week after all of the extra time we'd spent practicing together to get them ready for game day.

They'd even come over and sat with us through lunch today, which was a good sign. The freshman team was now almost evenly split between our table and Elijah's, which was a sign that things maybe were shifting our way and Elijah was finally losing whatever pull he might have managed the first week of school.

It was all temporary anyway. Varsity and JV guys, and their friends and girlfriends, tended to all sit together at one table and most of the guys were just waiting until they got off the freshman team and onto one of those so they could move and eat lunch there.

Part of me, the part that still felt the dream life, found all of this stuff to be pointless. In the long run, it didn't matter who ate lunch with whom. It was all high school nonsense.

But the rest of me was in high school and knew that, in a way, it mattered a lot. High school could be brutal for some kids, and which social group you ended up in would matter a lot.

Besides, if I could save people like Wayne and Bennett from Elijah's orbit, I was ultimately doing them a favor.

We pulled into the parking lot of Pennington Field and were sent off into the visitors' locker room. It was actually a really nice field, although that wasn't so surprising for Texas. Football was king here, and schools spent a lot of money on their athletic departments.

The sun was still pretty high in the sky as we warmed up for the game, which was a first. Normally, we didn't even get on the field until seven, so a five o'clock start was earlier than normal.

The sun and the heat weren't the things I focused on, though. More important was how Elijah was glued to Hunter's side all through stretching, whispering the whole time. I couldn't hear what he was saying, but Hunter's expression was somewhere between uncertain and concerned.

I could imagine what Elijah was saying. All of his cronies on the offense were riding the bench, and Hunter was the only one still on the field, able to throw the game. The fact that he'd been benched and still had not changed his mind was ... unbelievable. Well, unbelievable if I didn't know Elijah.

By the time we finished warm-ups and headed for the locker rooms to gear up the rest of the way and do our run out, Elijah looked smug, leaving Hunter behind, looking frustrated.

I sped up to catch up to him and then slowed to match his pace. Hunter almost flinched, like he thought I was about to take a swing at him, now that he was by himself.

Like he thought I was Elijah, willing to burn everything down for his own petty grievances. But Hunter didn't look angry or hostile like he normally did. He looked scared. Maybe Elijah didn't like him playing his best with us on the field or maybe Elijah just thought Hunter was somehow to blame for what happened to them. Whatever it was, Elijah had threatened him.

That much was clear.

"I don't know what he told you, but don't forget that he's where he is because he can't control himself. Don't screw this up and end up like him."

"You threatening me?"

"No, I'm giving you a heads-up. Do you want to spend your high school career riding the pine or stuck on JV, or do you want to have a chance to play D1 college ball?"

Hunter looked from me to Elijah's back. He was stuck somewhere between being pissed and being afraid, although it seemed pretty clear he didn't know which of us to be afraid of and which of us to be pissed at.

He chose to run, walking faster, to put some distance between us.

"Your choice, man," I called after him.

I had to say, I much preferred running out onto the field at home than playing in someone else's stadium. The home stands were packed while ours were only half full. Also, it felt like a lot of those on the visitors' side were people from Bell that couldn't get seats on the home side.

To add to the poor start, they got the coin toss, so they got the first drive. It had to happen, but it always felt like we started things off on the right foot by starting on the offense.

Our guys did a good job on defense, stopping their drive in just four downs, forcing it to end with a punt. I guess that was the good thing about my not being on defense. Elijah's friends on that side had no reason to throw anything. Hell, none of my friends really were on that side, either. All the guys Elijah had singled out as targets early in the year, were on offense.

"Alright, offense, let's go!" Coach Heidemann said, clapping.

We ran out onto the field and lined up. This was it. I'd convinced Coach to change the lineup and we'd done the work all week to be ready for this.

Now I had to show him something.

On the snap, Clark did his job, exactly as we'd been practicing it. It wasn't until that moment that I realized how much of my concentration had been used keeping an eye on Jake and Hunter, trying to figure out when the other shoe would drop and they'd turn on me.

Now, I could focus entirely on my reads. I didn't have to go past my first one. Miguel cut across the middle and managed to break free of his defender. It was a short route, Coach wanting us to feel out Bell's defense before we tried anything fancy. Miguel pulled my pass in cleanly and turned upfield. He gained eight yards before a defender managed to pull him down.

"Nice," I said, slapping him on the shoulder as we moved to the huddle.

The next call was straightforward.

"I-Right 21. Bennett, it's all you."

Clarke was starting to show that, even though he was a little smaller than Aiden, maybe he shouldn't have been riding the bench. He and Leon Prewitt opened a beautiful gap in the defense, and Bennett barreled through, getting twelve more yards before a linebacker pulled him to the ground, giving us a first down.

We hustled back to the line. It was the most excited I'd seen our team since the season started. Unfortunately, we weren't in practice and the other side got a say in what happened. The next set of downs was a lot rougher. A missed block, a broken route, and a very short one-yard gain put us at fourth and long, which ended our first offensive outing in a punt.

Coach, however, was in good spirits in spite of that.

"Good job, guys. You're starting to play some good football," he said, slapping me on the back as we came running back to the sidelines.

Behind him, I saw Elijah grimace a little. He looked to Hunter, who very purposefully did not look back at him. I'm sure it wasn't lost on anyone that Coach had not called a single play to Hunter the whole time. I know it wasn't lost on Hunter. I could see it on his face. He might have gotten to stay on the first string, but he'd lost Coach's confidence, and it was showing.

He had to be re-evaluating how secure his position was.

Thankfully, our defense held strong again, and soon we were back on offense.

Hunter was the last one to the line. Coach had held him back for a moment, saying something to him as he ran out to the field.

When Coach called the play, I'd been a little concerned. He was starting off with Hunter. I was glad Coach was making it clear, this was his chance and he'd better not screw it up.

I gave him a look as we lined up. He met my gaze, but didn't do anything else or give me any indication of what he was thinking. So be it.

I snapped the ball and put it in his gut. He cut to the outside, managing to run a bit wide and catch a solid block which Connor made, picking up yardage as he went more toward the sideline than downfield, trying to edge out the defense. He didn't manage to get past them, but he did pick up eight yards.

It was a solid attempt.

"Good job, Hunter," I said as we went into the huddle.

He didn't reply, but at least he nodded. A small sign that he'd heard me and accepted it. Maybe it meant there was some hope for him yet.

Everyone was pumped, and we started playing with it, moving the ball methodically down the line, with none of the mistakes of the first series. It wasn't perfect, not every snap got us yardage, but we did well enough to end up thirteen yards from the end zone. The first down, a running play, was stopped at the line of scrimmage.

On second down, I faked the handoff to Bennett, drawing the linebackers in just enough to buy time. Wayne ran a short route well and I hit him in stride. He juked the first defender, picking up another ten yards before getting tackled. The chains moved again, and our bench erupted in cheers.

In the huddle, I kept it simple: "I-Right 33. Bennett, punch it in."

The line dug in as the ball was snapped. Clarke and Leon bulldozed the defensive line, creating just enough space for Bennett to plow through for three hard-fought yards. He stumbled into the end zone, ball tucked tight against his chest. Touchdown.

The guys swarmed Bennett, clapping him on the helmet and shouting praise.

We didn't get a chance to duplicate that success the rest of the first quarter. Our defense was still doing a good job, but Bell's defense was nothing to write off. They did a good job locking us down and keeping our drives short.

The second quarter, their offense seemed to get some things to click and put together a drive that got all the way downfield, tying the score 7 to 7.

It seemed like we might go to halftime that way, as there was a lot more back and forth of short drives ending in punts. We did have a moment when it looked like we were going to finally break through when Casey Jackson intercepted a really ambitious pass, but he got pulled down pretty far back, and we then got held to just four downs before Bell got the ball back.

I think they knew we were wanting to get another touchdown on the boards before halftime because they really turned on the pressure as we neared the end of the first half. One of our last drives that started from a good position thanks to another interception, but their defense started to bring the pressure as soon as the ball snapped, sending their safety on a blitz. I was more than pleased to see Clarke read it perfectly, stepping up to meet him head-on. The collision bought me the second I needed to flip a screen pass to Miguel, who darted through traffic for six yards.

Two plays later, we lined up in the I-formation again. Hunter stood behind me, waiting for the handoff. The snap came clean, and I placed the ball right in his gut. Bennett crashed through the line ahead of him, absolutely demolishing a linebacker. Hunter followed the block perfectly, bursting into the open field for fifteen yards before getting dragged down.

"Now *that* is what I'm talking about!" Coach Heidemann shouted from the sideline as we ran back to the huddle.

The next run got stuffed at the line. We were closing in on their end zone again, and the defense was all over us. On third down and eight, the defense brought pressure, forcing me to roll right. Miguel broke off his route, finding space near the sideline just over the end zone line, right at the sideline.

I let it fly just before a defender reached me. Miguel went airborne, snagging the ball with one hand while touching one foot in the end zone as he came down.

The ref's arms went up. Touchdown!

We went into the locker room at 14 to 7. But we acted like we were up by way more than one touchdown. We were finally playing like a real team, and everyone could feel it.

Coach came in after us, raising his arm to get the celebration to calm down. But he did something I hadn't seen him do before.

Smile.

"That's what I'm talking about! You guys are finally playing like a real team out there. But let's not get ahead of ourselves. We've still got half a game to play, and we can't let this go to our heads. I want to see more from you guys. You've done a great job so far, especially our new stars. Clarke, those blocks were beautiful. Bennett, those were some great runs. You're really seeing the offense the way you need to. But we need more. They put the pressure on us for the last quarter, and except for that amazing last drive, they kept us locked down. I don't want that to happen again. If we're going to do this, we're going to do it for real, which means don't let them get in your heads. Don't let them. They got to dictate the pace of the first half, but we're going to change that around. I want you to decide how this next half goes. Alright. Bring it in."

The only people who didn't seem excited by everything that was happening were Elijah and Jake. Jake looked mostly devastated while Elijah looked furious. I'm not sure anyone else was paying attention to him, their teammate who seemed to be pissed that we were doing well.

Well, not 'anyone.' Hunter noticed. I could see him glancing over at Elijah several times. It was hard to read him, though. Was he worried about Elijah? Was he angry at him?

Who knew? What I did know was that so far, Hunter had stuck with the program. As long as he kept doing that, I didn't care what else he had going on. He could be an asshole, as long as he played *for* us instead of *against* us.

We ran out onto the field ready to tear it up. Unfortunately, this wasn't a movie, and a rousing speech and our enthusiasm didn't mean we'd then sweep the field of our enemy.

They had a say in things, too.

The third quarter became a slog. Coach was playing it safe, calling short passes and conservative runs that chewed up the clock, but didn't gain much ground. I hit Miguel and Wayne on slants and quick outs, picking up a few yards here and there, but nothing flashy.

We'd walk the ball downfield a bit before being shut down, and our defense would force the same. No one really gained much yardage.

Coach didn't want to risk it, and I got it. A mistake could shift the momentum, but it felt like a waste of all the excitement we'd had coming into the quarter. Worse, I couldn't help but think we were missing an opportunity. The way Bell's defense was lining up, their secondary wasn't ready for anything deep. But I kept my mouth shut and stuck to the plays.

I held my peace until the end of the third quarter, when the score was the same as it had been at halftime.

"Coach, they're playing up on every receiver. We need to try something longer."

"If I had a nickel for every time a freshman QB thought the only solution to a tough game was letting them chuck the ball downfield, I'd be a millionaire."

"Come on, Coach. It's not like that. You've seen their coverage. They're creeping up on every snap and are expecting us to keep it short, 'cause that's what we've been doing all night. You said we weren't going to let them dictate the game, but we're doing exactly that. We spent a whole quarter doing short passes and runs, and we're stuck, so let's try something different."

Coach looked unconvinced. I understood. I was just a punk kid telling a professional how to do his job. Living an entire adult life, well, most of one, in the dream gave me a perspective most fifteen-year-olds wouldn't have. I knew adults had a lot of experience that gave them a perspective that I didn't have as a kid, but I also knew that could get them stuck in their ways. Short-sighted.

I was trying to be respectful and just keep it to the facts, since kids normally relied on emotion instead of reason. I just hoped Coach was the kind of guy who didn't just dig in harder when challenged.

He studied the field for a moment, then sighed. "Alright, Sims. But if this backfires, it's on you."

I grinned. "Yes, Sir."

The fourth quarter started with a bang. On Bell's first drive, their running back fumbled after a crushing hit from Mason and our defense got the ball inside our 40-yard line.

Coach called the first play, a handoff to Bennett. I tried to not let it get to me. He said he'd let me pass. I just needed to be patient. I hoped.

This time at least, the running play worked better than it had in the third. Bell was rattled by the fumble and big run loss, and it worked to our advantage. Bennett followed Clarke through his block, cutting upfield and breaking two tackles before finally going down at their 35-yard line. The crowd on our side, what there was of it, roared. Even the guys on the bench were on their feet, with the exception of Elijah.

The next play, Coach called for a play-action pass. I faked the handoff to Bennett and watched as Bell's linebackers bit hard, since that's what we'd been doing all game. Miguel was already streaking down the sideline, running with everything he had, a good three steps ahead of his defender. I let it fly, dropping it right in Miguel's hands, and he caught it just over the end line.

Touchdown.

The celebration on our sideline was electric. Coach Heidemann was clapping as he barked out instructions for the kicking team. They got the extra point. The scoreboard now read 21 to 7, and for the first time all season, it felt like we were in control.

Bell's offense came back out looking rattled. They couldn't get anything going, and our defense shut them down, forcing a quick three-and-out. By the time we got the ball back, the energy on our sideline was sky-high.

On the next drive, Coach called for a run. The snap came, and I handed it off to Hunter. Connor bulldozed a path ahead of him, taking out two defenders in one sweep. Hunter followed, cutting through the gap and sprinting for a solid fifteen yards before getting tripped up.

Wildly, he actually smiled at me as we got into the huddle. Elijah's hate may be infectious, but nothing could beat the feeling of winning.

The clock kept ticking, and Bell started getting desperate. Their blitzes got more aggressive, but our line held strong, giving me just enough time to pick apart their defense with short passes. This time, I could see why Coach had gone back to the short game. After the long pass, the defense had started playing our receivers tighter and not cheating up as much.

He was watching though, that much I knew. When they finally started pulling their defense in tighter, to stop our runs and short passes, Coach gave the green light to go deep one more time.

Bell put on the press as hard as they had all game, trying to keep us from punching anything through. Miguel's receiver was still tight on him, but Wayne found a clear path downfield. Just as the pocket started falling apart around me, I launched it, the ball spiraled toward him.

Wayne misread the route, slowing down when he should've kept going. The ball sailed past his outstretched hands, landing on the turf. Wayne slapped his helmet in frustration as we regrouped.

I clapped him on the shoulder. "Shake it off."

Coach pulled it back to running plays after that, and they shut us down, ending the drive. From there on out, Coach went with clock management. We were already far ahead and the last thing Coach wanted was to give them a chance to intercept the ball and turn things around.

When the final whistle blew, the scoreboard read 21 to 7. We'd done it.

Our first win of the season.

Chapter 15

Friday was the first practice in a while where Coach didn't ride us like we were screw-ups. In fact, he was in a downright amazing mood. We did the least amount of warm-up we'd ever had to do before and spent a fair amount of the practice looking at film from the game, with Coach explaining where things went right and where we could still fix things.

I thought Coach might say something about the long passes I completed during the game and how we gave up a whole quarter by banging our heads into their defense with running plays over and over, but he didn't. I'd kind of hoped the success with that would have opened the door to a new kind of offense, where I got to really let loose, but I guess just running the ball forever was the way to go.

Elijah was still on the warpath, trying multiple times to corner me in the hall, but I managed to always be in a crowd. It wasn't that I was scared of him, but I just had too much going on to throw it away with a suspension.

Or worse, getting benched and giving my starter spot up to Gabriel.

Since practice was easy and the coach let us go early, I scrapped the extra practice with the guys and took off for home right after Elijah and his guys went back into the locker room. I thought maybe I'd made a mistake when Hunter slowed down and looked right at me as I headed for the street, but either Elijah was too lazy to go beyond chasing me to the parking lot or they didn't remember the way to my house because no one followed after me.

My walk wasn't alone, however.

I was walking quickly, mostly to put some distance between me and the school so I wasn't in direct line of sight if Elijah came running out, and turned a corner to see someone else making the walk toward my neighborhood.

It wasn't hard to figure out who it was, since the Chinese girl, whose name was Li, I'd finally learned, stood out. She was taller than just about everyone in the school and had long, straight black hair that was pretty distinctive.

I decided that seeing her walking was a sign and picked up my pace to catch up with her. Either she had the fastest walk of anyone I'd ever met, or she heard me and picked up her pace because I wasn't closing the distance between us very quickly.

"You're walking like you're trying to escape me," I called out, jogging to catch up.

She must not have seen me because she turned and looked a little surprised.

"What the hell do you want?"

"Nothing, really. I'm going the same way and just wanted to say hi," I said, falling into step next to her.

"How many times do I have to say I'm not interested?"

She picked up the pace even more, I guess trying to shake me.

"A few more times, probably," I said as I matched her stride. "Look, I'm not trying to be annoying, and I'm definitely not hitting on you; I just ... I feel really bad about how the guys treated you. The fact that I was ever friends with people like that ..."

"So I'm what? Your penance?" Li stopped abruptly, spinning to face me.

"I wouldn't put it like that."

"If you feel so bad about what your friends did, why aren't you trying to fix things with all of the other people those jerks mess with?"

"I am. Or I'm trying to. You're definitely not the only person I'm constantly chasing."

"I bet."

"No, seriously. You can ask around. I could give you a list if you want."

"And what makes you think any of us want your help making things right?" she asked.

"I don't think you want them to treat you like this, so you want ... something to change, right? I don't know exactly what to do, but I at least want to try. Is that such a bad thing?"

"I guess not," she said after a moment, turning and starting to walk again.

I walked in stride with her again. This time, she didn't speed up to lose me.

"It's more than that. I've also noticed you're always by yourself. That can't make you happy."

"I like being by myself. Just because you hate being alone doesn't mean I do. Not everyone needs a fan club."

She should check with the football players, and maybe even the cheerleaders. I definitely didn't have a fan club.

"Maybe that's true. But not wanting a fan club isn't the same as wanting to be alone all the time. And I don't believe you prefer it. Or maybe I can't believe it."

"Oh really? And why's that?"

"Because people aren't built for that kind of isolation. Plus, I've seen how you watch other people at lunch, especially the groups. And not in a 'God, I hate those people' kind of way."

Li stopped walking again. "That's seriously creepy."

"It's not like that," I said quickly. "I just ... I'm worried about you. I mean, after what Elijah and they did to you, I can get why you don't ..."

"You shouldn't," Li cut in. "I didn't ask you to feel guilty about me."

"No, but I feel guilty all the same. The question still stands. Don't you get tired of being alone all the time?"

Instead of answering, she started walking again. I didn't say anything or push her, just walked next to her.

Finally, she said, "It's not worth letting anyone trick me again."

"That's fair. I can promise I'm not trying to trick you, but there's no way for you to know that for sure. I get why you'd be hesitant."

We reached the corner and she looked north; I needed to keep going straight, so I stopped. Surprisingly, she stopped, instead of leaving me behind.

"Look, if you really want me gone forever, just say so and I'll respect that, otherwise I'm probably going to come back to check on you again. But maybe think about whether that's what you actually want."

Li adjusted her backpack strap, studying the ground. "I guess ... you can keep checking. But I'm not promising anything."

"I'll take it," I said with a small smile. "See you around, Li."

I turned and headed for home, leaving her behind. She was still like a wounded puppy who'd been kicked a few too many times. Skittish and ready to run.

I'd take our talk as a victory. It wasn't much, but it was something. And sometimes, 'something' was enough to start with.

Saturday was actually productive, and more than just doing the yard work and changing the oil in Eduardo's mom's car. At first, Eduardo was still really quiet while we worked, but I guess doing something boring for a long time with someone else finally got to him, because he started talking.

It started with some jokes and messing around, probably not the smartest thing to do when working with yard tools, but it was something. Then, just random conversation about nothing important. The kind of BS-ing guys do.

My knowledge from the dream life came in handy again when we went to change the oil in his mom's car. Eduardo had never done any kind of car maintenance, so I was able to walk him through it and teach him how to do it. I think that got him to open up more than anything else, and while we worked, he told me a little about his life in Midland.

Most of it was just the same as my life here, although I guess his was a little less rambunctious. What still wasn't clear, even after all of that, was how he'd end up initiating into a gang. Not that I ever really knew any gang people in my life, or my dream life for that matter, but nothing about his personality struck me as being that type.

He was too soft-spoken. Too afraid of people. And too kind-hearted.

Hell, that had been one of the things the papers had said about him after he was caught. That everyone who knew him was shocked he'd ended up in a situation like that, that he'd kill a deputy. At the time, I'd just chalked it up to the kind of nonsense the papers liked to write, because it made the story catchier, but they were right.

In exchange for the work, his mom made some kind of chicken and rice dish for lunch that was delicious.

And my time with him finally worked. Monday at school, I managed to get Eduardo to move over to eat lunch with me and the rest of the guys, who accepted him with open arms. It really said a lot about the people I was choosing to be friends with. Had I still been buddies with Elijah, he would have made Eduardo jump through hoops to even be talked to, and then constantly belittled him to make sure he knew his place.

Elijah's weekend seemed to have gone a lot less smoothly. He seemed to be unraveling. He tried to corner me again just before lunch but he was predictable as always and I was keeping an eye out for him, so I was able to avoid him. He had some kind of argument with Jake that ended up getting loud enough for us to hear Jake tell him, "That's not fair," and storm off.

I could imagine what Jake thought was unfair. It was following Elijah's 'plan' that ended up with him riding the bench through our first win. The other thing I couldn't help but notice was that Hunter wasn't sitting with them at lunch. He actually wasn't anywhere at lunch.

I thought maybe he missed the school day, home sick or something, but on the way to the field house to get changed for practice, I turned a corner and saw him standing by his locker.

He'd just pulled open his locker door and an avalanche of crumpled paper cascaded onto the floor around his feet.

"Son of a bitch!" Hunter said, slamming his fist into a neighboring locker.

He dropped to his knees and started gathering the wadded-up balls of notebook paper. My first instinct was to keep walking. Hunter had made it clear whose side he was on.

But, I'd been exactly the kind of jackass Elijah and the rest of them still were, and I was out here asking people for forgiveness and trying to get a second chance. It would be hypocritical to just write Hunter off.

And there was a more strategic element to not walking by. It was obvious where this came from. And why. Elijah had given Hunter a death stare throughout most of the game, especially every time Hunter completed a play instead of botching it. And I'd seen the two of them argue, both during the game and at Friday's practice.

Elijah was the kind of guy that any sort of deviation from what he wanted was the same thing as treason. Elijah wanted Hunter to keep burning down his high school football career in the name of a feud, and Hunter didn't want to.

So Elijah was sending him a message.

I walked over and crouched down next to him. Several of the pages had insults and slurs against him, mostly in the direction of questioning his sexuality.

"I don't need your help," he growled, snatching the paper from my hand.

"Okay," I said, standing up, but I didn't walk away. "But we both know Elijah did this."

For a moment, Hunter hesitated. He didn't look up or respond, and he resumed picking everything up, after that pause, but he'd heard me.

"Is this really the kind of friend you want? Someone who'd do this?"

Again, he didn't answer, but he did look both ways down the hallway, I guess making sure no one saw us talking. I got it. He was in a tough place. Maybe he thought if he just kept his head down he'd end up back in Elijah's good graces and still play well enough to keep from losing his spot on the team.

He was naïve if he thought that was going to work.

Hunter finished stuffing the last crumpled note into his backpack, I guess, planning on throwing them away somewhere else.

He said, "He just doesn't know when to stop."

Well, it was more of a mutter than actually saying it out loud. Like he couldn't stop the words from escaping.

"He's not just hurting you. He's hurting the whole team. You've got to see that."

He stood up, not looking at me or agreeing, but not walking off either.

"You saw how much better the game was on Thursday when he wasn't on the field. The rest of us just got to play some football. No head games. No bullshit. Don't you think it'd be better if it was always like that? If we could just focus on winning?"

"It's not that easy," he said, looking at me for the first time since I walked up.

"Why?"

He looked away again. He knew why, he was just afraid to say it, like if he did, it would become real.

"Look, I get it. He's been your friend for years. Remember, he was my friend first, so I know exactly where you're coming from. But friends don't try to destroy your chances just because you won't help them wreck the team."

"You don't know what you're talking about," Hunter said, but there wasn't any anger or animosity this time.

If anything, he just sounded tired.

"Maybe not. But I know Elijah can't stand anyone doing anything he doesn't approve of. And I know you're better than that."

"I didn't ask for your opinion."

The anger was back. I guess he realized he let himself slip. Or maybe he was scared about how close he'd come to actually agreeing with me.

"No, but you got it anyway." I shrugged. "Everyone makes choices, Hunter. It's never too late to make different ones."

He looked at me. For a second, I thought he might agree or at least acknowledge the point. Instead, the moment passed and he slammed his locker shut hard enough to make the whole row rattle. Without another word, he hitched his backpack higher on his shoulder and started walking away from me, toward the door that led out to the field house.

"See you at practice," I called after him.

He didn't respond, but his steps faltered for just a second before he rounded the corner. I waited a minute before heading toward the field house myself. The last thing he needed was Elijah seeing us together, forcing Hunter's hand.

Maybe I'd managed to get through to him. Maybe he'd be the first one to break away from Elijah's control.

I gave him enough of a head start that he was out of sight when I went through the door and headed toward the field house. By the time I got inside the locker room, I could see Hunter standing near Elijah and the rest of them making a halfhearted attempt to join them in conversation.

They had their backs turned to him and it was clear they were shutting him out. He gave me a look, but then turned his back to me too. Elijah, however, did turn his head to see who came through the door and gave me a smirk, which I found somewhat irritating.

This is what Hunter needed to see. That Elijah was always playing games. And yet, here he was, still trying to be friends with them, regardless of the fact that they were shunning him for not throwing away his football career.

Just when I thought there was hope for him. I just shook my head and headed toward my locker, where Miguel and Connor were already suiting up.

I'd made it about three steps when Coach stuck his head out of his office and yelled, "Sims! My office."

I sighed and stood there for a second, trying to imagine what had happened this time. Worse, how Elijah had been involved. It would explain the smirk he'd just given me.

I, however, couldn't keep Coach waiting, so I changed direction, heading to his office. Instead of finding Coach Heidemann inside, I found him and Coach Holloway, the head of the football program at Wheaton and coach of the varsity and JV teams.

"Have a seat, son," Coach Holloway said, gesturing to the chair in front of the desk.

I sat down, trying not to fidget. Whatever Elijah had done, if it involved Coach Holloway, it was big. There was a chance I wouldn't even be playing football after today, depending on what lie he passed around this time.

"I watched the tape from Thursday's game," he said. "And I wanted to tell you how impressed I was. You showed some ability for decent passing, although we'll have to really work on it if you're going to reach the levels I think you're capable of. The thing I was really impressed by, though, was the way you kept the offense moving, even when things weren't clicking. Being shut down for a full quarter and then managing to come out of it with your guys still giving it their all shows real leadership."

"Thank you, sir," I said, still unsure where this was going.

"Coach Holloway has a situation we think you might be able to help with," Coach Heidemann said.

"JV's having a rough season. Zero and three so far and from what I'm seeing, we're not in a position to start winning any time soon. The main issue is at quarterback, where we're just not getting the production we need at that position."

I'd met Jorden Kinsell, the JV quarterback, only once. Actually, he'd been the backup quarterback at JV until the guy who'd been at that position, whose name I was forgetting at the moment, had to transfer out of the district on the second day of preseason practice, before school started.

That left Jorden with no backup. I'd been practicing on the other end of the field and even I had noticed him struggling, with passes often sailing wide or falling short. I honestly didn't consider it would be that much of a problem, since the entire football department seemed to prefer running plays over passing, even at the varsity level.

"We'd like you to move up to JV," Coach Holloway continued.

To say I was floored was an understatement. They'd made it very clear that freshmen did not end up on JV or varsity. I got that this was a special circumstance, but I also knew this was a big deal.

I could also see problems coming from a mile away. If I was a struggling starter and they brought in someone from the freshman team, something they'd vowed not to do, to replace me, I'd be pissed. No way Jorden wouldn't hate me for taking his spot. I didn't know him, but I could see this being trouble.

Of course, I was leaving five guys who were definitely trouble behind, so even if he became difficult, it was still an upgrade.

"If that's what you think is best, Coach," I said.

"Good. I'm glad to hear it," Coach Holloway said. "Now, I want you to know that you're being phased in as our starter, but Dale

Eddins will remain team captain. You're young and this is going to be as much of a learning experience as your chance to show us what you can do. Still, I expect you to show the same leadership qualities you've displayed so far."

Dale was, I think, a running back, and maybe he was also a junior. I honestly wasn't sure. Most of the JV and varsity guys didn't hang out with the freshmen a lot.

That was just kind of how it was.

The only thing about this that was really bothering me was leaving Miguel, Connor, and the others behind to deal with Elijah and the rest on their own. It felt kind of like I was abandoning them.

Not that I was going to turn the offer down.

"Has anyone told Jorden yet?"

"We'll handle that," Coach Heidemann said. "We already talked to Gabriel, since he needs to start practicing today to get ready for Thursday. We'll talk to Jorden while you get suited up for today's practice. Because of some district rules, we can't move you to JV until after this week's game, so you're still going to be listed on the freshman roster this week. We plan on having Gabriel start to give him some experience, and will swap the two of you in and out throughout the game. It'll be a good way for him to get some experience on the field before he's on his own. In spite of that, you'll practice with the JV so you can get two full weeks of practice before you have to go out on the field with them."

That explained Elijah's smirk. He'd heard from his new pal Gabriel that he was going to practice as a starter today and had inferred from the news that I was being demoted. Why he'd think the coaches would drop me after our first actual win, I'd never know, but it was clear he'd think that.

He was going to be furious when he heard that I'd been put on the JV team and he hadn't.

"I'll want you on the sideline for Saturday's game, too. Unless we can find a way around the rules, you'll have to ride the bench, but I want you to see the team play for real before you go out on the field with them," Coach Holloway said, as he pulled a thick playbook from the desk and handed it to me. "Learn this inside and out. The basics are the same plays you've already been running, but the rest are more complex and there are more variations. I gotta say I'm glad you started working on audibles early because that's going to be part of it, too. I want you knowing every play by heart before you take a single snap as a starter."

It was bigger than my freshman playbook, that was for sure.

"When can I tell my teammates?"

"We're making the announcement today," Coach Heidemann said. "After we've informed each of you individually."

It was going to make this week crazy busy, but if that's what I had to do to get this opportunity, I'd take it.

"I won't let you down."

"I hope not," Coach Holloway said.

Chapter 16

"... worry about it. Mom will understand," Eduardo said as we walked into the cafeteria.

"Make sure she knows I'm going to keep coming to help, but I might have to switch to Sundays for now. JV plays on Saturdays every week, of which the evenings are going to be pretty packed. Maybe I could come earlier, but I want to see how the first few weeks go."

"No, Sundays are good. I'll check with Mom, but she'll be good either way."

"Cool. I'd come this Sunday, but I'm losing both Thursday and Saturday for doing homework, and I'm already starting to fall behind. So I need at least a full day to try to get caught up."

"No, hey, it's fine. I can't tell you how happy Mom is just for the little stuff you did last week. Trust me, she thinks you're an angel and keeps saying I need to be more like you."

"Ha, no, you don't want to do that," I said, and then stopped as something caught my eye.

Li, who hadn't been in the cafeteria on Monday, was back and sitting by herself again. We'd made some small progress on Friday, and I'd hoped to see her again yesterday, but she was here today, and I was still hoping to build on that progress.

"Hey," I said to Eduardo. "There's something I gotta do real quick. Could you let the other guys know I'll be there in a few minutes?"

"Uhh, maybe I should wait with ..."

"You'll be fine. Trust me; I'll be along in a minute. Okay?"

He nodded, took a deep breath, and started walking toward our table. I watched him for a moment, making sure he made it okay. The guys really had taken to him, I think mostly because they saw how hard I was working to get him integrated into the group. They were good guys and they'd welcomed him in almost immediately his first few days eating with us.

Which is why I was happy to see Miguel waving him over as soon as he noticed him, which seemed to make Eduardo relax. Or at least relax as much as he ever did.

Seeing that he was okay, I turned and headed toward Li, who had her head in a book and didn't look up until I put my lunch down and sat in the seat in front of her.

"Studying and eating, huh?" I asked, seeing that the book was some kind of math textbook.

Her eyes flicked up from her book and then back to it, as she said, "I guess."

It wasn't exactly a warm welcome, but at least she didn't tell me to get lost with her first sentence.

Progress.

"I meant to ask you something when we were walking on Friday, but I forgot. You weren't at lunch that day, and I didn't see you here yesterday. Don't you eat lunch every day?"

"I do, but sometimes I eat it while doing a tutoring session for people who don't have time after school."

"Ohh, I'd been wondering why you were leaving school around the same time my practice got out a bunch of times. I couldn't figure out what else was going on after school that would keep someone around. Do you tutor a lot of people?"

"Some."

"Is it like a job or ..."

She sighed and closed her book, I guess realizing I wasn't going to leave her alone any time soon. "Kind of. Not officially, I guess, but my mom sets it up with some kids' parents or whatever."

"But you get paid, right?"

"Yeah. Plus, it'll look good on my college transcript."

"Huh, that's interesting, actually."

"Why?" she said, her eyes narrowing.

"I've been trying to get out of remedial classes and convinced a couple of my teachers to help me get on level for next year, so they've been assigning extra work to me that's usually ahead of what we're working on in class. But it's a lot, and they said they'll only keep helping me as long as I show I'm up for the challenge. I've been going in and getting help from them when I can, but football takes up my entire time after school, and honestly, I'm starting to drown in it. Since you do tutoring, and I think we live kind of near each other, I think maybe tutoring could help."

"You're seriously asking me to tutor you?"

"Yeah, if it's not too much trouble and I can convince my parents and afford whatever you charge. Seriously, I need it. Football really is picking up, and the workload's getting intense."

"This isn't some kind of trick?"

"No. You can talk to my teachers if you want and confirm everything. Ms. White and Mrs. Mace have been doing the most work with me."

"I ... guess."

"Really?"

"Yeah. I mean, it's okay, you don't have to pay. That's just for the stuff my mom sets up."

"Well, if I need to, I will. I really could use the help."

"Just do the work and don't make me regret it, and we'll be even."

"Deal," I said, and then decided that since things were going well, I was going to shoot for the moon. "So, why don't you come over and sit with me and my friends."

"Why?"

"Why not? Wouldn't it be more fun to be with other people, and even maybe make some more friends? Really, they're good guys, and they're not just all football players. Eduardo is a friend of mine, he doesn't play any sports that I know of, and he started sitting with us last week. He's doing fine, see?"

Li looked past me to my table where Eduardo was listening to Miguel talk about something, nodding occasionally while Connor and Jamal were arguing about something I couldn't hear.

"Just a bunch of normal guys eating lunch. What's the worst that could happen?"

"A lot," Li said, but she kept watching the table.

"And if it does, you could move back to this empty table. It'll be more fun sitting with friends."

"We're friends now?" Li asked, raising an eyebrow at me.

"I hope so." I shrugged. "I mean, you did just agree to help tutor me. That's kind of 'friend territory,' right?"

Li stayed quiet for what felt like forever, studying the table.

Finally, she let out a small sigh and said, "Fine."

I tried not to show how pleased I was, keeping my voice casual. "Cool. Here, let me help you with that stuff."

I reached for her books, but she pulled them back. "I can carry my own books."

"Okay, okay," I said, holding up my hands. "Just trying to help."

We walked over to the table together, Li trailing slightly behind me. The guys looked up as we approached.

"Hey guys, this is my friend Li. She's gonna join us for lunch. Li, that's Miguel, Connor, Jamal, Tyrell, and Eduardo."

"Hi," Li said softly.

"There's space next to Eduardo," I said, pointing to the empty spot.

Li hesitated for just a second before sitting down. Eduardo gave her a small smile, which she returned after a moment.

"So what were you guys arguing about?" I asked Connor and Jamal, trying to get the conversation flowing again.

Connor immediately jumped in, talking about his feelings about some movie they were arguing about, which Jamal clearly didn't agree with.

No one brought a lot of attention to Li, but they weren't shunning her either. Mostly just letting her exist with them, which is what I think she needed, because she visibly started to relax after a few minutes.

Honestly, I felt like I was getting good at this.

Thursday, we were back on the field against Eastwood High School from El Paso. For the first time since the season started, Elijah looked overly pleased with himself instead of glowering at me the whole time. As predicted, he had taken the news that I had been moved to JV badly, complaining loudly to anyone who would listen about how, if they wanted to turn things around, he should have been moved to JV instead of me.

Never mind that the only win the freshman team had was while he had been benched.

At least practice had been better every day since I had been on the opposite end of the field with JV and varsity. We would warm up together and then switch in and out with them, one group on the field working plays while the other was either in the locker room or with the defensive or offensive coordinator. I had to miss today's practice, which would involve JV playing against varsity, as a buildup to varsity's game tomorrow.

Miguel and the rest had told me that since I'd left, Elijah had become more of a pain, walking around like he was the big man on the team now. Technically, Tyrell had been assigned as captain of the team for today's game, but the coach made it known they would be picking the new permanent captain soon. Gabriel should have been making a push for that spot, but he was deferring everything to Elijah.

Which was a mistake.

"Ready for the show? See how a real team plays?" Elijah said as we headed for the field house to do our run-on and start the game.

"Front row seat to watch us crush Eastwood."

"Break a leg out there," I said, and then muttered. "Preferably your own."

The fact that he was the reason we had done badly never seemed to enter his thick skull.

Coach Heidemann gathered us up in the field house and said, "Listen up, guys. Tonight isn't just about winning or losing. It's about proving we can work together as a team. I expect to see hustle and hard work, but I also expect you to all play the mental game like we've been talking about. Watch the other team, make your adjustments, and we're going to win this thing. Alright, let's go show them what Wheaton is all about."

The speech got everyone excited, and we ran out onto the field like we were going to roll over the other team. Unfortunately, motivation is just one part of the puzzle, and the rest of the pieces seemed to be missing.

The first quarter started rough. Gabriel was slow making his reads, and their defense was tough, putting a ton of pressure on our offensive line. He was barely getting his passes off before El Paso's defense crashed in. Our running game wasn't faring much better with a two-yard gain here, a three-yard loss there.

Every drive ended in a punt.

There was one close moment when Elijah broke free on his route, but Gabriel's throw sailed high, missing by a mile.

The rest of the quarter unfolded like a slow-motion car crash. Their defense kept bringing pressure, and Gabriel kept looking more rattled. When the inevitable happened, a blindside hit that jarred the ball loose, I almost saw it coming before it happened.

Their linebacker scooped up the fumble and rumbled into the end zone as the quarter expired. One kick later, it was seven-nothing, visitors. The crowd groaned.

The second quarter unfolded a lot like the first. Gabriel kept forcing passes to Elijah, completely ignoring wide-open receivers downfield. I watched Miguel break free of coverage three times, waving his arms frantically, but Gabriel never even looked in his direction.

Coach was nearly frothing at the mouth halfway through the quarter as yet another rushed throw sailed straight toward two defenders hovering around Elijah. The safety snatched it easily, and my stomach dropped as he sprinted down the sideline. Our guys managed to push him out of bounds, but the damage was done.

"What was that?" Coach Heidemann called out as Gabriel jogged to the sideline. "You had Miguel wide open on the crossing route."

"Didn't see him," Gabriel mumbled, ducking his head.

"Because you weren't looking," I said quietly, earning a sharp look from Coach.

Three plays later, Eastwood's running back punched it in from the five-yard line. The scoreboard flipped to fourteen to zero. Coach Heidemann walked up and down our sideline like a caged animal, clipboard tucked under his arm.

"He's playing favorites instead of football," Miguel said, dropping onto the bench next to me. "I might as well be invisible out there."

"Trust me, I see you getting open. But Gabriel's got Elijah-vision right now."

"More like Elijah-pressure," Miguel said, taking a sip of water. "It's just like I was telling you. About how he's been in practice."

"Just be patient. Coach sees it, too."

The half ended shortly after that, without much movement for either side. Things in the locker room, as we piled in for halftime, were tense, to say the least. Most of the team sat silently on the wooden benches, heads down, clearly defeated.

Almost everyone.

Elijah threw his helmet into his cubby as soon as he got to his locker and started pacing, yelling at everyone like he was the team captain.

"You call that blocking? My grandma could hold the line better than you guys!" He jabbed a finger at Connor. "Three sacks! Three!"

"Maybe if you ran your routes right, Gabriel wouldn't have to hold the ball so long," Tyrell said, standing up. "Or maybe you could release him and *allow* him to pass to someone other than you. Miguel has been open half the game, but he's throwing to you every damn time."

Half the team looked to Gabriel for some kind of response, even though everyone knew it was true. Gabriel didn't look up. Before Elijah could respond, Coach Heidemann walked in looking as angry as I'd ever seen him.

"Enough!" he said, clearly having heard some of that exchange. I don't care who you think is at fault. If we don't start acting like a team, this game is over. That was pathetic. I've seen all of you look better in practice than you did out there today. We've got two quarters to turn this around. You know what separates good teams from great ones? It's not talent. It's how they respond when things go wrong. I need you all to go back out there and perform in the next half! You understand me?"

A few players muttered halfhearted affirmations. Elijah folded his arms and stared at the ground.

"I said, do you understand me?" Coach said, raising his voice.

This time we responded louder, though the energy was still low. He nodded once, as if accepting that was the best we could muster. As we stood to head back to the field, Coach grabbed Gabriel's shoulder and pulled him aside. I couldn't hear what Coach said to him, but he occasionally jabbed the air or pointed at Gabriel for emphasis. Gabriel nodded a few times and looked like he was going to puke.

The third quarter kicked off, but it was clear from our first snap that nothing had changed. Gabriel hesitated, the pocket collapsed, and he scrambled out to his right, flinging the ball toward Elijah in desperation. It sailed wide, landing ten yards out of bounds.

Next drive, a glimmer of hope emerged. Gabriel finally decided to throw to Miguel, hitting him on a short slant for a gain of seven. The sideline erupted in cheers at finally seeing some kind of forward movement. The joy was short-lived. On the next play, the line gave way, and Gabriel was sacked for a loss of eight.

We punted. Again.

By the time the defense handed us the ball back, it was clear frustration was mounting. Gabriel dropped back on third-and-long, and instead of checking his options, he locked onto Elijah, who wasn't even open. The throw was high and late, picked off by their cornerback. He sprinted thirty yards downfield before we managed to reel him in.

Their offense capitalized on the mistake with ruthless efficiency. Three plays later, their running back darted through a gap and into the end zone. The scoreboard now read twenty-one to zero.

It seemed like this was going to be a complete blowout. We did have a moment of luck two drives later when Gabriel managed to hand off cleanly to Hunter just as their defense misread the play, leaving a hole open for him. Hunter might have been a jerk, or at least friends with jerks, but he wasn't a bad player and he took advantage of the opportunity he was given, breaking through for a fifty-yard run and our first points of the night. It was like a shot of adrenaline to the team. The extra point sailed through the uprights, and for a moment, we had a sliver of hope.

But it didn't last.

Late in the quarter, Elijah decided to take matters into his own hands. On a third-and-short, he caught a screen pass and, instead of cutting upfield for a safe gain, he juked left, then right, showboating. The ball popped loose, and their linebacker pounced on it.

Coach Heidemann threw his clipboard to the ground hard enough to break it, yelling at everyone and no one in particular.

Thankfully, our defense stopped it from turning into yet another score, but we'd wasted what little momentum we'd managed to build.

As the third quarter ended, Coach sent for me, along with Wayne and Clarke. It wasn't hard to tell what was about to happen.

"Blake, you're in at QB. Lowry and Reeves, you're in for Garner and Lehr."

Elijah's face twisted with fury. "What? You can't …"

He stopped as soon as he spoke, realizing how much he'd just screwed up. Everyone tried not to look at him or Coach, not wanting to get caught in whatever crossfire that might happen.

"I can, and I am. Now, get off my field. You're done for tonight."

When the defense finally stopped their last drive, I grabbed my helmet and jogged onto the field. It was actually weird, playing with absolutely no pressure. No one actually expected me to save us from this mess and I wouldn't be around tomorrow to see the results, I'd be at practice with the JV team.

They, however, were going to feel the pain, of that I had no doubt. Next week, Coach wasn't going to be able to sub me in, which meant he was going to have to find a way to get Gabriel to start playing football instead of playing catch with Elijah.

The team was feeling a little energized, I think hoping this meant they were going to finally make some progress.

I wanted to take advantage of that excitement as best I could, and so did Coach, not calling the normal first running play, but giving me an opportunity to pass out of the gate. At the snap, I dropped back seven steps, watching Miguel cut inside while Wayne streaked down the sideline. The safety bit on Miguel's route, leaving Wayne one-on-one. I released the ball just as Wayne broke free.

Wayne tracked it perfectly, snagging the pass over his shoulder and accelerating past the last defender. The crowd erupted as he crossed the goal line.

With the extra point, we'd closed the gap.

There was a little back and forth for a bit, with their defense scrambling to reset their play style to watch for my longer passes. To make up for the opportunities it gave us inside. Our defense, however, was energized, putting on some serious pressure.

At just under five minutes to play, Tyrell and Jesse collapsed the pocket, forcing an incomplete pass on fourth down deep on our side of the field.

Since they were covering deep a lot more than they had with Gabriel, we pushed downfield methodically. Hunter broke free for nine yards. Wayne caught a short pass for five. We just kept moving the chains downfield.

With two minutes left, we were second and seven on their thirty-five. The closer we got to their end zone, the more aggressive they became. They'd already blitzed once, and I was waiting for it to happen again.

As soon as I got the snap, I saw their linebackers charging. Unfortunately, Clarke missed his block almost completely, and part of our line started to collapse before I'd even gotten set for the pass that had been planned.

Everything slowed down. A defensive end broke free, heading straight for me. Instead of throwing it away, I stepped up into the collapsing pocket. The defender's hands brushed my jersey as I slipped past him.

Because of the way the pocket had collapsed, I saw an opening in the line, and I took it, pushing through the hole. I managed to dodge another grab for my jersey while Tyrell, who somehow realized what I was doing, really dug in and managed to hold two guys back just enough for me to get through.

I saw open field ahead. My legs pumped harder than they ever had before as I cut toward the sideline. I could see their linebacker and cornerback trying to cut me off, but Miguel managed to get himself in between me and the closest one.

Twenty yards. Fifteen. Ten. Their safety closed in, but I was faster than he was, so if he caught me, it was going to be just at the line.

I dove for the end zone as the safety grabbed my ankle. The ball crossed the plane just before my knee hit.

"Touchdown!"

The referee's arms went up. The sideline exploded.

Miguel was the first to reach me, pulling me up from the turf. "That was insane! Where did that come from?"

I couldn't stop grinning. "Sometimes you just have to make something happen."

Coach Heidemann met me at the sideline. "Now that's playing quarterback. Way to keep your head and make a play."

The extra point tied it at twenty-one all. We'd erased a two-touchdown deficit in just under a quarter. Most of the rest of the team was wild with excitement. With the exception of Jake, who looked pissed, and Gabriel who looked like he was going to be sick.

I'm sure Elijah, hearing us tie it up from the locker room, was on the verge of destroying stuff.

There was hardly any time left in the game, but they managed to get a field goal with only a few seconds left, winning the game. Not that it seemed to matter. From the way our team acted, you would have thought we'd won instead of lost.

Chapter 17

As good as Thursday's game went, at least my quarter of it, Saturday's game was a disaster. Jorden struggled the entire time, with four interceptions and a botched handoff, the last of which turned into a touchdown for the other team.

I was actually glad I got a chance to observe the game in person because the level of competition was way more intense than I was used to. Since it wasn't just freshmen, the guys were all generally bigger and faster than the teams I'd faced so far this year.

Our defensive players were monsters, and the only reason the game ended with a 7 to 0 loss. They crushed the other team's offensive line time and time again, getting three sacks against their QB.

Our offensive line, while fine, was not up to the same level, but they did well enough. Jorden did get sacked once, but it was because he just sat in the pocket, even as it collapsed on him, instead of staying mobile. I know that was the playbook we ran, to stay in the pocket and follow your reads till the last moment, throwing the ball away if it got too bad.

I even got the point of that. Scrambling could lead to sacks and fumbles, instead of tossing the ball out of bounds and stopping the clock. But it also threw away our down and brought us one step closer to having to clear the field for the defense, which I never wanted to do, especially when I could see room to get out of the way and stay on my reads.

Today was my first real practice with the JV starters. I'd been with the second string all of the previous week to give Jorden the time he needed to try and pull out the last game. It hadn't worked, but I knew why the coaches did it. I was excited for today, to really get into it, playing with the other JV starters, who were mostly sophomores with some juniors and a couple of seniors mixed in. Nervous, but excited.

"Look who decided to grace us with his presence," someone called out as I joined the rest of the guys stretching while Coach Holloway talked to varsity on their part of the field. "Peewees play at Frazier Park."

The other guys chuckled at the snub. Compared to the bullshit I'd had to deal with Elijah, I could deal with a little ribbing. I was the new guy and a freshman to boot, so it was to be expected.

I kept my head down and started my stretches, trying to ignore the side-eyes and jokes. The worst thing I could do was take it personally. They'd see it as blood in the water, and I'd become free game. More concerning was Jorden, who was off to my left, aggressively stretching his hamstrings and pointedly not looking in my direction. I could only imagine how he was taking my replacing him.

After about fifteen minutes, Coach Holloway blew his whistle and yelled, "Alright, gentlemen, bring it in!"

We jogged over to form a half-circle around him where I ended up near the back, which was probably for the best.

"I know you saw him out here last week, but starting this week, we've officially made the change to our roster, and Blake will be taking over as starting quarterback for the rest of the season."

The muttering started immediately, but I still ignored it, keeping my eyes on Coach.

"I know it's unusual to have a freshman on the team, let alone starting, but talent and dedication deserve recognition regardless of grade level, and I think we can all agree we'd like to start winning some games sometime this year. I expect everyone to work together and give Blake the same support you'd give any teammate."

"Sure thing, Coach," Brandon Porter, a junior defensive tackle said. "Though somebody better check their diaper, smells like freshman around here."

A few snickers rippled through the group.

When it died down, I said, "It's gonna suck when this freshman shows you guys up."

There were a lot of 'oohhhs' and some genuine laughter instead of snickers, this time directed at Brandon, who didn't crack a smile.

"Alright, enough comedy hour," Coach barked. "Receivers with Blake for passing drills. Rest of you split up by position. Varsity has the field first."

As we broke into groups, I grabbed a ball and started warming up my arm. I'd been doing drills in the backyard when I wasn't doing homework and spent some extra time Sunday afternoon at it. I knew this was a big step for me and I wanted to make as good of an impression as possible. It was hard to get a read on the receivers, who had a varying degree of enthusiasm.

"Let's see what you got, freshman," Dwight Baker said, setting up for the first route I was going to throw.

I watched as he ran the sloppiest post pattern I'd ever seen. It wasn't hard to see what he was doing. He was testing me, trying to throw me off my game. But I'd practiced and played with Wayne, who was unintentionally just as erratic. So, throwing to someone who couldn't seem to run their route wasn't something I was completely unused to.

I released the ball just as he made his cut, hitting him perfectly in stride. Dwight turned back, trying to hide his surprise.

"Lucky throw," he said as he got back to me and tossed me the ball.

"Sure was," I agreed, already setting up for the next pass. "Want to try your luck again?"

For the next twenty minutes, we ran through the route tree with each of the wide receivers. I also had the tight ends for a bit to give them some chances at receiving short lobs. They even stopped messing with me after a few goes, mostly because Coach Easley, the offensive coordinator, told them to knock off the horse shit and do it right, or he'd swap them for their backups.

Unlike Elijah, who would have taken that personally, they brushed it off and started trying. This wasn't mind games or trying to one-up anyone. They were just hazing the new guy, which I could deal with.

Varsity finally finished up and was ready to go to the coordinators, which meant we finally got a chance to scrimmage under the eye of Coach Holloway.

As we walked to the twenty-yard line, where we'd be running plays, Kevin Dean walked past and said, "Nice arm, freshman. But let's see how you do when you've got real pressure coming at you."

"Looking forward to it."

Actually, I was. The only way I was going to prove to them that I belonged there, was on the field.

Coach Holloway blew a whistle as soon as we were all roughly in our starting positions. "First series is all passing plays. Give Blake a chance to get settled before we start prepping the actual plays for this weekend."

What he meant was he wanted to see how I'd handle real pressure. As the defense lined up, I could see Kevin grinning behind his face mask. A junior on defense, and probably one who'd move to varsity next year, he was part experience and part skill, enough that he felt it was up to him to show the new guy what was up.

Challenge accepted.

The center snapped the ball, and immediately, I felt pressure from the left side. I'd already seen, from watching JV play, that the offensive line was much weaker than the defensive line. I'd thought I'd been ready for it, but the pocket started shrinking faster than I expected, even accounting for the imbalance. Whether that was on purpose or just a skill imbalance, I started to roll left to avoid being caught in it while I kept my eyes downfield.

I juked and just missed a tackle from Randy Killam, one of the defensive tackles, and was thinking about saying screw it and trying to make for the sidelines to see if I could pick up some yards before the line fell apart completely when Mickey Evans, one of the wide receivers, broke free of his coverage.

I hit him in stride for a clean fifteen yards as hands grabbed me around the waist, enough to tell me I was tackled, without actually taking me to the ground, which wasn't allowed in practice for obvious reasons.

A few whoops came from the offensive line, and Mickey was smiling as he tossed the ball back to Andre Price, our center.

"Let's see you do it again," one of the linebackers, whose name I didn't remember at the moment, said.

Not everything was perfect. The next play went south fast. The defense crashed through almost immediately, and I had to throw it away before taking a sack, well a touch that would have been a sack if it had been allowed. I got it out of bounds and kept it from being a turnover, but that was just about the only good thing I'd managed that play.

"What happened to showing us up?" Brandon said as we lined up for the next snap.

I didn't respond, focusing instead on reading the defense. They were showing blitz again, and I could see my guys eyeing each other, all but confirming they were not pushing hard, letting the defense through to test me.

Again, not malicious, but definitely hazing to see how I'd hold up.

As soon as I got the ball, the pocket started collapsing again, this time from the right. I made my reads as fast as I could, and everything was covered. I didn't just want to throw it away again, so I scrambled left, hoping someone would break free.

Thankfully, someone did.

Dwight, a junior I didn't really know other than by name, got free of his coverage as he ran on a deep post route. I didn't even think about it, or the guys closing in on me. I just let it fly, sending the ball spiraling to him for a twenty-five-yard pass.

He held it up and ran around whooping like he'd just scored, instead of stopping on completion like we were supposed to. Coach blew his whistle, calling us all back to the sideline.

"Damn," Kevin said, pulling off his helmet as he walked past. "Alright, you might have some game."

"A little," I said, grinning back at him.

This was what football was supposed to be. Competitive and fun. We could play hard, try to crush the other guy, and laugh about it after. It was a breath of fresh air after all the bullshit Elijah had put me through.

"Not bad, Blake," Coach Holloway said as we gathered back in. "You're handling the pressure well, but remember, scrambling is a last resort, not your first option. Sometimes, you need to trust your protection and let the play develop."

"Yes, sir," I said, though I noticed he wasn't exactly telling me to stop doing it.

Besides, my protection had let them through on purpose, to see what I'd do. I thought it was just for the moment and I hoped it wouldn't last, but I'd trust them as soon as they showed me they were playing for real.

"Alright, let's get back to running the playbook. We're still a running team, and that's going to be our focus, but I don't want the receivers getting complacent out there. If Blake shows us he can do this on the field this weekend, we might start working in some additional passes."

From the corner of my eye, I could see Jorden glower and look over at me, like it was my fault he hadn't been able to do his job. I wasn't trying to show him up. I was just trying to do my best and make the most of the opportunity I'd been given.

Thankfully, everyone else seemed to be much more rational and the rest of the practice went off beautifully. The offensive line stopped letting the defense through on purpose, and I started to get real looks from the few passing plays we ran.

Our defensive line was still better than the offensive line, and it was a challenge, but I didn't have any more reason to scramble the rest of the afternoon.

All in all, a good start to my time on JV.

Things went pretty well the next few days. The hazing more or less stopped, although they found plenty of opportunities to continue the kind of ball-busting that was a part of every sport. Lots of references to me being a child, needing my mommy, and a random pacifier in my locker were about par for the course, but I didn't take it to heart.

They didn't give me any more shit than anyone else. Well, maybe that wasn't true, but it was mostly because I was both the newest guy and being a freshman made me a particularly easy target.

On the field was where it mattered, and they stopped testing me and started trusting me. My football IQ was still lower than I wanted it to be, and I had a lot of studying ahead of me to get there. Not just studying our own playbook, but reviewing tapes and learning how to read the players.

The dream life might have given me a heads up as to where the sport was going to be going, but I'd been a fan after being forced out, not a true student of the game. And that was what I was going to have to be if I wanted to succeed now that I had a real chance at it.

Still, even with all of that, I was having fun again. No more Elijah and his guys trying to screw up plays. Just a team playing together and wanting to win together.

They'd even invited me over to sit at the JV and varsity table, which was a big deal for a freshman. It was quite the buzz when I politely declined, telling them I wanted to stay with my guys. They might not be on my team anymore this year, but I was certain they would be making varsity in a year or two and they were going to be the core I'd be playing with until I graduated.

I again got some mocking jabs, but I am also pretty sure I earned some respect from the guys. They said I was loyal to my people, which meant when the time came, I'd be loyal to them too. If I wanted people to start looking at me as a leader, if not this year than at least next year, that was groundwork I needed to lay down.

Unfortunately, it wasn't all fun and games.

Thursday, I was at lunch with my normal guys, but down at the far end of the table, kind of away from everyone, ready to bash my head against the table to make the pain stop.

"That's not right either," Li said, pointing to my answer about organism classification. "You've got the order mixed up again."

"Kingdom, class, phylum, genus, family, order, species. No, wait. Kingdom, class, order. Damn it," I said, dropping my head onto my textbook.

"You're getting closer." Li tapped her pencil against the top of my head. "Try this; Keep People Cheering Over Friday Game Scores."

I lifted my head. "What?"

"It's a memory device. Each word starts with the letter of the classification levels, in order. Keep for Kingdom, People for Phylum, and so on."

"So now I have to remember some random sentence instead?"

"It's about football. You seem to remember that big book of plays you're always carrying around. I figured making it about football would help, since it's the only thing you ever remember."

"I'm not sure whether to be insulted or impressed."

"Go with impressed and try it again."

"Keep … people … cheering …" I worked through each word. "Kingdom, phylum, class, order, family, genus, species!"

"Finally." Li made a note in the margin of my paper. "Now, try the next one."

I stared at the question about bacterial classification and felt my frustration rising again. "You know what drives me crazy? The girl behind me got half credit for this same answer on a quiz last week, but Walsh marked mine completely wrong. Apparently, my missing one meant I missed the whole question, but she missed three and got credit for the ones she did get right. God. I hate that guy."

"Maybe you should talk to your coaches about it. You're some big football star now, right? Start using it to your advantage like the other jocks in school."

"That's not fair. For one, that's what Walsh hates about me. He thinks anyone who plays a sport is just trying to coast by, and yet when I'm trying to actually do a good job, he thinks I'm pulling a fast one. And for two, since when am I a star? I'm on the JV team. That's not exactly big man on campus territory."

"Not according to them." Li nodded toward Miguel and Connor, who were talking about the game they had coming up today and how bad practice had been going for them. "They talk about your promotion like you're headed straight to the NFL."

"Well ... they're idiots. And since when did you start listening to them? I thought you were always too busy reading to notice anything else."

Just because I read doesn't mean I'm deaf."

"Sorry, I didn't mean ..."

"Let's try this next section again," she said, interrupting me and trying to get me to focus back on the work and not on her.

I tried to humor her, because I knew she hated when I pried too much, but my brain was starting to get fried and lunch was almost over. I just didn't have any focus left in me for this study session.

"I need a break," I said, pushing my textbook away. "Can I ask you something?"

"You just did."

"Why are you always so unhappy?"

"I don't know what you mean."

"Come on. You never smile. You don't take part in conversations, even here. You barely talk to anyone except when you're tutoring."

"Not everyone needs to be the life of the party, Blake. Some of us are fine being quiet."

"There's quiet and then there's ..." I waved my hand, trying to find the right words. "Look, this is high school. I know it sounds stupid, but for a lot of people, this is as good as it gets. Their peak moment. And you're just ... letting it pass by."

Li picked at the corner of my textbook, not meeting my eye. She had the same annoyed expression she had every time I pressed about anything, so I expected her normal sarcastic response.

Instead, she surprised me when she said, "It's different here. Everything's different."

"Different than what?"

"In Houston, where I lived before moving here, our apartment was in Chinatown. Our whole complex was Chinese families. I went to an American school, had American friends, but my life at home was ..." She paused. "I could walk down the street and get authentic hot pot, and the street signs were in Chinese. There, I was just like everyone else ... well, as long as I didn't venture out too far. Here, everyone stares at me and just refers to me as 'the Chinese girl.'"

I felt a twinge of guilt, since I'd referred to her as that in my head a bunch of times before I'd learned her name.

"Why did you end up moving here?"

"My mom bought Mrs. Downing's antique store when she retired. They were both big into antiques and knew each other professionally, and I think they became something like friends over the last few years. I know Mom would drive all the way here to buy inventory from her. Mrs. Downing wanted to sell the place so she could move to Colorado to be closer to her kids, so she gave my mom the chance to buy it."

"Wait, your mom runs that antique store on Main?"

The antique store was still called Downing's Antiques. If you went anywhere toward Main Street, you'd end up passing it, so it was kind of hard to miss. I didn't exactly shop for antiques much, but I would just have assumed someone named Downing still owned it.

"Yeah. She's really good at finding pieces, fixing them up, selling them to people who don't want to do the work themselves. My great-grandfather was some kind of master craftsman back in China, although I never got to meet him. The way Mom tells it, he could look at a broken piece of furniture and know exactly how to restore it. He raised her so her parents could try for another child and get a boy, and taught her everything he knew. I think it kind of crushed him when she married my dad and they moved to America."

"What did your dad do?"

"He was a researcher at the big medical center in Houston. Cancer research, ironically enough." The smile faded. "He died when I was eight. Brain tumor."

"God, Li. I'm so sorry."

"It's okay," she said, but it was clear she was still sad that he was gone. "After that, Mom had to figure out how to support us. She'd been doing restoration work as a hobby, just to keep busy, but suddenly, it became our lifeline after he died. We barely made it some months, but she kept us going."

"That must have been really hard."

"It was. But this store … it's the first time I've seen her excited about something since Dad died. She's there all the time, seven days a week from when they open until closing, but she's building something that's hers. Actually, she's there more than that. We live in the apartment above the store."

"Sounds kind of lonely though."

Li's shoulders lifted in a half-shrug. "We manage."

"You know, it might help if you got involved in some activities. Being smart is great, but studying is pretty solitary."

"What would I even do?"

"Well, what do you like?"

Li started to answer, then stopped herself. She looked around the cafeteria, maybe checking if anyone was listening.

"Promise you won't laugh?"

"Cross my heart."

"I like basketball." The words came out in a rush. "I used to play with kids, well boys, back in Houston. We'd go to the courts near our apartment complex almost every weekend. Mom hated it, but I still snuck out all the time to do it. After Dad died, I kept playing. It helped, mostly 'cause Mom was gone all the time, so I was always either alone or with some aunt or uncle."

"Your parents' families live in Houston."

"No," she said, laughing. "It's a Chinese thing. Any friend of the family that's older than you is your aunt or uncle. If they're older than your parents, they're your grandparents. It's just the way things are."

"Ohh," I said. "Did you play for your middle school team, back there?"

"God no. Mom would never have let me. She thought it wasn't the proper kind of thing for a girl to do, and that it would get in the way of my schoolwork. It's too bad. My gym coach asked me to join the team. I was good, but I was also like five inches taller than any girl in my school. Hell, I still am."

She wasn't wrong. I was closing in on six feet, and she towered over me. She was tall even among the tallest seniors, let alone the freshmen, which wasn't a good thing in high school. People who stood out often became targets, especially if they were quiet.

"I was good, though," she continued. "I beat everybody I played against in the pickup games, guys or girls. Even the high school kids."

"You should try out for the team when the season starts," I said. "You'll tower over most of the girls here, too. If you're as good as you say you are, you could really stand out."

"Mom would never ..."

"She would. You just have to sell it right. Look, lots of kids have good grades, right? But this is a small district, and we don't get much attention from colleges. You know what Texas does have, though? Sports culture."

"What's your point?"

"Athletic scholarships open doors. Even Ivy League schools recruit players, especially ones with good grades. And you're what, six-five?"

"Six-four," she corrected.

"Even better. That's the perfect height for a female center, and you're not even done growing yet. Add in good grades, and colleges would fight over you."

"Why do you care so much?" she said, suddenly turning hostile. "I don't need saving, Blake."

I didn't take it personally. I didn't think her sudden anger was about me. If I had to guess, she was afraid. Maybe of change. Maybe of getting rejected and not making the team. People tended to lash out when they were afraid, and it stopped a lot of them from ever achieving something.

Anything worth doing was a little scary.

"I'm not trying to save you. This is what friends do." I gestured between us. "You're helping me with school stuff. I want to help you find your place here. That's all."

"Friends?" she asked, sounding almost surprised.

"Yeah, friends. People who help each other out. Make each other's lives better. Or at least try to."

She looked down at her lap for a long time, and I just kept my peace, looking over at Eduardo talking to Tyrell, which was an unusual pairing, but those two were actually hitting it off, which I was happy to see.

"I'll think about it," she finally said.

"That's all I'm asking."

"Good." She tapped my science book with her pencil. "Now stop stalling and tell me the basic parts of a cell."

"You're ruthless, you know that?"

"Someone has to be."

Chapter 18

Saturday, I was at my first game actually on the field with the JV team. We were playing Whyatt High School from Fort Worth, which had a record of three and one as opposed to our 0-4, and they had a hell of an offense from the tape we'd watched.

Still, I was as pumped as I could be, to finally show what I could do on a slightly bigger stage. More so because this was a home game and our stands were packed. The away team's stands were fuller than I was used to from being on the freshman team, but that could also have been partly explained by it being Saturday instead of a Thursday, making it a lot easier for people to make the long drive to get here.

"Ready to show us what you've got, hotshot?" Jerry Roach asked, bumping my shoulder as we jogged to the sideline after ripping through the banner and screaming like banshees.

"Just try to keep up," I shot back with a grin.

We won the coin toss and the kickoff return went okay, getting the ball to our 25-yard line. Coach Holloway's first series of calls were all runs, which wasn't a shock. Wheaton was a running team, and everyone knew it. I hoped to be able to change some of that, but I knew I wasn't going to be able to do that in my first game.

Not that running plays were a mistake. The coach stuck to it because it worked.

As the snap came to me, I pivoted and handed Jerry the ball. He exploded off the left tackle, breaking through a narrow gap. He juked a linebacker and plowed forward, dragging a cornerback for an extra yard. Six yards. Not bad.

"Nice work," I said as we jogged back to the huddle.

"Just getting started."

The next play was a fullback drive. On the snap, the line held strong, pushing back Whyatt's defense as Joe Gardner barreled through the middle, bouncing off a linebacker and driving forward for three yards before the pile swallowed him.

"Third and short!" Jerry called as he trotted back to the huddle. "Let's move the sticks."

Coach went safe again.

I faked a quick drop back to hold the linebackers for a beat before turning to hand Jerry the ball. He followed Elton and Bryce, who double-teamed the defensive end just enough for Jerry to duck through the gap. He got hit almost immediately but twisted and fell forward, picking up two yards and the first down. The sideline erupted in cheers.

I almost whooped with joy as Coach called our first passing play. A short lob, but at least it wasn't handing the ball off again.

I dropped back, as the receivers all cut short routes. The defense bit slightly on the play-action, and Miles turned just as I released the ball. It was low but catchable. Miles scooped it up and turned upfield for four yards before being shoved out of bounds.

Not my most stellar work, but I thought it was at least acceptable. Coach didn't, I guess, since we were back to the ground game.

On the next play, Jerry took the handoff, bouncing outside to avoid a clogged middle. He turned up field, but a cornerback came flying in, wrapping him up after a modest three-yard gain. The defense was tightening up, and we knew it.

On third down, Coach called for another run, this time sending Joe up the gut again. The snap was clean, and the handoff smooth, but their defensive line basically knew what we were doing now.

Joe barely made it to the line of scrimmage before he was swallowed up, leaving us with fourth down. Coach waved for the punt team, and we jogged off the field. Not the worst drive ever, but the slow grinding didn't really get the team energized.

Whyatt took over and immediately showed why their offense was so dangerous. Their quarterback had an arm and his coaches weren't as afraid to let him use it as Coach Holloway was with us. They kept threading passes over the middle and connecting on deep outs. Our defense managed to bend without breaking, forcing them to settle for a field goal, but I couldn't help feeling a twinge of envy watching their passing game click so smoothly.

It also put us down by three.

The rest of the quarter saw us sticking to short runs and conservative passes. We chipped away at the defense, picking up small chunks of yardage on running plays, while I mixed in a couple of play-action passes to keep the defense honest, but so short it wasn't enough to actually get anything going and we struggled to string together enough plays to threaten the end zone.

I had a little bit of hope as the second quarter started when Coach called another play-action pass, giving me a chance to open the field up.

I faked the handoff to Jerry, the defense biting hard as their linebackers surged forward. Rolling out to my right, I kept my eyes downfield. Miles broke out of his short route, cutting toward the sideline. The corner covering him stumbled, just enough for me to release the ball. It spiraled cleanly, hitting Miles in stride. He turned upfield and managed to fight off the safety for an extra couple of yards before going down. Eight yards. Not bad.

It felt good to actually get the ball moving again.

On the next snap, I handed the ball off to Jerry, who took it off tackle. Elton and Bryce opened just enough of a gap, and Jerry burst through it. He juked past a safety and stiff-armed another defender, earning an extra five yards before being brought down with a fifteen-yard gain. The sideline erupted, along with the stands, as we started gaining some traction.

Not that it was all big plays. The next series was a steady grind. Three runs back-to-back chipped away at Whyatt's defense, giving us another first down, but just barely.

Coach gave me another shot at a short pass, and things went off the rails. I saw Dwight running a short crossing route, open by a step and I threw it just a hair too far ahead. Dwight stretched for it, but their linebacker read the pass perfectly. He jumped the route and snagged the ball.

Before Dwight could react, he was sprinting upfield. Elton Marti managed to trip him up after about ten yards, but the damage was done and the momentum shifted back to Whyatt. Their offense picked us apart with a mix of quick mid-range passes and solid runs, driving straight downfield. Despite our defense's best efforts, they punched it in for a touchdown with a short pass over the middle, and then added the extra point on top of it, putting the game at 10 and 0.

That really sapped us, although our defense seemed to take it personally and tightened up some. The next few drives were a slog on both sides. Whyatt's defense adjusted, stacking the box against our runs and forcing us to punt twice. Our defense returned the favor and kept Whyatt from scoring again. Both teams traded punts, and neither managed more than twenty yards per drive.

To say I was frustrated was an understatement. We'd started the quarter so well and my interception had taken the wind out of our sails.

Thankfully, it didn't last, maybe because they were having as many problems as we were. With two minutes left in the half, we finally started putting something together. It wasn't particularly easy and every yard was a fight. Jerry and Joe kept grinding it out, forcing third downs on almost every set of downs, but we converted each time.

Coach even let me throw again, in spite of my earlier interception, with short slants to Miles, Mickey, and Dwight, which gave us just enough breathing room to keep the chains moving. By the time we crossed midfield, the clock had ticked down to under a minute.

On first-and-ten from the twenty, Jerry followed Elton through a gap, dragging a linebacker for five yards, putting us at second-and-five. I kept an eye on the clock as we hurried back to the line.

The next play was a power run to the left. Bryce and Elton collapsed the edge, and Jerry bounced outside, picking up seven yards before being shoved out of bounds. First-and-goal at the eight with thirty seconds left.

Coach signaled another run. I'd hoped we would go for a short pass, but even passing teams tended to stick with the ground game at the goal line. The snap was clean, and Jerry barreled straight up the middle, fighting through a swarm of defenders. He gained four hard-fought yards, and we scrambled to reset. The clock kept ticking.

On second-and-goal, Joe took the handoff, pounding into the pile. He was stopped at the two-yard line. Third down. Ten seconds.

We hurried back to the line in a hurry-up offense, with me calling the play from the line, which was another handoff to Jerry. The snap hit my hands, and I turned to him. He charged forward, following Elton's lead block. The defense surged, but Jerry lowered his shoulder and pushed through the pile. His momentum carried him over the goal line as the referee's arms shot up. Touchdown!

The crowd roared, and the sideline exploded like we'd won the game, instead of ending up a field goal behind at halftime. I think they were just excited to see us do anything of note.

The extra point was good and we headed to the field house behind 10 to 7. It wasn't pretty, but at least we were back in it.

We were in good spirits, in spite of being behind, as we headed into the field house. Sure, we were down, but getting that touchdown right before the break had injected some life into the team.

"Alright, boys," Coach said as he began his mid-game speech. "They're good, but so are we. Defense, tighten up those zones. Don't let their receivers get behind you so much. You know they're going to throw a lot, so be ready for it. Offense, we're moving the ball, but we need to finish drives. Stick to the plan, and we'll wear 'em down. Got it?"

A chorus of "Yes, Coach!" came back to him.

As the players dispersed, I made my way over to him, waiting patiently for a chance to talk.

"What is it, Sims?"

"Coach, we're running fine, but their secondary's cheating up cause they know we're going to do it almost every play. Mickey and Dwight have been beating their guys consistently and they've been light in the backfield. If we open up the passing game a little, I think we can exploit that."

He shook his head before I even finished. "I appreciate the input, but we run our system, Blake. I've been coaching this game a long time and, believe it or not, I might know what I'm doing. You stick to running my plays. We don't need flash; we need execution."

"But ..."

196

"No 'buts,' Sims. You focus on what I call. That's how you help this team."

I bit back my frustration and nodded. "Yes, Coach."

As I turned away Jorden, who'd only been a few steps away, said, "Guess you're not as big a deal as you thought, huh?"

I shot him a glare but let it slide. He wasn't worth it.

Maybe talking to the coach had been a bad idea, though, because as the third quarter started, Coach pulled me and sat me on the bench, sending Jorden onto the field instead, with him looking smug.

I was seething on the inside, but I knew better than to argue, since that was what probably put me on the bench in the first place.

My exile didn't last long, however, as the first drive went downhill fast. On second down, Whyatt's blitz overwhelmed our line. To make it worse, Jorden hesitated in the pocket and their linebacker drilled him. The ball popped loose, and Whyatt's defensive end scooped it up, sprinting untouched into the end zone, leaving the score at 17 to 7 after the extra point.

Coach's experiment ended with that goal. "Sims, get back in there."

I grabbed my helmet and jogged onto the field after the kickoff put us at the twenty-five. I wanted to show him that keeping me in was the way to go, but Coach stuck to the ground game. Jerry took the first carry off-tackle, barreling forward for six yards. The next play was a fullback dive, and Joe fought his way up the middle for three more.

On third-and-short, I handed it back to Jerry. He followed Bryce's block, slipping through the line and picking up five yards to move the chains. The next series was more of the same. Jerry hit the hole hard, grinding out eight yards over two carries. On third down, Joe powered through for another three, keeping the drive alive.

It was slow football and it ate a lot of time off the clock that we really couldn't afford being a touchdown plus a field goal behind, but it was keeping the ball moving.

Jerry continued to hammer their defense, bouncing outside for seven yards on the next play. On second down, he juked a linebacker and dragged a safety for another six. The grind continued. By the time we hit their thirty-five, Jerry had racked up thirty-two yards over six carries, Joe had six yards, and Miles had two yards, both from one-yard punches that didn't get anywhere.

We had made progress, though, moving the ball forty yards down the field on ten plays.

Finally, Coach called a play-action pass. I took the snap and stepped back before rolling out, scanning for an open man. Mickey had a step on his guy down the sideline, but as I released the ball, their safety closed fast, breaking it up.

It wasn't an interception, but it also wasn't yardage.

We were back to the running game as nearly a fourth of the quarter had ticked down on our monumentally slow drive.

We lined up and the snap came clean. I stepped back and stretched out the ball for Jerry to grab as he ran past, but Whyatt blitzed and the pocket collapsed almost instantly, crumbling around us.

To make it worse, it was the right side that collapsed, and Jerry was running to the left, not looking at the linemen closing in behind him. He wasn't going to turn on the jets before it was too late, looking for a hole to punch through, and ending up getting blindsided by a linebacker.

We'd be lucky if he just took the loss. More likely, a hit like that would result in a fumble.

I had a split second to decide; hand it off and watch Jerry get buried or pull it back. I didn't even think. I just yanked the ball back and took off toward the opening their defense had left as they zeroed in on Jerry and where he'd be after he grabbed the ball. Their entire line was too focused on Jerry to notice me turning and running like my life depended on it, until I was out of the pocket and through the massive hole they left in their line with that blitz.

I bolted down the right side. Adrenaline surged through me as I sprinted past the line of scrimmage. Their cornerback saw me too late, backpedaling in a desperate attempt to adjust, dropping his coverage and coming for me. I juked left, then right, feeling the defender's hands swipe at air.

I heard our fans erupt as I broke free into open field, but I kept focused on my goal. The end zone was coming up fast.

Thirty yards downfield, I felt the burn in my legs. I could see their safety angling for me, but I was tight against the sideline without many options but to just run as fast as my legs could carry me. He finally closed the distance, diving at my legs and clipping me just enough to throw me off balance, sending me tumbling out of bounds at the three-yard line. The crowd exploded and my teammates rushed down to join me, slapping my helmet and practically knocking me over again just as I stood back up.

"Way to keep us alive, Sims!" Andre Price, our center, yelled as he helped steady me on my feet.

I grinned through the adrenaline, catching my breath as we jogged back to the huddle. I felt truly alive. First-and-goal, three yards out. We could do this.

Coach wasn't taking any risks after that scramble and called a fullback plunge. It was the right call. We had four downs and three yards. No reason to try anything fancy.

I faked a quick look after the snap, not that anyone thought I was going to throw it. The defense knew what play we were running just as well as we did. I slapped the ball into Joe's gut and he lowered his head, driving forward from behind our line, which surged with all its might.

Their linebackers hit him hard, but Joe kept his legs churning, pushing forward until he broke the plane.

It was less running and more pushing Joe's body across the line, but it worked. The referee's arms shot up. Touchdown!

The stands erupted again and the energy on the sideline was electric. Elton grabbed Joe, lifting him off the ground in celebration as the rest of us swarmed them.

I jogged off the field for the extra point, which ended up being good, putting us at 17 to 14.

"Nice run, Sims, but stop trying to do everything yourself. If the play isn't there, throw it away or make the play within the system. Scrambling will end up in a turnover and I don't want to see it. Got it?"

"Yes, Coach."

How could he see that just grinding away was not going to win us the game. Yes, I'd been lucky to get through, but had I thrown it away or handed it to Jerry, at best we would have ended up punting and we'd still be ten points down watching their offense start a drive.

"Good," he said, clapping me on the shoulder, I guess unaware of how frustrated I was.

The rest of the third quarter was more of the same grind. Mickey and Dwight kept finding openings in the secondary, but except for two passes, we kept the ball on the ground. Sure, we chipped away at Whyatt 's defense, but nothing substantial enough to threaten another score.

Thankfully, our defense held strong, keeping Whyatt from gaining any meaningful yardage either, so it didn't get worse. The quarter ended still 17 to 14, and it seemed that at best we were going to manage to tie this up, since these slow drives just ate up the clock without getting us touchdowns.

We went right into the fourth quarter with most of the excitement from my run and our touchdown burned out by more grinding plays. We just couldn't hold any momentum with this kind of ball.

Whyatt had a lucky early drive after a terrible punt from us set them up for the start of a drive at midfield. Their quarterback wasted no time, hitting a quick slant for eight yards. Our defense tightened up on the next play, stuffing a run for no gain, but on third down, they caught us with another slant, threading the ball through a narrow window for the first down.

Their pace picked up, running a no-huddle offense that kept our defense scrambling. Two quick outs later, they were within field goal range. Our defense managed to shut down the next three plays, but they were close enough to still put up points, and their kicker split the uprights from twenty-five yards out.

With that, the score was 20 to 14.

We weren't out of it, unless we wanted to be. There was still a lot of time in the fourth quarter to pick up a touchdown and a field goal and tie it up, but not if we ground it out. Unfortunately, it seemed like we wanted to be out of it.

"We're not out of it yet," Coach Holloway said as we prepared to take the field again. "Stick to our game and we can win this. Grind it out, wear them down. No need for heroics."

He had to see there wasn't time to grind anything out. Not that he'd listen to me.

The kickoff put us at our own twenty. Jerry took the first hand-off, barreling through the line for three yards before being taken down by their middle linebacker. The next play was a sweep to the left, but their cornerback sniffed it out, wrapping Jerry up at the line of scrimmage. Third-and-seven.

Coach called for a quick pass. I dropped back, half hoping one of the guys would say screw it and take off long, but they held to their routes, with Mickey breaking his coverage and crossing over four yards out.

I didn't have time to wait as the pocket started to collapse, and zipped the ball to him. He caught it and turned up field, but was brought down two yards short of a first down.

Coach signaled to go for it, which was a bit of a shock.

The play was a dive up the middle, which wasn't a bad call for fourth down with two yards to go. It was also exactly the play the defense thought we'd run. I took the snap, turned, and handed it off to Jerry. He hit the line hard, but their defense stacked the box, driving him back before he could stretch for the marker.

Turnover on downs.

Jerry slammed the ball into the turf as he got up, muttering under his breath. I felt the same frustration. The defense had been sitting on our running game all night, and we'd walked right into it over and over again.

Whyatt's offense came back out, chewing up the clock with short runs and quick passes, playing our game now that they were up and wanted to eat time off the clock. Our defense held as best they could, forcing a punt after a long, grinding drive, but by the time we got the ball back, less than five minutes remained.

Coach's conservative approach didn't change. The first play was another off-tackle run, this time by Miles, I guess hoping to catch them by surprise by handing it off to our tight end. Miles did pretty well, actually, fighting for three yards before being brought down. The second play was a fullback dive, and Joe managed two more yards. Third-and-five. I dropped back for a short pass, but their blitz came fast, forcing me to dump it off to Jerry in the flat. He was tackled almost immediately, leaving us short of the sticks.

Coach waved for the punt team. I wanted to scream.

"We're not gonna win by giving them the ball back!" I said to Jerry as we jogged off the field.

"Tell him that," Jerry muttered, jerking his head toward Coach Holloway, who looked pissed, like this was someone's fault other than his own.

Whyatt took over and ran the ball relentlessly, grinding the clock down to its final seconds. When the whistle blew, the scoreboard was still at 20 to 14. We'd lost ... again.

I ripped off my helmet as I trudged off the field, sweat dripping into my eyes. I was pissed.

Hey, you played a hell of a game," Mickey said, clapping me on the shoulder. "We'll get 'em next time."

"Yeah, man," Jerry added. "You kept us in it. Not your fault."

I forced a nod, but it only helped a little bit. I felt I'd played okay, and really everyone had, but it didn't matter when the game plan had us shackled.

As we reached the field house, Coach stopped me. "Good effort, Sims. Stick with it."

I wanted to tell him where to stick it, but I was not dumb enough to actually say it out loud.

Instead, I just said, "Yes, Coach."

I even managed to keep the bitterness out of my voice. I dropped onto the bench in front of my locker, staring at the floor as the sounds of post-game chatter filled the room. The praise from my teammates and the coach's platitudes couldn't really make me feel better.

This was my first game with JV and I know no one was expecting miracles, but we could've won the game if we'd just taken some chances. I think I would have preferred it if someone had screwed up. Then, at least, there'd be something to fix.

As it was, if we kept just grinding it out, we'd end the season in the middle of the pack ... at best.

Chapter 19

I wiped sweat from my forehead as I yanked another weed from Eduardo's mom's vegetable garden. In west Texas, October is still in the nineties … or, if we were lucky, it might drop into the eighties.

I actually didn't mind it, though. Maybe it was because of all the time spent practicing outside in the heat, but it seemed that spending time without the pads on felt a lot cooler. Then again, maybe it was remembering what it felt like to do construction with the foreman breathing down your neck because you have two other jobs to finish that day.

True, that last one was not from my actual life, but the memory of the dream was so strong it still gave me a point of comparison.

Also, I got to hang out with Eduardo. I'd started this off with the goal of keeping him from ending up in gangs, to protect my father, but surprisingly, I found that I really liked him. Past the shy, quiet exterior, he was a really great guy, worried about others as much as himself, funny and sarcastic.

So much so that it had started making me second guess if the dream was actually any kind of predictor at all. Yes, a few things in the dream matched real life, but those could have been coincidences. It just seemed impossible that the guy I was getting to know would end up initiating into a gang and ultimately killing someone.

That was the farthest thing from the Eduardo I was now friends with.

"It sucks she hasn't had time to deal with these," I said, pulling another handful of weeds out of the ground and tossing them into the pile I was making. "They're bigger than the vegetables."

"She was out here three weeks ago," Eduardo said. "They grow really fast."

"Damn."

"I know. She loves her garden, though, says it reminds her of her grandmother's garden back home. It's why I wanted to do this today while she was out with Alex. With Dad stuck in bed or making the drive back and forth to Midland every week, she doesn't have time to stay on top of it. I figured if we could at least keep up with the easy manual labor part of it, the weeds and whatever, it would take the pressure off her, so it can still be fun."

"Yeah," I said.

"We were at the game yesterday," he said after a few minutes of silent work.

"We?"

"Yeah, me and Tyrell."

"I didn't realize you two were hanging out," I said.

"That's the first time we did something after school. He was trying to explain some of what everyone did on the team and offered to go with me to your game and point stuff out, although I think that was an excuse. I think he wanted to go and everyone else was busy."

I knew they were getting along at lunch, but thinking of the two of them hanging out at the game was strange. They were very different people, both physically and personality-wise. It was good though, seeing him making friends.

"Or he wanted to hang out with you. You two have been hitting it off."

"I guess. He's a good guy. Anyway, he was saying the coach was really holding you back and playing right into the defense by running the ball the whole game."

It was nice to know that someone else could see that, too.

"I don't know about holding me back, but he isn't wrong. We were running the ball all damn night and Whyatt knew exactly what we were going to do every damn time. It was frustrating as hell."

"You should talk to your coach."

"Ha," I said, not able to stop the laugh from coming out. "That would be the day. I mean, I did say something about us playing into their hands, and he basically told me to shut up and do what I was told. He's the coach and I'm a freshman, so it's not like I have much pull."

"That isn't right, though. I mean, you're there in the middle of everything, who else would know better? But maybe I'm wrong. Alex may watch a lot of football, but that was the first game I've ever watched the whole way through, let alone been to."

"You're not wrong. Or I guess, I don't think you are, but Coach Holloway has been coaching for a long time and that was my first game at this level."

"Well ..." he started to say, and then stopped talking as we heard what sounded like a car with the loudest exhaust I had ever heard pull up out in front of the house.

It was loud enough that the windows were rattling a little bit, and it didn't just sound like a bad muffler. Living in a rural area, I heard a lot of old trucks with shoddy mufflers. I couldn't really put my finger on it, but this sounded more like someone had gone out of their way to make it sound like that.

That wasn't the thing that had my attention, however. Eduardo had not only stopped talking, but he'd gone stock still, his hands around a bunch of weeds still in the ground. His facial expression had gone from relaxed to as tense as I'd ever seen it.

"What's wrong?" I asked.

He didn't answer right away. Instead, his eyes darted from the side gate to the front yard to the back door, like he was expecting someone. And he wasn't wrong.

Before I could say anything else, the back door of the house swung open and a tall guy in his mid-twenties stepped out. The way he carried himself was with a confidence that bordered on cocky. He was dressed in a loose flannel shirt with the sleeves rolled up and jeans that looked too new to be casual. Tattoos snaked up his forearm, disappearing under the cuff of his shirt, and his hair was slicked back.

"What the hell you doing out here playing in the dirt?" he asked Eduardo as soon as he walked through the door.

"What do you want, Rafe?"

The quiet, almost perpetually defeated tone was back.

"What I want is for you to quit doing women's work and come for a ride with me."

"I can't. You know Dad's hurt and I'm helping out. Besides, I have a friend over."

"Ohh, I guess that explains it. Thought this was some backwards place where y'all hire white boy gardeners now," he said with a laugh.

I pushed myself up from the ground, brushing dirt off my jeans. "I'm Blake. Eduardo's friend from school."

The guy looked at my hand like it was a pile of dirty socks and then stepped around me, still looking at Eduardo.

"Come on Eddie, we got places to be."

"No. I told you, I'm busy."

"What was that?" the guy said, taking a step closer to Eduardo and his voice dropping down a notch, threateningly. "Did you just tell me no?"

"He said he's busy," I said, taking a step back and to the side, putting myself between him and Eduardo.

Everything about this guy bothered me. He was pushy, arrogant, and entitled.

This time, he did look at me. "This ain't got nothing to do with you, gringo."

"It does if I say it does. He said 'no,' so get the fuck out of here."

"What did you say to me?" he said, taking a step closer to me, his shoulders squaring up like he was getting ready to do something.

Eduardo stood up and moved sort of next to us, but he looked conflicted, almost terrified, his hands opening and closing at his sides as he visibly wrestled with what to do.

"I said get the fuck out of here. You really should get your hearing checked," I said.

Rafe's face flushed red. "This is my cousin's house, gringo. No white boy is gonna tell me what I can and can't do with my family."

He was right up in my space, close enough I could smell the cigarette smoke on his breath.

Eduardo seemed to finally come to a decision, because he pushed himself between us and took a step back, forcing me to do the same, putting distance between us and Rafe.

"Rafe, you need to leave."

"Are you serious right now?" Rafe's eyebrows shot up. "You're choosing this white boy over family? Over your own blood?"

"Mom's gonna be home any minute. You know what she'll do if she finds you here."

I knew that was a lie. His mother wasn't due back for at least another hour. But I kept my mouth shut. Eduardo's mom wasn't a big woman, but she clearly had some kind of effect on this guy, because I could see him thinking it over.

His eyes flicked from Eduardo to me and back again. The way his weight shifted forward made me think we were about to throw down right there in the garden. I tried to keep myself light on the balls of my feet, ready to react, but I wasn't going to throw the first punch. Not in Eduardo's house against his family, whatever this guy was to him.

"You need to leave," Eduardo repeated, more sure of himself this time.

The guy wrestled for another second, clearly torn between leaving and throwing down, and then said, "Whatever."

With that, he spun on his heel toward the driveway and stormed through the side gate, banging it open against the fence as he went through it. We both continued to watch the gate, I guess wondering if he was going to change his mind and come back, until the loud ass exhaust started up again.

Tires squealed as he peeled off out of the driveway, the sound of the car fading as it went down the street.

"So who was that?"

Eduardo went back to the garden, dropped to his knees, and started to yank out weeds again, with a lot more force than was necessary.

"That's my cousin Rafael. From Midland."

"He seems like a real piece of work."

"Yeah." Eduardo pulled another weed, tossing it harder than needed onto the pile. "We used to be close when we were kids, but he dropped out of school when he was a freshman and got involved with some people. I guess we grew apart."

Something clicked into place. This guy was how Eduardo ended up getting recruited into a gang. The reason Eduardo went down the path that ended with him in prison. Watching Eduardo's defeated posture until the end of that confrontation, the way he seemed to shrink in on himself, I could see exactly how it had happened. How he'd been pushed into doing something so far outside of who he was. How someone as quiet and reserved as Eduardo could get pulled into that life.

If I hadn't been here today, Eduardo almost certainly would have gone with him. Hell, the only reason he'd stood up to Rafe at all was because I'd done it first.

"Like what kind of people?"

"I don't want to talk about it," he said.

The whole thing clearly bothered him; I guess being torn between being loyal to his family and avoiding putting himself in bad situations. From the way his cousin had reacted when Eduardo had mentioned his mother, it wasn't hard to figure out what his parents thought of the family delinquent.

If I had to guess, this might be the reason his parents moved them out of Midland.

"What did he want you to go do with him?"

"I don't know. Probably nothing."

We both knew that was bullshit.

"That's a long drive from Midland, just to do nothing. He must have had something specific in mind."

"I said it was nothing, Blake. Just leave it alone, okay?"

"Sure," I said, holding up my hands. "Didn't mean to pry."

We went back to working on the garden, but my mind was racing. This was the real problem. It wasn't going to be enough to just be Eduardo's friend. I had to help him build up the confidence to stand up to Rafe on his own, not just when someone else did it first. The question was how. Eduardo was naturally conflict-avoidant, happy to fade into the background. Getting him to assert himself, especially against family, wouldn't be easy.

But I needed to figure out how to get him there, both to protect my dad and to keep Eduardo out of trouble.

Practice on Monday was more running plays. Actually, it was almost entirely running plays. Last week, we'd done at least some passing practice, and I couldn't help but feel it was intentional.

Sure, he'd gotten on us at the start of the practice about how we have to get better at opening up opportunities and then exploiting them, and maybe he was just trying to fix the weaknesses we had in the running game. But, it also felt a little targeted, like a message to me after my complaint about not passing enough and not going for deeper passes.

Maybe I was overthinking things, but it was still bugging me when we got back in the locker room.

I passed Coach Holloway's office and took a few steps toward my locker when I stopped, as my intrusive thoughts started to take over. That kind of thinking where you're standing at the side of a bridge and, even though you have no wish to hurt yourself or do anything bad, there's that thing in the back of your head asking "but what if you jumped?"

They were winning this time. I knew my best course of action was to just follow the program and trust that I'd get to the level I wanted. But then there was Kenneth. He was a great QB. I'd watched him throw some serious bombs way downfield in practice, but having watched some varsity film, that wasn't the game he was allowed to play.

They kept him locked down in the ground game and short dinky passes. As good as he was, he wasn't being heavily recruited, and it felt pretty related to this situation.

I'd spent a life where high school was my glory days and I lived for the past. Or at least I'd dreamed I had.

I didn't want to live that life again.

I turned around and found myself in the coach's doorway, knocking.

"What do you want, Sims?"

I closed the door behind me and sat in the chair across from him, which got an eyebrow raise from him. Maybe that was a bit presumptuous of me, but I wanted his full attention.

"I wanted to talk about ... about what it's gonna take to get where I want to be. Long term."

"Long term? You're a freshman and you just got on this team. Maybe focus on the short term for now."

"I am focused on that Coach, but you said in practice on Thursday that we had to practice for the team we wanted to be, not just 'cause it was on the schedule. I figured that was true for players, too."

He grunted, but crossed his arms and leaned back in his chair. I couldn't tell if he was impressed or annoyed that I'd thrown his own words back at him.

Either way, it got him to listen.

"I want to become a better player. A better quarterback. I want to get on varsity, hopefully next year, and win state at least once before I graduate. And after that, get on the radar for a college program that could lead to the NFL."

"You do realize every quarterback who's ever picked up a football wants that exact same thing?"

"Yes, sir."

"And you know how many actually make it? How much work it takes?"

"I'm guessing not many, but I'm ready to put in that work. Kenneth graduates this year. His backup's a junior. Which means by my junior year, it's just me, Jorden, and Gabriel competing for varsity. I know I have the skills to lead this team."

I didn't want to badmouth them directly, but I knew that Coach knew what I was saying. I was better than them and the obvious choice.

"Well, we'll see if that's true. Saying you're ready to do the work and actually doing it are very different things. As for getting to the next level, yes, you have raw talent. That much is clear. Raw talent that could make you an outstanding high school player, maybe even get you into a solid college program."

"But?"

"But the guys who make it to that elite level? It's not just about talent. They almost always come from money because getting there requires resources most families don't have."

"Not all of them."

"No, not all, but most. Those resources get them things like private coaching, and not just for specialized training. Speed coaches, conditioning experts, nutritionists." He ticked them off on his fingers. "Sports psychologists, media training, all of it. At that level, dealing with pressure becomes just as important as throwing accuracy. Not to mention elite-level camps that cost a small fortune to attend, even if you qualify."

"Ohh," I said.

"Look, Blake, you come from a good family. Your dad's a deputy, which tells me you've got discipline and support at home. But deputies don't exactly pull in the kind of money needed to afford the level of specialized coaching and resources I'm talking about."

I'd worked that out myself. I could only nod in response.

"Now, we've got trainers, coaches, and conditioning programs here to help all of our athletes improve. But there's a difference between what we do and what private coaching can provide. Those folks spend all their time working on one athlete. Speed work, conditioning, film analysis. Everything is customized. Here, we've got the whole team to think about."

"I get it, Coach," I said. "I just wanted to know what it takes. That's all."

"Good. Because the last thing I want is for you to start doubting yourself or getting discouraged over this. Like I said, you've got talent. And I'll be honest with you, if things continue the way they are, then you're right. By the time you're a junior, you'll probably be leading varsity. You've got what it takes to get there. But you've still got to do the work to get there."

Thanks, Coach. I appreciate that."

"Don't thank me yet. You're not there until you're there, you understand?"

"Yes, sir."

"Now, one thing I can do to help is talk to the track coach. You've got good speed, better than most quarterbacks I've coached, but again, it's just raw ability. It could be better, and that's something we can work on here. It's not the same as hiring a high-level speed coach, but it'll get you closer."

"That'd be great. I'd really appreciate it."

"I'm happy you're thinking about improving. Just keep working at it, son. Anything else?"

"Well ..." I hesitated for half a second, then decided to just say it. "Since we're talking about getting ready for varsity one day, I think the heavy focus on the running game isn't just limiting the team, it's holding me back, too."

Coach Holloway let out a laugh, shaking his head. "I walked right into that one, didn't I?"

"Maybe a little." I grinned, though I was trying not to push too hard. "I get why we run the ball as much as we do, but it feels like we're missing chances to develop a more balanced attack. And honestly, Coach, I think I've got the arm to make it work."

"I appreciate the hustle, really, I do. But I don't fix what isn't broken. We run the playbook we do because it works. It wins games. That's the bottom line."

I thought about trying to counter it, that we weren't exactly winning games now, but I knew I'd already pushed my luck enough.

"I understand."

"Good. Now get out of my office."

"Thanks, Coach," I said, standing up and leaving.

Not exactly what I'd hoped for, but not as bad as it could have been either. Maybe he'd think about it, and at least I was going to get to work with the track coach to get faster. So there was that.

The locker room had mostly settled down by the time I got out of the coach's office. Most of us had homework and family stuff during the week, so we didn't hang around after practice.

Plus, why shower at school when you could go home and shower?

There were a few varsity guys at the other end of the locker room still talking, but that was about it. I went to my locker, and dropped my pads and then stopped. My lock was gone.

Not gone. It was on the floor. Someone had cut it off.

Wrenching my locker open, at first I thought maybe nothing happened, since my school bag was still there. It took me another moment to realize my clothes were missing.

212

I turned in a circle, looking around the locker room, trying to figure out where they'd gone. Stolen was the obvious answer. And on purpose, since the lock was cut.

But then what?

I kept turning, hoping they didn't get taken somewhere else. I checked the trash cans and thankfully didn't see them there, along with the boxes and open places they could have been dropped, but still had no luck finding them.

I'd just walked past the small cleaning closet when something caught my eye, and I took a step back, looking inside.

There they were, inside the mop bucket, floating in what smelled like bleach.

"Come on," I muttered, fishing them out.

The bleach had already done its work - white splotches dotted my black shirt, and my jeans looked like they'd been tie-dyed by a kindergartener having a bad day.

"Something wrong?" Coach asked as he walked out of his office toward the door leading to the rest of the school.

"No, Coach," I said, hiding my clothes behind my back.

He shrugged and kept walking. It wasn't a great performance, but the coach seemed like one of those hands-off, if it isn't my problem, kind of people.

Which was for the best. I know schools like to think kids would tell a teacher if something happened, but that always made stuff worse. I could deal with this myself.

And I knew exactly who was responsible.

Chapter 20

The entire way home, I fantasized about getting my hands around Elijah's throat and choking him out. Admittedly, that was taking things a little too far. Sure, he was an asshole, and he'd ruined my clothes, but I'm not sure going to prison for attempted murder would be the best way to deal with it.

Still, it did make me feel a little better fantasizing about it.

I was just so furious because he kept doing this shit and kept getting away with it. There were absolutely no consequences for him. I knew that because there had been no consequences for me when I'd been just like him, but now that I was trying to turn over a new leaf and be a better person, it was like I was constantly considering the consequences.

I was certain that if Elijah was pissed off enough at someone, he could put his hands on that person and choke them and would only get a slap on the wrist.

It sucked that bad people got to do whatever they wanted without caring about it, but if you were even a little good, you had to constantly moderate yourself.

I walked through the door, ready to go upstairs and be pissed off for a while longer, when I saw Mom sprawled on the couch, one arm draped over her eyes, the other hanging limply toward the floor.

"Mom?" I said, my voice a little higher than I meant it to be. She shouldn't even be home. She had a shift at the hair salon that she was supposed to be at.

When she didn't respond, I dropped my bag and rushed over to her. Her face, what I could see of it, was covered in sweat, and her skin was waxy and pale. So limp, her arm just kind of lying on her face. I couldn't even tell if she was breathing.

I dropped to a knee next to her and started trying to figure out what I should do. I reached for her arm to check her pulse, but right before I grabbed her wrist, she moved her arm slightly, uncovering one eye and asking, "What do you need?"

The question was clear, not slurred or anything, but her voice still sounded really weak.

"Mom, you look terrible," I said sympathetically. "Are you sick? Did you ... Did something happen at work?"

"I'm fine," she said, obviously not fine. She tried to push herself up, but she slumped back against the cushions, clearly struggling. "Just have a headache, so I switched shifts with someone. Don't make a big deal out of it."

"You don't look fine. You look like you've been hit by a truck. You've been having a lot of these headaches lately."

"It's nothing. Just ... stress. The regular Tylenol isn't really cutting it anymore, so it just seems like it's worse than it is."

The fact that over-the-counter drugs weren't helping told me that it was much worse than she was letting on.

This went well beyond headaches. I moved away in my dream when I was nineteen, partly for work and partly to get away from Mom, who had spiraled into some really out-there stuff while still doting on Josh. I knew that she'd ended up getting sick in my dream, and I had a vague memory of it being connected to the headaches.

I wanted to kick myself for not paying more attention back then. And wondered, going forward, what should I do?

Yes, I sometimes hated Mom for the way she always sided with her little psychopath, but she was still my mother, and I hated seeing her like this.

Besides, she wasn't always mean. She could be nice sometimes, too.

What was clear, though, was that the headaches were more than just headaches. There was more to it than that, but I wasn't sure what.

"Have you seen a doctor about these headaches?" I asked getting off my knees and sitting on the edge of the table. "If regular drugs stopped working, then it has to be getting worse, right?"

Mom's hand fluttered dismissively. "Dr. Taylor wasn't any help at all. Just said they were tension headaches and to take some aspirin. Doctors always think a woman's pain is all in her head."

"I thought I heard Dad say that the last time you saw Dr. Taylor was like two months ago. Maybe you should get a second opinion? These headaches don't seem normal. What if it's something serious?"

"Blake, honey, please." Mom's voice had that edge to it, the one that said I was pushing too hard. "I know my own body. I just need better pain medication."

I didn't want to push any harder. She was already hurting. The last thing I wanted was to annoy her on top of that.

"I could run to the pharmacy," I offered. "Get whatever over the counter medication is strongest? I mean, they have to have something better than just Tylenol, right? Or I could get other stuff, like Ibuprofen or whatever; maybe it'll work differently."

Her face softened. "Would you? That would be wonderful. And stop worrying. I'll probably be fine by the time you get back."

I didn't believe that for a second, but I nodded anyway. "Want me to handle dinner when I get back? So you can keep resting?"

"That would be nice." She reached out and patted my hand as she closed her eyes again. Her skin still felt clammy. "Such a good boy. I love you, sweetie."

"I'll be right back," I said, hurrying out the door.

We lived close enough to Main Street that the pharmacy was only a few blocks away. The headaches did have a tendency to come and go, so I didn't doubt it might go away, but I also knew they'd still come back.

Fixing this would be harder than fixing Dad's thing, since it would require her to do something.

Maybe I'd talk to Dad about the headaches again.

Later that night, I lay on my bed, staring up at the ceiling, my eyes tracing over its textured pattern, kind of like a form of meditation. Mom had been mostly right. By the time I'd gotten home, she was sitting up and looked much better.

She still opened the bottle and downed a few pills as soon as I handed her the bottle, suggesting the headache wasn't gone, just better, but at least she didn't look like death warmed over anymore.

I left her sitting there, leaning back with eyes closed, and made one of the only things I knew how to make: spaghetti. It was something I'd taught myself as an adult in the dream life, and Mom was actually surprised when she came into the kitchen later and saw what I was making.

Josh was thankfully quiet through dinner, and so Mom had no reason to stop being nice to me, making this one of my best evenings in a while, in spite of my ruined clothes.

I'd talked to Dad after dinner, trying to bring up her headaches and how worried I was about it. He'd kind of blown it off. Well, that wasn't fair. He hadn't blown it off exactly, and it was clear he took it seriously, but it was also clear he wasn't going to talk to me about it.

I got where he was coming from, sort of. Back in my other life, the dream life, if some teenager had tried telling me how to handle something this serious, I probably would've dismissed them too. What did a kid know about these things?

Hell, even with that dream life still a solid memory in my head, I didn't know about these things or what to suggest even if he had listened to me. Construction work and welding hadn't exactly made me a medical expert.

But watching Mom suffer, knowing what might be coming, it was torture. I hadn't been around in that other timeline, but I knew it got a lot worse, and I wanted to avoid that for her. Again, not that I could explain that to them.

What was the point of getting this second chance if I couldn't actually change anything? Everyone just saw me as some kid who couldn't possibly understand adult stuff. The coaches were the same way every time I made a suggestion.

It was frustrating.

The only thing I could really have an effect on was myself. Which left me with my other problem; how to achieve my goal. I still wanted, more than anything else, to make football my career, which ultimately meant getting to the NFL.

Coach was right about needing high-level training to make that happen. He was also right that I couldn't afford it.

I'd left that problem working in the back of my mind all night as I dealt with more pressing matters, but it seemed that this was one area where my dream memories might actually be able to help.

I knew the dream was real. I was done second-guessing that. Enough stuff had played out either in the way I remembered it or at least affected by changes from the way I remembered it to tell me it wasn't just my subconscious making patterns.

Mechanics of how that actually happened be damned, I knew what was going to happen, which seemed like the kind of thing I could turn into money.

My problem was, I hadn't exactly been a Wall Street guy in that other life. I'd been a blue-collar guy, which didn't really lend itself to investments.

Sure, I could piece together some stuff. I knew the technology that would go mainstream, I knew some companies that would be huge. What I didn't know were any details. How those companies got huge, the sequence of when things would hit.

If I had time, I could just go for it, throw my money into Apple or Google, whenever it showed up, and let it roll into real money. But I didn't have time and I didn't exactly have much money to throw into anything. Stock could go up a thousand percent, but if you only put a dollar in, that would give me ... what, a thousand dollars after years of waiting.

Not exactly the solution to my problem. I needed something quick where I could take what little money I had and build on it, then again and again, so it had a chance to snowball into enough money to be useful.

And I had to do all that in time to hire private coaches early enough to do me some good.

I knew of some major events, too, of course. 9/11 and the start of like, twenty years of war in the Middle East. That big recession in 2008 that had crushed the construction industry for a long time. Who'd win the presidency and a few other major offices.

But that presented the same problem. Those events were years from now, and I didn't know how to make money off those things.

Thinking of 9/11 made me also wonder if I was supposed to do something about that? I mean, I knew when it was going to happen. That one, at least, I knew exactly when it would happen.

But how could I? How could I possibly explain that to anyone? What would I even say? 'Hey, in about seven years, some terrorists are going to hijack planes and crash them into buildings.' Right. That would go over well.

They'd probably think I was crazy. Or worse, once it actually happened, they might remember that kid who knew everything about it before it happened. And then they'd think I was somehow involved.

Once again, I was trapped knowing things I couldn't do anything about.

Then it occurred to me. There was something I knew a fair amount about.

Sports.

And not just sports, I knew specifics. I knew games that would be played. Big wins and losses. I knew who would win the championships.

Mostly, I knew it for football, but I knew a few other sports more generically, and still knew the big events. Baseball. Basketball. Hell, even a few other things.

The baseball strike was still going on - had been since August. I couldn't remember exactly when it would end, but I knew it was sometime this fall. Not much help there, though. How would I even make money off knowing when a strike ends?

There was the Oklahoma-Colorado game. I didn't remember the details exactly, but I knew it was an unexpected blowout of a top-ten team by a much lower-ranked one. Colorado was ranked high - fourth or fifth maybe? And Oklahoma just crushed them. Not just beat them, but demolished them in a way nobody saw coming.

And Dad loved boxing. He would talk about it a lot before he passed. There was that George Foreman fight around Christmas I think of this year. Maybe even sooner. I'd have to look it up, but I remembered Dad going on about how nobody thought Foreman had a chance.

I grabbed a notebook and started jotting notes, trying to capture everything I could remember about sports from that time. The Super Bowl upsets were months away, but worth noting down. The more I wrote, the more details surfaced.

There was something here. If I could verify the dates and details, I could start small. Build it up gradually, rolling winnings into the next bet. A risky way to gamble if you didn't know what would happen, but I did.

The only things that were changing right now were stuff I was affecting, and it's not like what I did out here in west Texas was affecting who won the Super Bowl.

I'd placed a few bets in my dream life. Nothing serious, just office pools and the occasional weekend wager. Enough to know how it worked, at least in theory.

Then reality hit.

Theory was great, but I was fourteen. It's not like I could walk into a bookie's office and place a bet. I stopped writing and thought. There had to be a way. Maybe I could convince someone older to place bets for me? But who would trust a kid with gambling advice?

There was only one obvious answer. I had to convince Dad to do it for me, 'cause I sure as hell wasn't waiting to start this until I turned eighteen.

Man, this was going to be one hell of a conversation.

Even though I'd released most of my anger about Elijah to deal with Mom and work through everything else, I hadn't forgotten it. I got up extra early to make the walk to school the next morning, thinking about all the shit he'd done this year.

Destroying my clothes might have been the last straw, but it wasn't the only one, and the closer I got to school, the angrier I got. I'd been trying to play this smart, to keep from getting in trouble, since the start of school, but I was just about at my limit.

Elijah lived on the other side of town, a little too far to walk, and his mom had to be at work early, so he usually was at school way before everyone else. I made my way into the building and down to the lockers near the door that led to the field house, since that was where most football kids got assigned lockers, I guess to make it easier to get to practice.

My plan worked. I turned the corner to find Elijah at his locker, putting books into his backpack. Also, as expected, he was alone. Elijah always hid behind Mason or Jake, meaning dealing with him would have required facing off against multiple guys. I'd do it if it came to it, but my odds were not great that way.

No, this needed to be handled one on one.

I was up on him just as he closed his locker and turned around. The moment he saw me, his eyes went wide and he looked terrified. He took a small step back, putting himself right against the locker, looking both ways down the hall, I guess hoping a teacher or maybe one of his buddies would show up and bail him out.

It's why I wanted to do this before school, instead of at the end of the day. There weren't a lot of classes at this end of the school, since it was by the athletics department just down from the cafeteria. Most teachers would be in the main part of the school on the other side of the building. His tough guy act was nowhere to be seen.

No help was coming for him.

Even though he was already against the lockers, I pushed my forearm into his chest hard, slamming him into them as hard as I could.

"What the fu..."

"What do I want?" I asked, interrupting him. "I want to beat the shit out of you for ruining my clothes yesterday, dumping them in that bucket of bleach water. That's what I want."

"I don't know what you're talking about."

We both knew he was lying. Hell, I'd only been about seventy-five percent sure it was him until this moment, since there were a few others, like Jorden, who could be the culprit. But the expression on his face gave it away.

For someone who was constantly pulling shit and then pretending it wasn't him, you'd think he'd be a better liar.

"Bullshit. I know it was you. You've been screwing with me all season, and I'm getting real tired of it."

"If you don't ..."

"If I don't … what? Stop? Let you go? Your friends aren't here with you right now, Elijah, and you and I both know you aren't man enough to fight your own fights. Are you so stupid that you don't realize you can't hide behind them twenty-four hours a day? You ready to start fighting your own fights?"

"I'm not afraid of you," he said, but his voice quivered as the words came out.

"Bullshit. You're terrified of me. You're scared of fucking everything. It's why you are the way you are, Elijah. Too scared to be a real man so you gotta tear everyone else down to your level. Well, I'm sick of it. I've been patient with you, Elijah. All year. Patient enough to let all the crap you and your buddies have pulled slide. But guess what?" I leaned in close, getting an inch from his nose. "That patience is officially gone."

He swallowed hard, his Adam's apple bobbing. "Look, man, whatever you think I did, I didn't …"

"Next time something like this happens," I said, continuing as if he hadn't said anything. "If you so much as look at me the wrong way, I'll find you when your friends aren't around. And I'll beat you within an inch of your life."

Elijah froze, his mouth opening and closing like a fish out of water. For all his tough talk on the field, all the swagger he showed when Mason and Jake were backing him up, there was nothing left now.

I wasn't naive enough to think he was going to just take it, though. He'd be terrified for a little while, but then he'd be embarrassed, and that would make him feel like he needed to do something.

"You aren't with someone all of the time, Elijah. Even if you come at me with Mason, I'll still find you later, when it's just me and you. This is your one chance to get smart. Stay out of my way. Don't fuck with me again. Don't fuck with my friends again. Or I'll make sure you never catch a ball again."

I released him and he dropped to the floor. He was shaking, not looking up and not meeting my gaze as I glared down at him. He was a beaten dog.

I turned on my heel and walked away, leaving him huddled there, the scared little boy he was.

I gave it a fifty-fifty chance whether he'd actually listen or try to come after me to save face.

Chapter 21

Everyone was excited as the bus rolled into Trinity High's parking lot next to their football field. After last week's game, practice all week had felt different, like the team was starting to think they could win after a long losing streak.

I was feeling it, too, something like excitement instead of nerves for the first time since moving to JV. It might have helped that this was my first away game with the team. When I'd played the away game with the freshman, it had basically been us and a few parents.

We didn't have the full caravan that varsity had, but we had a fair number of cars and a second bus carrying the JV cheer team, which is something we didn't have as freshmen. There was only a JV and a varsity cheer team, so we'd had to go without.

There were also a number of kids from our school who'd car-pooled and followed us. We didn't have the marching band, but it was a pretty good showing after playing to empty stands as a freshman at an away game.

"Alright, let's move!" Coach Holloway barked as the bus came to a stop. "Grab your gear and get on the field. Warm-ups start in fifteen!"

I stood and slung my bag over my shoulder and headed off the bus. Most of the grab-ass came to a halt as we made our way off the bus and toward the visitors' locker room.

It was time to get our game faces on. Well, for most of us.

I caught Jorden Kinsell glaring at me again, and he wasn't particularly subtle about it. Honestly, at this point, I didn't care. I had bigger things to focus on than his resentment over being benched. I was trying to be more 'adult' about everything these days, keeping in mind what I remembered from the dream version of myself, but if he was meant to lead the team, he would have played better.

Trinity got the kickoff and the game was on with their returner catching it cleanly at the five. Our coverage team swarmed downfield, forcing him out of bounds at their twenty-five.

Not a terrible way to start the game.

Trinity's offense started with basic plays, not that different from the stuff Coach gave us. We had a good stop on the second down when Donald Huff broke through their line and wrapped up their running back for a slight loss.

After their quarterback overthrew his receiver on third down, they punted and it was our turn to have a go.

"Remember," Coach said as I jogged past after calling the play. "Establish the run early. Make them respect it."

Not what I wanted to hear, but what I expected.

At least it went well. Jerry took the handoff smoothly, finding the hole our line created and then dragged a defender for an extra yard, setting up second and six.

Coach asked us to make them respect the run, and that's what we did.

On the next run, Joe powered through on a fullback dive, really hammering into their linemen. It wasn't a huge gain, but it put us at third and short.

The next play was a surprise. A quarterback sneak. We'd done it once in practice, but it hadn't gone well. I was tall and in good shape, but I didn't have the weight to really push through linemen like that play called for. I guess Coach thought we'd catch them off guard.

And he was right.

I didn't get very far and it felt like I'd hit a brick wall, but we picked up two yards when we only needed one for a first down.

I could feel the momentum building.

Jerry swept right on the next play, following his blockers for six yards again. That was starting to be his magic number, but for pushing the ball downfield a little at a time, we'd take it.

On the next play, the defense started to creep up and I called my first audible of the game. I sold the play-action hard on second down, the entire defense flowing with Jerry while Joe slipped through the middle, running for four more yards.

We were starting to gain some yards. Not fast, but it was working, and I could see their defense starting to get frustrated, which was exactly what they shouldn't do.

Jerry took advantage of it and broke free on a counter left, with twelve yards of green grass opening up before him. Our first serious yardage and our side of the stands, light though it might have been, went wild. We were rolling now.

We kept going. Joe pounded up the middle for another three on first down and I thought there was a chance we might make it all the way on this first drive.

Then things went wrong. Jerry got caught in the backfield on a pitch right, their defensive end reading it perfectly. An eight-yard loss and our momentum stalled. Third and long, our protection broke down. I spotted Mickey breaking open deep and I actually considered saying screw the short lob Coach had called, but I never got the chance.

Their linebacker came free on a delayed blitz. I tucked the ball and ran, finding space to the right. Six yards. I was proud that I'd managed to keep from getting sacked and even pick up a little of our lost yardage, but it still left us pretty far back on fourth down.

We were, however, in field goal range.

I ran off the field and the special teams ran out, getting us our first points of the game. 3 – 0.

Trinity's next possession had a few moments where it looked like they might get something going, but ultimately, they went nowhere. Especially after Spencer Marshal made a tackle on their running back, burying him hard in the dirt, and then their QB overthrowing his receiver by a good three yards.

We got the ball back with under a minute left in the quarter. Jerry took another handoff as time wound down, gaining three yards before the whistle blew and the quarter ended.

Not brilliant football, but a good first quarter.

We started the second quarter with a handoff to Joe, who plowed straight ahead, pushing through the line for four yards.

Classic Wheaton football, apparently. Head down, smashing into the other line.

Not the most exciting ball, in my opinion, but at least it was working somewhat this time and we had points on the board.

"Nice push," I said, giving him a light push as we lined up for the next play.

The defense shifted and was showing blitz. I rolled right on the snap, buying time as their linebacker crashed through. Since it worked the last time, I went with the same strategy, tucked the ball and ran, sliding after picking up five yards.

I could see Coach with his arms folded, glaring at me as I headed back to the huddle. I knew he wanted me to throw it away, but it felt like such a wasted opportunity, especially when they were heavy on one side of the line and I thought we had room to run.

We picked up eight more yards on the next play, this to Joe again, except he went on a counter instead of blasting down the center like every other time.

I guess Coach wanted to keep them guessing.

He was keeping me guessing with the next play when he surprised us all by calling a pass play. And not just a short dink, but a serious, honest-to-God pass.

I tried not to get nervous as we lined up. It kind of felt like he was giving me a shot, and I didn't want to let him down, or who knew how long it would be until I got a chance at another one.

I took the snap and faked a handoff to Jerry as I watched Miles haul ass fifteen yards and cut hard enough to get separation from his coverage. I let it fly as soon as he was clear. The ball sailed perfectly into his hands for a fifteen-yard gain.

We were so close to the end zone, for a second, I thought he was going to break free and make a run for the goal line, but he was taken down as soon as he tucked the ball under his arm.

He held onto it, though.

"It's about time," Miles said as he came back to the huddle.

I had to agree.

We were within spitting distance of the goal line and Coach had us back to the running game. The defense started to tighten up, trying to deny us the goal, but Jerry managed to pick up six more yards. Coach called another run, calling for Joe to go right down the middle, which had to be getting predictable by this point, except for once I agreed. He was good enough to push his way through the last few yards and get us the touchdown. Unfortunately, they really didn't want us to get it and held him to just three yards in a huge pileup. We were at third down and one yard from goal.

If we messed this up, Coach would have our asses.

We didn't do anything fancy, except for having Jerry make the run. He was smaller than Joe, but he was good enough to get that last yard for our first touchdown, followed by Gerald's extra point.

Ten to nothing.

There was a moment in Trinity's next drive when it looked like they might move the ball, but again it ended in disaster for them. They'd put together a handful of good downs including two really solid passes and it looked like they might have an immediate answer to our touchdown.

And then Luke Boniadi managed to strip the ball from their runner and recover it at their forty-five.

"That's what I'm talking about!" Coach Holloway shouted, practically jumping up and down.

Unfortunately, there just wasn't enough time left on the clock for any kind of drive to come together after that, and time ran out.

As good as the first half went, the second half was when things really heated up.

Our first drive began with a running play that picked up four yards and then another that picked up three. It was almost starting to become cliché that every second down was three yards, but I guess that was better than losing yards.

Then Coach did it again; called another passing play. I hoped this was a sign of something coming. I'd shown him I could throw for more than five yards, and I just needed to prove it wasn't a fluke.

Everything started out well. Mickey burst off the line, creating separation down the sideline almost as soon as he took off, and my protection held, giving me lots of time to set up.

I couldn't have asked for a better throw.

And then, as it landed in Mickey's hands, it slipped right through his fingers.

"Son of a bitch."

I looked over at Coach on the sideline when we got to the huddle. He didn't look pissed, but I hoped it wouldn't be the end of my being able to pass. It might have been incomplete, but I thought my pass was great.

"Sorry, man," Mickey said as he joined us.

"It's okay," I said, trying not to sound as annoyed as I felt inside.

It wasn't fair to be too hard on him. It happened sometimes. We only had three more yards to get the first down, but Coach didn't want to risk it, which made sense this early in the quarter.

Trinity started at their twenty-five after the punt, and they began to pick up yardage on some runs. I was hoping they had another screw-up, like what had cost them their last drive, but the screw-up was on our side this time.

Their QB managed a beautiful pass twenty yards down the sideline to a wide receiver, who left our safety hugging air, giving him nothing but open field. Our guys tried, but never caught him, giving Trinity their first points on the board and bringing the score to 10 - 7.

Coach was absolutely livid.

Again, it happens, but it put the score way closer than anyone wanted. At least the kickoff went okay, with us returning it to the thirty-two-yard line.

We were doing running plays again, just like the rest of the time. Five yards here, three yards there, managing just enough to keep us in the fight. We'd made it a good way down the field when Jerry had his own moment of luck, breaking free on a sweep and hauling ass twenty yards down the sideline, juking hard enough to get their safety to almost trip up on his own feet, and he was into the end zone.

With the extra point, we were back up at 17 - 7.

As we went into the final quarter, it seemed like that one big play was all Trinity had in them, because their offense completely gave up the ghost. They had a terrible kick return, a run that only managed one yard, and then back-to-back incomplete passes that had them punting almost as soon as the drive began.

I was ready for a final slow grind to the end zone, and it started that way with another run for Jerry that got nowhere.

Then Coach surprised me for a fourth time. Even with the incomplete pass last time, Coach called for another pass. This one wasn't a cut at fifteen yards, though. This one had my primary read as Mickey, who was going deep, and my secondary read as the closer-in receiver.

I guess Coach figured we were far enough ahead and we might as well go for something flashy. Or maybe he just wanted to see what I could do.

The defense showed blitz again, but I wasn't buying it. They'd been faking most of the night. The ball snapped and I dropped back, watching Mickey burn past their corner. Luck was on our side. The safety, probably expecting another run, was way out of position by the time he realized what was happening, and Mickey had a clear path a good two steps ahead of his coverage.

I let it fly.

It was one of those passes you knew was going to be on target the moment it left your hand. Mickey didn't screw up this time. He didn't even break stride, catching it in a full sprint and cruising into the end zone.

"Now that's what I'm talking about!" I said, slapping Andre on the shoulder as I started to walk off to the sidelines.

Gerald nailed the extra point, putting us up 24 - 7.

Trinity tried to answer and they battled for a few first downs before their drive fizzled out after a short completion and a stuffed run up the middle. Another incomplete pass later, they punted it away.

I honestly thought they were close enough for a field goal at least, but maybe they didn't have faith in their kicker. Not that it really mattered. The game was over by that point.

We just ran down the clock while Trinity burned through their timeouts, I guess hoping for a miracle.

I don't really know what their thinking was.

The final whistle had me feeling amazing. My first win on JV and I'd finally gotten some real passing yards.

I headed toward the locker room and when I walked by Coach Holloway he said, "I guess you can handle a few passes after all."

He didn't wait for a response, just turned and walked away.

I hoped beyond hope that meant we might start passing more and running less. End up with some kind of balanced offense. Maybe I'd been too hard on Coach. Maybe he'd been so wedded to the idea of a mostly running game because he'd had some bad passers at QB.

I just hoped I'd shown him that I wasn't going to continue that. I was here to play.

I'd slowed down as I'd worked that through my head and just started to walk again when something caught my eye. I looked up to see a blond cheerleader waving at me. As soon as she saw she caught my attention, she winked, did this little kick back thing with her foot, and then ran off to join the other cheerleaders without looking back at me.

I didn't have to wonder who she was. Melanie Barlow. In the dream life, I'd had a serious crush on her both years I was in high school and then seeing her around town for the next two years until she headed off for college.

I'd heard she'd gotten with some star athlete in college, and I think settled down and had some kids. After she'd left town, dream me had stopped paying attention. But he'd sure as hell paid enough attention to know who she was now.

And she was winking at me.

Yeah, I could definitely get used to this winning thing.

Sunday morning, I was up early because I knew Dad had to be at the station at nine, which meant he had to leave the house no later than eight. I wasn't usually a morning person, especially on weekends, but this wasn't something I wanted to talk about around other people, and I needed an answer in the next few days. With his schedule and what time I had to be at school, it was much harder to catch him alone on a school day.

As soon as I smelled the coffee, I got up and went down to the kitchen, where I found him sitting at the small kitchen table, the newspaper open and a cup of coffee already next to him.

"Nebraska really crushed Pacific," he said as I sat down.

Football. It was the main language we spoke to each other.

"Yeah. I watched some replays on ESPN when I got home last night, and Pacific's defense looked lost out there. They've got a young secondary, and I think their coordinator's new this year, too."

"It helps that Nebraska's running game is unstoppable," I said, but in an offhanded way.

I had too much on my mind to talk about football in any intelligent way, and I think he caught onto my distraction. Or maybe it was my nervousness.

He folded his paper, set it aside, and asked, "What's on your mind?"

"What do you mean?"

"Blake, I can't remember the last time you were up this early on a Sunday, and it wasn't so you could sit and shoot the breeze with your old man. So, what's bothering you?"

"Busted. Okay, yes, I did want to talk to you about something, although honestly, I do wish we'd sit down and talk more."

Although I was on the path to keep from losing him, there was a part of me that really wanted to spend more time with my dad. The other weekend we'd hung out for an afternoon and it was still one of the best times I'd had. It was hard because he was working a lot, or with Mom, who wasn't my biggest fan half the time, or I was preoccupied with homework and other stuff.

It wasn't until he pointed out that we never did things together that I realized time was getting short between us even if the stuff in my dream never came true. I'd be off to college in four years and I'd have less and less time with him.

I really did need to make spending time with him a priority.

"I'd like that, too," he said, reaching over and patting my arm. "But why don't you go ahead and spill whatever you actually wanted to talk to me about."

"So last week, I talked to Coach Holloway about what it takes to get to the next level. I've been working on getting my grades up, but my goal is still to get picked up by a really good college program and do well enough to get drafted. I know, I know how unlikely that is and that's why I've been working just as hard on my schooling, but it doesn't mean I've given up my dream."

"I've never asked you to. I just want you to do it smart, so that if you don't get what you want, you still have a plan."

"I am. I promise. Anyway, he said that while the coaches at school will work with me to improve as much as they can, and they do have a lot of kids get into D1 and D2 programs, that there was a big difference between that and making it into the NFL. He also pointed out that if I checked, the bulk of the guys that do make it come from families with money. He said the reason for that was that the only way to really ensure you get to that next level is private coaching and specialized training, along with elite-level camps, clinics, and showcases. I imagine in college, the training will pick up, but there are a lot of kids playing college ball who want to be a starting quarterback at one of the big programs. There's a lot of competition for those spots."

"I guess that makes sense. I'm glad to see you're taking this all so seriously."

"I am. I've also been thinking about how to pay for it, since from what I've been able to find out it's really expensive, and I have an idea.

"A way to pay for it myself."

"That's admirable, son. How much are we talking about?"

I took a deep breath. "Between ten and fifteen thousand dollars a year."

Dad choked on his coffee. "Fifteen thousand dollars?"

"Yeah. Like I said, a lot. But that's for a full year of coaching from a private coach, plus a speed coach, consulting with a nutritionist and regular checkups, as well as attending the majority of the football camps I could find."

"Blake, that's ..."

"I know, way more than we can afford. But like I said, I have a plan. One that could work to get me started by this summer or maybe by the end of the year. But you're going to hate it."

"What is this plan?" he asked, using his cop voice.

233

He didn't do it often, but sometimes it leaked out. Like I was a perp about to lie to him.

"I need you to really hear me out, okay? I am dead serious about this and I'm not just doing this on a whim."

He gestured for me to continue.

"The Oklahoma - Colorado game is coming up and I remember you talking to that old college friend of yours in Nevada about the Super Bowl last year. The one who helped you place that bet."

Dad placed little bets in office pools, and I knew he gambled here and there in Vegas a few times, but last year he was positive all of the experts were wrong and, in spite of the Cowboys being favored, that Buffalo would pull it out. He'd been wrong and the Cowboys had not only won, but it'd been a blowout.

Mom had been pissed at him for a week for wasting the money.

"No."

"Dad ..."

"Absolutely not. Sports betting? That's what this is about?"

"Dad, hear me out," I said. "I'm not asking you to gamble for me. I'm asking you to place one bet, one time ... with *my* money."

That was a lie, but I figured it would be easier to slowly walk him into this rather than trying to sell my plan all at once.

"Blake, gambling is against the law, even if you do it through a friend."

"Come on, Dad. It was also illegal when you placed that bet on the Super Bowl."

"That was different."

"How? I'm just asking you to do the exact same thing, but with my money this time."

"Stop." Dad held up his hand. "You're fifteen. Do you understand how easily this kind of thing can get out of hand? Are you really prepared to throw your money away like this? And if you win, are you going to be able to just stop? I've seen a lot of gambling addicts in my time, and this is how it starts."

"I'm not a gambling addict. I have a plan, and this is the only way I could think of to make it happen."

"That's what every gambler said when they first started."

"Dad, I've been working so hard. My grades are up. I have all A's for the first time since elementary school. I'm starting on JV as a freshman. I'm not the same kid I was even two months ago."

"And I'm proud of you for that. But it doesn't change …"

"It's my Christmas and birthday money," I interrupted. "Mine to spend how I want."

"Why are you so sure about this game? What makes you think you know something all the experts don't?"

"I can't explain it. I just do. I am absolutely positive I'm right."

"Nobody knows for certain how a game will end. That's what makes it gambling."

"I do." The words came out before I could stop them. "I really can't explain it."

"Blake, if you know something that's set up ahead of time, that's not just illegal gambling, that's fraud. A felony."

"It's not that. I swear to you now, that's not it."

He was quiet for a minute, I think trying to get a read on me. I knew it was a big ask, believing in my confidence but not taking the next logical step to some kind of fixed game. I couldn't even be mad at him for it. The real explanation was so fantastical, there was no reasonable way anyone would believe it.

"You're smart, son. But you're being naive. There's no such thing as a sure bet. That's how people lose everything … thinking they've figured out some special angle nobody else sees."

"I'm not trying to figure out angles. I just …" I trailed off, frustrated. "I need you to trust me on this."

"This isn't about trust, Blake. It's about protecting you from making a mistake that could snowball."

"But that's exactly what trust is. Letting me make my own decisions. Hell, letting me make my own mistakes."

"There's a difference between letting you learn from mistakes and enabling potentially destructive behavior."

"Come on, Dad. You're acting like I'm asking to join a gang or something. It's one bet. My money. And I swear to you, I wouldn't ask if I wasn't absolutely sure."

He sighed and pinched the bridge of his nose. "Blake …"

"I'm not going to let this go. I've done everything in my power this year to show you I'm worth trusting. I've done everything

235

you've asked and all the stuff you wanted but didn't ask me to do. I don't know how I could do more than I am right now. You can't then shut me down the first time I ask you to trust me."

He didn't answer right away. "Alright. If, and this is a big if, I help you with this, there has to be ground rules."

"Name them."

"First, this is absolutely a one-time deal. Win or lose, we're never doing this again."

"Agreed."

"Second, your grades stay up. You promise me here and now that you will keep on the path you're going."

"I promise."

"Third, I handle everything. You don't talk to anyone about this. Not your friends, not your classmates, and absolutely not your mother. As far as anyone's concerned, this never happened."

"Deal."

"Fourth, if you lose, that's it. No crying about it, no asking me to cover it, no trying again to win it back. You accept the loss and move on."

"Absolutely."

Dad took a long drink of his coffee. "How much are we talking about?"

"Nine hundred and sixty-five dollars."

"And what exactly do you want to bet on?"

"Oklahoma over Colorado by thirty points."

Dad's eyebrows shot up. "That is a very specific bet."

"I know."

He tapped the side of his mug for a second and said, "No. We can't make that bet."

"But you just said ..."

"I said I'd help you place a bet. If we walk in with that kind of specific bet and win, it raises red flags. Nobody bets that precisely unless they know something."

"Oh." I hadn't considered that. "So what do we do?"

"We spread it out. Four sixty-five on the spread the books are offering, four hundred on the closest spread to thirty points, and a hundred on the money line."

I did some quick math in my head. It wouldn't pay as much as my original plan, but it was better than nothing.

"That works."

"Not even a question about what I just said? When did you learn about sports betting?"

"I told you, I've been doing my research."

"I can see that." Dad stood up, shaking his head. "I can't believe I'm agreeing to this. I must be losing my mind."

"You're not. You're trusting me."

"Maybe." He grabbed his coffee cup, downed it and put the dirty cup in the sink. "I'll call Pete tonight after my shift."

"Thanks, Dad."

He paused in the doorway. "Blake?"

"Yeah?"

"I really hope you know what you're doing."

"I do," I said, but he was already gone.

I sat there for a while, staring at my hands. I did know what I was doing, sort of. The memory of that game was clear enough, even if I couldn't remember the exact score. Oklahoma had destroyed Colorado. I just hoped spreading the bets out like Dad suggested wouldn't cut too much into the potential winnings.

The next step was going to be even harder. If Dad didn't like the idea of me betting, he was really going to hate me rolling the winnings into the next bet.

Chapter 22

The little bell over the pharmacy door clinked as I pushed it open. After Dad went to work, Mom never came out of her room. I thought she was working, until I heard a noise from the back of the house and went to investigate.

She was lying there, listless, in the dark. Apparently, she called in sick to work again. The stuff I'd found for her last week had seemed to help, and she hadn't had another attack except for a small one the day after I'd found her home on the couch. I'd actually thought maybe we'd found the solution, but apparently not.

So I was back at the pharmacy, hoping to find something else. I'd already gotten the extra strength pill with what looked like the highest dosage on the side of the bottle last time, but that only worked for like a week.

"Back again, Blake? How's your mother doing?" Mr. Sullivan, the pharmacist, asked from behind the counter.

"Not great. The last ones didn't help much. She's taking more and more of them, but they're barely touching the pain anymore."

"Did she go to see Dr. Taylor like I suggested?"

"I think so, but I don't think anything was prescribed."

I actually knew she hadn't. I'd heard her and Dad arguing about it a few weeks ago, and she'd blown me off last week when I'd suggested it.

Mr. Sullivan pursed his lips, considering. "There's a newer medication we just got in. It's not much different than the medication you got before, but it's supposed to be formulated for migraines, so it's worth trying. But Blake, she really needs to see a specialist. These headaches aren't normal."

"I know," I said, like she'd listen to me at all.

"Just …"

Whatever he was going to say was cut off when the front door burst open with such force the bell nearly flew off the wall. A small Chinese woman stormed in, her shoes making a flapping sound like they were flip-flops as they tried to keep up with her stomping. Her black hair was pulled back in a severe bun, and she looked familiar. It took me a moment to realize she looked like what I imagined Li might look like when she got older.

Well, if she got older and shrunk by more than a foot.

She made a beeline for the counter, stopping right in front of me.

"Are you the boy who talked to my daughter?" she said, poking a finger at my chest. "Li is a good student. She does not have time to waste playing games. You need to stay away from my daughter!"

I took an instinctive step back, caught off guard by her intensity. Mr. Sullivan had paused mid-reach for the medication he'd been talking about from a shelf behind him and was just staring at us.

I also knew her last name wasn't Zhu, like Li's. She'd explained the other day that married couples didn't take each other's last names, and kids usually had the last name of the father while the mother kept her maiden name. It seemed strange to me, having an immediate family with different last names, but who was I to knock how other people lived?

"Mrs. Sun, I wasn't trying to …"

"No! I know boys like you. You all think because I have a tall, pretty daughter that she needs a boyfriend. That she needs sports. What she needs is to study!"

"That's not what I…"

"You know what happens to girls who play sports? They spend all their time practicing or dating boys who play other sports, and their grades start to slip. Because they're good at sports, teachers think it's fine to have students who get Bs or Cs. You know what those girls don't do? They don't go to Harvard!"

"Mrs. Sun, Li's really talented. She told me about playing in Houston, how happy it made her. With her height and skill …"

"The only skill that matters is the one that will get her into a good college and give her a good job."

"But she's lonely. Until recently, she would spend all her time sitting by herself, not really talking to anyone."

"Good! Less time talking means more time studying. You think friends will help her get into medical school? You think running around in a sweaty gym will help her become a doctor?"

"No, but ..."

"No 'buts!' You leave Li alone. She's to study, get good grades, and go to Harvard. She'll become a doctor like her father. I don't want boys filling her head with silly ideas about sports."

It was hard to really get a grip on the conversation. Li's mom was like a tornado, hitting me from every side. It did put a lot of why Li was the way she was in perspective, though. I'd only had to deal with this for sixty seconds, and it was already too much for me.

I couldn't imagine what it would be like to live with this.

But ... it wasn't any secret what her mother actually wanted. That was one benefit of her approach. It was very clear what her goal was. It was even a good goal, although I worried how that would leave Li once she got out into the world, out from under her mother's roof.

"Mrs. Sun, please. I understand you want what's best for Li. But basketball scholarships can actually help with college applications. Schools like Harvard look for well-rounded students, and they're not great on admissions even if you have perfect grades. No matter what a school's policy is, though, they will put that aside for a good athlete."

"You think I don't know about American colleges? I've researched every top school."

"I have no doubt. Then you know sports can open doors. Li is really tall for a girl and if she's even half as good as she said she was, she'll be able to open a lot of doors that might otherwise be closed to her. Give her not only a real chance at a good school, but options for several."

"And what do you know about it?"

"I don't know if she told you, but I play football, and I want to go to a good school, so I've spent a lot of time looking at sports scholarships. I know Li's unhappy and lonely, which could hurt her grades, too, since it would make her unfocused."

240

She didn't say anything for a minute, just glared at me with such intensity I thought maybe she was going to hit me in the stomach or something for daring to talk to her daughter.

Instead, she said, "You will come to dinner, tonight. Seven o'clock sharp. We will discuss this properly then."

With that, she turned around and headed for the door at the same speed she'd come in.

"I ... what?"

"Seven o'clock. Don't be late. And bring information about these scholarship programs!"

The bell jangled violently as she yanked the door open and stomped out and down the street. To say I was shaken by the whole encounter was an understatement.

Mr. Sullivan, apparently, found it amusing.

"She's something, isn't she," he said, chuckling to himself as he handed me the medication and started to ring it up.

"No kidding," I said as I paid for it.

I was honestly a little frightened that I might not make it out of this dinner alive.

Several hours later, I found myself in front of Downing's Antiques, a building I'd seen in passing but had never actually been this close to. There was a closed sign in the window, and part of me just wanted to turn around and walk away.

Except I'd already committed myself to do what I needed to do to make up for how Li'd been treated in the dream life and how she was being treated by Elijah and the rest now. So instead of running, I pressed the small buzzer by the door and waited, smoothing down the nicest shirt I owned.

I was so nervous, I felt like I was waiting for a first date. Or maybe an execution.

After about a minute, I saw Li through the window, weaving through the shelves of trinkets. Instead of unlocking the door and stepping back to let me in, however, she stepped through it, pulling the door shut behind her so we were both outside.

"I'm so sorry about my mother," she said as soon as the door was shut behind her. "I swear I didn't know she was going to ..."

"It's fine," I said, cutting her off. "You told me what she was like, so I should have expected this. If I can help you get her to agree to let you play, it's worth a try."

"Thank you," she said, squeezing my arm for a moment before opening the door again and ushering me into the shop.

After locking the door behind her, she led me through the shelves, which were filled with small and medium-sized things of all shapes and sizes, from pots and picture frames to trinkets. The other half of the shop was cluttered with chairs, tables, and furniture, and I didn't even know what its purpose was.

The second floor was completely different from the shop below. It was just a modest apartment with a mix of simple self-assembly furniture and Chinese decorations.

The kitchen and dining area were both just at the top of the stairs, and Li's mom was by the stove still working on the food when we got up there.

"Sit. You there. You there," she said, turning around and pointing at places across from each other at the already set table.

Li was avoiding eye contact as I sat down, clearly as uncomfortable with all this as I was. Her mom began bringing over dishes as soon as we sat down. A big bowl of steaming rice, vegetables in some kind of sauce, slices of beef and green onion, and a plate filled with buns that had some kind of meat inside.

"Now," Mrs. Sun said, sitting down after putting the last dish on the table. "Tell me about these sports scholarships. How do colleges choose which athlete to take? What are the requirements? What percentage of players receive these scholarships, and how good are the schools that offer them?"

I opened my mouth to answer, but she continued before I could speak.

"What kind of grades are needed if you have this scholarship? Which schools give most of the money? Do you just play and get them, or do you have to do something to apply for them?"

"Well," I began, fumbling with my chopsticks as she started spooning food onto my and Li's plates. "I can only speak for football, but …"

"Yes, I understand you play football, not basketball," she interrupted. "How different is the process?"

"The basic recruitment process is similar. But football and basketball have different ..."

"What percentage of students get full rides? Li says Harvard has sports teams. Could she play there?"

I was starting to get flummoxed by all of the questions, and I didn't know how to use chopsticks, but there were no forks, and it felt kind of insulting to ask for one, so I was trying to do my best while paying attention to what she was saying. Which ended up with me trying to copy Li's movements and dropping one, which bounced off the plate and onto the floor.

Li hopped out of her chair, grabbed the dropped chopstick, and went to get me another pair.

"Thanks," I said as she handed it to me. "For Harvard ..."

"First, tell me about the recruitment timeline," Mrs. Sun cut in. "When do scouts start watching? What grades must be maintained? How many games do they watch?"

"Māmā, ràng tā shuō yīxiàr la," Li said.

I didn't know what she said exactly, but I recognized the exasperated tone I sometimes used with my mom when she was embarrassing me.

"Fine. You answer now," she said, jabbing a chopstick at me.

"For football, and I'm pretty sure basketball too, colleges usually start looking at players in their sophomore or junior year, depending on how good they are. The very best players start getting attention in their sophomore year, everyone else in their junior year. They evaluate players based on their performance in games, their physical attributes, and their potential for development. Scouts also usually attend tournaments where they can see multiple players at once, and it's a good place to get on their radar. Those players who they think will benefit their programs, either because of their ability to help them win or their popularity to increase attendance, will usually get offers, which is to say, they get asked to commit to going to that school and receive some kind of scholarship.

Mrs. Sun, who was clearly holding herself back until I stopped to take a breath, asked, "And what are the chances of getting these scholarships?"

"It varies by division and school. Division I schools offer the most complete scholarships. I can't speak for women's basketball, but it's usually like a couple of thousand scholarships given out each year across all the schools in that division, which is less than in football and men's basketball. The competition is tough and there are a lot of kids who want them, but Li would have advantages. Her height, and from what she's told me about her skills …"

"And Harvard?" Mrs. Sun pressed.

It had been hard to get information without the Internet, but I did look up a few things before I came over because I knew this would be something she asked.

"Yeah, that's the tricky part. None of the Ivy League schools offer athletic scholarships but they do have a strong women's basketball program, and being an athlete can ensure you get admitted even if they would not choose you otherwise. They want their team to be competitive."

"So why do it then?"

"Like I said, if you have both good grades, are a well-rounded student, and can help their teams, you will very likely get an offer to go there, sometimes even without directly applying. But, there are also very highly rated teams like Duke, Notre Dame, and Stanford that do give full-ride athletic scholarships and are extremely good schools. So it gives you choices in both directions."

"But sports takes time away from studies. Time Li needs for AP classes and SAT preparation."

"I understand your concern, but I think she can manage both. I've actually improved academically since joining the football team after years of being a terrible student. I'm getting all A's for the first time, even with getting a lot of extra assignments to enable me to move up from remedial classes and I got promoted unusually quickly to a higher team in the football program. And Li is much smarter than me. If I can handle it, she definitely can."

"You are doing well in school now?"

"Yes, ma'am. And from talking to my counselor, colleges want more than just good grades. They look for leadership and involvement in the school's community."

"Like student government?" Mrs. Sun asked.

"Exactly. But that's mostly a popularity contest. You need a lot of friends and connections in the school to win those positions."

Mrs. Sun set down her chopsticks. "I have asked about you, Blake Sims. Your coaches say you have talent. Your teachers confirm you are a good and hardworking student."

After meeting me, it did not surprise me that she would call either the coaches or teachers, although I had to wonder how she knew who my teachers were. The answer wasn't hard to figure out, though.

I glanced at Li, who seemed to be trying to disappear into her chair, very pointedly not looking at me.

"My concern is not just academic," Mrs. Sun continued. "There are other ... social elements. Parties and boys that might distract her."

"That's also a problem when you're not in sports. Actually, I've found sports help with focus and discipline," I said. "I think Li's already proven she's great at managing her time. If she's already very busy with everything, she won't have time to get out of control. If she wants student government, she will need to go to some social functions to make the friends she'll need, but I think she can manage it. Plus, teams need their athletes to pass so they stay eligible to play, so the coaches help give them the resources they need to maintain their grades."

"Yes, I have researched this extensively since our meeting at the pharmacy. From what I have found, I believe you are correct in saying student athletes have better college acceptance rates. I will allow her to participate in basketball."

"Really?" Li asked, shooting up in her chair, looking from her mom to me and back again.

"Yes," she said, and then stabbed her chopsticks at me again. "You will help Li prepare for basketball tryouts."

"I ... what?"

"You know about sports and how to best prepare for athletic success, yes? You are very clearly a successful athlete, so you will help her practice and prepare. You two may work together after school when your homework is complete and on weekend days, time permitting. You will call ahead and get permission to practice. You will provide a plan to get her ready to make the team by the end of the week."

"Māmā!" Li protested, but her mom held up her hand.

"You want to play, yes? Blake will help you succeed. He will also assist you in making the right connections to become class president by junior year."

"I'm not sure I can guarantee ..." I started.

Her mom gave me a look that stopped me cold. "You convinced me basketball was worth pursuing. Now you will help ensure it benefits her future. Class president looks very good on college applications."

Li was staring at her plate, but I could see the smile she was trying to hide. I knew the feeling. The way we got there might be unorthodox, but she was being allowed to play a game she clearly loved.

How could I stand in the way of her getting that?

"Of course. I'll do my best to help."

"Good," Mrs. Sun said, standing up. "Sit there. I have made sesame cake to celebrate this decision."

She brought over a plate with what looked like little fried balls covered in sesame seeds. They were actually really good - crispy on the outside and chewy inside with some kind of sweet filling.

After we finished eating, Li's mom announced it was time for me to go home. Li was really quiet as she walked me downstairs through the shop to the front door.

"I'm so sorry about all this," she said as she unlocked the door. "I didn't think she'd ..."

"Make me your personal basketball trainer and campaign manager?" I laughed. "It's okay. I meant what I said about wanting to help."

"Still. Thank you. For everything."

"Li!" Mrs. Sun's voice carried down from upstairs, followed by a string of Chinese words I didn't understand.

Li winced and said, "I have to go. See you tomorrow?"

"Yeah, tomorrow."

She gave a quick wave before disappearing back inside. I stood there for a moment, wondering what exactly I'd gotten myself into. Helping Eduardo, all the extra schoolwork, and now helping Li.

I had to be crazy!

Chapter 23

Wednesday was the first chance I had to practice with Li. She had tutoring until almost dinnertime on both Monday and Tuesday, and I still had a lot of studying to do for the week, between school and watching a game video. As part of the extra work I'd asked Coach for, to start making improvements in my game, he sent me home Saturday with a video of the game. I was supposed to make notes in specific formats, and bring them back to him so he could see how I evaluated the game.

What that really meant was watching the game several times through, once making general notes and identifying sections to look at, then reviewing them more closely, even playing them at half speed so I could really focus on finding the strengths and, more importantly, weaknesses in our gameplay.

It was an interesting assignment, and I was actually learning a lot by doing it. At least, it felt like I was, and that I was making progress in practice, starting to see the patterns from the game and then on the field without the coaches having to point it out to me. I wasn't getting everything. I probably wasn't catching most of the little errors made and tendencies our guys had, but it was something.

We didn't really have scouting videos of the other teams, although Coach said varsity did, at least during the playoffs. So mostly, it was for seeing our own errors and mistakes, rather than using it to predict the other team's.

"Looks like you've got a fan club," Mickey said as he juggled the ball.

We were off to the side working with Coach Easley, our offensive coordinator, on short five-yard passes that Coach Holloway liked to run as part of the push-and-grind game that he preferred.

These tended to be quick passes, but they also had me throwing into heavy traffic, and that could end in interceptions if I wasn't careful. It's what had gotten Jorden in so much trouble in the first part of the season.

I looked over at the stands and saw Li sitting up several rows wearing basketball shorts and a baggy T-shirt, looking mildly uncomfortable with her backpack perched on her knees. I gave a wave, and she waved back kind of shyly.

"Not a cheerleader, just my friend. She's trying out for the girls' basketball team, and I'm helping her train."

"Hey, you don't have to get defensive with me," he said, grinning and putting more into the statement than he said out loud.

"Sims, get your head into practice," Coach Easley yelled, whacking the back of my helmet.

"Sorry, Coach," I said and went back to throwing.

After practice ended, I waved the guys off as they headed to the locker room and went to the stands. I knew I'd be meeting Li, but I thought we'd meet at the court, and I didn't want to keep her waiting, so I'd brought my bag out with me. Some of the guys made some kissing noises at me as I headed to the bleachers where Li was coming down to the field to meet me, which caused her to blush.

"Don't mind them. They're idiots."

"It's okay," she said, but I could tell it was making her very self-conscious.

We made our way down the track, off the field, and down the sidewalk to circle the building where the basketball courts were set up behind the teacher's parking lot. They were also used for tennis courts and sometimes even volleyball, but usually tennis, since the basketball and volleyball teams usually played inside the gym.

That meant, for us right now, that a tennis net was stretched down the half-court line, which basically kept us to half-court play only, but that was fine. It wasn't like we were doing a pickup game or anything. Later on, if we needed more room, we could go to Frazier Park, but it usually had people playing pickup games after school until it got too dark to see.

That might be good when I needed to see her play against other people, but for now, we'd work on the basics.

"You're really good," she said suddenly. "At football, I mean."

"You watched the whole practice?"

I hadn't realized she'd been there long enough to see me throw more than a handful of times. I thought when the guys called her out, that she'd just arrived, since I hadn't noticed her before that, and even though Jorden wasn't starting anymore, he was still getting to throw in practice, meaning I spent a lot of the time watching her after I noticed her just waiting around while he got to do his thing.

"Most of it. I don't know much about football, but even I can tell you throw really well. And you're fast. You were outrunning a bunch of those other guys out there."

She must have been there early because we didn't scrimmage at all today, and the only time we'd run was for warm-ups and then doing some sprints before breaking into groups with the coordinators while Coach Holloway worked with varsity.

"Thanks. I think I could do even better if Coach would let me be more mobile. You know, scramble when it makes sense, pass more. But that's not my call."

"Why not? Aren't you the quarterback?"

"It's complicated. High school football has a lot of … politics. Coach Holloway likes a specific style of play. Conservative. Ground and pound."

"That sounds painful."

I laughed. "For our runners, more than me, since they have to keep charging headfirst into the other team's line. But hey, we won last week, so I can't complain too much."

"Still, you looked really good. Like you knew exactly what you were doing."

"Thanks. I've got a long way to go, though. Especially if I want to make it to the NFL."

"Is that what you want? To play professionally?"

"It's all I've ever dreamed of."

Actually, it's all I've ever dreamed of twice, technically. In this life and in the dream life.

"That's … kind of amazing, actually. To know exactly what you want like that."

"You don't?"

"I mean, according to my mom, I'm going to Harvard to become a doctor. But that's not exactly my dream."

"Basketball?"

"Ha," she said, laughing out loud. "No. I mean, I like to play and if I could play in high school and college, that would be great, but no, I have no dreams of being a professional athlete."

"Then what?"

"I'm not sure. I don't think I've really thought about it. It's just been, do viola lessons, do Chinese lessons, get A's, get on the honor roll. Just the next thing and the next thing, following the plan put in front of me."

"Don't you think maybe you should consider what *you* want to be doing? I mean, it's your life and you're just starting. Do you want to look back in thirty years and realize you're living your mother's life, instead of your own?"

"No," she said after a long pause. "But it's also not that simple. It's … it's a Chinese thing. It's hard to explain."

"Okay. I won't push. Just think about it. Okay?"

"Yeah."

We got to the court and, thankfully, no one was there. That wasn't that big of a surprise. There weren't any lights, so we had maybe an hour of playtime before it got too dark, and most people didn't want to cut games short once they got going.

"So, I talked to one of the guys on the varsity boys basketball team about what tryouts are like and what you should expect. Sorry, I don't know any of the girls on the team, but one of the JV guys on my team knows him and connected us."

"What did he say?" she asked, her normal reserved demeanor slipping for a second.

"So it's two parts. One is running everyone through drills to see your fundamentals, and then they'll split you up for scrimmages, so they can see you play. We can't really do the scrimmaging because there's just the two of us and all that," I said, waving at the tennis net at half-court. "But we can at least work on the fundamentals."

We started with dribbling exercises, or at least what I thought were the exercises. I'd watched a fair amount of basketball in my dream life and I talked to some people over the last few days, which wasn't the same as actually knowing what I was talking about, but it would have to do.

Li seemed to be really good at handling the basketball. She had a ton of control, switching hands easily without looking down at the ball, something I couldn't do, going in between her legs, and even changing hands behind her back at one point.

"Where did you learn that?"

"Some guys I played with at the park back home thought it was cute having a girl wanting to learn to play basketball, and kind of adopted me. They taught me all kinds of stuff and had me practice."

"Ohh, so when I'm calling out dribbling drills, you must be getting a real laugh."

"No! I really app…"

"I'm joking. If you know actual drills, let's do them."

She started again, and her drills were a lot more complicated than the ones I'd had her do, including speed dribbles, stopping and cutting back while controlling the ball, and switching from between the legs, behind the back, and around the other side, pulling up for a shot. I didn't know how useful all of that was, but it looked really impressive."

We continued with free throw shooting, each of us taking turns at the line. Li's shots were consistent, with her hitting almost ninety percent of them. I hit closer to fifty percent, and that was rounding up. After that was rebounding, which consisted of me bouncing the ball off the backboard, trying to simulate a shot that didn't go in and her trying to get the ball in one short go.

This was the most questionable of the drills because it was very different from having someone else against you, contesting the ball, but it was what they'd told me would happen at tryouts, so it's what we went with.

Again, she was really good at it, always seeming to know where the ball was going to bounce and getting a hand on it. It helped that she was tall, but even with that, she was really good at getting into position.

Finally, we tried some contested shooting. She'd start a few steps back and come in for a shot, and I'd get my hand up in the way, not really trying to block it, but trying to make the shot harder. She was really solid close up, but her shooting in the mid-range was closer to seventy percent with my hand in the way, and that was again not having anyone really putting pressure on the ball, trying to move it, and a whole team operating around you. I'd heard somewhere a good shooting percentage was in the forties, which made sense with everything that would be happening.

Although I didn't know if that was true or not.

She was a lot worse from behind the three-point line, only hitting two out of ten shots. None of that seemed to matter to her. She was grinning and having a great time. It was the happiest I'd ever seen her. The serious, no-nonsense girl had completely disappeared, and a kid just having a good time took her place.

She was glowing.

"Having fun?" I asked during a water break.

"So much." She was practically bouncing on her toes. "I forgot how much I loved this."

"It shows. You're really good, Li. Like, really good."

"Thanks." She ducked her head, but I could see her pleased smile. "My mid-range game needs work though. I can post up all day, but if I want to be more than just height under the basket …"

"Yeah, it and your three-pointers are definitely weaker, although I wouldn't say they're terrible."

"Threes don't matter as much. I know I'll be playing post. But being able to hit those elbow jumpers would make me harder to defend."

"Okay, well, I guess we know the areas we need to focus on next time. Speaking of which, we should probably wrap it up. Same time Friday?"

"Definitely." Li gathered her things, then paused, "Hey, Blake? Thanks for this. For helping me, I mean."

"No problem. That's what friends are for, right?"

"I guess maybe that's true," she said, a weird smile on her face.

Saturday, the game against Cooper High went a lot like the last game did, although with a much closer result. The biggest difference was that they were a much better defensive team than Trinity, and had our standard short game locked down.

Not that it stopped Coach from continually running it.

The only good part was that their offense was much worse than their defense, and our guys were able to lock them down. It helped that their coach seemed to come from the same school as Coach Holloway and kept to a short game.

At least I got to throw two long passes this time. Neither resulted in a touchdown, and the running plays that followed them got shut down. Still, I got a solid twenty-three-yard pass in the second quarter and a nineteen-yard pass in the fourth that got us close enough that instead of punting, we got to kick a field goal, which is how we won 10-7.

It felt extra vindicating because this was my second time playing against them, although this time with the JV, not the freshman team. Even so, it felt good that I didn't have Elijah trying to burn the offense down this time.

"Good game, Blake," Andre said from the other side of the bus aisle as we made our way back from Amarillo.

He'd been one of the few upperclassmen who hadn't given me grief when I moved up to JV. Not that they'd been mean, but he'd avoided participating in the hazing.

"Thanks."

Not that I thought I had a lot to be congratulated on for the win. My two real passes didn't get us a touchdown, and I'd even avoided scrambling beyond just getting out of the pocket when it collapsed so I could get a short pass off.

"If Coach would've let you air it out more, I think we could've won by more. Three completions out of the last four, that's nothing to shake a stick at."

"I suggested it, but I think every QB suggests they should get to pass more, so I'm not sure it counted for much," I said, shrugging.

"Maybe. But anything would have been better than just smashing face-first into their D all night."

"Tell me about it," Joe said.

Coach had him driving it in over and over all night, and he'd taken a hell of a pounding. I felt kind of bad for him. Still, we'd won two games in a row, and everyone was in good spirits, joking and having a good time.

It was amazing what a small winning streak could do.

When we pulled into the school parking lot, Andre leaned over and said, "Hey, we usually hit up Silver Spoon after games, win or lose. You should come."

I knew they did that, but I hadn't taken it personally when I hadn't been invited the last two times. They didn't know me, and I was an interloper. It felt good to get the invite, though. Like I was finally part of the team.

"Sure."

"Cool. Need a ride? I've got room."

"That'd be great. Just need to call my dad real quick, let him know."

"No problem. I'll wait by my car, it's the blue Civic."

"Give me five minutes," I said, hustling off the bus.

As I climbed off, Coach slapped my shoulder and said, "Good game tonight, Sims. Way to manage the clock."

"Thanks, Coach."

I might not say the same thing about his play-calling, but a win was a win, and I'd take the accolades.

I jogged into the field house and into Coach's office, which he left open for players to be able to call home when the buses got back from away games. Dad answered on the third ring.

"Hey, it's Blake. Some guys invited me to go to the Silver Spoon and are going to give me a ride over. Can I go?"

"Yeah, but see if you can get a ride home when you're done or call me to pick you up, okay?"

It was a short walk from the diner to our house, but it was already ten, and it was a good guess we'd be there pretty late, so I understood his concern.

"Sure."

"Okay. How'd you do tonight?"

"Good. We won, although it was close. Coach let me throw two long passes."

"Good job. I'm proud of you. Okay, have fun tonight and call me if you need a ride."

"I will."

I hung up, grabbed my stuff, and jogged out to the parking lot. This kind of an invite was a big deal and the last thing I wanted to do was screw it up by taking too long and have them leave without me. I'd been playing with the team until now, but I wasn't really part of it yet. I understood that. I was the only freshman on the team, and a late addition, but this could go a long way to making things easier.

Thankfully, Andre was next to his car, talking to Nathan Huff, a junior and one of the backup defensive ends, and Spencer Marshall, a senior and one of our linebackers.

"Sorry to keep you guys waiting," I said as I jogged over.

"No sweat, man. Throw your bag in the trunk and let's get going. You're in the back with Nate."

These were three of the biggest players on the team, and Nathan took up a good part of the back seat. The diner's parking lot was already crowded when we got there, with cars filling most of the parking spaces, small clusters of players, cheerleaders, and even some students who'd just come to watch the game gathered together near cars with open doors, music blasting out of them.

It was like a party.

Inside the diner was even wilder. Every booth was taken and the few regular people, not part of the football group, seemed a little shell-shocked by the sudden deluge of teenagers around them. Every booth was overfilled and most had kids just hanging around next to them, talking.

There were people everywhere.

I thanked Andre for the ride and broke off, squeezing into a booth with Miles, Mickey, Jerry, and Joe while Andre and the others went to join the line guys.

"That's two," Jerry said when I sat down.

"All thanks to our new freshman," Miles said, grabbing me by the shoulders and shaking me.

"I'm just handing the ball to these two and standing back. I'm not sure much is thanks to me."

"You're our good luck charm," Jerry said. "And besides, now that they're figuring out you can throw, they can't just all cheat up and beat up on me and Joe."

"I don't know," Joe added, rubbing his hurt shoulder. "Felt like they were beating up on us pretty good tonight."

"Yeah, but they stopped doing it as much after that first pass in the second. Besides, isn't this better than getting beat up and losing?"

"I guess."

"Hey, you could always go talk to Coach," Mickey said. "I'd be all for more long passes and less waiting for you guys to get ground into the mud."

"I bet you would," Jerry said.

The argument over passing or running went on like that for another thirty minutes. That's the way it went. We were all a team, but inside that team, offense and defense were two separate groups, and on the offensive side, the line and the backfield were also separate, mostly because in practice we broke into those groups and so that's who we spent the most time with. And in the backfield, it was running backs versus receivers, with me being lumped with the receivers, since I passed the ball versus running with it.

Everything was a competition, no matter how far down you drilled.

We didn't really eat meals, but most of us got drinks, milkshakes, and snacks like onion rings or a basket of fries. I wasn't sure how that worked out for them, being packed but not selling full meals, but this late in the evening, the diner was usually pretty empty, so maybe, on average, it worked out.

Freddie, the owner, didn't kick us out and it was a Mustang tradition going back forever, I think, so we all kept coming.

We continued, going back and forth on why passing or running was better, and getting into it with the defensive guys, who started shouting across the diner that the only reason we stayed in the game was 'cause they locked down the other side. They had a whole chant and everything.

While they weren't wrong, I wasn't going to let them come after the offense like that and joined in shouting them down. It was all in good fun and we were having a blast.

All the shouting made me thirsty, though, and finally I got up and headed over to the counter to get a refill. There was only one waitress working this late and while we'd all leave some cash to make sure us being a pain in the ass wasn't too bad, I didn't want to add to her stress by asking her to get it.

Also, it would have taken forever, since it was work to keep up on all the refills for the fifty or so kids packed into the place.

Even at the counter, I had to wait a while for Freddie to get to me.

"You were amazing tonight."

Melanie Barlow had materialized next to me, her long blonde hair falling in perfect waves. I'd had a weird, déjà vu kind of thing when she'd waved at me last week on the field, remembering how hard I'd had a crush on her. Will have? Will have had?

"Uhh, thanks. Though most of the night was just handing it off."

She waved at Freddie, pointing to her drink. I couldn't help but notice that it was still half full. She didn't actually need a refill. I realized she'd used it as a pretext to come and talk to me, which caused my stomach to do a little flip.

"Come on; those passes though? And the ones in the last game. Everyone knows you're what this team needed. We're all talking about it. They've lost all season and, once you joined, they start winning? Nope, be as humble as you want, but that's no coincidence. I think we could really start winning if Coach Holloway let you start playing for real."

"I'm not being humble; I'm just not trying to take away from what everyone else is doing. And I'm not sure that's ever going to happen. Coach keeps a pretty tight leash on the playbook."

"I guess," she said, shrugging. "So, how are you liking JV so far? Must be weird being the only freshman."

"I thought that might be true, but it's actually been pretty great. The guys have all really accepted me."

"Yeah, I noticed that. I mean, you're here tonight, right? So, how's the year treating you? We're in Mrs. Mace's class together, right?"

"Yeah, I think so."

I actually knew so. I'd definitely noticed her in class, but I thought she hadn't noticed me. Why would she?

"What did you think about that poetry assignment? I thought it was kind of brutal."

"Yeah. I just don't have the brain for it."

"But you're doing lots of extra work, right? Trying to get out of the remedial classes and move up? You can't claim you're not that smart."

"You know about that?"

"Everyone knows. We see you being assigned all the extra homework and getting tutoring from that Chinese girl."

"Li," I corrected.

"Sure. So anyway, I was thinking ..."

"Melanie," one of the other cheerleaders called from across the diner, interrupting her. "Come on, we're heading to Katie's!"

"Just a second!" Melanie called back before turning to me. "I should probably go. But this was fun. Maybe we could study together sometime? You could show me that big brain of yours."

I swallowed hard. "Yeah. Sure. That'd be cool."

"Great," she said, smiling and laying her hand on my arm for a second, squeezing before letting go. "See you Monday!"

She flashed one last smile my way and bounced over to join her friends, leaving my head spinning. What had just happened? More importantly, what was I going to do about it? The memory of future-me's crush on her was crystal clear: the way it had consumed me sophomore year, how devastated I'd been when she'd started dating a senior.

But that was a different timeline. A different me.

Things could be better this time.

Chapter 24

We ended up staying until Freddie kicked us all out of the diner around eleven-thirty. While that wasn't all that late, we'd also played a full football game and spent two hours each way on a bus. I was about dead when one of the juniors dropped me off at home.

I slept until almost noon, when a knock at my door woke me up.

I cursed myself for how late I'd slept. Between giving up time to train with Li and how much of my Saturdays were eaten up by football, I really didn't have the time to be sleeping away my only totally free day.

I hopped out of bed and half-shambled to my bedroom door, pulling it open and finding my father, dressed for work, standing on the other side.

"You won," he said, stepping past me into my room and closing the door. He looked almost shell-shocked. "Every single bet."

"Wha... How much?"

"You now have three thousand four hundred and thirty-eight dollars. That's twenty-four hundred and seventy-three in profit. How? How on earth were you so certain this was how the game was going to go? Vegas only had a fourteen-point spread; they didn't see it going this way. And you were positive."

I knew this moment was coming, and honestly, I'd been dreading it. If there had been any other way to place the bets, I would have, because there was no way to explain how I knew what I knew. I almost thought up a lie but abandoned it just as quickly. Dad was really good at spotting lies, and even if he wasn't, the entire crux of my argument was 'trust me.'

I'd be shooting myself in the foot if I tried to bluff my way through this.

"Blake?"

"I was thinking if I should try to make up a reason, but I decided not to. I want you to trust me, and that means I have to be completely honest with you."

"This isn't something you get to decide, Blake. If you're involved in something illegal ..."

"I'm not," I cut in. "Nothing illegal. No one else was involved in how I knew the outcome. But yes, I did know how the game was going to end. Mostly. I knew it was going to be a blowout and somewhere in the range of thirty points."

"How? Explain it to me."

"I can't. There's no way to describe it that won't sound completely crazy. I need you to trust me on this."

"This isn't something I can just trust you on. This could end badly if you're doing something you shouldn't. I mean jail time badly."

"I'm not. I can promise you that. Look at the evidence. I didn't just know they'd win, I knew the exact score, more or less. There's no way to throw a game like that, and me, a kid living in West Texas, would have to have inside information on what would be the biggest scandal in sports history, if the game was being thrown. Hundreds of people would have to be involved. I know it's hard to believe, but I'm being straight with you instead of making up excuses."

He was quiet for a long time, staring hard at me. I could see he was in cop mode, trying to figure out what I was thinking. If I was lying.

"You make a good point," he finally said.

"Good, 'cause I want you to place more bets."

"Blake, I told you this was a one-time thing."

"I know what you said. But this isn't enough for what I need. These next bets are just like the last one, guaranteed. I know exactly what's going to happen."

"How?"

"I can't tell you."

"Then I can't place the bets."

I sighed. Round and round we went. Part of me wanted to tell him everything, about the dream, about his death, about Joshua. But, I couldn't stop his death if I was in the nut house.

"If that's how it has to be, then I won't be able to bet. Because there's no explanation I can give you that will make sense. All I can say is that I know what's going to happen."

"Blake ..."

"So instead," I continued, rolling right over him. "We need to figure out another way to come up with twelve thousand dollars. And fifteen thousand the year after that. And another fifteen the year after that. Or I give up on my dream of being drafted."

"That's not fair."

"It is. Maybe I make it on just talent, but the people I'm competing against, many of them will have help on top of their talent. I'm trying to find a way to make my dreams happen without putting you and Mom in debt. And I think I've proven something is happening here that can pay for it."

Dad was back to the cop stare. I kept my mouth shut, knowing pushing any harder right now would backfire.

"I must be absolutely crazy," he finally said, shaking his head.

"That makes two of us."

"What are these bets you're thinking about?"

"I don't know if they even take pro bets like this, but on the twenty-third, some NFL records will be broken. The Rams are going to have the longest kickoff return in history: a hundred and three yards. And Tyrone Hughes of the Saints is going to set the record for most kickoff returns in a single game. It's going to be a crazy game."

"That's ... incredibly specific." Dad crossed his arms. "A game score is one thing. Those kinds of record-breaking performance? That's not something anyone could arrange."

"I know. And I still can't tell you how I know."

"Maybe. What else?"

"November fifth. George Foreman is going to win the heavyweight title."

Dad's eyebrows shot up as he exclaimed, "No way in hell. Moorer's undefeated. Thirty-five and O. Foreman's in his mid-forties. It's a miracle that fight is even happening."

"I know how it sounds. But that's what's going to happen."

"Jesus." Dad started pacing my room. "Okay. Even if, and this is a massive if, you're right about all this, we need to be smart about this. We can't just keep winning. Someone's going to notice."

"What do you mean?"

"We need some losses mixed in. Strategic ones. Small enough not to hurt too badly, but enough to make the pattern look natural."

"I hadn't thought about that."

"Who wins the Rams-Saints game?"

I wracked my brain, trying to pull up the specifics. "Pretty sure the Saints take it. Close game though."

"Okay. Here's what we do. Five hundred on the Saints to win straight up. We'll put a hundred on a high over-under that we know will lose. That offsets some of the winning pattern. Then another hundred on the longest return record. Not both records though. That'd be too suspicious for anyone to predict. "Then we take everything you've got and put it on Foreman."

"Okay. Sounds good."

"I must be out of my mind. I need to make these calls somewhere else. Just in case. The last thing your mother needs is to hear me placing all these bets."

"Dad …"

"Sure, just … don't make me regret this," he said, waving off what I was going to say, and heading back downstairs.

I didn't say anything. I knew I was pushing him hard enough as it was. This was going to work, though. The problem was, I needed more. I needed more stuff to bet on after this. And maybe something outside of sports.

I spent the next several hours alternating between homework and working on my list of stuff to gamble on. Actually, it wasn't as hard as I thought it would be. The dream was still pretty clear in my head, every year I lived of it. Hell, sometimes, I remembered stuff from the dream better than I remembered stuff from my own life.

Still, it had to be something that dream me had been paying attention to, which did put a big limit on the things I remembered.

A few hours later, I headed downstairs to grab something to eat, having slept through lunch. I was almost to the bottom of the stairs when I heard my mother's voice coming from the kitchen. I stopped cold and started to turn back around. I wasn't hungry enough to deal with whatever was making her sound so angry.

"No, that's not acceptable. None of these medications are working."

I stopped in my tracks. I knew it was wrong to eavesdrop, but I was getting more and more worried about her health, and it sounded like Dad had finally gotten her to go see the doctor.

There was a pause, and I could hear her pacing, clearly listening to whatever the other person was saying.

"Don't tell me to be patient. I've been patient. For weeks now, I've tried everything you've prescribed, and nothing helps."

Another pause. I eased down a few more steps, careful to avoid the squeaky third one from the bottom.

"The Imitrex isn't touching it anymore. Neither is the Fioricept. And the preventatives you gave me might as well be sugar pills."

There was another long silence.

"I don't care what the insurance company approves! I need something that works. These headaches are killing me. I can barely function."

The pacing stopped. When she spoke again, her voice was quieter. She sounded like she was begging. Pleading with him.

"You don't understand. I can't … I can't live like this."

The quiet voice was gone after the next long pause.

"Then what good are you?" she yelled.

The sound of the phone slamming into its cradle made me jump. Then came the soft sounds of crying, muffled like she was covering her face with her hands.

I backed up the stairs as quietly as I could and went back to my room. She'd be mad if she knew I was listening, and I knew she didn't want me seeing her like that.

I needed to talk to Dad about her. He needed to get her to a specialist. There was something wrong, and it wasn't just headaches. If they were just treating the symptoms, then they'd never find it.

I couldn't spend all of Sunday at home doing homework, though. I also had to go to Eduardo's to help out, as part of the plan to keep him out of the gang. After meeting Rafe and seeing how much influence he clearly had over Eduardo, it was all the more imperative.

It also meant that there was still no rest for the weary. I could have kicked myself for sleeping so late.

By early afternoon, I found myself on a ladder hammering another nail into a fresh facing board along the south side of the house. The wood was good, sturdy cedar Eduardo's dad had brought back from work, or somewhere. I'd seen the rotted facing boards and suggested they change them out, both because they looked kind of bad and because the rot could spread into the side boards or even to the edge of the roof, which would allow rodents and other small pests into the attic.

Eduardo's mom had loved the idea, and had wanted to get the facing boards changed for a while, but she said if it was going to be done, it was going to be done right. Which meant using a good solid wood and painting it well.

And a lot of work would be done by Eduardo and me.

"Hand me another nail?" I called down to Eduardo, who was holding the ladder steady.

"So Melanie Barlow really just came up to you?" He asked as he handed a few more up.

I'd been telling him about the after-game trip to the Silver Spoon on Saturday, partially to get him to join us next time. He was comfortable with the other freshman football players we ate lunch with, but I really thought that if he were friends with more of the guys – guys Elijah and the rest wouldn't dare cross – he'd be insulated from their bullshit almost entirely.

He'd also have backup if it ever came to it. I could just imagine what Rafe would do if he came face to face with Andre, Spencer, or Nathan, each of whom, individually, outweighed Rafe by a hundred and fifty pounds.

They would have been okay with it. There were enough friends of friends at the diner Saturday night, people who didn't play but were part of the circle, that he wouldn't have been out of place at all.

Of course, getting Eduardo to believe that wasn't an easy task. So, I was trying to sell the upsides.

"Yeah, caught me totally off guard. She was all 'we should study together sometime' with this look, you know?"

"No, I don't. Girls don't look at me like anything."

I paused mid-swing. "That's because you practically dive under a table whenever one walks by."

"I do not," Eduardo protested, but his voice went quiet like it always did when he was uncomfortable.

"Dude, Friday in the cafeteria, Sarah Marti asked if she could borrow a pencil and you nearly knocked over your coke, you freaked out so bad."

"That's different. I wasn't expecting ..."

"That's exactly my point," I said, as I finished securing the board and climbed down a few rungs. "You're acting like girls are going to bite you or something."

"Easy for you to say. You're a big-shot quarterback. Girls are lining up for you. Besides, have you seen her brother? He's a house."

"Not even close. My last relationship went down in flames and she's now dating Mason of all people. And being a quarterback has nothing to do with it. You just need to talk to them like regular people. And Elton is a pretty good guy; he's not going to pound you for talking to his sister."

"Right, regular people who are pretty and smell nice and make me forget how words work."

I couldn't help laughing. "See? You're funny when you relax. Girls like funny guys."

"Blake ..." Eduardo's voice had that warning tone.

"I'm serious! You're a good dude. Smart, decent-looking ..."

"Blake, please stop describing me."

"Fine, fine. Just think about it," I said as I climbed back up. "Pass me another board."

We got back into the rhythm of it, and I started talking about a fight that broke out on Friday in the cafeteria over some kind of nonsense. It wasn't a real fight, just one of those things that happen in high school, but that could be kind of funny.

Once we finished the last board, Eduardo and I headed inside, the amazing smells from the kitchen hitting us. I swear, even if I wasn't trying to stop what could happen in the future, I might still have spent half of each Sunday here fixing stuff, just to get the food his mom made us as a reward.

Mine wasn't a home-cooking kind of family, but even the times we did, it was nowhere close to what she fed us. It was a good thing I did so much exercise every week, or I'd have weighed three hundred pounds by now!

We were coming from the rear of the house after washing up when Alex, Eduardo's brother, came thundering down the stairs, almost bowling into us.

"Hey, watch it," Eduardo said.

Like all older brothers, he found Alex much more annoying than Alex really was. It was that sibling reflex. I could kind of relate to that, although Alex was a good kid, and mine was an honest-to-God psychopath … but still.

"Mom said I should help!"

"When did she say that?"

"I don't know. Like twenty minutes ago, but I had to finish something first."

"Yeah, so you just happen to come offer to help when we're on the way back in, after we're done. Just like always."

"We appreciate the offer, though," I said, patting Alex on the shoulder. "There's always next time. We're going to have to change out the gutters. They're cracked pretty good on that side of the house."

"Ohh," Alex said, clearly not wanting to actually do any work.

I swear, the kid needed to learn a poker face. Eduardo wasn't much better, shooting me a look for backing up his brother instead of piling on with him.

"So I was talking to Tommy Newton, and he knows you and I are friends, and he said his brother Calvin said you were really throwing well. He said you threw for like forty yards against Trinity."

Calvin Newton was one of our cornerbacks. I actually didn't know him super well, only in passing, so it was interesting that he was talking to his family about me.

"It was only thirty-five and I'm only as good as my receivers, but yeah, I've been having some good games."

"It sucks that the coach still makes you run the ball all the time. You guys would be winning every game if you could throw more."

"Ha, I'll tell Coach you think so. Maybe he'll listen to you, because he doesn't listen to me."

"No," he said, getting shy at the idea I might mention him to anyone.

"Hey, you want to come see a game sometime? I could probably get you down by the field before kickoff. Maybe even sneak you onto the sidelines for a minute."

Alex's eyes went wide as he yelled, "For real?"

"Blake, you don't have to ..." Eduardo started.

"ARE YOU SERIOUS?" Alex practically bounced off the walls.

"Mijo, inside voice," Eduardo's mom said, coming out of the kitchen, probably trying to find out what all the ruckus was about.

"Mom! Blake said I could come to his game! And go on the field!"

"Did he now?" She raised an eyebrow at me, but her smile was warm. "Well, that's very nice of him."

"Thank you - thank you - thank you!" Alex wrapped his arms around my waist in a tight hug.

"Okay, I think it's just about time to eat. Eduardo, you and Alex go clean up the tools and put away the ladder, and then get Alex washed up and come eat. Blake, come sit down and eat something."

"I should help clean up outside ..."

"No, no, no," Mrs. Guzman said, her tone leaving no room for argument. "You've done more than enough. Sit!"

"But Mom ..." Eduardo protested.

"Now, please." She pointed toward the door. "Blake is our guest."

"Really, I don't mind ..."

"Mijo," she fixed me with that look all moms seem to master. "Sit."

I sat.

Eduardo looked annoyed and I gave him an apologetic look. He shrugged and took his brother by the shoulder, herding him toward the door. We both knew what mothers were like. We were helpless against them.

The smell of whatever was cooking got even stronger as she took a big spoonful and dropped it on a plate with some freshly made tortillas.

"Those two," Mrs. Guzman said, shaking her head. "Always fighting."

"They're just playing. You should see me and my brother. They're angels compared to us."

That might just be the biggest understatement in history.

"Yes, normal brother stuff that drives their mother crazy," she said, but she was smiling.

"I met Rafe the other day," I blurted out.

I had actually wanted to find a moment alone with Eduardo's mom to talk about Rafe ever since he had come over, but I hadn't had the chance. He was clearly the biggest issue with keeping Eduardo on the straight and narrow, and I needed to know more about him.

The change in her expression was immediate. Her smile vanished, and it looked as if she had smelled something rotten.

"When?"

"He showed up here. You and Alex were out shopping, and I was working in the garden with Eduardo."

"That boy has the devil in him. He's no good. No good at all."

"I got that impression."

"He's the reason we moved here. Away from Midland, away from ... all of that. Eduardo doesn't know the whole story. But Rafe, he's involved with very bad people. Dangerous people. And he doesn't care who he drags down with him. Eduardo looked up to him because he was the older cousin and had a car, but he's into too much. I was very scared for my baby. He wouldn't be the first in the family that boy has poisoned."

"What do you mean?"

"Two of Eduardo's cousins are in prison because of Rafe. Long sentences. They were good boys, like Eduardo. But Rafe ... he has a way of making trouble sound exciting. He causes good boys to make bad choices."

"So you moved away."

"It's been hard on Hector, with all the driving, but we couldn't ignore the signs. The way Rafe started showing up more often, talking to Eduardo about easy money, about respect. Just like he did with the others. I didn't know he was coming here. Has he been around more than that one time?"

"Not that I've seen. And Eduardo stood up to him when he was here. Told him to leave."

The relief on her face was palpable. "He did?"

"Yeah. It wasn't easy for him, but he did it."

"Good. That's so good." She reached across the table and squeezed my hand. "You know, Blake, since you and Eduardo became friends, I've seen such a change in him. He's more confident, more focused in school. He talks about the future now."

"I'm glad. I'm really happy we met. He's my friend. Honestly, getting to know all of you has been amazing."

"Mom!" Alex's voice carried from the back door. "Eduardo won't let me put the tools away!"

"Because you'll mess it up!" Eduardo shouted back.

"Will not!"

Mrs. Guzman rolled her eyes, but her smile had returned.

"Dios mío! Those two ..." She pushed back from the table. "Excuse me, Blake. I better go make sure they don't kill each other."

I watched her hurry toward the door, thinking about everything she'd said about Rafe. I wondered what he had done to get the other two cousins locked up. And if Eduardo knew about it.

Chapter 25

"Come on, I'm just trying to understand what happened," I said as Eduardo and I walked into the cafeteria.

I'd first asked about his cousins the previous night, after we all finished dinner just before I'd gone home, but he'd found a way to keep dodging the question. I really wanted to get a better idea of how Rafe had gotten his cousins to make such huge mistakes. His mom would have answered, but kids would never tell parents, or aunts, everything.

They would tell their cousin.

"It's complicated."

"Yeah, I get that. But how did he convince them? You said one of them tried to rob a bank or something? Like, what the hell, that isn't small stuff. How do you convince someone to do something that'll put you in federal prison?"

"It was an ATM. He hooked it to the back of his truck and tried to haul it away so they could break into it later. And I don't know, he just … did. That wasn't the first thing that Rafe had them do. It just kind of escalated."

"Okay, I get that, but how did it start."

"Blake, can we drop this? Please?"

I tried not to make a face. I didn't want to keep pushing him, and maybe even push him away, but if he talked about this stuff, he might be less likely to follow in their footsteps. Still, there was a limit to how much I could ask in a short amount of time before it went from friendly checking to actually annoying.

The decision was more or less made for me when Mickey Evans appeared beside us, practically materializing out of the lunch crowd.

"Blake! We were talking, and we think you should join the rest of us, instead of sitting off by yourself," he said, jerking his thumb toward the back of the cafeteria where the football players and cheerleaders held court. "Time to upgrade from freshman territory."

I looked over at my usual table where Miguel, Connor, and even Li were already sitting. It didn't seem right, abandoning all of them just 'cause I had a chance at an upgrade.

"Thanks, but I'm good where I am," I said. "Those guys were there for me when I needed backup. Can't just ditch them now that I moved up to JV."

Mickey looked over at that side of the cafeteria, first at my group of friends, and then his gaze slid over to where Elijah and his crew sat. The rest of the team couldn't have been oblivious to the politics that had been going on on the freshman side of the team, even if they did choose to ignore it.

"Yeah, those guys seem cool," he said, looking at them then glancing with an odd expression at Elijah and the rest. "Go ahead and bring them along."

If they disliked Elijah even half as much as I did, it meant I'd have fewer problems when he moved up from the freshman team and in with the rest. That was maybe the best thing about getting to JV early; it helped me set up some insulation against him.

Eduardo, however, was looking green and I knew how Li would feel about moving to a whole new area with a whole new group of people. It would do her good. Eduardo too.

I made up my mind.

"Sure. We'll be over in a minute.

"Perfect."

Mickey grinned and headed back to the other football players.

"That was decent of you. Most guys would've bailed the second they got invited to sit with the older kids," Eduardo said after Mickey left.

"I'm not most guys. And you're going, too."

"Me?"

"Yes. I'm not leaving any of my friends behind. Let's go break the news to them."

"You're serious?" Eduardo asked as we walked toward our usual table.

"Dead serious. Think about it, this'll be great for everyone. The freshman guys need to build relationships with the older players they'll be teaming up with next year." I gave him a light nudge with my elbow. "And you and Li need to get out of your shells more."

"I don't need ..."

"Not taking 'no' for an answer," I cut him off. "Consider it part of your personal growth plan. You and I are sticking together."

Eduardo let out a dramatic sigh and said, "Fine."

"Good. Hey guys," I said as we got to the table. "We're moving. Over there."

I pointed to the table with the varsity and JV teams and almost all the cheerleaders.

"About time," Jamal said. "We'll miss you, man."

"No, you don't get it." I made a sweeping gesture that took in everyone at the table. "*We're* moving. All of us."

"For real?" Connor's face lit up.

"Sweet!" Miguel was already grabbing his tray.

"What?" Li's eyes went wide. "No, absolutely not."

"Yes, absolutely yes," I countered. "Come on, it'll be fun. It's already decided. Everyone up."

Miguel, Tyrell, and Connor were already standing and helping Jamal to his feet. The guys' excitement was almost infectious, except Li and Eduardo seemed immune. To look at them, you'd think I was leading them in front of a firing squad."

"I can't believe I'm doing this," Li muttered, but she picked up her tray.

"You'll thank me later," I promised.

As our group made its way across the cafeteria, I caught sight of Elijah watching us. He wasn't even trying to keep the jealousy off his face as he saw where we were going. Part of me felt satisfied seeing him stew, knowing he was seeing the end of any chance of his becoming the big man on the team. I looked away, though. Antagonizing him would only make him more likely to do something stupid out of desperation.

We reached the JV table where Mickey had already made space for us.

"Welcome to the big leagues," he said with a grin.

"Thanks for having us."

We were off to one end, kind of an add-on to JV, with me as a buffer between my guys and the JV team, with the cheerleaders between JV and varsity. The two long tables they'd pushed together were absolutely packed.

Even better, a few of the freshman cheerleaders were seated down on this side. Most importantly, one in particular.

"Uhh, I'm here, Li, you sit across from me and Eduardo, you sit there," I said, pointing at two seats.

They were both kind of in a daze and did what I said. It wasn't until Eduardo had put his stuff down and looked over to a brightly smiling Sarah that he paled and looked over at me, shooting me a glare. I gave him the same smile Sarah was giving him.

"You two know each other, right?" I said, trying to be very helpful.

"Yeah. We have math together. Hey," Sarah said.

"Uhh, hi," Eduardo replied oh so smoothly.

Sarah had it in hand though. I saw her brother Elton giving Eduardo a hard look and thought I might need to talk to him at practice, let him know Eddie was a good guy and he didn't have to worry.

"And this is Li. She's trying out for the basketball team soon."

"Nice," Drew, one of the sophomores, said. "Welcome to the cool kids' table."

Li just kind of bobbed her head, unable to find her voice. I wasn't worried. This was how it went for both Eduardo and Li the first time they moved to our table. Miguel and the rest settled in alright on their own. It helped that they were already part of the football program, so this was just an upgrade, not a whole new thing.

"Since when did we become a daycare?" Jorden said from a few seats down, ruining the mood. "This is getting ridiculous. There's barely room to breathe."

Jerry rolled his eyes. "Drop it, man. They'll all be on the teams next year anyway. Plus, we need Blake with us."

"Oh yeah, can't function without the golden boy," Jorden snapped, shoving back from the table. "You guys used to have some pride."

He stormed off, tray in hand. He kind of lost steam after a few steps, trying to figure out where to go. Unfortunately, Elijah had been watching and waved him over. Great, just what I needed. My biggest JV critic teaming up with my least favorite freshman. But what could I do? Jorden had hated me since the moment I took his starting spot.

"Good riddance," Andre said, watching Jorden drop into a seat next to Elijah. "That guy's been blaming everyone but himself for his problems since day one. I'm sick of hearing it."

A whole lot of the guys kind of mumbled agreement or shook their heads.

"Man, I'm not gonna miss that drama," Ronald Lewis, one of the other seniors on JV, said.

Everyone agreed and then went back to what they were talking about. I was just happy I had them solidly on my side. It was setting up so that I'd have plenty of backup over the next four years.

The conversation shifted to lighter topics. Li gradually relaxed as Sarah drew her into a discussion about their shared AP Biology class. Eduardo even managed a few contributions here and there, though he still looked ready to bolt at any moment.

Yep. I'd done a good thing.

At one point I kind of glanced down toward the middle of the two tables where the cheerleaders were all gathered, and Melanie caught my eye. She gave me a sly smile and then a slow wink that made my stomach tighten up. She didn't get up or anything; she had a good spot among the senior cheerleaders. I kept looking over, stealing glances, and caught her doing the same thing several times.

Not a bad way to start the week.

The flirting looks and smiles kept happening every time I saw Melanie, all through Tuesday and into Wednesday, which was a lot more now that we were eating lunch together, or at least at the same table.

She didn't stop to talk to me, either at lunch or the times we saw each other after school, while the cheerleaders were practicing over on the track and we were on the practice field. I would just catch her looking at me, and she'd give me that sly, playful smile she had.

To be honest, sometimes she caught me looking at her. I found myself drawn to her. Part of it was because of the crush I had on her in the dream life, but the rest was all right here and now. She was beautiful, for starters. Golden-blond wavy hair that reached just below her shoulder blades, these captivating green eyes behind thick lashes, a smattering of cute freckles across her cheeks and nose that really stood out on her fair skin that was much less tanned than most of the other cheerleaders.

She could say so much with those eyes, too. It's what made those glances get to me so much, I think. Those eyes really drew me in.

If I didn't have memories of dating as an adult from the dream, I might have let this go on for weeks. It was painfully obvious she liked me and I certainly liked her, but I would have been too scared to pull the trigger. But I remembered some of the lessons dream me had learned.

She was probably as nervous as I was. And if it didn't work out, so what? The worst she could say was no.

Which was why, when I saw her coming down the hall toward me with some of her friends in between the last two periods, I veered toward her, kind of cutting her off and separating her from her friends. She gave a little giggle and moved to duck around between the wall and me, but I put my arm out, blocking her path.

Not touching her, but making it clear I wanted her to stop and talk.

"Oh!" Melanie's surprise was so obviously fake it was almost funny. "Blake, you scared me."

"Did I? I'm surprised because you've been watching me since you turned the corner."

"Someone thinks highly of himself," she said, but the small smile she couldn't hide as she looked away for a second said she liked my direct approach.

"Just calling it like I see it. What are we going to do about this thing between us?"

"Thing? I have no idea what you're talking about."

"No? Ohh, my mistake then," I said, dropping my arm and starting to turn away. "In that case, there's this other girl …"

Her hand shot out and grabbed my forearm. "Wait."

I turned back, fighting to keep my expression neutral. "Yes?"

"Maybe …" She looked down at her shoes, then back up through her lashes. "Maybe there is something."

"That's what I thought," I said, stepping closer to her. "So let's do something about it. Jimmy's, Friday night?"

"Friday?" She pursed her lips, pretending to think it over. "I might have plans …"

"Cancel them."

"Pretty confident, aren't you?"

"Should I not be?"

"I suppose I could move some things around. Now move, I have to get to class."

"Good, it's a date." I stepped back and extended my arm, "After you."

Instead of walking around me like a normal person would, she somehow managed to squeeze past me, even though there was plenty of room, brushing her chest against my side. The move was so calculated it would have been funny if it wasn't also so very effective.

I stood there, watching her walk back toward her friends. Just before she got to them, she glanced back over her shoulder, shooting me that knowing smile of hers again.

As soon as she rejoined her friends, they immediately huddled around her, giggling and sneaking obvious looks in my direction as they hurried down the hall."

When they were out of sight, I turned and headed to my next class, feeling pretty good about myself and the way that went.

That feeling didn't go away for the rest of the day. I was riding high all through practice, although Coach did have to yell at me once to get my head in the game when he caught me looking over at Melanie.

The guys found it hysterical and teased me for the rest of practice, but I didn't care. Nothing was going to knock me off the high I was riding.

Dad's cruiser was in the driveway when I got home, which meant he'd had the day off today, since it was also there when I left for school. I honestly had trouble keeping up with his schedule since it changed kind of often. Midlands was a big city for West Texas, but it wasn't actually a big city, and its police force was on the small side, which meant any small change, such as someone needing a day off or someone having to be in court, could reshuffle the whole department's schedule.

At least for the deputies.

"Hey, how was school?" Dad called from his recliner when I walked through the door.

Mom wasn't around, so I assumed she was in her room lying down. I guess she could have been at work, but she'd missed a lot of days lately cause of her headaches, and odds were her car was just in the garage.

"Amazing. Practice went great. Coach finally let me open up the passing game during the scrimmage."

Dad perked up, muting the TV. "Yeah? They finally letting you show what you can do?"

"God, I can only hope. Ohh, also, I don't know if you're working on Friday, but I'm going to be out Friday night, okay?"

"Sure? Something with the team?"

"Nope. I have a date."

"Good. We haven't seen much of Brandy lately. Everything okay there?"

"Actually, we broke up about a month ago. This is someone new. Melanie. She's a JV cheerleader."

"I'd ask if you were okay, but having a date with a new girl tells me you're probably doing fine."

"Yeah. It was for the best. Melanie's great, though."

"Well, have fun," Dad said, grabbing the remote to unmute it and then paused. "You remember the rules, right?"

I couldn't help rolling my eyes. "Don't do anything that ends with someone dead, pregnant, or in jail. Got it covered."

"That's my boy," Dad said, and unmuted the TV.

I laughed and headed upstairs. My weekends were pretty busy, and I had a lot of homework to do, since I was supposed to go to Eduardo's again on Sunday. With a date on Friday night, that wouldn't give me much room for doing homework, so I needed to get busy tonight.

I walked into my room, tossed my bag across the room to my desk, and then froze in place. Something was wrong. It took a moment for the smell to hit my brain. It was like the worst parts of the locker room, but concentrated. Stale and eye-watering.

I turned several times, looking around the room, trying to figure out where it was coming from. My bed covers were messed up, pulled back in places they shouldn't be. I yanked them away completely and saw it. A massive yellow stain in the center of my mattress.

I didn't even have to take a guess at what had happened. I knew.

"Son of a ..." I spun and stormed back downstairs, taking the steps two at a time.

"Dad!" I said when I got to the bottom of the stairs and around the corner into the living room. "I need a new mattress. And I'm putting a lock on my door."

Dad sat forward in his recliner. "Hold on there. What's going on?"

"Josh pissed on my bed."

"Blake, that's a pretty serious accusation."

"Yeah? I think it's a pretty serious thing for someone to do."

"How do you know it was Josh?"

"Because I'm not an idiot. I know you didn't do it ... and I know I didn't do it ... and unless Mom's gotten really creative with her revenge for me not making my bed, that leaves exactly one suspect."

"Why would Josh do something like that?"

"Are you serious? You know why he'd do something like this. Hell, it shouldn't even be surprising. I've heard you and Mom fighting about how he's been out of control for weeks. This isn't even the worst thing he's done."

"What do you mean?"

"Remember when Mom grounded me for 'hitting' Josh? He stole one of my Peewee medals, and when I caught him, he slammed his own face into the doorframe and then told Mom I punched him. He's a vindictive, evil little piece of shit."

"Blake …"

"No, Dad. Josh is messed up. Like, *seriously* messed up. And everybody keeps acting like it's fine, like he's just going through a phase or something. But normal kids don't do this stuff."

Dad sat there for a long moment, his jaw working. I know I was being too hard on him. He'd been arguing with Mom to get Josh into treatment. The fact that Mom was blocking it wasn't entirely Dad's fault.

Finally, he stood up and said, "Alright. Let's get that mattress out to the garage. We can put it out with the heavy trash next week. You can use my old sleeping bag tonight, and we'll get you a new mattress tomorrow."

"That's it? We're just going to pretend this didn't happen?"

"I'm not pretending anything, but right now, you need a place to sleep, and I need some time to think about how to handle this."

"Fine, but I'm putting a lock on my door."

"No. Blake, that will just cause more problems around here that we don't need."

"So what? I'm just supposed to leave everything I own where Josh can get to it? My room isn't safe. Nothing in this house is safe while he's here. We can pretend all day that everything's fine, but we both know that Josh is a problem. And if you won't let me protect my stuff, then fine. I will go stay at Eduardo's or something."

An empty threat. The Guzman's didn't particularly have room for me, and it wasn't like I wouldn't run the idea by them first.

"That is not an option, and I don't care for you threatening me."

I took a deep breath and tried to dial back my anger. Dad wasn't the 'you better respect me' kind of dad, but that didn't mean it was right for me to disrespect him either.

"I'm not trying to threaten you, Dad. But you have to see that this is out of control. This isn't normal teenage stuff, anymore."

Dad didn't respond, but I could see him considering.

"Look, I get it," I continued. "I'm not trying to tell you what to do about Josh, that's between you and Mom. But you have to at least let me protect myself and my stuff. If you're not going to force the issue with Mom about getting Josh help, then at least let me keep my things safe."

He still didn't say anything, but I'd made my point. Anything more would just be repeating myself. So I shut up and let him decide.

"Fine," he said finally. "We'll put a lock on your door."

"Thank you. I'm sorry for being a pain in the ass about this. It's just ... I've got a lot going on right now. I need to focus on school and football, and I really don't want to make things even harder by getting into fights with Josh."

"I know, and you're not a pain in the ass. I'm sorry you've been caught up in all of this. Come on, let's go move that mattress and find you a sleeping bag. We can stop by the hardware store tomorrow after school."

"What about Josh?"

"Let me worry about Josh. You focus on your stuff."

Chapter 26

We didn't get the lock on the door until Friday afternoon. Dad wanted to wait until Mom was out of the house to 'not cause an argument,' which I guess I could see his point. But it also meant I put stuff I cared about in my backpack and hauled it with me to school on Thursday.

Josh was escalating and I really didn't trust him not to do anything stupid, even for just the one day.

At least we got the mattress on Thursday. Mom saw us but was lying down on the couch and, other than looking at us carrying the mattress in, didn't really have much to say.

I really did feel better when Dad put the new lock on my door. I talked him out of just replacing the knob with one with a lock, since I thought Josh could get that open pretty easily, and instead had him install a hinge and I put a padlock on it, so that Josh would have to literally destroy my door to get in.

While that wasn't out of the realm of possibility, at least that might finally be him going too far and actually get him in trouble.

By Friday night, though, I'd put all of that out of my mind as I got ready for my date. I dressed in jeans and a nice button-up shirt, going for nice but not too fancy. Jimmy's wasn't exactly the Ritz, and church clothes felt like a bit of a stretch for there.

I was actually way less nervous than I'd thought I'd be. Maybe it was because I'd experienced dating in the dream life, so it wasn't as scary to me as the few dates I'd been on in middle school. I'd been a wreck before the first dates I'd been on with Brandy in eighth grade, before we became a couple.

Now, I felt alright.

Dad was working the night shift tonight and left as soon as we got the lock on my door and Mom had gone to work for the first time in a week, so that left me on my own.

Thankfully, Melanie's place was between my house and the school, so the walk wasn't bad, and we weren't far from Broad Street where Jimmy's, the burger place where we were going, was located.

Her house was a little two-story place that appeared really well kept, like someone had put a lot of care into the way the yard looked, and the front porch light was on.

It was just starting to get a little cool out so I'd worn a jacket, but otherwise, it wasn't too bad. I rang the doorbell and a few moments later, an older woman opened the door. She seemed a little too old to be Melanie's mother, maybe in her mid-fifties with silver-streaked hair, but there was a resemblance there.

"You must be Blake," she said, giving me a warm smile. "Come in. Melanie will be down in a minute."

I stepped into the entryway, noting the family photos on the walls. Except for a few pictures with a man around the same age as the woman who answered the door, all of the pictures had just Melanie and two other women in them. In the pictures with the man, Melanie was really little, but the other women confused me. There was the older lady who answered the door and then another woman who looked maybe ten or fifteen years older than Melanie.

The age gap was a weird combo, and I could only guess that she was Melanie's older sister, although why waiting so long between kids was a wonder.

Before I could contemplate it any further, footsteps on the stairs drew my attention. Melanie appeared, wearing a blue dress that made her eyes pop.

It wasn't overly fancy, but it was still very nice and for a moment, I wondered if I'd miscalculated wearing the jeans.

The other woman in the picture appeared from what looked like the kitchen and solved the mystery when she said, "Hi. I'm Donna, Mel's sister."

"Uhh, hi," I said, not expecting to meet so much of her family on the first date.

"Okay, we're leaving!" Melanie grabbed my arm. "Bye, Mom, bye, Donna!"

"Have him back by eleven," her mom called after us as Melanie practically dragged me outside.

Once we were down the block, Melanie burst out laughing. "You looked like you were about to pass out in there."

"Did not," I tried to sound offended but couldn't help grinning.

I'd been so calm and collected when I'd left my house. What had happened?

"Please, you were so nervous. It was kind of cute, actually."

"I just wasn't expecting to meet your whole family."

"Yeah, I'd hoped to get to the door myself, but I couldn't find my earrings. You survived, though."

"Barely."

She'd been smart enough to wear tennis shoes which actually went with the mid-thigh length dress, although it was a little cold for that. I saw her shivering and pulled off my jacket.

She looked surprised and then smiled when I put it around her shoulders.

"Well, look at that. Chivalry isn't dead."

"Not if I have anything to say about it," I said.

We weren't the only people walking. There were other people about, taking evening strolls and even some kids I knew from school heading somewhere.

"So, the other day, you were telling me about the extra school-work you're doing. I've asked around and everyone says you're really busting your ass."

"I'm just trying to keep my options open."

"But everyone says you're amazing at football."

She said it as if to say, why would I need any other options?

"Football's great, but it's not guaranteed. One bad hit and that's it, you know? I don't want to be that guy who peaks in high school, working at the scrap yard, telling anyone who'll listen about his glory days."

She nodded slowly. "That makes sense."

We fell into silence for half a block. Although we'd done this flirting thing back and forth, we hadn't actually spent much time talking to each other before now.

"What about you?" I asked as we approached the restaurant. "What do you do besides cheerleading?"

"Promise not to laugh?"

"Never."

She rolled her eyes. "I'm teaching myself Japanese. I want to study abroad there in college."

"That's actually really cool. Why would I laugh at that?"

"Because most people think it's weird. They assume I just watch anime or something."

"Do you?"

"Sometimes, but not much," she admitted. "But that's not why! I think the culture is fascinating. The way they blend traditional and modern, it's amazing."

She launched into an explanation of Japanese architecture as we reached Jimmy's, her hands moving animatedly as she talked. She actually knew quite a lot about it. That was honestly very surprising. I'm not sure what I expected her to say, but that wasn't it.

Jimmy's was packed with the Friday night crowd. There weren't a lot of restaurants in Wheaton, and half of those were fast food, so this one could get pretty busy. And tonight was no different. Thankfully, one of the hostesses was also on the JV squad with Melanie and got us a booth near the back.

It was warmer in here, enough that Melanie took off my jacket, but she didn't hand it back. Instead, she folded it over and sat it on the seat next to her after she slid into the booth across from me.

"I love this place," she said, picking up a menu she probably didn't need. "Everyone acts like it's just a burger joint, but their chicken is amazing."

A waitress with frizzy red hair and a nametag reading 'Darlene' appeared with her order pad. "What can I get y'all?"

"Cheeseburger, fries, and a chocolate shake," I said.

"Grilled chicken salad and a Diet Coke for me," Melanie said, handing back the menu.

"Diet?" I raised an eyebrow.

Melanie was in amazing shape and got a ton of exercise from cheerleading, so the diet soda was a little unexpected. Most girls around here just drank coke or sweet tea.

At least the ones I knew.

"Hey, cheerleading requires a certain look. Besides, their salads are huge. And I plan on stealing some of your fries."

"Ohh, you do, do you?"

"So, what's up with you and Elijah? He's in my math class, and to hear Brandy talk about you guys, you backstabbed them and ruined their chances for making JV. She went on this huge rant about you the other day at practice."

"Ha. They never had a chance to make JV. I only did 'cause I got lucky. Elijah got put on the second string because he was trying to throw games in some kind of head game power play. He has no one to blame for how he ended up but himself. And Brandy chose to be with Mason. She picked her bed. Literally."

"She says you made up the stuff about her cheating with Mason."

"I didn't make up the fact that less than twenty-four hours after we broke up, she was dating him. But hey, maybe that's a coincidence."

Darlene arrived with our drinks. I took a sip of my shake while Melanie stirred her soda, and we fell into a kind of uncomfortable silence for a minute.

"What about you?" I asked, breaking the lull in conversation. "How's cheerleading going?"

"It's fun, mostly. Competition season is coming up, so practices are getting intense. Coach keeps changing the routine because some of the girls can't get the timing right on their stunts."

She talked for a bit about what she'd experienced in junior competitions and what she hoped for from the ones coming up. I pointed out that if she moved to Japan for college, I wasn't sure how much cheerleading there would be, but she didn't have the same goal as me. This was just something she was doing through high school.

The jukebox kicked on with "Sweet Home Alabama," and Melanie perked up.

"You like Skynyrd?" I asked.

"Love them. Donna got me into it before, well, when I was little. Dad's vinyl collection was like her prized possession growing up."

"Was?"

286

Something flickered across her face. "He passed when I was little."

"I'm sorry."

"It's okay. I barely remember him." She took a long sip of her drink. "What about you? You strike me as a top forties guy."

"I can appreciate both."

Our food arrived, and conversation flowed easily between bites. We were actually getting along a lot better than I could have hoped. I was reaching for the ketchup when familiar voices approached.

"Well, well, well." Jerry stood at our table, flanked by Patrick, Miles, and Elton. "What do we have here?"

"Looks like our QB finally scored," Patrick said with an exaggerated wink.

"Don't you guys have somewhere else to be?"

"Nope," Miles grinned. "This is quality entertainment."

"Speaking of entertainment," Elton said, "what's with you playing matchmaker with my sister and that new kid?"

"Eduardo's a good guy," I said. "And Sarah seems to like him."

"Yeah, well." Elton crossed his arms. "If anything happens to her ..."

"You'll come after me. Got it."

"As long as we're clear," he growled, but there was a hint of a smile on his face.

"Alright, let's leave the lovebirds alone," Jerry said, herding the others away.

They settled at a table across the restaurant, occasionally throwing thumbs up and kissy faces our way.

"Sorry about them," I said.

"Don't be. It's sweet how they look out for each other." Melanie stole one of my fries. "Even if they're huge dorks about it."

"I guess we should get the check," I said, spotting Darlene heading back our way with it.

"Thanks for dinner," Melanie said when I pulled out my wallet.

"My pleasure."

Outside, the temperature had dropped further, and Melanie shivered before slipping my jacket back on. Without thinking, I reached for her hand. Her fingers interlocked with mine, and she gave a small squeeze.

"So, what's it like having an older sister?" I asked as we walked. "Must be nice having someone to look up to."

"Donna's ... complicated. We don't really talk much anymore. What about you and Joshua? What's he like?"

"He's going through some stuff right now. It's been hard on everyone, especially my mom."

"What kind of stuff?"

"It's hard to explain. Just ... stuff."

"That's rough. I'm sorry."

"Yeah, well, it is what it is. So tell me more about your architecture obsession. What got you interested in that?"

"Nice deflection," she said, but went along with the subject change. "I saw this documentary about Japanese temples when I was twelve, and something just clicked. The way they use space and light, how every detail has meaning ..."

She continued explaining various architectural styles as we walked, her free hand gesturing expressively. I wasn't really following half of it, but I was enjoying just hearing her talk. Hearing the sound of her voice.

Much too soon, we reached her front porch.

"I had a really good time tonight," Melanie said, turning to face me as we stepped onto the porch.

"Me too."

We stood there for a moment, neither moving. Her eyes met mine, and I found myself leaning forward. She tilted her head up slightly, and our lips met. The kiss was soft and brief, but perfect.

When we pulled apart, Melanie's cheeks were flushed pink. She bit her lower lip, trying to hide a smile.

"Goodnight, Blake," she whispered.

"Goodnight."

I waited until she was safely inside before heading home. The walk back felt shorter somehow, maybe because I spent most of it replaying the evening in my mind.

I was still floating when I got to the house and walked in the front door, thinking nothing would take this feeling away. I was reliving that kiss with Melanie over and over.

My good feeling came to a screeching halt as soon as I walked through the door.

"Blake Andrew Sims, get in here right now!"

She was standing in the middle of the kitchen, arms crossed, with Josh hovering behind her with a smirk on his face, since she couldn't see him. She looked pissed and I knew he'd done something to try to get me in trouble.

I wanted to wipe that stupid smile off his face.

"You want to explain why there's a lock on your bedroom door?"

There it was. Josh had tried to get into my room and saw the lock. My room was past his down the upstairs hallway and the bathroom was before his, so he wouldn't just happen to see it walking by. He'd have to walk down to my room to see it.

"It's there to protect my stuff, and Dad approved it. He installed it this morning for me."

"You went to him without discussing it with me?" Her voice climbed higher. "I'm your mother. You don't get to make decisions like this behind my back."

"Behind your back? I just said Dad literally installed it himself."

"Only because you went to him without talking to me. You're always trying to pit us against each other, telling me one thing and him another, or not telling him when I tell you no. I won't have it."

"I didn't do anything like that. And how does he even know I have a lock on my door unless he tried to get into it while I was out?"

"That's not the point," Mom cut in. "I won't have you hiding things in there. For all I know, you could be doing drugs ..."

"Drugs? Are you serious? You know they randomly test athletes, and I'm not going to do anything that will put my football career in jeopardy. You want to know what I'm doing in there? Homework. That's it. The only reason I need a lock is because he keeps stealing my stuff ... and he literally peed on my mattress."

"That's a lie," Joshua said, stamping his foot.

"Blake, I will not have you spreading lies. You can't blame your brother for things you have no proof of."

"Proof? Why do you think Dad and I brought that new mattress in a few days ago, or why there's a mattress out in the garage right now waiting for heavy trash day, with a big yellow stain right in the middle of it? Unless someone broke into our house to piss on my bed, or you're suggesting that you or Dad did it, then it had to be Josh!"

She didn't even acknowledge what I said. "I will not have you spreading lies in this house, Blake."

"He's been sneaking out at night, too!" Josh said.

"What? Is this true?"

"Seriously? He says something completely made up and you just believe him, but anything I say is automatically a lie?"

"Do not talk back to me like that! I want that lock off by tomorrow."

"No. Dad approved it, and it's staying. You can talk to him about it."

"It's not fair!" Josh screamed, stamping his foot and storming up the stairs, stomping on each step as hard as he could.

"Get out of my sight." Mom's voice was ice cold.

I headed upstairs, furious. How the hell could she be so blind to how he was acting?

What's worse, I could hear Joshua's theatrical sobbing through the door, and then, of all things, Mom talking to him, trying to soothe him. Like anything had been done to him at all, instead of him not being allowed to break into my room anymore.

I guess the night could have been ruined after all.

Chapter 27

Saturday, we played L.D. Bell High School. I'd already played their freshman team in an away game early in the season, but this time, we were playing at home, which meant we didn't have to do the four-and-a-half-hour bus ride.

It had been my only win on the freshman team, and we repeated it again with a 21-7 win. Weirdly, that was also the score we'd won by when I'd played them as a freshman. The only down part for me was that the hope I'd been holding onto that Coach was changing his mind about letting me make more passes, because we were focusing on it more in practice, didn't happen.

He gave me four real pass plays, which was two more than the last game, one in each quarter. I completed all four. None were monster passes, mostly in the twenty-yard range, but two converted into touchdowns, which was the first time on JV where the majority of the points on the board came from plays where I was passing, instead of running plays.

I could only hope that he saw I was having success with the passes, although I didn't think he did. I think he saw it as their team wasn't expecting long passes since we still hardly ever did it, so they kept our guys out of double coverage, making it easier to complete passes.

I liked to think I could still have completed them, but who knows? He had been a coach for longer than I'd been playing the game, at least in this life, so maybe he knew something I didn't.

Not that I was going to stop pushing for more passes.

The other good thing about playing a home game was that it wasn't that late when we all got to the Silver Spoon. This time I was sitting in a booth with Melanie sitting on one side of me and Joe on the other, with Mickey and two other JV cheerleaders, Hanna and Emily, sitting across from us. I think Joe was annoyed he had to sit next to me on the far inside of the booth while Mickey was sandwiched between the two girls.

I tried to feel bad for him, but I was flying high. Between winning the game and Melanie holding my hand under the table, I'd completely forgotten about the stuff with Josh and Mom the night before. Well, not forgotten, but it wasn't bugging me as much as it had most of the day.

Neither had talked to me about it the next morning and when I saw Dad and tried to talk to him, he said just leave it alone and let him handle it. They hadn't taken the lock off my door by the time I had to leave for the game, at least, so I guess he managed to talk Mom down.

I was just happy to be with my friends. Joe was in mid-story, recounting his glory moments from the game, being as loud as humanly possible.

"... see me? Blam. Right through the line. That's my tenth touch-down this season."

"Because Coach just loves shoving your big ass down the middle of the line," Mickey said.

"Whatever," Joe said, annoyed as all three girls laughed.

"Well, I thought Blake stole the show with those two touch-downs. Coach Holloway really should let you guys do more of those long passes."

"That's what I'm saying," Mickey said.

"Only 'cause it gets you the ball and a moment of glory," Joe said.

"Well, if that isn't the pot calling the kettle black," I said.

"Jesus, the testosterone is getting thick over here. Maybe we should go and let the boys finish arguing," Melanie said, half standing up.

"No, no, no," I said, not letting go of her hand and pulling her back down. "We were just messing around. It's the oldest rivalry in the offense: receivers versus runners."

"Fine, but only 'cause you're cute," she said, which got an 'ooo-hhh' from Mickey and Joe. "Are you going to get a milkshake?"

"I don't know. Still deciding."

"Sorry, I think I misspoke. Order us a chocolate milkshake. I don't want a whole one, so we can share."

I shook my head and laughed, as she got up to let me out so I could go get it. I could hear Mickey making kissing noises as I walked away, and I flipped him off without turning around.

The diner was packed. Wheaton was a football town and the whole place lived for high school sports, so even the regulars were happy to have the team here, even though we weren't the varsity. Many of them had been to the game and would stop and ask kids about the season or give suggestions.

It was a real town affair.

As I waited in line, I looked back at Melanie. We'd only been on the one date and had the one kiss, and that was yesterday, but already, it felt like this was going somewhere. She'd been all over me during the portions of the game and after when we had a chance to socialize, and she'd been glued by my side ever since we got to the diner.

It seemed impossible that this girl I'd been crazy about in my dream life was here with me. We weren't official or anything, but I think we both felt the chemistry hard and knew where this was going.

I got back to the booth with the milkshake, which included the mixing container that held the extra and my soda, and slid back into the booth after Melanie got up to let me in.

"... going with to homecoming," Emily was saying as I sat down.

I suddenly noticed that Hanna was a junior, same as Mickey, Melanie and I were freshmen, and Joe and Emily were sophomores. That seemed like too much of a coincidence, especially since Melanie and I'd gone out on a date.

I smelled a rat and looked over at Melanie, who seemed to read my mind and rolled her eyes at me.

"What about you, fresh? I'm assuming you two are going since you're a couple now."

"We're not a couple," Melanie protested. "We've only been on one date."

"Still, it went well. What about it? Want to be my date to homecoming?"

Melanie took a long sip of our milkshake, making me wait.

"I suppose I could clear my schedule," she said finally, squeezing my hand under the table.

"Way to put pressure on the rest of us," Joe said.

Emily looked across the table at Joe, expectantly. The silence stretched uncomfortably as Joe shifted in his seat, his usual bravado, at least with us guys on the field, gone. It also proved that this had been a setup all along to get Emily and Joe together.

"So, uh, Emily," Joe started, stumbling over the words. "Would you maybe want to, I don't know, go to homecoming? With me?"

"Very smooth," I said, earning an elbow to the ribs.

Emily studied Joe for a long moment, during which I thought he might actually pass out.

"Sure," she said finally. "Why not?"

"Really?" Joe's voice cracked on the word.

He was actually surprised. Poor fool didn't realize he'd just been set up. Not that it was such a terrible fate. Emily was pretty and seemed nice, although I didn't know her well.

"And then there was one," Mickey said, looking at Hanna. "Good thing we already figured this out, right?"

"Did we?" Hanna asked innocently. "I don't remember agreeing to anything."

Mickey's face fell. "But I thought ... I mean, we talked about ..."

Hanna burst out laughing. "Your face! Of course we're going together, you idiot."

"When did this happen?" Joe asked.

"I'm honestly shocked. I've never seen someone with so little game. Hanna, did you hit your head or something?" I asked, grinning at Mickey.

"Shut up. Both of you."

We burst out laughing.

"We started talking a few weeks ago," Hanna confirmed. "And went out last weekend. It took forever to get him to realize I was trying to get him to ask me out. All he wants to talk about is football and some pass he caught two weeks ago."

"It was a really good catch," Mickey protested.

"It really was," Joe agreed. "The way ..."

"No," Melanie cut him off. "We are not spending another hour discussing every play of the game. Some of us were actually there and saw it happen."

"But don't you want to hear about ..." Mickey started.

"I will dump this milkshake on you," Hanna threatened.

Hanna reached for the glass and Mickey quickly leaned back, hands raised in surrender.

"We're all going to the homecoming game first, right?" Emily asked. "Did y'all wanna do something after? Dinner?"

"That could work," Hanna said. "School dances are usually lame, so I really just want a few dances, get our pictures, and see them announce the homecoming court. We can go after that."

The girls got down to planning our evening, which was going to apparently include the three of us, and confirmed this was a setup. They'd maneuvered it so each of them ended up with the guy they wanted to take them to the dance, and seemed to already know they were all going together, well, with us in tow.

Emily was the oldest and clearly the leader, but I was impressed how Melanie didn't just take a backseat even though she was the youngest of the three. She was vocal, made her opinions known, and wasn't just a follower.

It was pretty attractive, actually.

"Still slinging wieners, Melanie?" Brandy said as she walked by our table, bringing our conversation to a halt. "Nice to see you dating down, Blake. Not that you were ever that high up to begin with."

Melanie worked part-time at Superdog, a drive-in-style place that mostly did hotdogs, as one of the car hops. Brandy's dad was the local lawyer, which meant she had money and had a bad habit of looking down on people who didn't. I guess 'cause Dad was a cop and we were kind of middle class, I got a pass from that usual snobbery.

At least while we were dating.

Pre-dream me didn't really notice her attitude but current me absolutely did. It actually turned my stomach a bit that I ever dated someone like that.

The dig clearly hit home, though, because Melanie's hand tensed in mine for a second before her other hand gripped the edge of the table, and she started pushing herself out of the booth.

I didn't let go of her hand, pulling her back down. "Don't."

"Did you hear what she just ..."

"Yeah, I heard. Trust me, she's not worth it."

Brandy stopped a few feet past our table, turning back with a smirk. "What's wrong, Blake? Don't think the slut can fight her own battles."

"I'll show you who's a slut," Melanie said, standing up again.

"She's not worth it," I said, pulling her down a second time. "She's just bitter I dumped her and is being a bitch. The best thing we can do with her is ignore her."

"Coward," Brandy spat. "You two deserve each other. You don't know what you're missing."

I couldn't help myself. "That's true. But everyone else sure as hell does."

Brandy's face flushed red. For a second, I thought she might actually come back to the table, but instead, she spun on her heel and stormed toward the door, shouldering past a group of sophomores who were just walking in.

"What a bitch," Hanna said, shaking her head.

"I don't understand," Melanie said. "We were friendly at the start of the year. She even helped me with some routines during pre-season practice."

"Yeah, well, that was before you went out with me," I said.

"So what? She was dating Mason like two seconds after you guys broke up."

"More like during," Joe muttered.

Mickey kicked him under the table.

"I should have hit her," Melanie said, stabbing her straw into what remained of our shake. "Right in her stupid face."

"While that would have been entertaining," I said, "I'm glad you didn't. But I like that you wanted to."

"Of course I wanted to. No one talks to my ..." she trailed off, blushing slightly.

"Your what?" Mickey teased.

"Shut up," Melanie and I said in unison.

"They're already finishing each other's sentences," Emily said. "How cute."

"I think I preferred when we were talking about football," Joe said again.

"You would," Hanna said. "But seriously, what's her deal? I mean, she's the one who cheated."

"She's probably jealous," Emily said.

"Jealous of what?" Melanie asked.

"Well, look at you two. You're clearly into each other. Meanwhile, Mason's already eyeing Katie Johnson, like she'll give him the time of day."

"Wait, what?" Joe asked. "Since when?"

"Since Tuesday. Keep up."

"How do you even know these things?" Mickey asked.

"Because, unlike you boys, we actually pay attention," Hanna said. "Speaking of paying attention, let's discuss color schemes and what you boys are wearing to homecoming."

Sunday was packed with homework and doing stuff at Eduardo's house, but I managed to get it all done and was ready for school on Monday.

Honestly, now that JV was gelling and I wasn't actually in practices with Elijah and his group anymore, school was really clicking on all cylinders. Ever since I'd moved to the JV table, they'd more or less started avoiding me. I hoped that meant that Elijah didn't want to alienate the older players if he didn't have to, although I knew there was an equal chance he was just waiting and plotting his next move.

Either way, I was going to enjoy it. Melanie had switched seats and was sitting with me at lunch and, although I knew he hadn't made a move yet, Eduardo was talking to Sarah more and it seemed like something there might be working. Although, time would tell.

Until Elijah did something, I'd just live my life and enjoy how well things were going.

"Blake!" Coach Holloway called from his office as I walked into the field house to get suited up for practice. "Come here a minute."

I changed direction, weaving between the metal lockers, and again wondered what I'd done to get called in the moment I walked into the locker room. Of course, this wasn't the first time he'd done that, and every other time it had been no big deal, but the eyes of every other player followed me as I headed toward him, making me self-conscious anyway.

Inside his office was another man wearing a Wheaton Athletics polo shirt and track pants. I knew he was a coach here at the school because I'd seen him once or twice, but I didn't know who he was other than that he wasn't part of the football program.

"Blake, glad you're here. This is Coach Greer, head of our track program," Coach Holloway said, gesturing to the other man.

Coach Greer extended his hand. His grip was firm but not crushing.

"Nice to meet you, sir."

"Likewise. Coach Holloway here's been telling me about the goals you and he discussed."

"He has?"

"We have," Coach Holloway said. "When we discussed your goals, one of those involved finding the resources and training to begin getting you ready to compete at a higher level of play. I'd mentioned that one of the things we could help with was improving your speed and footwork, and Coach Greer here was the resource I was thinking about."

"I caught your game on Saturday," Coach Greer said, sitting on the edge of Coach Holloway's desk. "I was particularly impressed by that ten-yard scramble you did in the third quarter. You nearly broke it wide open."

"Yes, sir. Just couldn't quite get past them."

"But you were close. Your base speed is good, but I noticed areas we can improve. Your turns could be quicker, your agility needs work, and we can definitely boost your acceleration and top-end speed."

I nodded, thinking about that safety who'd caught me. If I'd been a half-step faster ...

"Yes, sir, I like the sound of that."

"I'm not here to waste my time, so this isn't something I normally do for players. But, Coach Holloway tells me you're willing to put in the work. Says you're not afraid of extra training."

"I'm not."

"Good, because I'll hold you to that. If you want to get some improvement in time for next season, I'm going to have to work the hell out of you. You might regret agreeing to this."

"I won't quit. I told Coach Holloway I was willing to do whatever it takes, and I meant it."

Coach Greer studied me for a moment, like he was trying to decide how much I meant it. "That's what I like to hear. Now, I know you've got football practice in the afternoons, so we'll need to work around that."

It wasn't hard to figure out what he meant by work around that. I wasn't going to be able to skip any of my classes and I still needed conditioning, which really only left one time slot. I just hoped it wasn't too early.

"Starting next Monday, you'll meet me an hour and a half before school starts. Mondays, Wednesdays, and Fridays."

"That early?" I said, in spite of myself.

I tried to stop the words, knowing it would contradict what I'd just said.

"If you want to get this training, then yes. That early. The morning sessions separate the committed from the curious."

I did the math quickly. If practice started at six-thirty, I'd need to be up by five-forty-five at the latest. Maybe earlier.

"Blake?" Coach Greer prompted. "Does that schedule work for you?"

The thought of losing those hours of sleep made me want to groan, but I kept it off my face.

"Yes, sir. I can handle it."

"You sure? I don't want you committing and then leaving me standing on the track all by myself."

"I'm positive," I said, meeting his eyes directly. "This is important to me."

Coach Greer nodded slowly, seemingly satisfied with my response. "Good. Then I'll see you Monday morning, six-thirty sharp. Don't be late. I start on time, with or without you."

"Yes, sir, I'll be here."

Damn. There went my mornings.

Chapter 28

I hurried into the gym, rushing enough that I nearly slipped on the recently polished floor on my way in. I'd told Li at lunch that I didn't think I could make it to the tryouts because I had practice at the same time it was going on.

I still made a try for it, asking Coach if I could be late to practice so I could see my friend try out for the basketball team, explaining that I'd been helping her get ready for it and really wanted to support her. To my shock, Coach had said yes, although in a very Coach Holloway kind of way, adding that I needed to hurry my ass back when the tryouts finished and put in double the work once I did.

I honestly hadn't expected it, but I also wasn't going to look a gift horse in the mouth. Instead, I hustled my ass to the gym, hoping I hadn't missed anything.

Luckily, they were still stretching and warming up when I got there. I climbed the bleachers, settling into a spot with a good view of the court. Li stood out among the other girls, not just because of her height, but something about the way she held herself, like she was trying to fold in on herself despite being nearly six-foot-four.

I'd seen her when she'd let her guard down a little bit, when we'd been practicing for tryouts, and she'd almost ... grown. It also made it easy to see when she pulled back into her shell, trying to hide from everyone.

When she caught my eye, I flashed her a thumbs-up and my biggest grin. The tiny smile she sent back looked more like a nervous twitch, but I'd take it.

"Ladies!" the basketball coach yelled, waving them over to her. "Circle up!"

I couldn't hear what she said to them, but she would say a bunch of stuff then point to one end of the court, clearly giving them instructions. After a couple of minutes of this, the group broke up into lines, apparently to do dribbling exercises.

Li's first runs weren't great. She was hesitant and that made her a lot less smooth than she normally was.

"You've got this, Li!" I shouted.

A few heads turned in my direction, including the coach's, but I didn't care. Li needed to know someone was in her corner.

I'm not sure if it helped, or even if she heard me, but she did start to relax and do better as the drills continued.

They moved on to passing exercises. She did a lot better on these, including a particularly nice bounce pass through the two players assigned to block it that had the coach making a note on her clipboard.

The shooting drills came next. This was what we'd worked on most. She was really good with layups and close shots, but her mid-range had been really weak. She started with layups, her long strides eating up the distance to the basket.

She made each one without a problem.

I got a little tense when they moved to the mid-range jumpers. Her first attempt clanked off the rim and I worried she'd let it get in her head. Instead, she looked up at me in the stands, took a deep breath, squared up, and released. The ball arced through the air and dropped straight through the hoop.

She made the third of her attempts, too, bouncing it off the backboard and into the net.

The three-point drills were really rough, and she missed all three, but I didn't think they'd hold that against her. She was a big body to put under the net, and wouldn't be way out on the three-point line much.

They ran through more drills – defensive slides, rebounding exercises, full-court sprints. Li wasn't always the best, but she held her own and was near the top on the ones she wasn't the best at.

Then, it was the moment of truth. The coach split them into teams for a scrimmage. Since everyone had to try out every year, she was up against people who'd been on the team last year.

Which meant Li was up against Taylor Stine, the senior who was on last year's varsity team and played the spot Li was trying out for. She wasn't nearly as tall as Li, only about six feet even, but she had a lot more experience than Li playing actual, organized games.

They lined up against each other for the tip-off. When the whistle blew and both girls jumped, Taylor got there first, tipping it to her point guard who took off down the court. A quick pass to the wing resulted in a jump shot that bounced off the rim.

Li grabbed the rebound but held the ball too long, letting two defenders collapse on her, one of whom grabbed the ball, resulting in a jump ball.

The next few minutes were rough. Li stayed close to the hoop on offense but kept her hands down, not really showing she wanted the ball.

In one play, the white team's point guard drove toward the basket, drawing the defense before dishing it to Li in the post. Instead of going up strong like we'd practiced, Li immediately passed it back out.

I couldn't take it anymore and jumped to my feet. "Come on Li! You're bigger than them! Take the shot! Be aggressive!"

"Young man!" The coach yelled up at me. "Sit down and shut up during my tryouts!"

I dropped back onto the bleacher, but I didn't care. I just wanted her to find her confidence. I knew if she could, and she'd make the team for sure.

And she did. Or at least she started to. The next time down the court, Li planted herself deep in the post, both hands up, calling for the ball. When it came, she didn't hesitate. One dribble, then a perfect drop-step move that left her defender behind. The ball rolled off her fingers and through the net.

"Yes!" I whispered, pumping my fist.

The blue team tried doubling her on their next possession, but Li spotted her teammate cutting to the basket. Her pass threaded between the defenders and resulted in an easy layup.

Then came the blocks. Two shots in a row, she smashed the ball right out of the other player's hand. The second one started a fast break that ended in another white team basket.

The blocks, I think, were what made her finally forget she was at a tryout and just start playing basketball. And it showed.

She started taking passes, using her size to box out the defenders and making some really good layups. She also started doing some good rebounding, especially on offense, taking missed shots and putting them back up for points.

The rest of the scrimmage belonged to Li. She scored three more times from the low post and had two more beautiful blocks, really using her size to push the other team around, including Taylor Stine.

I wasn't sure how long they were going to go, since there wasn't a scoreboard or clock or anything, but after one of her teammates launched a three that bounced off the board that Li then rebounded and put back up, the coach blew her whistle, ending the scrimmage.

I got up and started walking down the bleachers, since that was the end of the tryouts, but I looked back as they all gathered around the coach and saw a much more relaxed, happy Li looking back at me.

I gave her another thumbs up, and she grinned her big goofy grin that I recognized as her actual smile, and not the timid, tight-lipped one she gave most of the time.

I couldn't stay to see what else was going to happen, since I didn't want to make the coach regret giving me this chance, but I knew the scrimmage was the last part of the tryouts and they wouldn't list the results for like a week.

I was glad I got to come see her, though. She'd done amazingly and I was really proud of her.

"Here, try this one." I slid the pre-algebra worksheet closer to Melanie, tapping a finger on problem number four. "It's all about isolating the variable, see?"

When Melanie had asked to come to my house to study, I'd envisioned a heavy make-out session. True, we'd only had a few fairly chaste kisses so far, but a boy could hope. I was honestly surprised when she pulled out her math textbook and sat down at the kitchen table.

She'd apparently really been struggling in school and said she was in danger of failing the math class for this six weeks, which would mean being benched for cheerleading.

Which she really didn't want to happen.

I think Ms. White may have suggested that she start getting tutoring, and I also think she suggested I do it, which was almost as big of a surprise as the no make-out session. Yes, I'd maintained all A's so far and I was doing really well on the algebra stuff she'd been assigning me, so I could skip that step and go right on to one of the other on-level maths for sophomores next year.

That didn't mean I should be teaching anyone else math.

But I also didn't want to let Melanie down. I really liked her, and, while we weren't official, we were starting to spend more and more time together. So, how could I say no?

"But what about the negative sign? Doesn't that mess everything up?"

When she leaned in to look at the problem, a strand of her golden hair came loose and fell on my arm. It tickled a little bit, and I hoped she'd never move.

"Nah, just treat it like any other number. Move it to the other side but remember to flip the sign. Positive becomes negative, negative becomes positive."

I had to focus hard to keep myself on task as I pointed to each part of the equation, trying not to get distracted. She smelled like vanilla and cinnamon. It was nice.

"Oh, okay." She bit her lip, then started writing. "So, like this?"

"Exactly."

Mom had hovered for the first ten minutes that we'd been studying, I guess to see if we were up to any funny business, as if we'd start going at it right there on the kitchen table. Finally, after her fifteenth trip into the kitchen, she told me that she had a headache and was going to go lie down, and that me and my 'friend' weren't to leave the kitchen.

I didn't love the way she said friend, like I was nine again, and we were two kids just playing, instead of Melanie being the girl I was dating, but I knew better than to sass Mom when she got her headaches. They gave her a short fuse, and I'd prefer not to get into some blowout fight with her with Melanie sitting there.

While she wrote, I caught a glimpse of motion in the doorway behind her. I expected Mom would be coming to check on us again, but Josh's face appeared around the corner. He hovered there, no expression, just watching.

I guess Melanie felt me tense up, because she stopped writing and glanced back. She offered a polite smile, but he didn't return it.

"Need something?" I asked.

Joshua didn't move from the doorway. "Just getting some water."

I said nothing else, waiting for him to leave. He held my gaze for a moment, then stepped to the sink and filled a glass. I think Melanie could feel the tension, because she shifted in her seat and pretended to go back to the problem, even though her pencil didn't move an inch.

I exhaled once he was gone, but the mood felt off now.

"He always that friendly?"

"Pretty much," I said, having absolutely no way to explain my brother was a psychopath in the making. "I try to ignore him."

We returned to the pre-algebra worksheet. I guided her through the next question, reading it aloud. "If 'n' is three more than half of 'm,' and the sum of 'n' and 'm' is twenty-one ..."

She dropped her pencil. "I'm lost already."

I slid my notebook toward her so she could see the steps. "All we're doing is turning that sentence into an equation."

We went back and forth on it for a few minutes. Some of this stuff we'd covered weeks ago and even had a quiz on. I wasn't trying to judge, but if she didn't know any of it, then she must have really bombed the quiz, which would explain her low grades.

"I appreciate this. Really," she said after we finished the problem, placing a hand on my arm.

I liked the feel of her touch. Her hand was warm and soft. We'd only gotten one more problem in when I heard movement behind me again. I looked up to see Josh in the doorway again, glass in hand, although it was empty this time.

Melanie saw him, too, and shot me an uneasy look. She had every right to be. He wasn't even looking at me. He was just staring at her, barely blinking.

"What?" I said, meaning it to sound every bit as harsh as it did.

"Trying to find the remote."

"Why would the remote be in the kitchen?"

"Who knows? You lose stuff here all the time."

"Get lost."

He scowled at me, but turned and left the room again.

"I can handle random weirdness," she whispered, "but he's creeping me out."

"Ignore him. He's doing it on purpose."

"Okay, but if he stands there one more time, I'm calling him out."

I didn't know if I wanted to see that, or if it would be a bad idea.

"We're almost done, right?" she asked, trying to make her voice sound lighter.

"Two more, then you're free."

She angled her body closer, resting an elbow on the table. I pointed out the next equation. She wrote down each step, biting her lower lip when she hesitated. It took her a couple of tries, but she got it right.

"That's it," I said. "You figured it out."

She flashed a wide grin. "It's a lot simpler with you showing me."

"Blake, let your brother into the kitchen," Mom called from her room. "It's his house too. I don't have the energy for this."

Of course, the little shit went and lied to Mom. He almost certainly didn't mention he was being a freak and staring at Melanie like a psycho.

Melanie looked at me and I just shook my head. There was no easy way to explain how screwed up our family was. Besides, I knew what was coming next.

Josh reappeared in the kitchen, setting his glass by the sink and then opening the fridge, rummaging through it. He found an apple and took it out, leaning against the kitchen counter while he slowly ate it, staring holes into Melanie's back.

306

"Seriously, Josh, can't you do that in your room?"

He took another loud bite. "I like it here."

This wasn't how I wanted the afternoon to go.

"You're bothering us," I said.

He didn't budge. "I can go wherever I want in my own house."

I guess Melanie had had enough, because she finally turned to him and said, "Could you leave us alone, please?"

He ignored her and took another loud bite.

I got up and took a step toward him. He hurriedly backed away, but not too far, and yelled for Mom.

"What did I say about noise, boys?"

"He won't leave us alone to study. He's just …"

She cut me off. "Both of you settle down."

I glared at Josh, trying to make it very clear I was within an inch of beating the shit out of him. He must have gotten the message because he finally left the room.

"We should probably do this at your house next time," I said.

"Yes, please," she said, shutting her textbook.

"No. Let's at least finish this. We have the unit test next week and I want you to do well. If you aren't on the field cheering, how can I possibly play well?"

That got a smile out of her. She bumped me with her shoulder and then opened her textbook again. We managed to get most of the problems done and were on the last one when I heard the old floorboards in the hall creaking. I didn't need to guess who was out there.

I called out, "Josh, cut it out."

Silence. Then, his voice from the hallway: "I'm not doing anything."

Melanie started gathering her things, shoving papers into her backpack a little too forcefully.

"I think I should probably get going," she said. "My mom wants me home for dinner."

It was barely five. I doubted that was true, but I wasn't going to call her out on it. She was clearly uncomfortable, and who could blame her?

"Yeah, okay. Let me walk you out."

This wasn't how I'd pictured our study session ending.

I followed her down the hall, pointedly not looking at Josh, who'd relocated to the top of the stairs.

"I'm sorry about him."

"It's fine," she said, although her tone said otherwise. "He just … made me feel uncomfortable."

"I know. I get it." I reached out, touching her arm lightly. "I'll deal with him."

"No. Just … let it go, okay?"

"Okay," I agreed reluctantly.

She gave me a small, forced smile. "I'll see you tomorrow?"

"Yeah, definitely."

I opened the door for her, and she stepped out onto the porch. As she turned to leave, I noticed Josh in the hallway. He was just standing there, watching us. I saw Melanie shudder.

"Bye," she said quickly, practically running down the steps.

I watched her go and felt almost sick to my stomach, thinking I'd just screwed up whatever chance we had. When she was out of sight, I closed the door and turned to face him.

I think he could see how angry I was, because he turned and ran upstairs, slamming the door to his room closed. Part of me wanted to go up there and beat the shit out of him, but I'd just be in trouble again, even when he was doing everything he could to instigate a fight.

What I did know was there was no way I would bring her back here again.

Chapter 29

Melanie wasn't exactly cold to me the next day at school, but things after our disastrous study session seemed off. It was homecoming day and everything was crazy, so maybe it was just the whole day that felt off. We had no practice that afternoon, even though we had a game the following day, because of all the prep for the dance and for the varsity homecoming game. This included a pep rally that took up the last two periods of the day.

Varsity was pumped. Today, they were playing Midland, our biggest rival, even though we'd lost to them the last three years in a row. Melanie confirmed we were still on for the dance and that I was picking her up with Mickey, who had a vehicle and was driving us and his date.

All the commotion really put me behind, so I was just getting dressed in jeans and my jersey when I heard his jeep pull up. I grabbed my letterman jacket, which they'd handed out to the JV and varsity players today, and ran out of the house and down the driveway carrying a suit bag with my clothes for the dance.

Hanna was already sitting beside him in the passenger seat.

"Finally," Mickey called. "We thought you bailed."

I tossed my bag in the back and said, "Not a chance."

"We picking up Melanie next?"

I nodded. "She's ready, or so she said."

We pulled up to Melanie's house and I hopped out, going to the back and pulling the homecoming mum I'd picked up that afternoon out of my suit bag. The thing felt like it weighed twenty pounds, and it actually might have.

Between the massive blue and gold flowers, the endless cascade of ribbons with bells on the ends, it was exactly the kind of over-the-top Texas tradition that made absolutely no sense but you had to do, anyway.

"Man, you went all out," Mickey said from the driver's seat. "That thing's bigger than she is."

"That's kind of the point, isn't it?" Hanna said. "The bigger the mum, the more you like the girl. You should take notes."

Hanna was already wearing her mum and it was also ridiculously big, although maybe a little bit less so than the one I got Melanie.

I rang the doorbell, and Melanie answered wearing her JV cheerleading uniform, her dress bag draped over one arm. Her smile lit up her whole face. It was the first real one I'd gotten since she literally ran away from my house the day before.

"Hey! Come in for a second while I grab my stuff."

I followed her inside, where her mom and sister Donna were waiting with a camera.

"Just one quick picture," her mom insisted.

"Not yet," Melanie protested.

She looked at the mum, clearly waiting for me to give it to her.

"This is for you. I hope it's not too ..."

"It's perfect!" Melanie threw her arms around my neck, careful not to crush the mum between us.

I helped pin it to her uniform while her mom snapped what had to be thirty pictures. The bells jingled with every slight movement Melanie made.

"About yesterday," I said as we finally escaped and walked back toward Mickey's jeep.

"Don't." Melanie squeezed my hand. "That wasn't your fault. And I'm not going to let your brother ruin tonight."

I took her dress bag and carefully laid it over my suit bag to keep it from getting messed up, then helped her up into the back seat. Her damn floral arrangement was almost like a barrier between us, taking up half the back seat.

"He did good, didn't he?" Melanie asked Hanna when she looked back at us.

"He really did. Mine is just flowers. No writing. No bells. Most guys don't have a clue what looks good."

I'd had them put "cheer" across the middle part of the circled flowers, and a little megaphone and two pom-poms. The lady at the store thought it was a good idea, and I was really glad they approved.

"Hey, I asked you to homecoming, didn't I?" Mickey said as he pulled away from the curb, not missing the dig against him.

"After Joe asked Emily and you panicked about being the only single guy on the team."

"I did not panic! I was being strategic."

"Strategic about what?"

They were actually kind of funny. Apparently, they'd been friends forever and had dated very briefly in middle school, and since then, they had remained friends. I wasn't sure what caused Hanna to set her sights on him again, but my memory was that she had asked him to homecoming or at least engineered it so he asked her.

At school, we split up at the locker rooms to store our dance clothes in our lockers. As part of the team, we were all expected to wear our team gear in support of varsity.

The stands were already packed when we found seats with the rest of the JV team and cheerleaders, and our guys were already on the field stretching and warming up.

It seemed like the whole town was here, probably because they were, and every one of them started cheering and stomping when our guys ran out onto the field for the start of the game.

Except for the few times we'd made it as far as the division playoffs, this was the biggest game of the year for us. Midland was the nearest school to us and kept beating us year after year, making them our all-time rival. I'm not sure if they felt the same, although their side of the stadium was packed as well, so maybe they did.

The first half was a real back-and-forth affair. Both teams traded scores, neither able to pull away decisively. We'd surge ahead, then Midland would answer right back. It was a nail-biter, the kind of game that kept you on the edge of your seat the whole time, not that any of us were actually sitting.

Coach was, of course, sticking to the running game. He was a big believer in "if it's not broke, don't fix it," although considering we *always* lost to Midland, I guess in this case it was, even if it is broke, don't fix it.

The guys and I were really into the game, screaming our heads off every time one of our guys finally broke into open field or our defense had a good stop. Melanie and the girls, on the other hand, were really only half paying attention, going from watching the game to socializing, and Melanie was at the center of all of it. She wasn't even at our seats half the time, running off to talk to kids in our class who weren't part of the athletics program.

"Blake!" someone called from behind us.

I turned to see Eduardo and his brother coming down the steps toward me. His parents were way up at the top of the bleachers and waved to me when they saw me turn around.

I waved back and moved over to make some room for them between me and Mickey. He wasn't part of our group, but he'd been with us at lunch enough that most of the guys just kind of accepted him being there.

"You guys made it."

"Alex wouldn't stop bugging me until I brought him," Eduardo said.

His little brother bounced excitedly next to him, decked out in Wheaton gear.

"This is so cool!" Alex said. "We're gonna win, right?"

"Course we are," Mickey said. "Just gotta start throwing the ball more."

Alex launched into a diatribe of plays and possible ways the team could break out of our rut if we had more of a passing game. It was all kind of surface-level stuff, but the enthusiasm was there. In a few years, Alex would really be one of those guys who knew everything about football.

You could just hear it in his voice.

"You're still coming to my game tomorrow, right?"

"Hel... I mean, heck yeah. Remember, you promised to get me on the field."

"You did?" Mickey asked, looking over them at me.

"Before the game, just for a minute."

"Hey, it's your life."

I was less worried about it. Coach wasn't the hard-ass he made himself out to be. I figured if I presented it right, he'd let me bring them down for just a minute.

We went into halftime tied at fourteen to fourteen. I'd looked back at the previous years' records and honestly, this was the best showing we'd had against them in a long time. We were pretty evenly matched, and it seemed like we might be able to pull it off.

They called the cheerleaders down and Melanie and the rest of the JV squad hurried to join varsity cheer on the field, leaving their big mums with us, since they obviously couldn't actually perform wearing those things. The few senior JV players went down with them.

The marching band began setting up as the announcer's voice crackled over the speakers.

"Ladies and gentlemen, please welcome our senior football players, cheerleaders, and band members for our annual homecoming recognition ceremony!"

The seniors lined up, first the football players, mostly still in their gear only with their helmets off, interspaced with the few JV guys in jerseys, cheerleaders and dance team members in their uniforms, and band members in their stiff outfits and big hats. Parents joined them on the field as the announcer read each name, listing off achievements, where they were going to college, and future plans.

Once all that was done, the cheerleaders and the dance team took center field. The music started, some pop song I vaguely recognized, and they launched into their routine. It looked pretty good to me, but I didn't really know much about dance. All I knew was that Melanie told me they'd been working on it for weeks.

"They're really good," Eduardo said.

The routine built to a series of impressive stunts, although most of them were done by the seniors. Melanie and the other JV girls were there for support as much as anything else.

The crowd cheered as they struck their final poses.

As the cheerleaders cleared the field, the marching band took their places. The drum major blew her whistle and they began their big halftime show.

There was something about a high school football game that was just amazing to experience.

Unfortunately, the rest of the game didn't live up to that high point. At first, it was more of the back and forth. We'd score, they'd answer. They'd score, we'd answer.

Neither defense could seem to keep up with the other's offense.

Midway through the fourth, Midland kicked a field goal to put them up by three. Our offense got the ball back with just under two minutes left, one timeout, and seventy yards to go. It was do-or-die time.

Kenneth actually did a decent job moving the ball down the field, mostly running plays, of course. He got us down to their twenty-yard line with thirty seconds left and then, on second down, they set up for what I knew was a passing play. I think the coach was hoping for a short dink to get us within distance of the goal line to power through and win the game, probably calling a timeout as soon as the pass was completed to stop the clock.

None of that plan worked out.

The pocket collapsed almost as soon as the ball was snapped. Kenneth scrambled to his right, looking for an open receiver, but there was nothing. He tucked the ball, trying to make a run for it, but a Midland linebacker caught him from behind.

Kenneth went down hard, the ball popping out of his hand before he hit the turf. Everyone piled on it. The whistle blew, and the clock stopped. When everyone got up, one of their players had the ball. We'd turned it over. Worse, Kenneth didn't get up.

A hush fell over the stadium as people started to realize he was still down. Trainers rushed onto the field, surrounding him. They worked on him for what felt like an eternity, but was probably only a few minutes.

Thankfully, they were able to get him to his feet. He looked shaken as they walked him off the field. Although he was walking under his own power, he was clearly shaken and not able to continue.

The crowd applauded, relieved that he was at least able to walk, but the mood had shifted. The energy was gone.

Our defense took the field, but it was all over. They made a run and then let the clock wind down.

We'd lost another game against Midland. It was a lot quieter and less exciting as we made our way down the bleachers and headed toward the field house.

"Man, that sucked," Mickey said.

"Yeah, but at least Kenneth is okay. It could have been a lot worse."

We all nodded our agreement. At the halftime show presentation, he'd announced signing with North Carolina State. Although they were only ranked twice in the last four years, it was still a decent program and he had a full ride. Getting injured now and losing that would be a major blow and the thing everyone who played football feared.

We split off at the locker rooms to go get changed. It was one of the benefits of being in one of the athletics programs; we had our own lockers inside the locker room to keep a change of clothes in. Other kids, unless they wanted to go home, had to just go into a school bathroom to change.

I'd brought my Sunday suit, which was about as nice as I could get. It fit well and wasn't baggy like a lot of guys' suits, so it looked nice, and homecoming wasn't a tux-worthy event.

Most of the guys did the same, and all of us felt kind of uncomfortable. The girls might like playing dress up, but we preferred to be dressed for practice rather than a big to-do any day of the week.

Once we were all changed, we headed out of the locker room, meeting up with the girls outside.

Melanie looked great in her dress, a short, dark blue thing that showed off her legs. Her hair was down, loose around her shoulders, and she was wearing makeup, but not too much.

"Wow. You look nice," I said.

"Thanks," she said, smiling. "You too."

All of the other girls look great, too, although once we got their mums back on, most of their dresses tended to be hidden behind the flowers and ribbons.

The group of us walked over to the gym where the homecoming dance was being held. It had been transformed. Blue and silver streamers hung from the ceiling and banners were stretched across a bunch of the walls. Hanna had been on the decorating committee and was smiling ear to ear as we all looked around, impressed.

A DJ booth was set up on the stage, and music was already playing with some people on the dance floor.

"Pictures first!" Melanie pulled me toward the photo backdrop.

The photographer, a short woman in a bright sweater, had set up a small arch with a sparkly backdrop. She instructed us to stand a certain way. Mickey and Hanna went first, and we watched them pose. Then it was our turn.

Melanie looped her arm around my waist. She stood on her toes a bit to match my height for the photo. The camera clicked. She giggled because the flash was blinding.

On the next one, Melanie turned, pulling my arms around her waist with her back to me in the standard prom pose. They gave us a number so that we could order them in a couple of weeks. Melanie was pleased though, which is all that really mattered to me.

After the pictures, we joined the rest of the JV squad near one of the tables that had been set up along the periphery of the dance area for kids to congregate. Melanie immediately dove into conversation with the other cheerleaders while I hung back with the guys.

"Man, look who actually showed up," Mickey said, nodding toward the entrance.

Eduardo walked in with Sarah, both looking slightly uncomfortable but happy. Sarah wore a forest green dress while Eduardo had on what looked like a brand-new suit.

"Good for him," I said. "Didn't think he'd actually ask her."

"More like she asked him," Joe said. "Emily told me Sarah's been watching him for weeks."

The opening notes of "All-4-One" started playing, and Melanie appeared at my side, grabbing my hand.

"Come on, we have to dance to this one."

I let her pull me onto the dance floor, wrapping my arms around her waist while she placed hers on my shoulders. We swayed to the music, and for a moment, everything felt perfect.

But only for a moment, because one of the JV girls I didn't know well came up and grabbed her and said, "Melanie, everyone's here. We're taking a group photo."

"I'll just be one second," Melanie said to me, already pulling away. "Save my spot?"

Before I could answer, she disappeared into the crowd. I made my way back to the guys, who were busy critiquing everyone's dancing skills.

I was glad Eduardo showed up, but I kind of wish Li had, too. I explained to her that if she wanted to get into student government, it wasn't going to be enough to just be on the basketball team. She had to start socializing, and this was a perfect place for it. She'd been adamant that she didn't want to be here, although she'd used her mom as an excuse, saying she'd think it was a waste of time.

"We should get dinner in about an hour," Joe said, checking his watch. "Maybe an hour and a half?"

"That's way too soon," Emily protested. "We haven't even really danced yet."

Mickey let out an exaggerated groan. "We've been dancing for like twenty minutes."

"That was just the warm-up," Hanna said. "You can't rush these things."

"Hey, just go with it," I said. "Make the girls happy and our life gets a lot easier."

Emily pointed at me. "You guys should listen to Blake. He's wise in the ways of women."

"Yeah, that's why they all want me," I said, striking an exaggerated pose.

"Maybe don't listen to Blake after all," Hanna said, causing everyone to laugh, which was what I'd been going for.

I spotted Eduardo and Sarah standing awkwardly near the edge of the dance floor. I'd kind of been keeping an eye on Eduardo, trying to make sure he had a good time. While this was a good thing for him, and probably a big deal, it was huge for avoiding the future I was trying to prevent. From the reading I'd been able to do, one of the precursors to someone joining a gang is not having structure or support in their lives. The gang offers that, gives them a home to go back to. Especially, if they have nothing to lose.

If I could give Eduardo enough so that he had something to lose, and reasons not to go, it would be a step further to making sure that he was never out there stealing a car and that my dad never got shot.

"Hey, they should come to dinner with us."

Joe frowned. "I don't know ..."

"Sarah's cool," Emily said quickly.

I was surprised she wasn't already hanging out with the other cheer girls, either the ones with our small group or the other half of them across the way, trying very hard to ingratiate themselves with the varsity girls.

But it made sense. It was one of the reasons I thought she'd be a good fit for Eddie. She wasn't quite like most cheer girls. She was smart, driven, and seemed more ... reserved and quiet. Eduardo was all of that except for being driven, a quality I hoped she'd rub off some on him.

Plus, she was cute as hell.

"Eduardo's alright, too," I added. "Just quiet. Come on guys, eventually, I'm going to get you all to come around on him. He's my buddy."

The group exchanged looks before Hanna shrugged. "Sure, why not? The more the merrier."

Melanie returned, sliding her arm through mine. "What'd I miss?"

"Making dinner plans. You up for Napoli's later?"

"Perfect." She tugged my hand. "But first, more dancing."

The DJ switched to "This Is How We Do It" and Melanie pulled me onto the floor. I wasn't much of a dancer, but I did my best to keep up with her. She laughed as I attempted some truly awful moves.

"You're terrible," she said, laughing.

"I contain multitudes of talents. Dancing just isn't one of them."

We made it through several songs, switching between fast and slow. During "Stay" by Lisa Loeb, Melanie rested her head against my chest as we swayed.

I honestly was having a great time, just dancing with her, being close to her and holding her. After how worried I'd been last night, it felt like this was a good sign that Josh wasn't going to ruin our relationship.

"Can you get me something to drink?" she asked after we'd danced to like six songs. "I need to talk to Jessica about something real quick and I'm dying."

"Sure thing."

I headed to the refreshment table while she headed over to some of the varsity girls, digging in my pocket for change. I was a little distracted, and didn't even see Elijah until he stepped into my path.

"Well, if it isn't the great Blake Sims."

I tried to step around him. "Not now, Elijah."

He blocked my way again. "Must be nice, having Melanie on your arm. Though I notice she spends an awful lot of time running off to talk to other people."

"Move."

"Especially the varsity guys. Kenneth in particular." His smile turned nasty. "But hey, maybe she actually likes you. Or maybe you're just her stepping stone to bigger things."

"Say one more word about her."

"What? Just telling you what everyone else can see. She's playing you, man. Using you to get closer to varsity. Of course, she's going to have to spread those legs if she really ..."

I stepped forward, my fists clenched. I'd been able to ignore his BS so far, but he was stepping over the line and I was ready to say fuck it and take a swing. Thankfully, before things could escalate, Mickey, Joe, Dan Cunningham our backup center, and Dean Kevin, one of our defensive tackles, appeared on either side of me.

"Problem, here?" Mickey asked, voice cold.

After another moment, Andre and Jerry joined us, forming a wall behind me. He looked at each face before taking a step back.

"No problem. Just having a friendly chat." His eyes locked on mine. "See you next season."

He stalked away as Melanie bounded up, practically vibrating with excitement. The guys, seeing that the moment was over, headed back to their dates, Dean and Andre slapping me on the shoulder good-naturedly.

I must have been doing something right to get those guys on my side like that. Or maybe it was just Elijah doing his best to annoy people.

"Blake! You'll never believe what just happened!"

I paid for a drink and handed it to her. "What's up?"

"Kenneth said I should try out for varsity in the spring! He thinks I have real potential!"

I know it shouldn't have and that Elijah was full of crap, but the moment she said Kenneth's name, everything he said popped back into my head.

"That's ... great."

"I know! He said he talked to Jessica and she said I was all but a shoo-in. If I get in sophomore year, it means I will have a good platform to make co-captain junior year and captain my senior year."

I tried to focus on her words, to be supportive, but I couldn't. Her entire face lit up talking about Kenneth's praise.

No. I was letting Elijah get in my head. Melanie had given me no reason to doubt her. She'd been nothing but sweet and genuine since we started dating.

The DJ's voice came over the speakers. "Alright, couples, last slow dance of the night."

The opening notes of "I'll Make Love to You" filled the gym.

Melanie stepped into my arms, and we began to sway together. I pushed what Elijah said out of my mind and tried to focus on just her, and how she smelled and felt.

Until I noticed her gaze drift across the room to where Kenneth swayed with his girlfriend, his arm in a sling from the game injury.

I tried to ignore it, but I couldn't. As we turned slowly on the dance floor, I couldn't quite convince myself it was just in my head.

"Hey," Melanie said softly, drawing my attention back to her. "Everything okay? You seem distracted."

"Yeah, just tired from the game I guess." I forced a smile. "Ready for dinner soon? They're talking about Napoli's."

"Starving. Though we should probably wait for the song to end first."

"Probably smart. I hear it's rude to abandon your date mid-dance."

She laughed and laid her head on my shoulder. I held her close, trying to focus on the moment, on how right she felt in my arms. But my eyes kept drifting to Kenneth, wondering if I was seeing things that weren't there or missing things that were.

Not the fairytale ending to the night that I'd hoped for.

Chapter 30

The rest of homecoming went well. We all went to dinner, joked, and had a good time, and I put the stuff about Kenneth out of my mind. Odds were, if she did have a thing for him, it was one-sided. I mean, he was a senior. He wouldn't be chasing freshmen. And it wasn't like I didn't look at girls still, even though I was more or less with Melanie.

Hell, we hadn't even said what we were yet. It was just my insecurities getting to me. After knowing that Brandy, who was the first girl I actually "dated," cheated on me, it was hard not to see that in Melanie.

The funny thing was, I knew I'd gone through this in my dream life. I knew worrying about shit like this didn't matter. If they were going to cheat, they were going to cheat, and no amount of worry would stop that, so it was better to just live my life. I could remember bad dates, getting cheated on, and even cheating on girls as I'd grown up.

The thing was, while I could remember all the things that happened, I didn't really have any of the feelings associated with them. Which was maybe why, even though I'd gotten over it in my dream life, I still had to deal with how it made me feel now, second-guessing myself, even knowing that was what I was doing.

Maybe it was that thing where you can tell a kid the stove is hot, but he won't take it seriously until he touches it.

Or maybe I was just a wimp.

The evening had ended well. She had her gym bag still, so she switched back into her tennis shoes at the restaurant and we told Mickey we'd get home on our own. Honestly, I think Mickey was happy to ditch us. He might be my friend, but Hanna was all over him at the restaurant and I think he thought he had a shot with her, and didn't want a couple of freshmen spoiling it for him.

So we walked, holding hands, for the five blocks back to her house. She'd been in an amazing mood, which she shared with me on the front porch when I "dropped her off." We didn't exactly do any hardcore making out, since her mom and neighbors could see us, but we were clearly past the first date peck thing.

Even better, there'd been no BS with Josh when I got home this time, so I got to go to sleep feeling amazing.

Which was a good thing, because today was our homecoming game. Coach had still had us do mostly running plays the previous week, but we did even more passing drills this week, so I really hoped he was planning on changing up the game plan a bit.

I went out to the field for warm-ups a little early because I was expecting Alex to be there. I knew Coach liked to be on the sidelines early, making sure everything was ready for the game, and I wanted to ask him if Alex could come down on the field for a bit, but I wasn't as early as I hoped. They were already there, way early, in the front row near the fifty-yard line, when I got out to the field. Alex practically vibrated with excitement when he spotted me.

"Blake! Blake!" Alex yelled, waving frantically.

Eduardo grabbed his brother's shirt to keep him from tumbling over the railing.

I grinned and waved back, then jogged over to Coach Holloway, who was indeed already on the field.

"Hey Coach, my friend's little brother's been dying to see the field up close. Mind if I bring him down for a minute before warm-ups start?"

Coach Holloway glanced up at the stands and grimaced in his normal way, but I could swear it softened slightly at Alex's obvious enthusiasm.

"Make it quick, Sims. I need you stretching in ten," he said, sounding as gruff as ever.

The man was committed to his persona.

"Yes, sir, it won't take long."

I headed toward the Guzmans. Eduardo's mom had her hands full trying to contain Alex's bouncing while Eduardo looked equal parts embarrassed and amused.

"Tranquilo, mijo!" Elena scolded Alex gently as I neared them.

"Hey, Mrs. Guzman. Mind if I borrow Alex for a minute? Coach said I could show him around."

Elena's eyes crinkled warmly. "Of course, Blake."

I reached up and helped Alex climb carefully over the railing. His eyes went huge as he took in the field from ground level.

"It's so big!" he breathed, spinning in a slow circle.

"Pretty cool, right? Come on, I'll show you the best part."

I led him toward the nearest goalpost, watching his face as he craned his neck up at the towering yellow bars.

"Go ahead," I encouraged. "You can touch it."

Alex reached out reverently and placed his palm against the metal pole. "It's so much taller than on TV."

I just smiled while he explained the details of field goals and his favorite players. I could imagine his family weren't big football people. I knew Eduardo preferred soccer, since he kept reminding me that it was *actual* football and ours wasn't real football.

At least I had Alex on my side. I introduced him around to a few teammates who were arriving. Joe gave him a high five and Mickey let him throw the ball to him a few times. I knew they were doing it as a favor to me, but Mickey at least got into it. Alex's excitement was pretty infectious.

When Melanie and some of the other cheerleaders walked by, Alex suddenly got shy.

"Hi, Blake!" she said, coming over to me. "Who's your friend?"

"This is Alex, Eduardo's little brother. Alex, this is Melanie, Hannah, and Emily."

"Hi Alex!" they chorused, making him duck his head and shuffle behind me.

"He's usually a lot more talkative," I said with a laugh.

"Oh sure, blame it on us. We'll see you out there, Blake. Nice meeting you, Alex!"

As they headed off to their warm-up area, Alex peeked back out.

"They're pretty," he whispered.

"I agree," I said.

"Sims!" Coach Holloway yelled from across the field. "Time's up."

"That's my cue, buddy," I said, guiding Alex back toward the stands where Eduardo and his mom were waiting. "Up you go."

I lifted him over the railing, making sure Eduardo had a good grip on him before letting go. Alex immediately started chattering about everything he'd seen.

"... and Blake let me touch the goal post and I met the cheerleaders and ..."

"Breathe, dummy," Eduardo laughed.

"Thank you, Blake," Elena said warmly after slapping Eduardo on the back of the head for calling his brother a dummy. "This means so much to him."

"Any time, Mrs. Guzman. Thanks for coming to support us." I gave Alex a final wave. "Cheer loud, okay? I'll be listening for you."

"I will!" Alex promised. "I'm gonna yell super loud every time you throw a touchdown!"

"Alex, inside voice," Elena reminded him, but she was smiling.

I jogged back to join my teammates for warm-ups, grinning. His enthusiasm was contagious and I couldn't wait to get out there and play.

I got to go out with Andre and Dale for the coin toss. While I had done them with the Freshman team, this was my first time out for JV. Dale was captain and Andre was co-captain, but I guess the coach decided I was doing a good enough job that I could at least join them.

Monterey's QB was their captain and, from what I had seen in the videos we watched of them from last year, he had one hell of an arm. On top of that, there was another player with him. Their center was a freaking mountain. He had to be at least two hundred and fifty pounds and made Andre look small by comparison. He was going to give our defense some real trouble.

The ref held up the coin. "Monterey is the visiting team. Call it in the air."

"Heads," their QB said.

The coin spun and landed. "Tails. Wheaton, it's your call."

"We'll receive," Dale said.

The kickoff actually went pretty well with the receiver running it back to our thirty-two. And then it was running plays, as always. Joe managed to plow through for three yards for our first down. Not a ton of yards, but movement.

The next play was another handoff; this time, Jerry broke through for six. Slow and steady marching down the field was Coach's game. Except, the defense obviously knew our game. The defense was playing tight, clearly expecting what we were going to do.

At least on the next play, Coach called for a pass. But then Coach often calls a short pass on third down, and their coverage was all over Mickey. Thankfully, Mickey knew his job and, after cutting across on a slant route, he turned back hard, losing his defender for a second and giving me the opening I needed. I drilled him for an eight-yard gain, and he held onto the ball as he was hammered into the ground right after he caught it.

It wasn't pretty, but it was a first down.

The drive continued that way, just grinding it out. We made it all the way to their seventeen before things stalled out.

Coach called another passing play on third down, and Mickey couldn't shake his defender this time. I dumped the ball onto the ground, in front of Mickey and on fourth down we went for a field goal. Gerald split the uprights, and we took the lead at 3 – 0.

Gerald's kickoff was great, and our special teams pinned them deep, but it didn't matter. Their quarterback came out firing, picking apart our secondary with these amazing passes. Seven plays later, they were in the end zone with their first score of the night.

Our next few drives were rough. They had our number, stacking the box against the run, then dropping into coverage when we tried to pass. I tried a few audibles to try to shift things around, but nothing was working. We were just too predictable, going to the same plays over and over.

Coach kept calling runs, trying to establish something, anything. Four yards here, five there. But it wasn't enough.

"They know exactly what we're doing," I said to Mickey as we headed for the huddle after another incomplete pass.

"No shit," he said, sounding as frustrated as I felt.

Sure enough, they stuffed Jerry for a two-yard gain, forcing us to punt.

Things were very different on the other side of the field. Their offense was a machine, mixing runs with these long passes that our defense just couldn't seem to counter. Not all of them were perfect, of course, but next to how little ground we were gaining, they made us look like chumps. It didn't help that our defense was gassed from being on the field so long. By early in the second quarter, the score was 14 to 3. The next drive was even more frustrating. Two yards. Four yards. Two yards. One yard. Coach called timeout and tried to pep talk us, half bully us into making something happen, but nothing changed. How could it? We kept running the same plays over and over.

We couldn't move the ball.

Montgomery kept on rolling. On their next drive, they only needed six plays to put the score at 21 – 3.

We got the ball back with just over two minutes in the half. Part of me hoped Coach would let us do something different. We had passing plays in the damn book, we'd even practiced them. Why wouldn't he let us run them?

But nope. Handoff for one yard. Handoff for three yards.

Their final drive of the half, with less than a minute left on the clock, was just salt in the wound. They marched down the field and kicked a field goal to make it 24 – 3.

As we headed to the locker room, I couldn't help but feel frustrated. We were better than this. But being predictable was killing us. Their defense knew exactly what was coming on every play.

It was like this every freaking game, even the ones we won. And I was getting tired of it. As we headed toward the field house, I caught up to Coach Holloway near the entrance.

"Coach, we need to change things up. They've got our playbook figured out."

Coach Holloway's face tightened. "Blake, we've been over this. We're not going to ..."

"He's right, Scott," Coach Easley, our offensive coordinator, said, coming up to us, clipboard tucked under his arm. "They're calling our plays before we run them."

"We stick to what works," Coach Holloway said.

I know I should let Coach Easley try and talk some sense into him, but it was so damn frustrating how pigheaded he was.

"Except it *isn't* working. I don't mean any disrespect, but it's frustrating as hell to keep running into their teeth and having to punt the ball. We're predictable. Look at their offense. Long passes, short passes, runs. They're making it hard as hell for our guys to set up against them."

Coach Holloway looked furious and said, "Get in the locker room, Sims."

Great. All that, and the only thing I'd managed to do was get in the doghouse with him. You'd think he'd want a quarterback who actually wanted to win. I went inside and dropped onto the bench next to Mickey.

"What'd he say?" Mickey asked.

"Nothing useful."

Mickey grunted. I guess they appreciated that I was the one putting my neck out there, since we all wanted the same thing. But I'd rather win than just have their appreciation.

Coach Holloway's halftime speech was all about execution and effort, completely ignoring our actual problems. The guys looked defeated.

As we headed back out for the second half, I grabbed Mickey's arm.

"Hold up. Get the others."

Mickey nodded, corralling Jerry, Joe, and the rest of our offensive backfield into a small group just inside the locker room.

"Don't look like we're just counting minutes 'til the end of the game," I said. "We're not done yet."

"Come on, Blake," Jerry said. "They're up by twenty-one. We're cooked."

"Only if we give up," I said. "That's the only way we actually lose, if we quit trying."

"But Coach won't ..." Dwight started.

"Forget what Coach won't do. Think about what *we* can do. We turned this season around and we've been winning games. Playing his playbook. Every other team's known we're going to run the ball, and we still made it work. We can do it again."

"Blake!" Coach Holloway yelled from outside. "What are you doing? Get out here!"

I couldn't tell if the guys were buying into it or not, but I wasn't ready to throw in the towel yet.

Thankfully, our defense managed to finally hold them on the first drive. I wasn't sure the team could recover if they just came out and scored again the second they took the field.

Coach called another run play, but I'd had enough of that garbage. He might pull me and put Jorden back in, but I didn't care.

"Right Slot, Thirty-two slant," I said as we walked out onto the field.

"But Coach said …" Mickey started and Dale cut him off.

"You heard the call. Run it."

I gave him a slight nod and he gave me a look like it was my funeral. Coach would know I'd ignored him and called my own play, and it wasn't like I was going to throw my guys under the bus for my decision. I hoped Dale knew that and was glad he backed me up.

The snap came back clean and Mickey took off. He didn't break for his slant until ten yards out, going at an angle but still heading downfield. When he did, his coverage turned back toward our line, I guess thinking he was going to keep it under ten yards, since that was what Coach always did. The defender actually slid and hit dirt as he tried to stop his momentum to get going back the right way.

It had them looking like idiots and Mickey was all alone. Mickey broke hard inside on his route, and I hit him in stride. He turned it up field for eight more yards before their safety brought him down.

"Hell, yeah!" Jerry whooped as we hustled to the line.

Another run signal came in. Another run play. Coach's eyes were trying to burn a hole through me as he watched me walk to the huddle. This time, I sent Dwight deep. The safety crept up again but kept looking over at Mickey, I guess afraid we'd try that play again. Dwight blew past his corner and was hauling ass. Their guy took off after him, but he was a step slow, again seeming to expect Dwight to cut back for a shorter pass. I dropped it right over his shoulder for thirty-three yards.

Coach was losing his mind on the sideline, but I didn't care. We were finally moving the ball.

From their thirty-seven, I changed the next play to a post route, back to Mickey this time. He burned his coverage again, but this time their safety seemed beside himself since I also sent Dwight hauling ass again. He'd decided to position himself to stop Dwight. I hit Mickey all alone and he was gone, all the way to the end zone.

"That's what I'm talking about!" Mickey yelled, spiking the ball.

"What the hell are you thinking," Coach screamed as I got to the sidelines while our kicker put up the extra point.

"Winning."

"You will call the plays I give you," he said.

"Then bench me. Coach, if you're too stubborn to actually win games, send me back to the freshman team. I'm not trying to disrespect you, and I'm not trying to be difficult, but have you been watching their defense? That was only possible because they were positive ... *positive* ... that we were just going to keep trying to march the ball down the field. Their offense is tearing us apart. The only way we come out of this game without being blown out is to stop being so damn predictable."

"Get out of my sight," he said, turning back to the field as our defense set up.

I honestly didn't know if that meant I was done and Jorden was going on or if that just meant get away from him for right now, but I chose the latter and tried to disappear into a group of offensive line players.

Coach Easley slapped me on the shoulder as he walked by and gave me a small smile, which I hoped meant he had my back. He went and stood next to Coach Holloway while Monterey showed that I was right. They tore through our defense, putting up another touchdown, making the score 31–10.

The entire time Coach Easley was in his ear. I could see Coach Holloway's jaw working the entire time, and he was clearly pissed, but maybe Coach Easley had a better chance than I did of getting through to him.

And apparently, he did because the first play Coach called when we got back on the field was a long slant. Again, we caught the

330

defense napping, and Mickey picked up fourteen yards. I could see them scrambling on the sidelines, and I knew their coach was trying to change his playbook for the game on the fly, so we couldn't keep this up forever, but for now, it was working. Three more passes and a run, just to keep things interesting, I guess, and we were back in the end zone. 31 to 17.

Still a long way from winning, but we were now actually playing some damn football.

Our sudden comeback seemed to have knocked a little wind out of their sails, as their next drive stalled out and they had to punt.

The next play Coach called was a running play, and I went with it. He was calling some passes and I wanted to see what he was going to do, plus, the defense was starting to pull back to have better coverage on our passers, so there was a good chance Coach was hoping to keep them off balance.

Also, there was probably a limited number of times I could directly defy the coach before he benched my ass.

It was the right call. I handed it off to Joe and they did not bum-rush him this time, allowing him to pick up eight yards. Part of me worried Coach would go back to just running plays after that worked, but the next play he called was for me to pass again. This time, it was an out pattern to Mickey, which picked up another twenty-nine for us, followed by eleven more on a quick out to Miles, putting us within nine of the goal line. I threw a short pass to Dwight, who we honestly didn't throw to that often, which got us into the end zone and put us at 31 – 24. after the extra point.

The momentum had shifted and Monterey's offense had slowed down a touch, but they weren't out of it yet, as their quarterback led them right back down the field for another touchdown, extending their lead to 38 – 24.

We were really cooking now, though. A touchback put us at our twenty again, and everyone was fired up. Eighteen yards to Mickey. Seven on the ground to Jerry. Twelve more through the air. Joe rumbled for eighteen. Twenty-two to Mickey. Then Miles punched it in from the three.

We were still behind at 38 – 31 after the extra point, but I felt like we could do no wrong, and the crowd was right there with me.

They were going absolutely nuts as we fought our way back from what had seemed like a certain loss.

Monterey's next drive ate up the clock but ended with a field goal for a score of 41 – 31. Their quarterback must have been getting tired because he had three incompletes on that drive, the most in a single drive so far.

We were far from done, still down by ten. A minute earlier, we'd put ourselves within striking distance, and there was still time on the clock if we could stay focused and make fast drives. We didn't have time for grinding out yardage.

Not if we wanted to win.

On the first down, Miles slid around me as I took the snap and I turned, slamming the ball into his gut. He barreled into the opposing line a little left off the middle. He had a good eye and saw an opening and went for it, breaking through for six yards before they wrestled him to the ground.

A decent start, but we needed bigger plays.

On second down, we had another pass play. Mickey ran a slant, planted, and cut inside just as I let the ball fly. He grabbed it and managed to push past the corner for a few extra yards before he got taken down.

Another first down.

We were now at the forty, and Coach called another pass. I guess their defense had had enough, because as soon as I snapped the ball, they all-out blitzed and the pocket started to collapse on top of me.

There wasn't time to go through my reads, and I just kind of let instinct take over. I pulled the ball in, ducked left, and angled toward an open space along the numbers. One linebacker lunged for my legs, but I twisted away and took off. I sprinted well past midfield before they brought me down. Standing up, I felt good about myself until I looked at our sidelines and saw Coach scowling at me.

I knew he wasn't a fan of my scrambling, but it was that or get taken down for a loss.

My way worked.

We hurried up to their forty-five, and the next signal was a simple inside run to Jerry. I handed it off, and he surged into a small hole near the left tackle. He pushed for eight yards, which was just enough to keep the chains moving.

At second and two on the Monterey thirty-seven, the call was for a short pass to Miles. Through the first half, these passes had mostly connected, but the receiver had been pulled down almost instantly, and we'd picked up next to no yards. This time, things went a little differently.

I fired a short bullet, and he wasn't instantly pulled down. The one defender with him tried to wrap him up, but he managed to juke to the right and lose him, running downfield to the twenty-five before they finally caught up to him and pulled him down. They couldn't guess what play we were going to run, and it was giving us a lot more options.

And we had another fresh set of downs.

We were back to running after that. Joe took the ball and followed Elton's block, shedding an arm tackle to cross the fifteen, then stumbled forward for a couple more yards. We ended up around the twelve, another first down.

We were really moving.

Coach had signaled another short pass, but Mickey didn't run his route right. Instead of cutting at the ten, just short of the goal line, he slanted toward the goal line, but he got bumped by their safety. I hesitated, almost changed targets mid-throw, but the corner was drifting to Dwight. Mickey pulled free, and I lobbed it right in front of him. Touchdown.

The extra point put us within a field goal of tying the game, 41 – 38.

They opened their drive with a run up the middle for two. Our line seemed to be adjusting, but that quarterback of theirs was dangerous. We held them to get a fourth down, and they decided to go for it instead of punting. The guy managed to toss a screen that squeaked out four yards, just enough for them to keep their hope alive if they wanted to push it.

That was enough to get them going, and five plays later, including a hell of a long pass that, thankfully, our safety managed to stop, still ended up marching into the end zone, pulling their lead back up to 48 – 38.

We managed to score again on the next drive to put us within three, 48 – 45. I thought we were going to end up just trading touchdowns after each drive as they pushed a killer set of drives downfield, getting just under thirty yards away from the goal on a fourth down.

They chose to go for the field goal, to widen the lead a little bit, and we all held our breath as the kicker lined up and sent the ball sailing toward the goal. From my vantage point, it looked like it was going to go in, sailing just inside the left goal post, but either my angle was bad or we got a very lucky gust of wind, because it banged off the yellow-painted metal and careened outside the goal.

No good. Our sidelines were already celebrating after the missed field goal, but I wasn't in the mood to start partying. We were still in this, but the clock was getting dangerously low.

Our next drive almost took the wind out of our sails as both Mickey and Miles dropped passes. To be fair, the one to Miles, I pushed a little bit, trying to get it just out of the reach of his coverage, and he could only get his fingertips onto it, but the one to Mickey was in his freaking hands.

I shook it off. Not every play was going to go perfectly. Even guys in the NFL dropped passes.

Although we didn't have time for this, we ended up having to punt, which just ate up more of the clock. We were so close; I didn't want to lose by a field goal.

Not after this comeback.

Monterey could see it, too. They started playing to eat up the clock, letting snaps take as long as possible and doing everything they could to keep the clock from stopping.

When their drive ended and they punted, we only had fifty seconds left on the clock.

This was probably going to be our last drive. We had to make it count.

"Alright, let's go!" I yelled, clapping my hands together. "Fifty seconds, plenty of time! Whatever you do, get out of bounds or call a timeout. Stop the clock!"

We hustled onto the field, the crowd roaring. Everyone, on both sides of the field, was on their feet.

It had become a serious ball game and everyone knew this was it.

Mickey took off on a slant route as soon as the ball was snapped. Both teams had really been moving the ball the last two quarters and their defense was slowing down, either from being on the field so much or because they could feel the game slipping away from them.

Either way, it was helping us and Mickey's coverage was a half-step slow. I saw the opening and fired the ball right as Mickey made his cut. He snagged it cleanly and turned up field, managing to get to the sideline before their safety could close in.

Coach signaled for a hurry-up offense and we sprinted to the line of scrimmage. They hadn't expected it at all, and the defense was still getting set when I snapped the ball.

Miles broke straight up the seam between their linebacker and safety. I pump-faked toward Mickey on the outside, pulling the safety a step in that direction, then threaded the needle to Miles for fifteen yards.

He was too far from the sidelines, so I started signaling for a timeout as soon as he was down. Thankfully, the ref saw me.

We huddled up on the sideline, everyone breathing hard and smiling like idiots.

"Listen up," Coach said, actually looking excited for once. "We've got one more timeout and forty seconds. That's plenty of time if we're smart. Blake, you've got the hot read if they blitz. Otherwise, work through your progression."

I nodded, trying to catch my breath. It had been a long night already and it felt like we hadn't stopped running since this drive started.

Mickey gave me a quick fist bump as we headed back out.

On the next play, the snap was clean, but Monterey's defense had adjusted during the timeout. Their coverage was really tight, and I couldn't find an opening. I tried to force it to Mickey but the ball sailed high.

"Shake it off!" Coach Easley yelled from the sideline. "Next play!"

I didn't need the encouragement. I was in the zone as much as I'd ever been.

Jerry lined up in the backfield on the next snap. Their linebacker showed blitz, so I knew he'd be open in the flat. As soon as the ball hit my hands, I flicked it out to him. He turned up field, juking past one defender and breaking another tackle. When they finally dragged him down, he'd picked up twenty-two yards.

As soon as Jerry was down, I called for a timeout. It was our last one, and time was getting short. We couldn't risk the clock running while we got set.

Coach Holloway didn't have a lot to say to us. The playbook was still the same. Keep it moving, stop the clock. We couldn't mess with running plays though, not until we were at the goal line, and I worried Monterey knew it. One run stopped short, and we'd eat up the clock getting reset. It was too risky to hope we'd be able to get out of bounds and we had no more timeouts.

We had twenty-three yards to go.

The next play was supposed to be a quick out to Miles, but their coverage was perfect. I had to throw it away to avoid the sack.

"Twenty seconds!" Someone yelled from the sideline.

This was it. Third down, twenty-three yards out, and twenty seconds. Either we made this, or we kicked a field goal and tied it up.

I wasn't going to settle for a tie.

The play call was for Mickey to run a corner route, but I saw their safety cheating over to his side pre-snap. We'd gone to Mickey too many times.

"Blue 80! Blue 80! Set ... hut!"

The ball hit my hands and I dropped back, watching the coverage develop. Mickey broke toward the corner, drawing both defenders. They knew I threw to Mickey more than Dwight, and I guess they thought that, under pressure, habit would take over.

But I saw Dwight. He was angling toward the back corner of the end zone, while their defense was focused on Mickey. Dwight only had his own coverage on him.

We could make this happen.

I let it fly, arcing it just beyond the defender, to where *only* Dwight could get to it. The ball seemed to hang in the air forever as Dwight sprinted under it. He leaped, extending fully, and pulled it in. His defender hit him just on the goal line, knocking him out of bounds.

The rest of the players basically stopped moving, looking for the call. Did his foot touch the ground before he was hit? Did the ball cross the goal line?

The referee's arms went up. Touchdown.

The sideline erupted. Mickey jumped on my back as we ran off the field, and we were all screaming like banshees.

"Did you see that safety bite on Mickey's route?" Coach Easley asked, slapping me on the shoulder.

These guys never stopped coaching.

"That's exactly why I threw it to Dwight," I said, still trying to catch my breath. "Knew they'd be watching for Mickey after the last few plays."

Gerald nailed the extra point, putting us up 52 – 48. Fifteen seconds were left on the clock. Unless something went very right for Monterey, we'd just won this game!

The kickoff went through the end zone for a touchback. They needed to try to get something to break, a long pass and a crazy run to get a Hail Mary touchdown.

They did just that, with their receiver catching a deep pass. Our safety was on him though, wrapping him up and falling over backward, pulling the receiver with him, away from the sidelines.

Monterey was forced to burn their last timeout to stop the clock.

"Watch for the hook and ladder!" Coach yelled as we lined up.

Sure enough, their tight end caught a short pass and immediately tried to pitch it back to their running back, who was trailing the play. Their tight end was hit by our safety and the ball hit the ground and bounced crazily as players from both teams dove for it.

Players piled on, with what seemed like everyone on the field from both teams trying to jump on the loose ball. Meanwhile, the clock ran out. 00:00!

The stadium went crazy!

We won. We freaking won!

Chapter 31

Everyone was ecstatic as we got back into the field house to get changed, roughhousing and joking, sailing high on our victory.

Well, almost everyone.

"Blake! In my office. Now!"

Coach yelled a lot, even when things were going well, so it took me some time to adapt to his tone. I was starting to get the hang of it, at least enough to know that this wasn't his 'I need to see you a minute' voice. This was his 'you're in deep shit' voice.

I didn't really have to work hard to guess what I'd done this time.

He was standing at the door and slammed it behind me when I walked through with enough force to rattle the framed photos of past Wheaton teams on the walls. I didn't take a seat. I just stood there, put my hands behind my back, and waited for the shit storm I knew was coming.

"What in God's name were you thinking out there? You completely abandoned the playbook. You ignored every single play I called, and did whatever the hell you wanted instead!"

I kept my mouth shut. The way the vein was pulsing in his forehead, I knew this was just the beginning.

"We have a system here, Blake. A system that's worked for twenty years. You don't just throw that out because you think you know better than your coaches!" He walked back behind his desk, jabbing his finger at me for emphasis. "What if those passes had been intercepted? What if their defense had figured out what you were doing or your teammates didn't pick up on the changes you alone had decided to implement? You put the entire team at risk with that cowboy routine!"

Coach stopped pacing and planted both hands on his desk, leaning forward. "This is what audibles are for. That's your safety valve if something's not working. That you're allowed to do. But completely ignoring my calls? I will not tolerate that kind of disobedience."

Coach had worked himself up something good and after he stopped yelling his chest was still heaving as if he'd just run a sprint, apparently waiting for my response. I kept my mouth shut, waiting until he actually asked me to say something.

"Well? You got anything to say for yourself?"

"No, sir. You're absolutely right. It's your team, and you're in charge."

That seemed to catch him off guard. He blinked, some of the red draining from his face. I may not have the feelings of the person I was in the dream life, but I remembered some of the lessons I'd learned.

Dream me had been chewed out by coaches, by bosses and foreman, and on two occasions by judges. Those experiences taught me something that most people, let alone kids, never seemed to learn. When someone is in a position of authority over you, and they're pissed at you, no amount of reasoning or facts or good points are going to win you the argument.

Trying to get respect or save face was just going to piss them off more and make things worse.

The best thing you can do is admit what you did was wrong, even if it's only wrong in their eyes. And that's it. Don't beg for forgiveness, don't try to make them see reason, and don't try to save face. Just eat the shit you are being handed and shut up.

If you give them a few minutes and don't escalate things, they will calm down enough to be reasonable. Eventually.

"I knew I was disobeying your calls when I did it," I continued. "I did it knowing there would be consequences. There's no excuse for that. While it worked out and we got the win, I recognize it could have gone wrong."

Coach Holloway sank into his chair, deflating slightly. I don't think he expected that, and it took the wind right out of his sails.

"Oh. Well ... okay then. Good. Just ... Don't do it again."

"May I say something, Coach?"

He waved his hand. "Go ahead."

"While what I did was wrong, and I do recognize that it's important to play inside your rule book and not go rogue, I would like to ask if it's possible that we use what we learned tonight."

"And what is that, exactly?"

I chose my words carefully. He might have calmed down, but if I tried to throw it in his face, or make this a me versus him thing, or tried to come in with an 'I was really right,' it would just set him off again.

"I think it's clear that using the same playbook every game has made us predictable. We saw that in the first half when they shut us down, completely."

Coach's jaw tightened, but he didn't interrupt.

"I know you believe in your playbook, sir, and I'm not saying it's wrong. I'm just saying we might be sticking to it a little too closely. I promise I won't go rogue like that again, but I thought it might be worth just looking at ways we could be a little more versatile and expand our options."

"Our system has worked for two decades," he said again.

"Yes, sir, I know. But is it possible our opponents know that and are using it against us?"

Coach drummed his fingers on his desk, considering. He was really tied to the way he'd always done things. Really, really tied to it. Had tonight not been a near miracle of a comeback, I don't think this argument would have worked, even if we'd managed some success in the second half. The way it played out, though, I hoped it would be enough to finally get him to budge.

After what felt like an eternity, he let out a long breath of air and said, "I'll think about it."

It wasn't a yes, but it was better than an outright rejection. Sometimes, that's the best you can hope for with authority figures.

"That's all I'm asking. Am I excused, Coach?"

"Yeah, get out of here."

He waved me toward the door, already lost in thought.

I pulled open the door and had half-stepped through when he said, "Blake. That was a damn good game tonight, even if you did give me an ulcer. Don't ever do it again."

"Yes, sir."

It was freezing and dark as I walked from the side street and into the school parking lot, on my way to the outdoor track. It was wild seeing the lot almost completely empty. School didn't start until eight, and most kids tried to cut it as close as possible to get those extra few minutes of sleep.

I looked forward to the middle of next year, when I'd have my license. If I could talk Dad into getting a clunker, then I could drive to school and turn my twenty-minute walk into a two-minute drive. Plus, it would make all the difference on the days it rained.

I was surprised to see not only Coach Greer, but also our conditioning coach, Coach Kerr, standing on the track, both holding coffees and looking none too pleased to be up this early either.

"Morning, Coaches," I said. "Surprised to see you here, Coach."

"I wanted to see what Coach Greer has planned for you so we can coordinate your conditioning program to match it," Coach Kerr said, standing there in a t-shirt, seemingly immune to the cold.

"Let's warm up first," Coach Greer said. "Two easy laps, then stretching."

I dropped my backpack and duffle bag but left on my letterman jacket and jogged around the track, letting my muscles loosen gradually. The cold made everything feel stiff, but by the second lap, I'd found my rhythm. After stretching, Coach Greer called me over to the straightaway. I'd even gotten warm enough to dump my jacket on my bags.

"We'll start with fundamentals," Coach Greer said. "Has anyone ever shown you proper arm movement technique for running?"

"Arm movement? Uhhh, I don't think so."

"Watch." Coach Greer demonstrated, his arms pumping smoothly at his sides. "Elbows at ninety degrees, hands moving from cheek to cheek, face to back pocket. Keep those shoulders relaxed."

I tried mimicking his motion, but Coach Greer shook his head.

"You're too tense up top. Like I said, relax. You're pumping your arms, but you're also letting gravity do a lot of the work. Keeping it smooth will help. Your coaches taught you about coiling the muscle, right? Like a spring? I know a lot of guys feel like they have to tense up when they're going for power, but there's more than one way to tense your muscles up. There's compression that helps explosion, and there's tension that fights against it. You're fighting yourself."

"Even carrying the football, your free arm needs to move right. Efficiency matters," Coach Kerr added.

I tried again, focusing on keeping my shoulders loose while maintaining the arm drive.

"Better," Coach Greer said. "But you're crossing the midline. Arms straight back and forward, not side to side. Every bit of sideways movement is wasted energy."

We spent fifteen minutes just on arm mechanics. Coach Greer stopped me repeatedly, tweaking small details I'd never considered before. By the end, my arms felt different. More controlled but somehow freer. Of course, we'd see how that translated when I was running with a football in my arms.

"Next, let's look at your basic leg mechanics," Coach Greer said. "High knees are crucial. You need to get that lift, then drive it down and back into the track. That drive down lets you get extra force when you push off, pushing you forward faster. Good leg mechanics are an easy way to add some speed."

"Like this?" I demonstrated what I thought he wanted.

"Close." Coach Greer positioned himself next to me. "Watch my knee height. Each step should bring your thigh parallel to the ground. Then snap that foot down. You're pushing the track behind you, not just running on top of it."

I tried matching his movement, focusing on driving my knees up high.

"There you go," Coach Kerr called. "That's the explosive power we want. Use your whole leg, hip to toe."

Coach Greer had me alternate between high knees and butt kicks, drilling the movements. Again, I wasn't sure how this would apply, but if I did get into the open field and was trying to outrun their safety when scrambling, I guess it could come in handy to really put on the speed and outrun everyone.

"Remember," Coach Greer said between sets, "speed isn't just about how hard you push. It's about directing that force the right way. Wasted movement means wasted energy."

"And on the field," Coach Kerr added, "wasted energy means slower cuts, weaker breaks, and missed opportunities."

I nodded, catching my breath. "I get it. It's like the difference between just throwing punches versus throwing them with proper form."

I'd seen that on a video online somewhere, a bunch of experts breaking down fight scenes in movies.

"Exactly. Raw power isn't enough. You need to channel it," he said, checking his watch. "Let's do some high knees for thirty yards, walk back, then butt kicks. Focus on form over speed."

As I worked through the drills, both coaches watched closely, calling out corrections. Coach Greer focused on the technical aspects: knee height, foot placement, and timing. Coach Kerr studied my movement patterns, occasionally making notes in a small notebook.

"Good progress," Coach Greer said after several rounds. "But remember, relaxed doesn't mean loose. Think controlled power. Every movement should have purpose."

I wiped sweat from my forehead, surprised to find myself sweating this much in the cold. "It feels different when I get it right. Like I'm using less energy but moving better."

"That's exactly what we want," Coach Kerr said.

After I finished learning the mechanics, Coach Greer led me to a set of starting blocks a little way down the track.

"Coach, we won't have those on the field," I said.

"I know, but this is about the mechanics of acceleration. Pushing off hard from a dead stop and building momentum fast. It'll help with your cuts and direction changes, too."

He checked the blocks and demonstrated the proper "set" position. "Hips slightly higher than shoulders, eyes down the track. You want to build tension in your legs, like the loaded spring we talked about before."

I got into position, and Coach Greer immediately adjusted my stance. "Hips higher. Head down more; you want to drive forward, not up."

"Like this?"

"Close. Now, feel that tension building in your quads and hamstrings. When I say 'go,' explode forward. Push with both legs, drive those arms."

"Go!"

I launched forward, but Coach Greer stopped me after three steps.

"You're popping up too fast. Stay low longer; think about driving forward, not standing up."

We worked on starts for what felt like forever. Each time, Coach Greer or Coach Kerr would point out something new, my arm drive was off, my first step wasn't powerful enough, I wasn't staying low enough.

"Again," Coach Greer said. "This time, imagine you're trying to push the track behind you with each step."

I settled into the blocks, tensed, and exploded forward at his command. This time felt different, more powerful, more controlled.

"Much better!" Coach Kerr called out. "That's the explosive power we're looking for."

Once we finished with that, Coach Greer set up cones at spaced intervals as timing gates for short sprints, one set at twenty yards and then the next at forty.

"Now let's put it all together, doing it how you would in a game. Focus on acceleration through the whole distance."

My first few runs were decent, but Coach Greer noticed something.

"You're decelerating before the finish. You're used to slowing down when you reach your target. It's a pretty common error for a lot of new runners. In track, you run through the finish line, not to it. Same principle applies when you're running for the end zone. Never stop until *after* you've passed your target. Don't even slow down."

I lined up again, determined to maintain speed through the finish. Push, drive, stay low, arms pumping. This time, I focused on accelerating all the way through.

"Two-point six seconds," Coach Greer called out. "Better. You know, if you could shave a few more points off that, you'd be pretty good on the track team. Our fastest runner last year could put up about two-point four seconds for the twenty-yard dash. Okay, one more set, then we'll move to ladder drills."

This was closer to what I was used to, a series of connected squares laid out on the track. We used something similar in football practice.

"High knees through each square," he demonstrated. "Quick feet, stay on your toes. Then we'll do lateral steps, in-and-outs."

I felt confident and thought I did pretty well, now that I was back in familiar territory.

"Lighter steps," Coach Kerr called out. "You're stomping through it. Think quick and nimble."

After the ladder, came cone drills, another setup I was familiar with. We weren't spending a huge amount of time on any of these, but I figured Coach wanted to get a baseline of where I was at and show me the kind of stuff we were going to be working on.

Even so, I'd felt really pushed all morning. By the time we stopped the sun was up and the parking lot was already starting to fill with cars. I also saw Miguel and Connor standing by the fence watching me. I gave them a small wave, just enough to acknowledge them without Coach yelling at me for not paying attention.

"Remember," Coach Greer said as we packed up. "Everything we did today builds on itself. The arm mechanics help with acceleration, the bounding helps with power, the ladder drills with foot speed. It all connects."

I nodded, breathing hard. He told me to come back out Wednesday at the same time, and I was honestly looking forward to it. It felt like, finally, we were making progress.

"Good work today," Coach Greer called as I headed for the locker room. "Keep up this kind of effort and we'll have you sprinting for real in no time."

I grinned. I was already looking forward to the next session.

Coach hadn't been wrong about being sore. I ran a lot in football practice, but the level of running we'd done the previous morning had been way more intense than I had expected. Adding football practice to it later that afternoon and some more aggressive conditioning from Coach Kerr in conditioning class, had me waking up the next morning feeling the pain.

It got a little better by mid-morning as I switched out textbooks from my locker, although I knew practice today was going to be a challenge.

I'd just closed my locker when a sudden commotion erupted behind me. I turned to find students pressed against the lockers and leaping out of the way to clear a path for a wild-eyed, six-foot-tall Chinese girl barreling down the hallway at a full sprint.

"Blake! Blake! Blake!"

I'm glad there was enough commotion to get my attention, because I turned just in time to see Li coming at me like a human torpedo. I dropped my bag as she launched herself at me, wrapping her arms and legs around me in a full-body tackle-hug that nearly sent us both reeling. I staggered back, barely maintaining my balance, my sore legs groaning in protest.

"I made it! I made varsity!" Li squeezed me tighter, practically vibrating with excitement. "The only freshman! Can you believe it?"

"Can't ... breathe ..." I wheezed, though I couldn't help grinning at her enthusiasm.

"Oh! Sorry!" Li unwrapped herself and dropped back to her feet, bouncing on her toes. Her usual reserved demeanor had completely vanished, replaced by pure joy. "But Blake, I did it! Coach Weyland posted the list this morning and my name was there! Right between Maria Braxton and Taylor Stine! I'm a bench player and Taylor's backup, but I'm still on the team."

I noticed the growing crowd of students watching us with varying degrees of amusement and curiosity. I would have thought that, at least, would get Li to calm down, since she was usually very cognizant of being the center of attention. She was so caught up in her excitement that she was completely oblivious to it.

"I knew you could do it," I said, taking a small step back to establish some space. "You worked harder than anyone."

"I was so nervous at first," Li continued, words tumbling out rapid-fire. "During the final scrimmage, I kept second-guessing every move. But then I heard you yelling from the bleachers and something clicked. I remembered everything we practiced and just ... played. Like I used to do back in Houston."

"Pretty sure your coach isn't my biggest fan for that."

"I don't care! If you hadn't been there ..." Li shook her head. "You have no idea how many girls got cut. Toni Martin's a junior and she's been playing since elementary school. Cut. Madison Hayes is a senior and was on the team last year. Cut. Coach Weyland kept us waiting forever while they deliberated."

"See? You had nothing to worry about."

"Oh! And my mother! Get this. I called her from the coach's office and she said, in her exact words, 'Good. Perhaps your friend isn't an idiot after all.'"

"Wow. High praise indeed," I deadpanned.

"From her? That's practically a ticker-tape parade," Li said as she grinned. "She thinks everyone who isn't her is an idiot. Being in the non-idiot category is like winning a Nobel Prize or something. She even said I could keep training with you, as long as my grades don't slip. Which they won't, obviously."

The warning bell rang, causing Li to jump. She suddenly seemed to notice all the eyes on us, her cheeks flushing as her usual self-consciousness returned.

"I should get to class," she said, voice dropping to its normal quiet tone. "But lunch later? I'll tell you everything about the final cuts."

"Wouldn't miss it. Congrats again, Li. You earned this."

She looked around nervously and then, surprisingly, gave me one last quick hug before darting off through the dispersing crowd. I grabbed my backpack off the ground and headed to class, still smiling. It was good to see her let her hair down a little. Being that tense all the time couldn't be good for a person. I turned and started toward my third-period class when I caught sight of Melanie standing by her locker. The smile died on my face as I met her eyes. Cold, narrowed, clearly displeased. Without a word or acknowledgment, she turned and walked away, leaving me standing alone in the emptying hallway.

What the hell had I done?

Chapter 32

Thankfully, whatever had annoyed Melanie wore off by the end of the day, and we talked on the phone that night for almost an hour. The fact that I had to do it sitting on the couch, with the cord wrapped around from the kitchen to the living room, made me miss cell phones from my dream life.

It was one of a dozen subtle reminders I'd get each day about all the stuff dream me had taken for granted, that were missing from my life. Thirty years didn't seem all that long until you realized all the things that had not only been invented but had become indispensable.

The internet and cell phones were the ones I think I missed the most.

While I was still wondering what had gotten her so riled up, I was also happy to just let it be. Friday night, I walked over to her house ready for our date. I was really looking forward to it. My initial excitement about Melanie, mostly framed by my memories from the dream life, had started to be replaced by real affection for her here and now.

She was incredibly sweet, was maybe the most supportive person in my life when it came to football, and we had so much fun together. There was still that little thought in the back of my brain that Elijah had planted, but after homecoming, there hadn't been the inkling of anything supporting it, so I just kept ignoring it.

I was smiling when I got up to the porch and rang the doorbell, just thinking about her. The girl had really done a number on me.

My smile faded when she opened the door. She was still in the same oversized Wheaton High sweater and jeans she'd worn to school and her eyes were red-rimmed and puffy, like she'd been crying. As soon as she saw me, she looked away, which was never a good sign.

"Hey," I said. "Everything okay?"

"Blake, I ..." She twisted the sleeve of her sweater. "I'm not feeling well tonight. I should have called earlier."

Before I could say anything, movement past Melanie from the direction of their living room caught my eye. I could see Donna, Melanie's sister, sitting curled on the living room couch. Even from here, I could see her eyes were red and puffy and it looked like there were tear tracks on her cheeks. As soon as she noticed me looking, she got up and walked quickly out of the room.

I could see why Melanie would lie and say she was not feeling well, since whatever had happened, it had been serious. I had enough demons in my family, literally in Josh's case, to know this wasn't the kind of thing you wanted to discuss with outsiders, even the person you were dating.

At least not right as it happened.

I mean, I'd made excuses for Josh's weird behavior the other day, but I hadn't actually explained to her what was going on there either. Not even the more reasonable 'my brother is a little sociopath' explanation, leaving out the dream stuff.

Melanie saw me looking past her and turned just in time to see Donna retreating from the room. Her shoulders tensed.

"I'm really sorry about tonight," she said, starting to close the door. "I just need to ..."

"Wait." I caught the edge of the door. "What's wrong? Did something happen?"

"Nothing happened. I'm just ..." She started to say something else, then stopped. "I'm not feeling well."

"Mel," I said, trying to keep my voice gentle. "I can tell you're upset. Whatever it is ..."

"I said I'm fine." Her words came out angry, but her eyes were pleading. "I just need to be alone right now."

"Okay." I held up my hands, letting go of the door. "I'm not trying to push. I just want you to know you can talk to me, if you need to. I'd just listen if you want, if you think it would help."

Her expression softened.

"Blake, I," She started, wrapping her arms around herself. "Thank you. Really. But I can't ..."

"Can't what?"

"Nothing. I just need some space tonight."

"No problem. I get it." I stepped back. "I'll head out, but call me if you need anything, okay? No judgment. Otherwise, I'll see you at the game tomorrow."

I turned to leave, but she took a step forward, coming halfway out the door, and grabbed the back of my jacket. "Wait."

I stopped and turned. She was biting her lip, conflict written all over her face as she grabbed my wrist.

"The thing is ..." she started.

Whatever she was going to say was cut off by Donna, who'd come back into the living room doorway and was looking at her sister, hard.

"Melanie!"

Melanie's grip on my wrist tightened. She glared at her sister, furious, the two glaring at each other.

"You should probably go," Melanie said finally, letting go of me.

"Are you sure?"

"Yes," she said, her voice cracking. "Please."

"Okay," I said, reaching out and gently touching her shoulder. "But remember what I said. Call if you need me."

She nodded without looking at me and took a step back inside, shutting the door. I turned to walk off the porch and down the path to the street when shouting erupted from inside, stopping me in my tracks.

"I don't want to hear it!" Melanie screamed. "You gave up any right to tell me what to do fifteen years ago!"

There was a beat and then a door slammed somewhere in the house. For a second, I just stood there, trying to figure out what that meant, but then I realized I was still standing on her porch. I didn't want her to catch me and think I was eavesdropping, especially since, whatever was happening was pretty serious. I quickly walked out to the street and then went back to a normal walking pace as I headed home.

I tried to think about something I might know from the dream that would explain what was going on, but Melanie and I had never actually been friends in that reality. I'd noticed her and been infatuated, but I'd been kind of a jackass with Elijah and a lot of the cheerleaders had avoided us. By the time I'd started to figure out that wasn't a great way to be, Dad had died and I'd dropped out of school.

Whatever she'd gone through, I had no idea what it was. Which meant I could only wait for her to tell me what was going on, and, hopefully, be able to help then.

Saturday night, we had our turn at taking on Midland High School after they beat our varsity team at homecoming. Of course, we had a bigger disadvantage, having to face off against them in their stadium. Even with that, I was pumped.

All week, Coach had not only had us practicing more passing plays, and he specifically told us that, after how well things had gone in the second half of the last game, he was changing up the playbook. This included some new formations, which even I hadn't expected to happen. The seniors and juniors seemed completely in shock, and we all knew how far out of character it was for Coach Holloway to ever change the way he did things.

The guy was stuck in tradition in the worst way.

Or at least, that was the prevailing wisdom. Considering I thought that with either the game last week or my argument afterward, he'd actually changed his mind, I didn't think that was fair to him. At least not anymore.

Midland was going to see a whole new Wheaton JV team, and I couldn't wait to show them we weren't going to be pushovers.

To say the home crowd was hostile would be an understatement. The bleachers overflowed with maroon-clad fans ready to see their team crush us, and they were screaming with all their might. Thankfully, our town folks showed up, even though we weren't the varsity. I wouldn't say our stands were overflowing, but they were far from empty. True, of all the away games we'd play, this was the closest, but it was still heartening to know our neighbors would take the time to drive out and support us.

"Big game tonight," Coach Holloway said as we gathered for warm-ups. "We have a new playbook. I know you've all wanted to shake things up, so now's your chance. Show me this was the right decision and let's make some history."

Wheaton had lost every game we'd played against Midland High School for the last eight years, including varsity, JV, and freshman teams. So to say he'd put a lot on our shoulders was an understatement.

We at least started with some good luck at the coin toss, where Jerry called heads and it landed in our favor. We opted to receive the ball.

We followed that up with a solid kickoff return that the kick returner got to our thirty before being dragged down. Not a bad start.

In the huddle, I could feel the tension. "Strong right, twenty-six dive on one." We still kept the first play simple with a running play. We knew their defense was solid, but Jerry managed to follow Cecil's block through the hole for six yards.

Not earth-shattering, but I'd take it for a first drive.

On second down, the defense shifted to cover our three-receiver look, leaving Mickey one-on-one outside. At the snap, I hit my three-step drop and fired the ball as Mickey broke his route. The pass hit him in stride for a quick ten yards.

The momentum built as we pushed into Midland territory, making steady progress with a mix of mid-ranged passes, short passes, and runs. After two more runs, we had another good pass to Miles, who I hit just as he cleared the linebacker. He made the catch and picked up fifteen yards, giving us a first down at their thirty-five-yard line.

Their defense was applying a lot of pressure, but with the playbook more open, every time they started to react to a series of longer passes, we'd insert running plays and then switch back to passing.

It was how football was supposed to be played. Almost like a game of chess between the coaches, trying to read the other guy's mind and guess which play he was going to run.

Unfortunately, our luck didn't hold out. Midland's defense tightened up and Jerry got stuffed for a two-yard gain followed by a passing play where none of our receivers could shake free, forcing me to throw the ball away. That was followed by a third down where I had to go with the shortest option in my reads, which only got us two yards, putting us at fourth and six, and effectively ending our drive.

The drive had shown that we could be competitive with a less rigid game plan, but we were also against one of the strongest defenses in the division. Gerald's punt pinned them inside their fifteen. A good defensive stand here could get us right back in scoring position.

Midland had other plans, though. We'd heard the freshman running back they had was a Walter Payton in the making, and the word on him hadn't been wrong. On their first play, he found a crease between Malcolm and Ronald, breaking into the second level for eight yards. The next play, he bounced outside containment for twelve more.

"Come on, defense!" I yelled from the sideline. "Wrap-up!"

They tried mixing it up with a quick slant to their tight end. Luke came up to make the tackle after a five-yard gain. But two plays later, their freshman found daylight again, nearly breaking Wilbur's ankle tackle attempt as he cut hard. Ernest had the angle but this guy had rockets on his feet and we couldn't catch him. Twenty yards later, he was celebrating in our end zone.

The extra point sailed through, 7-0.

I gathered the offense as we prepared to take the field again. They'd all seen what I'd just seen, which made everything a lot more serious real fast.

"We can't do anything about what happens on defense," I said, trying to keep everyone focused. "Let's focus on what we can do and play our game. There's plenty of time left so let's answer them back right here."

But watching their defense celebrate that score, I knew we were in for a fight. The crowd was totally into it now, and Midland's sideline was jumping.

We started with a run play again, this time from our twenty-one, but I didn't think this was Coach reverting to his old ways. I think he felt we needed to wear their defense down, but part of me wanted to air it out, take some shots downfield. We'd proven we could move it through the air on that first drive. We should do it again.

I took the snap on first down, and gave Jerry the ball, but Midland's defensive end crashed inside, forcing Jerry sideways. He bounced off a tackle but ended up losing a yard as he tried to get outside. On second and eleven, Mickey ran a short crossing pattern. He got a step on his man, but the pass found his hands at the same moment a linebacker got to him. Mickey was driven back, though he held on to the ball. We gained about four yards, not enough to spark anything big, but we were chipping away at their defense.

That wouldn't last. Midland's defense was freaking everywhere, pushing our line and all over our receivers. I swear I wanted to count and make sure they hadn't snuck extra players on the field.

On the snap, their linebackers rushed us, but Andre and our guys held strong long enough for me to make my reads.

Unfortunately, my reads sucked. Dwight tried to shake his corner on a post route, but he was stuck to Dwight's hip. Mickey's route was completely jammed up, and Miles was surrounded. The pocket started to collapse, so I tried to throw over the middle and drop it into Miles's hands, since my other two receivers were impossible to hit. Miles jumped and reached for it, but a defender got his fingertips on the ball and the pass ended up incomplete.

We ended up having to punt again. Not the answer to Midland's drive I'd hoped for. Worse, the snap was terrible and soared over Gerald's head. He jumped for the ball, but only got a piece of it, and it hit the ground behind him. He raced to grab it and, with defenders rushing in, he had no choice but to cover it. The official's whistle signaled the end of that fiasco, with Midland getting their first down deep in our territory.

Coach was livid. While the rest of the first quarter was marginally better, it was not the rousing start we'd hoped for.

Thankfully, our guys kept from repeating that mistake and the defense stopped the drive there when Midland managed to bang a very doable field goal off the right goal post, keeping us within a touchdown of tying it up.

Coach finally broke the pattern of starting every drive with a run and instead called for a deep post route for Dwight. That allowed for some separation as Mickey ran a short route on the opposite side of the field and Miles cut a little in front of Dwight, so they couldn't just swarm us.

Instead, they went for their next favorite move, to try to plow over the line and get to me. I could feel the pressure in the pocket as I made my reads. My first time through, everyone was covered, forcing me to go through a second run of reads, which would probably end up with me having to dump the ball before I got all the way back around again, unless someone got open in a hurry.

Thankfully, just as I switched from Miles back to Dwight, he cut inside his defender, giving just enough separation to make the pass doable. I stepped up in the pocket and released the ball. Dwight stretched out, snagging it in stride, picking up three more yards before his defender managed to get a hold of him and pull him down.

After a six-yard run, we were back to a pass play, although this one had everyone running shorter routes. The defense brought pressure, sending both outside linebackers and forcing me to backpedal as I looked for open receivers. I wasn't going to get my full read and Mickey was going further out, so I skipped him and looked for Miles.

Thankfully, the rush on the center had left him open enough for me to get the pass off before I got hit. With the defender closing in, I planted my back foot and fired the ball between two of their guys. As soon as it was out of my hand, I got hit and plowed into the ground.

I didn't get to see what happened, but the ball ended up twenty-five yards farther down the field, so he must have made a hell of a move to break free and get that far, since he'd only been about ten yards past the line of scrimmage when I'd hit him with the ball.

It also put us within four yards of the end zone with four chances to get it across the line.

We didn't need all four. On our first down, Jerry took the handoff and a solid block from Cecil opened up enough room for him to score.

With the extra point, we had them tied up 7-7.

It was back to our defense, and they tried hard, but Midland's running back was a different breed. Every time we thought we had him contained, he'd find another gear or make a cut that left our guys grasping air.

Our defense finally held them inside our red zone and managed to at least slow them down. They even got a little of their own back when Malcolm stuffed their star running back into the dirt for a loss and then Luke broke up a pass attempt. Midland ended up having to settle for a nineteen-yard field goal.

This one didn't bang off the post, and they were back up, 10-7.

We had two minutes left in the half, and we all knew it was important to get something going, so we went into halftime ahead. There was something to be said for the psychology of being behind at the half, and a lot of teams didn't manage to come back from it.

Our first play was another long pass to Dwight, with Mickey and Miles both keeping it close this time. I was a little worried that they would figure out we were running something similar to the play we'd run on that last scoring drive, but they bit when I faked a handoff, pulling the ball out of Joe's stomach as soon as I went to put it there and stepping back.

For the second drive in a row, I hit Dwight at twenty yards out. We followed that up with a run, just like the last time, and got six more yards right up the middle.

Coach didn't keep us on the repeat after that and changed it up. At the snap, Miles faked like he was running outside, then broke for the post and the safety bought it. Miles was two steps ahead of his coverage and their safety was out of position as he pulled the ball in. He turned and hauled ass downfield, staying just outside of their corner's reach until he crossed the goal line, giving us our first lead of the game, at 14-10.

That lead didn't last, though, with a hell of a return of the kick-off followed by one of the best runs I'd seen all year. They managed to get in range for a long field goal with seconds left on the clock.

Going into the locker room ahead 14-13 had everyone pumped. It was one of the harder games we'd played this year, but for the first time it felt like we were actually playing football instead of just going through an old playbook, regardless of what happened.

I'd like to say the second half started off a lot better. But it didn't.

Midland took the kickoff, and their running back showed why everyone was talking about him. He bounced off Ronald's tackle attempt, then spun away from Malcolm before Ernest finally brought him down at their forty.

The biggest problem wasn't just the running back. He was good, but we couldn't just focus on him since their quarterback was also pretty decent. When we put too much attention on the running back, the QB would pick up fifteen yards on us with passing. When we tried to stay on top of the receivers, their running back would grind out the yards. Our guys got hands on him, but he'd power through or bounce off. Even when we had him stopped, he'd fall forward for positive yards.

The drive ended with Midland crossing the goal line and taking the lead from us again, 20-14.

Our first play after the kickoff was so close to being perfect. Dwight broke free, cutting across to the center of the field and I hit him with this beautiful pass that had to be close to thirty yards, only for a yellow flag to go flying as we were called for holding.

The rest of the drive went about the same way. A run for a two-yard loss followed by a pass Mickey couldn't quite get his hands on and then a punt where their returner managed to pick up way more yards than we would have wanted, putting them in a really solid position.

Our guys managed to keep them from getting much forward momentum, but they were lined up for an easy field goal and kicked it through, putting the score at 23-14.

After a not-terrible start to the game, or at least one that kept us within reach, the third quarter had gone terribly for us.

The fourth quarter had started with us getting the ball back. I wasn't ready to give up yet, but a lot of the guys seemed to be losing faith. I knew if we didn't get something going soon, we really would be out of it. It seemed like that might be what was destined to happen when, on our first drive of the quarter, our first two plays went nowhere, with an incomplete pass and a run stopped at the line of scrimmage. We had one more shot before we'd have to punt, and I didn't want to end our first drive of the quarter four and done.

Coach called another running play, trying to throw off the rhythm we'd been in so far. The play was a handoff to Joe, but I could see their defense creeping up as we got set. They'd predicted our run and were ready to hammer us at the line again, but they were favoring the left side, giving us an opportunity.

We'd worked on what was not quite a trick play, but one we hadn't really used. In college, they'd started having halfbacks receive short passes occasionally, and I knew it was going to be a thing in the NFL in the coming years, which is why I'd pushed for us to try it.

Coach let us play around with stuff like that, although he'd made it clear this wasn't a play he ever wanted to see us use.

So I'd see how he'd feel about it now.

"Orange 32! Orange 32! Hut!"

The ball hit my hands clean and Joe, instead of taking the ball and trying for a power play to punch through, faked taking it into his stomach and then ran to the left, right into their teeth while Jerry slipped through the line. The defense bit hard. I had already taken a step back and was planted by the time they realized Joe didn't have the ball. I fired it to Jerry in the flat as soon as I saw him look for it and hit him right in the numbers.

He turned up field, picking up ten yards and a first down before they wrapped him up and took him to the ground. Not the best pass I'd ever made, but having one of our running backs take the pass put Midland in a tizzy.

I looked over at Coach on the sideline and he was just shaking his head. He was smiling, so maybe he wasn't pissed after all. He made the sign to run the same play again, although I knew he meant run the running play he had called.

"I cannot believe that shit worked," Joe said as we got back into the huddle.

"I can. Watch out, I'm coming for your position next," Jerry said, grinning at Mickey.

He was going to be insufferable after this.

It had done the trick, though, and broke the spell Midland had over us since we'd gone in at half time. We managed to start converting after that, marching the ball down the field in short spurts before opening it back up with longer passes. Not every play was perfect, of course. For every fifteen-yard pass we made, we had an incomplete pass or a run stopped at the line.

Still, eight plays later we were at third and six. We were going to score, one way or another, but I wanted seven points and wasn't ready to settle for a field goal.

I hadn't needed to worry. I snapped the ball, put it in Jerry's stomach, and he managed to plow in behind Cecil getting just over the goal line as everyone collapsed on him.

With the extra point, we were at 23-21, putting us in range to go ahead if our defense could hold them.

Unfortunately, our defense didn't hold them. Their running back broke through our line on their very first play of the drive, spinning away from our safety and breaking into the open field for a sixty-three-yard run, making the score 30-21.

It would have been incredible if it hadn't been done to us.

And then fortune smiled on us. After we burned a lot of time off the clock with Coach marching the ball down the field, going back to the old playbook, we put another score on the board, bringing us to 30-28. While I didn't love how much time had gotten eaten in the drive, Coach's switching back to our old playbook did work, since they'd prepared for the 'new' us, they kept expecting the passes that never came.

That wasn't the fortunate thing, though. On the first play of their next drive, it looked like their star running back was about to have another crazy run when he cut hard to avoid a tackle, and something happened. I don't know if his cleat got stuck or what, but his leg turned and his foot didn't, and he went down hard, grabbing his ankle.

He did manage to walk off, but he was limping pretty badly as he did it. Midland's offense kind of fell apart after that, not able to really get much going on the drive they had to punt the ball away.

Not that they were all the way out of it. They still had a solid defense. If they could lock us down, it didn't matter if they scored or not.

It really looked like that might be how it was going to work out, when the next two drives, both ours and theirs, died after the first series of downs, forcing a punt in four plays.

That worked in their favor, and the clock kept ticking away.

The next time we got the ball, we were at our twenty with less than two minutes to play. I think we all knew this was going to be our last drive.

As if to completely change it up again, Coach ditched the old playbook after just having picked it back up. On our first play, Mickey broke free on his route, and I hit him in stride for fifteen yards. I followed that up by hitting Dwight on a long thirty-yard pass to give us two first downs in two plays and move us forty-five yards downfield in the process.

The next play was another pass, the third in a row, to Miles this time, who managed another ten yards before getting pulled down, putting us at their twenty-five with forty-five seconds left on the clock. I don't know if their defense had gotten tired or just lost their head of steam because we followed that up with two more good plays putting us at second down and goal at the eight with ten seconds left on the clock.

We were out of timeouts, so if we didn't convert this time, we had to get the clock stopped, or there was a good chance we wouldn't get to play the fourth down before time ran out.

In the huddle, I could feel everyone's eyes on me. "Trips bunch right, divide on one! Miles, you're primary. Dwight, be ready on the back side."

Coach would normally have called a running play this close to the goal line on a second down, but again, we couldn't risk time running out. We needed it caught and out of bounds or in the end zone.

I snapped the ball and fell back, going through the reads. Miles was covered. Dwight had a step ...

I never saw the defensive end break through, and none of my guys called it out. One moment I'd been pulling my arm back, about to rocket a throw to Dwight for the game, and the next, I was hit on my blind side by a freaking freight train. Worse, he didn't just put me in the dirt, he hit me low and lifted up, sending me over his shoulder and bending me in half.

The entire world went upside down, and then I smashed head-first into the cold turf, which might as well have been concrete.

Then the world went black.

Chapter 33

It was weird, opening my eyes, waking up with the dark sky and stadium lights above me. It took me a second to even remember where I was, let alone why I was lying on the ground.

The world returned in stages, starting with bits of sound that slowly separated into distinct voices. Then feeling. My helmet felt tight, pressing against my temples, like it was trying to squeeze my skull. I'm not sure who, but someone thankfully slipped it off, taking away a little of the pressure.

"Blake? Blake, can you hear me?" Coach Holloway's face swam into focus above me as vision returned next.

"Yeah," I managed, though my voice came out raspier than intended. "Yeah. I think so. What happened?"

Nobody answered right away. Just looked at each other. Aside from Coach Holloway, Mr. Lassiter, the head trainer, and Coach Easley, I could see Mickey and Joe just on the edges of the circle that formed around me. Mr. Lassiter knelt down next to me and held up a small penlight, shining it in my eyes. I blinked a little against the harsh light as he had me follow it back and forth, before putting it away and feeling carefully along my neck.

"Any pain here?" he asked, pressing gently at the base of my skull.

"No, it doesn't hurt. I'm fine," I said, starting to push myself up, but the world tilted sideways.

Coach Holloway and Coach Easley both reached down and steadied me and, when they saw that I was determined to stand, grabbed me under the arms and helped me to my feet.

"Let's get you to the locker room," Mr. Lassiter said.

As soon as I was up, I pushed away from them to stand on my own. It was a little shaky, but I didn't want to be carried out on a stretcher. I looked around at the stands, where people had started cheering as soon as I was vertical. I couldn't help but notice the scoreboard which read Midland 36, Wheaton 28.

The clock read zero. The game was over, but as I walked off, I saw that Midland's special team was headed onto the field.

"What happened?" I asked again, pulling Mickey and Joe in to help me walk off the field.

"Andre slipped on the turf," Mickey said. "The whole line just ... collapsed. Their defensive end came through completely un-blocked."

"You were stepping back to throw," Joe added. "The ball went flying when you got hit. One of their linebackers snagged it and took it all the way for six."

"Shit." I rubbed my face, trying to clear the fog. "Why didn't anyone yell out a warning? I could've at least braced for it."

"I think we were all just shocked when we saw him coming through. It happened so fast ..." Mickey said before he was inter-rupted by a cheer from the opposite stands as they kicked the extra point, bringing our loss to 37-28.

We'd been so close.

"We've got to be ready for that," I said, frustrated and a little angry looking at the scoreboard. "A heads up and I could've tried to run it in. Worst case, thrown it away and we could have kicked for a field goal. Instead ..."

"Blake!" Melanie yelled, running up to me and then stopping, clearly unsure if she should hug me or not. "Are you alright?"

I pulled away from Mickey and Joe, taking an unsteady step on my own, pulling her into my arms. "Yeah, just stiff."

She wrapped her arms around me and I could feel her trembling slightly. Over her shoulder, I could see Mr. Lassiter glowering at me, clearly wanting me to continue on to the training room.

"The trainers want to check me out in the locker room before we head back," I said, carefully extracting myself. "I'll find you at the bus?"

"Promise?" Her eyes searched my face.

"Promise." I managed a smile I didn't quite feel. "Just need to get cleared first."

I shooed her along, but she kept looking over her shoulder as she walked back toward the rest of the cheerleaders. I tried to give her a reassuring smile, in spite of what I was feeling inside. We had fought so hard to get back in the game and were within inches of winning the game, and one hit had erased it all.

"Let's get you checked out properly," Mr. Lassiter said, putting a hand on my shoulder.

Ten minutes of poking and prodding later, the trainers released me to go get changed for the bus ride home, declaring me not permanently broken. Although, Mr. Lassiter did say if I felt dizzy or nauseous in the morning to go see my doctor.

Everyone was in the locker room getting changed when I got there and the whole place felt like a funeral. No one was joking or laughing or really even talking. It was a big change from how things had been even when I'd first come on board and the team was losing. I think being that close to beating Midland and then having it all fall apart had hit them hard.

None more so than Andre. He was sitting on the bench in front of the locker he'd put his stuff in, still in his pads, staring at the floor. Other than me, he was the only one who hadn't changed clothes.

"Hey." I dropped onto the bench next to him. "You okay?"

Andre didn't look up. "I should be asking you the same thing. I screwed up. Bad. I cost us the game."

"It happens," I said, but he didn't look like he was buying it.

"No, it doesn't happen," Mickey said one bench over, angry. "He's right, he cost us the game. We were right there. We could have beaten them, and that amateur shit cost us the game."

"Back off," Terry cut in, stepping between them. "Like you've never messed up before?"

"Not when it counted like that!" Mickey shot back.

"Really? 'Cause I remember you dropping a pass in the third that could have been a touchdown," Terry said. "How is that any different?"

"That was different ..."

"How?" Joe demanded. "We would have already been up if you'd caught that ball!"

"It's different because Blake got hurt!" Mickey shoved past Terry. "Do you want to go back to how we were at the beginning of the season, when we couldn't win a game to save our life?"

While he wasn't wrong about the beginning of the season record, Jorden was still on the team and in the room with us, and he'd definitely heard Mickey, turning red and glaring at me, like I'd done something to make him say that.

Things started to go downhill from there, with more guys taking sides, the shouting ramping up. My head throbbed from the noise. I pushed myself to my feet, swaying slightly.

"Hey!" I said, trying to project my voice to cut through the noise, but nobody heard me. "SHUT UP!"

As if to make my point, I slammed my palm into one of the locker doors, banging it closed with a loud clang. That did the trick. The room went quiet.

"This stops now," I said. "You want to talk about mistakes? Fine. I overthrew a bunch of passes tonight. Mickey dropped a big pass. Andre missed a block. We had that bad snap on the punt that kind of screwed us. We all made mistakes. We'll keep making mistakes. This isn't a scrimmage, we're playing against guys who want to win just as much as we do, and shit doesn't even go right in practice every time."

"But we could've," Mickey started.

"Could've what?" I said, cutting him off. "Could've won? Yeah, maybe. But we also could've gotten blown out. Do you remember how things were at the end of the third quarter? Midland's undefeated for a reason. Instead, we had them scared and were close to winning."

I paused and looked around the room, making eye contact with each guy I could see, making sure they were paying attention. "No one person is responsible for how we do. We win as a team. We lose as a team. And we are going to lose games. Hardly anyone gets an undefeated season. What matters is what we do when we lose. Do we give up and go for each other's throats, or do we learn from it and get better for the next time."

For a minute, no one said anything. I think they knew I was right and just needed someone to say it. They all looked like kids who'd just been busted with their hand in the cookie jar.

"Alright, I don't know about you guys, but I'm ready to get the hell out of here. Let's pack up and get to the bus."

That broke the spell. It was quieter than before, and there still wasn't a lot of laughing and joking around, but they did start talking again.

Mickey looked at me and then walked over to Andre and said, "Sorry, man. I was being a dick."

"I would have, too, in your place. We're good," Andre said, whacking him on the shoulder.

I reached down and grabbed my bag, dropping it on the bench so I could start shoving my crap in it. I really was ready to head home. As I unzipped it, I looked up and saw Coach Holloway, standing in the back of the room, watching us. When he saw me look at him, he gave me the briefest of nods and then left without a word, headed to the bus.

"Come on," Joe said as I threw the last of my stuff in my bag. "Melanie's probably worried sick by now."

"Yeah," I said, zipping it up. "Let's not keep her waiting."

When I woke up the next morning, the headache was still there. It wasn't exactly the same, having moved from the front of my head to the back of my skull, a steady, dull drumming that didn't seem like it would ever go away. After about thirty minutes of lying there, staring at the ceiling and praying I could just pass out again, I finally gave up and decided to head downstairs, hoping some coffee or breakfast might do something to take the edge off, at least a little.

When I stumbled downstairs, I found Dad leaning against the kitchen counter with his coffee cup in hand. He was already in his uniform and clearly about to head out to drive to work. I looked at the clock on the wall. He was either going to be late for his early shift or crazy early if he was working this afternoon.

I could also tell that something was wrong. He was doing that thing where he was trying to have a stoic non-expression while he stewed about something. It might have worked for people who didn't know him, but I did. He was seriously annoyed.

I also knew he hated to be pestered when he was like this.

"Morning," was all I said instead.

He closed his eyes for a second, took a deep breath, and when he opened them again, he seemed a little calmer. While I would always be impressed with how well the man controlled his emotions, being able to just shut them off like that, I would have preferred he shared with me what was going on inside his head.

Having lost him in the dream life, I really did not want to waste any time in this life hiding what we were thinking and feeling from each other.

"You got in late last night," he said, his voice completely neutral. Gentle even.

"Yeah. Since Midland is close enough, the game didn't start until seven, which means we didn't get done till almost nine and didn't get back to the school till ten-thirty. I was wiped out and didn't even go out after the game, just came home and passed out."

"How was the game?"

"Not good. We were a few yards away from beating them with like ten seconds to go and Andre missed his block. I got completely blindsided and fumbled."

"No. Are you okay?"

"I am now, but I was hit so hard I went upside down, bent in half and was knocked out when I hit the ground."

"You what?" he said, setting his coffee down.

"I'm fine, Dad," I said, holding up a hand to stop the freak-out that was about to happen. "Mr. Lassiter checked me out and said it didn't look like I had a concussion or anything. Other than a headache this morning and some soreness, I'm fine."

"Maybe we should get you to a doctor. Head injuries aren't something to mess around with, and a headache could be the sign of something worse."

"I know, and if it keeps up for a few days, I will. From what everyone is saying, it's normal to have a headache for a day or so after a hit like that and the trainers said I was okay. I don't want to freak out if it's nothing, so let's just wait a day and see."

"Fine. A day. But if it's still there tomorrow, I want you to see the doctor."

He had some kind of expression on his face that wasn't exactly worry. I'm not sure what it was, and I knew he was concerned for me, but I also knew that there was something else on top of that.

Probably whatever was bothering him when I came downstairs.

"I promise."

"Good. I guess before I go, I should also give you some good news. You nailed every single bet you gave me to place. I just can't believe you were right about Foreman. No one saw that one coming."

"Great," I said, not even a little surprised. "How'd we come out?"

"For you, really well. You're now up to twenty-nine thousand, eight hundred and forty-eight dollars. You have to tell me how you're doing this."

"I can't. I know it's probably really frustrating to keep getting the same non-answer, but there's no way to explain this that would make sense. It doesn't make sense to *me* either. All I know is that I'm absolutely positive what I know is going to happen, and I've been proven right every single time. You just said it yourself, no one saw the Foreman result coming. But I did. I'm really hoping this is enough to prove to you that this is real and that you believe me."

He didn't look mad or upset like the last time we talked. If anything, he looked … resigned.

"It kind of has to, doesn't it? No one gets that lucky."

"No. No one does. I'm not sure how long I'll be able to do this, so I want to ride what I know for as long as I can. Thirty grand is a lot, but I'm still not anywhere near what I'm going to need for three or four years of the kind of training I want to get. I'm going to need hundreds of thousands of dollars when it's all said and done, and if this goes away, so does any chance of getting that."

"So you want to keep going?"

"I have to. If it all falls apart, all I've lost is my initial nine hundred, and losing my best chance of going all the way with football is way worse than losing nine hundred dollars.

He stopped and looked at me again, considering.

"Okay, I'm not going to stop you. I guess you can consider me convinced and in on all of this."

"Good, because there are three games coming up that I know are going to go against the odds. They won't be blowouts like Foreman, but they'll add up. The Patriots are going to beat the Vikings in overtime, in spite of the Vikings being favored by a small margin. The money there is obviously betting it will go into overtime. Next, Nebraska is going to beat Colorado — who are favored — in a big blowout. I think by twenty points, basically killing Colorado's season and relegating them to the Fiesta Bowl. And last, the Lakers will defeat the Rockets in double overtime next week, I think, whenever their first game is. Since the Rockets won the championship and are looking good so far, I think they're favored, which will make it an upset, but I don't know how bad of one."

"The Lakers were really good last year, too," Dad pointed out.

"True. The Rockets are going to have another great year and are going to win the playoffs again this year, giving them two back-to-back."

"You're kidding?" he said.

"Nope. Not much we can do with that now, and they're going to be a pretty dominant team, so it's not going to be a shock when it happens, but they will have stiff competition."

"Man, I'm not sure if knowing this kind of stuff takes the fun out of sports or not."

"Maybe, but being able to win a bunch of money should put the fun back in it, right?"

"No kidding. I know you said you need a lot more than the thirty thousand, and you're right, none of these are going to have the kind of jump that the Foreman fight gave us. I think I might kick in some of my own money and put it together with yours. We've had a lot of bills recently and could use the money. I'll give you a cut of my part of the winnings, too, since this is all because of your gift, or whatever."

"Dad, you don't have to do that."

"I think I do. The extra money would help us. And like I said, you've made a believer out of me."

I guess that is what I asked for, so I shouldn't have been surprised when I got it. I could also read between the lines when he said we had a lot of bills recently. I knew Mom's doctor visits were starting to add up, and I also knew they were going to get worse.

Who was I to try to keep this all to myself? Besides, I was relying on him to keep us flying under the radar, so he wasn't going to go crazy with it or anything.

"Okay," I said.

"Okay," he echoed, pushing away from the counter. "I need to head to work. You sure about that head?"

"Yeah, I'm good."

"Okay, but I have your promise. If it's still there tomorrow, we go to the doctor."

"Sure thing," I said, watching him grab his bag and head out the door.

I'd actually forgotten about my headache during most of the talk about betting, which was another sign to me that it wasn't too serious.

Not that I wasn't ready for it to be gone. As soon as Dad said something about it, it came roaring back to life. Or at least I started noticing it again.

I was feeling better though, enough to be hungry anyway. I went to the fridge to see what I could make for breakfast and figure out when to call Eduardo and let him know I needed to take a pass today after that hit last night.

I'd just put my hand on the fridge when I heard something coming from the dining room. I hadn't seen Josh all day, he usually kept to his room anyway, and I'd assumed Mom was lying down, so I went to check and see what it was.

I was wrong about Mom, since she was sitting at the dining room table, surrounded by a number of books and a bunch of little bottles and jars.

"Mom?" I asked, stepping closer.

She jumped slightly, like I'd caught her doing something wrong. "Blake, honey. You startled me."

I picked up one of the books. It was titled 'The Natural Path to Wellness'. Then I looked at the others. 'Healing at Home' and 'Eastern Remedies for Modern Ailments.'

"Put that down," she said, reaching for the book. "Those aren't for you."

I moved around the table, reading the labels on bottles. Most weren't in English, and the ones that were had names I couldn't pronounce.

"What is all this stuff?"

"It's nothing for you to worry about," she said, starting to gather the bottles into a pile. "Just some natural remedies I'm looking into."

"Natural remedies? For what? Your headaches?"

"Among other things," she said. "Dr. Taylor just keeps pushing pills at me without looking for the real cause. These books talk about addressing the root of the problem, not just masking symptoms."

I had this sudden memory. Well, not memory really. More of an impression. In the dream life, before Dad had died, I'd been pretty self-absorbed. I knew Mom was having some kind of medical problem, but I never really paid attention to it.

I did have a vague memory of her getting into some kind of Eastern philosophy or something. I remember she started doing yoga at some point, which for West Texas in the nineties, had been notable.

Until right now, I hadn't realized all that was connected to her headaches. Considering where I knew the headaches were going to take her, I also couldn't imagine this would be a good thing.

It also probably explained Dad's bad mood when I'd found him in the kitchen.

"Mom, maybe Dr. Taylor's just trying to help you until they can figure out what's causing the headaches."

"Help?" She let out a bitter laugh. "All he does is write prescriptions that don't work and tell me it's probably stress. As if I don't know the difference between a stress headache and what this is."

"Then maybe we should find another doctor. One who will ..."

"No," she cut me off. "I'm done with doctors who think they know everything but don't actually help. People have been alive and doing just fine for thousands of years before the big pharmaceutical industry convinced us to start taking pills, trying to keep us sick to make money off of us, pretending we need all that crap."

I picked up another bottle, this one filled with what looked like dried flowers or herbs. "Yeah, but there was also a really high death rate from stuff we can cure now."

"That's not the point," she said, snatching the bottle from my hand. "Modern medicine is all about treating symptoms, not the person. These methods look at the whole body, the whole person."

"Mom, please. This stuff isn't regulated. You don't even know what's in half of these …"

"That's exactly what I'm talking about!" She slammed her hand on the table, making me jump. "You sound just like those doctors, thinking you know better than everyone else. I've done my research. I know what I'm doing."

"I just want to make sure you're being careful …"

"I'm the parent here, Blake. I don't need my fourteen-year-old son telling me how to handle my health. This is my decision to make, not yours."

"But Mom …"

"No." She stood up, gathering the books and bottles into her arms. "I don't want to hear any more about this. You need to remember your place. I appreciate that you're concerned, but this isn't your business."

I watched her stack everything into a neat pile, knowing anything else I said would just make her dig her heels in deeper. When Mom got like this, trying to reason with her was impossible.

"I'm sorry," I said as she stormed out of the room.

I stood there for a minute before I headed back upstairs. My appetite was completely gone. Dad was right to worry. This wasn't going to end well.

Chapter 34

My headache and most of the soreness was gone by Monday morning, but Mr. Lassiter still had me come by first thing, even before I started training with Coach Greer, so he could check me out again.

He said I looked good, that there was no sign of any lasting damage, and cleared me for practice, although I found out that afternoon that he told Coach Holloway he didn't want me getting hit during practice this week.

We only had one more game this season and it was coming up on Saturday, although we had the first week of playoffs next week. If we got to the championships, the games would go right to the last day of school for the semester, although competition this year was tough.

Although we didn't normally do any hitting at practice, I guess Coach was taking it extra careful with me, because he sat me to watch film all through Monday's practice, and Tuesday, I was only allowed to throw. I wasn't even allowed to take part in the scrimmage.

Andre had it a lot worse. Coach was definitely punishing him for what happened on Saturday, critiquing every little thing he did wrong and generally being all over him. Part of me wanted to tell the coach to take it easy on him, since mistakes happen, but there was a big difference in giving the team a talking-to and saying something to Coach.

Andre was at least holding up to it well, without complaining or pouting. I think he'd kind of wanted something like this, as maybe a form of penance. He'd felt really bad about it and had tried to apologize every time he saw me at school the day before.

He wasn't the only one going through it.

After practice, Melanie was waiting by the gate that led out toward the field house. She didn't meet me every time after practice but if the timing worked out, between when cheer practice finished and her ride was ready to go, she came by to see me.

It was a great way to end my school day, for sure.

She broke into a smile when she saw me, bouncing forward to wrap me in a hug before giving me a quick kiss. The PDA between us had ramped up after homecoming. We hadn't talked about us being official or anything, but I think most people had assumed we were together, and we'd just kind of gone with it.

Even in my dream life, the 'what are we' conversation had always been awkward, so if she was willing to just roll with it, so was I.

"Want to walk me home?" she asked.

I paused, surprised. "Don't you usually get a ride with Emily?"

"Changed it up today." She shrugged, turning and walking down the sidewalk toward the field house. "Coming?"

I just shook my head and jogged to catch up. That was the first hint that something was wrong. Melanie liked routine and she liked riding with a senior every day. I guess it made her feel like she wasn't just the average freshman.

I got my stuff from the field house and we started the short walk to her house. It meant a little longer walk for me, but if she wanted me to walk with her, then I would.

The more we walked, the clearer it was that something was off. Melanie was usually a chatterbox, filling any silence with stories about whatever drama was happening, and there was always drama, or just ... whatever. She abhorred silence.

So the fact that she was quiet was telling.

"Okay, what's wrong?" I asked after we'd gone a block without speaking.

"Nothing."

"Come on. You wanted to walk 'cause something's bothering you and you want to talk about it. So hit me with it, instead of making me drag it out of you."

She thought about that for a second and said, "Brandy's been running her mouth."

"About what?"

"About me trying out for varsity. She's telling everyone I'm not good enough and I started dating you so they'd consider me. That I'm not good enough to make it on my own."

I frowned. "Why would dating me matter for varsity cheerleading?"

"Don't be stupid, Blake." She stopped walking, turning to face me with her hands on her hips. "Everyone's talking about how you turned JV around. The way you played against Monterey. People notice that stuff."

"I mean, I'm still just on JV ..."

"You'll be varsity next year," she cut in. "Everyone knows it. And you'll probably start your junior and senior year. Kenneth only got one year as a starter since he was backup last year, and Ben will only have next year before he graduates. You'll be the first quarterback to start two years in a row in forever."

"That's a lot of assumptions."

"It's not assumptions, it's obvious. They may not say it to your face, but everyone's talking about how you won the Monterey game all by yourself, and how you almost brought us back to win against Midland until Andre slipped. Why do you think Jorden's so pissed? He knows he's going to have to stay on JV and you're going to sail right past him." She started walking again, slower this time. "I got lucky, you know? Landing you right before you broke big."

I know she was complimenting me, but the words hit me wrong. For a second, I remembered what Elijah said about Melanie using me to get closer to varsity.

But I only thought about it for a second. Looking at her face, the genuine worry in her expression and how she looked at me when she said she got lucky, I knew that wasn't true. It was just my own insecurities playing me.

"No," I said, reaching for her hand. "I think I got lucky."

It had been the right thing to say, and it got me a little smile, but she wasn't done with her venting.

"It's just bullshit. She cornered Tammy after practice today, going on about how I'm not ready, how putting me on varsity would be a mistake."

"They've seen you practice. She has to know that isn't true."

"Does she? We mostly practice separately from them, and other than Hanna and Emily, everyone else is backing Brandy. She's been telling people I'm too busy 'cause I have to work on a hardship permit and how it would look to have someone like me on the team."

"What does she mean like you?"

"White trash. I heard she was telling people her daddy gives her an allowance bigger than my paychecks. Like, it's somehow shameful that I have to work because we need the money. Like that makes me trash or something. She's also telling everyone that Donna had an abortion her freshman year, and disappeared the last few months of school because of it."

"How would she know anything about your sister? There's a huge age gap between the two of you."

"Her gold-digging mom. That's why she has money; she married Brandy's dad who was, like, twenty years older than her and rich. Her mom went to school with Donna; they were on cheerleading together in middle school. And now she's telling everyone how Donna gained all this weight freshman year and then vanished, and when she came back that summer she was skinny again."

I'd only met Brandy's parents a couple of times. They'd always been busy any time I went to her house. At the time, I'd thought it kind of cool how much free rein she was given.

"Melanie ..."

"It's not true. None of it's true."

"Brandy's always been like this," I said. "She'll step on anyone to get ahead. What if I talked to some of the varsity guys, Kenneth especially? His opinion carries a lot of weight with both teams."

"No," Melanie said instantly. "Absolutely not."

"But ..."

"I'm not having my boyfriend fight my battles for me. They already think I'm dating you to get ahead. If you go out and defend me, it'll only get worse."

"That's not what I ..."

"I know, and I appreciate it, I do. But I need to handle this myself."

"Okay, but if it gets worse, let me try to help," I said.

She just smiled and squeezed my hand. This was all well outside of my area of expertise. Even in my dream life, girl politics was nothing I'd really understood.

But I had noticed she'd called me her boyfriend.

That was something.

We were getting close to Thanksgiving break, with only one full week of school left to go, and my teachers were so focused on midterms that they put a hold on any more extra work to get me on level until after we got back from break.

I didn't mind. While I definitely wanted to do everything I could to be on level next year, we still had another full semester to get there and I'd been go, go, go since the second week of school. I could use a break.

Better yet, all the extra classwork meant I was ready for the tests. I'd do some studying over the weekend and the day before, I had to take each of my midterms, but I didn't need to stress about it.

So I finally had some free time.

I was supposed to have what was becoming our regular Friday night date the next night with Melanie but she said she had some stuff to do. Thankfully, Eduardo was free.

The last thing I wanted to do when I had a night off from schoolwork was to just sit at home.

He hung around at practice, watching us play, and sometimes talked to a few of the guys from the lunch table. After practice, instead of walking home, we headed down Broadstreet to the bowling alley. It was easily fifteen blocks, almost all the way down to the factory on the western side of town, but it was also the only place with arcade games aside from the dinky sit-down Pac-Man game at Napoli's.

Although they only had six cabinets, and most of them were several years old, it was as close as our town got to an arcade. They'd also just gotten Street Fighter in at the end of the summer, but I'd been too busy to actually get to play it, so I'd had to listen to Eduardo tell me about it while we worked on his house.

Of course, when I'd suggested we head to the bowling alley so I could finally play it for myself, it didn't click that Eduardo had been playing it all year, which gave him a big head start.

I figured out my mistake pretty quickly, though.

I pushed the buttons on the Street Fighter II cabinet rapidly, desperately trying to counter Eduardo's Ryu with my Ken, but it was no use. His Hadoken caught me mid-jump, and my character crumpled to the ground.

"Yes!" he said, pumping his fist in victory. "Seven straight! You might want to stick to football, cause you suck at this."

"Yeah, keep talking trash. Game's rigged," I muttered, fishing another quarter from my pocket. "Has to be."

Eduardo laughed. "Sure, that has to be it. Mr. Quarterback, big-man-on-campus, can't accept he just sucks."

I laughed and put in another quarter. I could take the teasing.

"So how are things with Sarah?" I asked, trying to distract him long enough to get some hits in.

It didn't work and he kept kicking my butt as he answered, his eyes never leaving the screen.

"Things are good. We talk a lot during lunch. And, you know, sometimes between classes."

"I saw you two holding hands in the hall yesterday."

Childish, yes, I know, but he was too timid. She was doing everything she could to signal him that she liked him, and he was taking kiddie steps. I knew he was shy, but he needed to get over that fear if he didn't want her to get frustrated and find someone who would show their interest.

"Have you kissed her yet?" I prodded when he didn't say anything.

The fact that I was able to land several hits when his hand suddenly froze in place said everything I needed to know.

"So that's a definite no. Man, you really need to make a move. She likes you. I guarantee if you ask her out, she'll say yes."

"I just ... I want to get comfortable first."

"Comfortable with what? With her? You just said you guys talk at lunch every day and sometimes between classes. If you want to get more comfortable with her, you're going to need to take it to the next level."

"No, I mean just … comfortable in the school. You've been around these people your whole life, remember? I'm new here."

"You were new three months ago; you can't keep using that excuse forever. You've got friends at school. What else is there to get comfortable about?"

The match ended, with me losing brutally again, even with him distracted.

He stepped back from the cabinet and said, "There's a lot to get comfortable with. It's just different here. I still feel like an outsider, and probably won't feel comfortable until that stops happening."

"Why do you feel like an outsider?"

"Because it's different. Not at school necessarily, but every-where else. In Midland, there was a big Hispanic population and my family knew all the other families in our community. That's not true here. Heck, two weeks ago, they held the annual Día de los Muertos celebrations. It's the first time I've missed it since I started going years ago. There is nothing like that here."

"Oh."

I hadn't considered all that. For me, Midland seemed about the same as Wheaton. Sure, it was a city and not a little town, but it wasn't that different. But then the people I talked to there, mostly Dad's coworkers' families, were the same types of people as I knew here, so of course it would be the same for me. I stood there awkwardly, not really knowing how to respond.

"Plus, at school, all my friends are your friends. I'm just the add-on."

"Now that's BS," I said firmly. "You may have a point with the community outside of school, but in school you're not an outsider anymore. Yeah, maybe that's how it started, but that's changed. I know you hang out with Miguel and Connor and the rest of them sometimes even outside of school and I've seen you with other guys in the halls. They like you for you now. And Sarah isn't holding your hand because you're friends with me."

"I guess."

"No guessing. They're your friends, too." I pulled out another quarter. "Just remember to still hang out with me sometimes, after you and Sarah get serious."

He gave a self-conscious laugh, and I couldn't tell if it was because of what I said, or the thought of him and Sarah getting serious.

"Actually," I continued. "I was talking to my dad the other night. You know, since I spend every Sunday at your house, and your mom keeps feeding me, he thinks you need to come over for dinner. Return the favor."

"Oh, no, that's okay ..."

"Sorry, I didn't mean to phrase that like it was a question. We're not taking no for an answer," I cut him off.

"I don't know ..."

"Come on. Your mom's probably sick of feeding me every Sunday."

"She's definitely not sick of feeding you. She loves how much you go crazy about everything she cooks. I think if she could trade me and Alex in for you, she would."

"Well, then at least come and get to know your new parents after we swap."

Eduardo laughed and said, "Okay, fine. When?"

"It'll have to be Sunday night. That okay?"

"Yeah. I have to check with Mom, but it should be okay." Eduardo turned back to the game cabinet. "Now, are you ready to lose again, or did you want to try one of the other games?"

"Oh, I'm not done here." I dropped my quarter in. "I've got you figured out this time."

Our final football game was on Saturday against Dunbar High School from Fort Worth, and we couldn't have had a worse day for it. Friday night, storm clouds rolled in and it rained like crazy the entire day. I thought the game would be called because of rain, since the field would be a mess, but we showed up, suited up, and nothing.

The game was going to happen as scheduled, no matter what the field was like. It was so bad, they even took us and the other team inside the school to warm up, because the field was so muddy and the rain was coming down hard.

I didn't know if it was because it was the end of the season and they had playoffs starting next week or what, but we were going to play in this mess.

When we jogged out onto the field, there was no banner to rip through and the band was mostly under umbrellas, keeping their instruments dry. Even the cheerleaders were all huddled under ponchos and umbrellas on the running track.

I didn't blame them. It was a cool sixty degrees but with the rain, it felt freezing. My fingers were already numb by the time we headed out for the coin toss, which set the tone for the night when the ref dropped it and it disappeared into the mud. Eventually, they found it and Dunbar won, choosing to receive.

"This is gonna be a nightmare," Mickey said as we walked back to the sidelines.

"No kidding."

Coach Holloway gathered us around before kickoff. "Weather's working against both teams tonight. Play smart, protect the ball, and let's end this season right."

Dunbar's first drive proved how bad it was going to be when their running back slipped in the mud trying to cut, going down hard and losing two yards. Two plays later, they punted after a short completion failed to convert.

We ran out onto the field, ready to start and I swore every time I stopped moving, I started to sink into the ground. I had a towel under my shirt to wipe my hands off, but even before the first snap, it was just as wet as everything else.

My first pass, just a short toss to Mickey, slipped right through his hands. I followed this up with my own disaster when, on second down, the ball squirted out of my grip as I went to throw it, causing it to sail wide, thankfully out of the reach of any of their players, so at least it wasn't an interception.

I did manage a short scramble on third down to pick up four yards when the protection broke down, but it wasn't enough for a first down and we had to punt.

And so it went for the next few drives. Passes dropped, runners slipped, the ball seemed to have a mind of its own in the worsening conditions. And the rain showed no signs of letting up.

Finally, Coach called what I think may have been the earliest timeout we'd ever used just to give us a break.

"I think we need to go back to the old playbook," I said to him as soon as we were back on solid ground at the running track. "I can't get anything to land and the receivers' hands can't hold onto the ball. I haven't completed one pass yet."

"I was thinking the same thing, actually," Coach said. "Just keep it simple; try and keep your feet under you. The season is going to be what it's going to be; I don't want any of you getting hurt."

Things got a little better after that. I think the other team had the same idea because nearly every play from both of us ended up being a running play after that.

It still was absolute chaos. Running backs sliding, linebackers colliding and both falling backward. It was maybe the worst game of football I'd ever played.

Twice, Coach tried to get the refs to call the game, and both times, they shut him down.

Not that it was all terrible. Midway through the second quarter, backed up on our own 13-yard line, the disasters lined up in a way that couldn't have worked better. The snap was high and I had to jump up to reach for it. When I landed my foot kind of slipped, causing me to stumble backward. I was supposed to be handing off to Joe, but my change of direction caused him to have to change direction, and he slid in the mud, landing on his side.

By that point, the pocket was starting to come apart and some of their linemen were crashing through, not leaving me any chance to pass it or find someone else to toss it back to, so I turned and ran.

When I cut left, I barely managed to keep my feet under me as a linebacker dove past, causing Joe to have to roll to keep from being stepped on. The entire line was a mess, but I could see a gap diagonally in front of me. I took off, running as fast as I could without falling down, keeping to a more or less straight line, as anyone who was trying to cut was finding themselves on their ass as often as not.

The mud worked in my favor, as the guys who tried to cut me off or catch up to me went slipping and sliding as they tried to change directions.

Eighty-seven yards later, I crossed the goal line, my lungs burning from the cold air and my hip hurting a little bit from the effort of trying to keep from falling down.

The small crowd erupted, and my teammates mobbed me in the end zone. There was no way I think I could ever repeat what just happened. The longest run I'd probably ever make in my football career, and it was pure dumb luck.

Nothing more.

Late in the quarter, the rain finally stopped just as Dunbar got the ball back, and it helped them mount their first real drive of the game. Their quarterback started picking us apart with short passes, working his way down the field, and capped it off with a twenty-five-yard completion to their wide receiver putting them in a scoring position.

Their quarterback scrambled in from the one-yard line after our pass rush lost containment in the slick conditions, answering my earlier touchdown and tying us up.

Going into the half, it was one of the wildest games I'd ever even heard of, let alone been in. Two touchdowns in the game so far, both run in by the quarterback, one for each team. Combine that with the incredibly low rushing and passing yards for a full half of football, and it would be one for the record books, although not in the way I'd like to get there.

Coach met us at the door of the field house and said, "No big speeches today. Get warm and dry. I know you're banged up, but we've still got another half of football to survive. You guys are doing a good job with what you have to deal with. Keep it up."

If he kept this up, he was going to lose his reputation as a hard-nosed asshole.

The second half was a little better. While the ground was still quicksand-like, at least the rain had stopped so our hands would be mostly dry, although we had to change out the towels every other drive because they got so completely covered in mud.

I managed to get one of my first completed passes of the game when Mickey caught it, picking up nine yards. We kept moving downfield in fits and starts, using Coach's old playbook.

Our line holding was still a problem, though. Once the linemen impacted, all bets were off and three times, I had to scramble when blocks were missed after our guys lost their footing. Sadly, my scrambles didn't end in another huge run, but instead with me on my ass in the mud for a loss, ending our first drive of the half with a punt.

The rest of the third quarter continued that way, with each of us making a little progress, followed by a disaster and a punt. There were times we were all so covered in mud it was hard to tell who was on what team.

Honestly, it made no sense for us to keep playing. There had been several twisted ankles on each team and one arm on Dunbar's side that seemed to be broken after a bad fall.

Whatever the actual reason the refs let this mess keep going, it was dangerous and Coach was actually kind of pissed about it.

Halfway through the fourth quarter, both teams started to slow down. We were tired, fighting through the mud and I think we were all ready just to get the damn game over with and take a shower.

Not that we were giving up.

The disasters had been kind of small through the third and most of the fourth quarter, just ending drives but not leading to major turnovers, until we had a third and nine with about four minutes left to go. I snapped the ball and took a few steps back right as Andre and Bradey, who was in the line right next to him, both slipped. Andre went to a knee and Bradey fell straight on his face as the opposing lineman took a small step back allowing him to fall.

I'm not sure if it was intentional or not, but it worked, because there was now a huge hole in the line and the pocket completely collapsed.

I spun away from their lineman, nearly losing my footing. Taking off to the right, I hoped to see someone open, and managed to cut away from a lineman who came charging at me, keeping my footing while he slipped.

That left a hole open for me, and I went for it, continuing to veer right as I ran, closing in on the sidelines. We were close to the end zone, and I did not want to screw up and drop the ball when I got hit 'cause the ball was muddy and slippery.

Their safety was slow, however. Maybe he was tired or maybe he was just having trouble keeping his footing, but he didn't have the speed to catch me, and I got into the end zone several steps ahead of him, putting us up by seven after we made the extra point.

I think that just about did it for everyone. The last few minutes of the fourth quarter, both teams just kind of gave in. The rain started again with a minute to play, and everyone was half-assing it.

As a game of football, this might be one of the worst ever played, although who knows? From the stands, maybe seeing all of us slipping and sliding around on a destroyed field was worth it for the amusement alone.

It also had a distinction of, I think, maybe being one of the first games where every touchdown was scored by a quarterback.

Which was nuts.

I just hoped the UIL, or whoever was in charge of the refs, actually took notes and kept this kind of game from happening again ... because it sucked!

Chapter 35

I set a glass pitcher on the dining room table and double-checked the place settings. We'd moved a few chairs around to make space, and Dad had insisted we use the "nice" tablecloth, the one my mother usually saved for Easter. I was surprised he didn't pull out the good plates, but I think there were limits to what Mom would allow.

The tablecloth looked odd next to the chipped everyday plates, but I wasn't complaining. It wasn't like Eduardo was going to really notice. At exactly six, the doorbell rang.

It was so exact I had to wonder if he'd been standing outside the door, waiting. I could hear my father coming down the hall, so I hurried from the kitchen to get there first.

Eduardo was in pressed slacks and a buttoned-down shirt, way overdressed considering my ratty blue jeans and t-shirt. He was holding some kind of plate with something covered by plastic wrap.

The poor guy looked nervous. Not 'talking to Sarah for the first time' nervous, but definitely uneasy.

"Hey man," I said.

"Hey. Thanks for inviting me."

I stepped aside so he could come in. "No problem. What's that?"

"Mom made a flan for me to bring."

"Ohh, that was really nice of her," I said and led him toward the kitchen.

Dad was already in there, checking on the pot roast, the one thing he knew how to make.

"All done?"

"Yep, it's looking good," he said.

"Here, Eduardo's mom sent this over for dessert," I said, handing the plate over to him.

"Ohh, nice," he said, taking it from me and sticking it in the fridge, then he turned to Eduardo and extended his hand. "And I assume you're Eduardo."

"Yes, Sir," he said, shaking it.

It looked like a firm handshake. Good. Dad was always one of those 'you can tell a lot about a person by their handshake' kind of people.

"Good to have you here. I appreciate your family giving Blake so much of your time these last few months."

"My parents are thrilled to have him. He's done so much work around the house, I swear they would marry him if you'd allow it."

"Really? Like, what has he been fixing?"

"All kinds of things. Fixed the back fence door, replaced the rotted eaves on the back of the house, even fixed the leaky faucet that's been driving Mom crazy for forever. She was really impressed, although it's got her on me 'cause I never wanted to learn this stuff from my dad like he did from you."

"Me?" Dad said, surprised. "Trust me, I've never been very handy and didn't teach him any of that. Actually, where did you learn all of it?"

I shrugged. "I don't know. I read a few DIY books and the rest just ... made sense."

That was as good of an explanation as I was going to be able to give him. It wasn't like I was going to explain that I had almost thirty years of construction work under my belt, or at least the knowledge of it from my dream world.

I think Dad was getting suspicious though, putting this together with the gambling thing and starting to really wonder where I was coming up with all of this stuff.

At some point, I was going to have to come up with a better story than 'trust me.'

"Well, that's something," he said after another beat. "Let's sit down for dinner. I'm gonna get your mom. You get the pot roast out of the oven."

"Sure," I said and grabbed some oven mitts to pull it out. "Mom's not feeling great, so Dad cooked and this is pretty much the only thing Dad can make. It's not bad, though."

"I'm sure it'll be fine."

"Come on, don't get all modest. I've had your mom's cooking. Trust me, this is not going to live up to your mom's cooking."

"Hey, I resent that," Dad said with a smile as he and Mom walked back into the kitchen.

"You haven't had her cooking yet," I said, spooning some of the food onto a plate and handing it to Eduardo to set on the table. "Wait till you try her flan. She is amazing."

Mom gave me a look, but she'd never been much of a home cook either. We tended to eat boxed meals even before she got sick. Other than the occasional pot of spaghetti or Dad's pot roast, I'm not sure we ever ate anything that could be considered 'homemade.'

Although, to be fair, Dad's pot roast was good. He'd also made some dehydrated mashed potatoes which would be okay after being mixed with the gravy from the pot roast.

"We'll see," he said as I prepared two more plates. "I'll take over here. You go get your brother."

It was all I could do to keep from rolling my eyes. The last thing I wanted to do was go and deal with that little psycho. Thankfully I was saved when he came thundering down the stairs all on his own.

He dropped into his normal chair, which didn't have a plate in front of it, and then reached across and grabbed the one in front of my seat, the little shit.

As soon as it was in front of him, he dug his fork in and got a big scoop full, ready to shovel it into his mouth.

"Joshua! We haven't said grace yet," Mom said.

Josh frowned but dropped his fork on his plate and crossed his arms, making it very clear he wasn't happy about it. I motioned for Eduardo to take the extra chair we'd put out and grabbed a new plate for myself.

As I sat down, Dad put his hand over mine and looked at me expectantly.

"Uh, sure," I said, bowing my head. "Dear Lord, thank you for this food, and for Eduardo being here. Please bless our family and keep us safe. Amen."

"Amen," Dad echoed.

As soon as the word left his mouth, Joshua dug into the food like he hadn't eaten in days. I noticed Mom had pushed her own plate out of the way and had replaced it with a glass filled with some kind of thick green liquid that looked awful.

I saw Dad's brow crease as he noticed it, too, but he didn't say anything about it.

Instead, he looked at Eduardo and said, "Blake mentioned your dad works in Midland too; what does he do?"

"He works construction. He just got on with the people building a new shopping mall on the north side of town."

"Oh yeah? I've driven past that place a few times. Looks like they're making good progress. I may have to stop by and say hello, thank him for all the times he's fed Blake."

"Uhh, yeah. I'm sure he ..."

"Why do you need to go talk to a bunch of wet..." Joshua said, interrupting him.

"Joshua!" Dad yelled, cutting him off.

Josh glared at Eduardo, like he'd done anything other than just sit there and have a nice conversation, slumping back in his seat and stabbing at his food as he did.

Eduardo looked over at me, kind of nervously, and then awkwardly tried to change the subject. "What's it like being a police officer, Mr. Sims?"

Dad gave him a small smile. I think he was happy Eduardo was the one to change the subject, since there was no way to keep what happened from being weird.

"It's good work. I like helping people, making a difference. But it can be grueling. Long hours, tough situations."

Mom finished the last of her foul-smelling green drink and pushed back from the table. "If you'll excuse me, I need to lie down."

"Of course, honey," Dad said softly.

We watched her head upstairs before Eduardo tried to get the conversation going again.

"That game yesterday was intense. I've never seen mud like that."

"That game should never have happened. I had words with Coach Holloway about it," Dad said with more intensity than I'd expected.

"Dad, it wasn't that bad ..."

"It absolutely was that bad, Blake. That field was a safety hazard. I made it very clear to Coach Holloway that putting kids at risk like that is completely unacceptable."

"I think he's right," Eduardo said. "Everyone in the stands was just waiting for someone to slip and hurt themselves on every play."

"I guess. Although, it let me get what'll probably be my longest run for as long as I play football. Who ever heard of a quarterback getting eighty yards on a scramble? No way that would have been possible if the field wasn't trash."

"You're just lucky you didn't get hurt," Dad said, not letting go of his position.

Josh finished eating and just left the table, not excusing himself or saying anything. I think Dad was just happy to have him go, since he didn't want to get into it with him when company was around. Things got a lot more relaxed once Josh left. We talked about school, football, and what it was like to live in Midland.

I couldn't really contribute to the last part, but they both knew a lot of places and it was something they could talk about, which was the whole goal of this dinner. The closer Eduardo got to us and especially Dad, the less likely the future where he killed Dad in a carjacking would ever happen.

"I shouldn't have had that second helping," Dad said, patting his stomach and pushing the dessert plate back. "Going to get too big for my vest at this rate. Tell your mom her flan was amazing."

"I will," Eduardo said, laughing.

"Let me grab my keys, and I'll give you a ride home."

"That isn't necessary," Eduardo said. "It's not that far of a walk."

"No, it's late, I insist."

"It's okay, let him take you," I said.

"Okay. I appreciate it."

As Dad disappeared into the living room to get his keys, I said, "Thanks for coming, man. I'm sorry about my brother."

Eduardo waved it off. "Don't worry about it. I know what annoying little brothers are like."

"No way. Alex is way better than Joshua."

"Yeah, maybe. Your dad's really nice, though."

"Yeah, he's alright," I said as Dad came back into the room. "See you tomorrow at school?"

"Yep, see you then," he said, following my dad outside.

Even with Josh doing his best to derail things, that had gone well. While I knew I wasn't done with this until I got him completely separated from Rafe, it was starting to seem like I'd done it.

The future where Dad died was done and gone, and this new future was starting to look pretty good.

The week flew by, even with having to take midterms. Everyone was ready for the weeklong holiday. At least the teachers were smart enough to make sure we were done by Thursday, since everyone knew that the day before a long break was more or less wasted.

More so this week, since tonight was our first playoff game, and a big pep rally was scheduled to send the team off, which would take up the last hour or so of the school day. It basically turned the entire day into a party and the teachers were having a hell of a time trying to keep everyone in check.

All bets were off as the bell rang and we were sent to the gym, with basically the entire student body trying to squeeze into the hallway that led to the gym and through the only set of doors into it.

At least we didn't have to fight for a place to sit. There were spots for the JV and freshman teams, for the dance team, for the band, and chairs up behind a podium under one of the baskets for varsity players to sit.

Not that we took our seats until Vice-Principal Ford got behind the podium and tapped the microphone a few times.

"Students, I expect exemplary behavior today. I know you're all excited to head home and start your Thanksgiving break, but we will be holding detention today for anyone who causes a scene. So unless you want to start your break an hour and a half after the rest of your classmates, I suggest you sit down and mind yourselves."

She gave a particular look toward a section of bleachers made up of mostly seniors. At the last pep rally, they'd caused all kinds of problems, with stupid chants interrupting the speakers and passing around a beach ball someone had snuck in.

The seniors seemed immensely proud of the scrutiny, grinning at each other like they'd been given a shout-out from the stage at a concert. Mrs. Ford gave a nod to the band director and the band struck up the fight song, which was clearly a cue for the pep rally to begin, since right after that both the varsity and JV cheer squads burst through the doors, running into the gym.

While the JV girls positioned themselves facing our section, the varsity cheerleaders created two lines, holding up a massive paper banner decorated with "Run Through State!" in blue and gold letters. Melanie had positioned herself well and was practically directly in front of me, giving me a big grin.

Principal Robbins switched places with Vice-Principal Ford and said, "Tonight marks the beginning of our run for the state championship! Let's hear it for our varsity Mustangs!"

The crowd erupted as Kenneth led the varsity team busting through the banner, ripping it apart dramatically and running into the room. They charged around the gym in their traditional victory lap, slapping hands with students in the front rows.

After they got to their seats and took their places, Coach Holloway took the spot behind the mic. "What a season it's been, Wheaton! Eight and two, and we're not done yet. These boys have fought through every challenge, every setback, and tonight they get to show what they're really made of. But they need your support in the stands tonight! Who's ready to watch the Mustangs make history?"

The crowd responded with thunderous cheers.

"Alright, that's what I want to hear. Now get up on your feet and let's show your quarterback some of that Mustang pride!"

Kenneth leapt up and practically bounced to the mic. He was pumped, and everyone could see it.

"When I say 'Mustang,' you say 'Pride!' Mustang!"

"PRIDE!" the crowd roared back.

"MUSTANG!"

"PRIDE!"

I know it's typical to think of kids as being jaded and not really caring about anything, but kids in West Texas loved football and went absolutely feral for their teams. Especially when it came to playoff season.

Everyone was stomping and cheering as the cheerleaders all moved to the center of the floor in front of the podium and started doing a routine, with the band playing.

It was a party atmosphere.

They also took a moment to introduce the varsity basketball teams, which would be starting their season near the end of the month. It was wild to see Li out there with all of the other girls, towering over most of them, and looking nervous as hell.

Well, nervous and a little proud. She saw me and gave a little wave, which I returned.

Finally, Principal Robbins returned to the podium to wrap things up. "Have a wonderful Thanksgiving break, everyone. And remember, be safe. We want to see all of you back in a week to finish this semester off right. I also hope to see many of you at the game tonight. We're all going to be there supporting our Mustangs as they start their journey toward the state championship!"

As students began flooding toward the exits, I spotted Brandy making her way over to Tammy. Why couldn't she take a break from her constant scheming? Everyone was in a good mood, happy to be headed home for a week of vegging and watching TV.

This was the last thing we needed.

I saw Melanie looking over at them and knew it was going to ruin at least the rest of the day for her. We had a date tonight, and it was almost certainly going to be the only thing she wanted to talk about.

At least I didn't have to go to practice after this. With the season over, we were done with afternoon practices, except for those who signed up for the seven-on-seven tournaments in the spring, but even those practices wouldn't start up until almost March.

I'd still have training with Coach Greer, and that was switching to after school, now that football was done, thank God, he'd put us on hold until after Thanksgiving, too.

So, for once, I would actually go home after school. As long as Josh stayed in his room, I would have a good afternoon sitting in front of the TV, rotting some brain cells.

As I passed by the trophy case, someone yelled out from behind me, "Blake, hold up."

I turned to find Kenneth jogging toward me, which was a little surprising. We were on the field at the same time during practice, and we both sat at the same lunch table, except I sat at one end with JV and he sat at the far end with varsity.

We existed in very different parts of the same world, so for the life of me I couldn't think of a reason he'd be coming over to find me, let alone run out of the gym to catch up to me.

"Hey man, got a minute?"

"Sure. What's up?"

"It's been so crazy this week, I haven't gotten a chance to say it yet, but I wanted to tell you how great you've been doing since you got moved to JV. I don't know how you got the balls to ignore Coach's play calling and then managed not to get benched, but you've been absolutely killing it since then."

"I have no idea either. I think I went temporarily insane."

"Well, it worked out for you. I went to see your last game and man, that mud bowl against Dunbar? That first scramble of yours was freaking nuts."

"Thanks, although I just got lucky. That whole game was pure chaos. Had the field not been such a mess, I would never have managed a run like that."

"No way, don't sell yourself short. They may not have been as long, but you managed some good runs in other games, too. You're fast as hell, and you're way better than I was as a freshman. You're going to be a monster when you get to varsity."

"I hope so," I said, and then wasn't sure what else to say. "Looking forward to tonight?"

"Yeah. We got a good draw for the first round, and I think we'll sail through easily. Next weekend is going to be the big problem. I looked at the bracket, and if Midland wins their game tonight, which we both know they will, we'll have to face them on Black Friday. I don't know if you saw the homecoming game, but it was kind of brutal."

"You never know what might happen."

Actually, I did know. This was the height of Midland's dominance of our district, and they'd get to state three times in the next five years. In my dream, at least, they lost this year and next year, before I'd had to drop out of school. We had been building a strong team that I thought, or at least liked to think, would have been able to pull it out the following year.

Not that it was going to change what happened this year. Coach might have changed the playbook for me, but I guess Kenneth never pushed back and just accepted the plays he was getting.

"I'm not sure if I share your opinion, but I like your optimism," Kenneth said with a smile. "Anyway, just wanted to say hi since we haven't really talked before. Try to hang out with us more, okay?"

"Sure."

He gave a wave and started to head back inside when I said, "Actually, could I ask you something?"

He stopped. "What's up?"

"Would you maybe talk to Tammy about the varsity cheer squad for next year? It's just …" I shifted my weight. "I'm dating Melanie, who's on the JV squad right now. She's really good, but my ex, Brandy, who's also on JV, is trying to keep her off the team. She's still mad about me breaking up with her, and she's taking it out on Melanie. She's been in Tammy's ear a lot, telling her all kinds of things, trying to convince her to keep Melanie off the team, even though she absolutely deserves it."

Kenneth rolled his eyes. "Yeah, Tammy's mentioned there's drama with the JV squad. I swear, the squabbling they all do, it's exhausting."

"Tell me about it. Look, I know it's not really your problem, but I'd appreciate any help to even things out. Melanie shouldn't get punished just because Brandy's jealous."

"No, I get it. That's messed up." Kenneth nodded. "I'll talk to Tammy, see if I can get her to look past whatever BS Brandy's spreading."

"Thanks, man, I really appreciate it."

"No problem. It's the downside of dating cheerleaders, right? I'll see you at the game, right?"

"Yeah, wouldn't miss it."

"Good," he said, slapping me on the shoulder and heading back toward the gym.

I felt oddly satisfied. It was a small thing, but maybe it would help protect Melanie from some of Brandy's schemes. Though knowing Brandy, she'd probably just find another angle of attack.

But Tammy was more likely to listen to Kenneth than Brandy, so I hoped it would at least slow her down.

Chapter 36

I stumbled down the stairs still squinting from the sunlight that was just a little too bright. It was almost noon and I'd slept half the day away, but since this was the first day of vacation, that was fine by me. Football was done, and my weekends just got a lot less busy.

What I wanted more than anything at the moment was a glass of water. I'd gotten in super late from our celebration with the guys from varsity after their crushing 32-7 win in their first playoff game.

The fact that we'd even been invited along was amazing. While they had practically the same celebration ritual of going to the Silver Spoon that JV had, normally only varsity players and cheerleaders went after their games.

Kenneth had somehow noticed me in the stands and yelled at me to meet them at the 'Spoon' as he headed back to the field house after the game.

Mickey, Hanna, and Melanie had been sitting with me, so I brought them along, which turned out not to be a problem. Better yet, Melanie and Hanna had been pulled over by Tammy and the cheerleaders when we got there, while Mickey and I went to sit with some of the guys, and they spent the whole night flitting between our table and the varsity cheerleaders like hyperactive hummingbirds.

It was nice seeing her so happy, and it paid off for me. It was pretty late when Freddie chased us all out, so I'd walked her home. She spent the entire walk just chattering away about all the funny things Tammy had said, how great Tammy was, and just gushing about the whole night. As soon as we got to her door though, she was all over me.

We'd been keeping things pretty tame so far, but she took things up several notches. It wasn't a full-on make-out session, considering we were standing in front of her house, but she definitely rewarded me for getting her a night with the varsity girls.

I'd been in such a good mood when I got home that I'd just lain in bed for an hour, staring at the ceiling, reliving the evening. And now I was paying the price for staying up so late.

My eyelids felt like they were lined with lead, and my brain still felt fuzzy. And it wasn't just because I stayed up late. Josh was banging around just after the sun came up, either building furniture or just being loud to be an asshole.

I was pretty sure it was the latter.

I'd tried to block him out with some music, but I couldn't find my headphones in my room and didn't have enough energy to go hunting for them then. Thankfully, he didn't do it for long. He'd been disappearing in the afternoons and on weekends, more and more, going who knows where, and coming back when it was dark. I know it bugged Dad, but Mom kept saying he was going to play with friends.

Like he had any friends.

But whatever. There wasn't anything I could do to convince them to take his actions more seriously. Mom was ... I don't even know why she put up with it, and Dad was more concerned with Mom's health and didn't want to fight with her about it.

Mostly, I just wanted to get some water, find my headphones, and head back upstairs to sleep a little longer.

I finished my water and headed into the entry hallway where I'd dropped my gym bag last night. I'd been so tired when I got home that I barely remembered throwing it down. I must have been really tired, because it was half unzipped. Although how I could have carried it around all day half open was beyond me. I knelt beside it, ignoring the heavy smell of old sweat that had soaked into the fabric.

It still had my clothes from gym the day before that I'd have to get to eventually. I dug past those, some random gear still in the bag, and a towel, and didn't see them. I pushed everything around again, wondering how I could miss them in a bag that was only half full.

And my brain caught up. There was no way the bag had been open. I remembered that it was closed when I got home.

It wasn't hard to figure out what had happened.

Mom and Dad would never have messed with it. If anything, they would have seen it and yelled at me to move it out of the hallway. Josh, on the other hand, would absolutely steal my shit. In a heartbeat.

Actually, he was more likely to do that now. Ever since Eduardo came over for dinner, he'd been even more of a pain than usual.

I shoved everything back into the bag and headed upstairs to his room. He was still out, doing whatever it was he did, and I went into his room.

The place was a pigsty. Stuff was everywhere. I knew Mom came in and picked up his dirty clothes, to do his laundry, something she hadn't done for me in a long time. This wasn't the first time he'd stolen stuff from me, and over the years, I'd worked out some of his most common hiding places.

I carefully moved his dresser away from the wall, but found nothing there except dust bunnies and a forgotten sock. I then checked under his bed. Getting on my hands and knees, I found two crumpled pieces of paper. Pulling them out, I recognized my old practice schedules from the start of the season. He'd torn them into pieces and then wadded them up.

Annoying, and he probably thought it was a "gotcha" to me, but we got these all the time as the practices changed. The fact that I hadn't even noticed they'd gone missing said that they weren't all that important.

I got up and looked around the room. Those were the two places he'd tended to hide stuff. Something tickled at the back of my mind. A few months ago, Mom had found something of mine in the garage and was annoyed that I'd leave something there. I hadn't known what she was talking about at the time, but now …

I headed down to the garage, which was a mess of boxes and old junk, too full to actually put a car into. Dad kept talking about cleaning it out, but we never did.

I made my way to where the Christmas decorations were stacked against the back wall, which was about where Mom had mentioned finding my stuff. I hadn't actually checked at the time, just taken my stuff from her, and now I was kicking myself for not paying more attention.

I started digging behind the boxes. He wouldn't just leave them in the open. He liked to hide stuff under and behind things. After a few minutes, I thought maybe I'd misread the situation, and they weren't there, until a section of drywall caught my eye. Moving closer, I could see it had been cut open and then pushed back into place.

I pulled it out carefully. It was still partially attached, so I couldn't move it all the way out of the way, but I opened it enough to see a shoebox sitting there, with my headphones resting on top.

Little bastard.

I grabbed my headphones and started to put the drywall back when something stopped me. I saw the shoebox and wondered just what else of mine he'd squirreled away. I picked up the shoebox and was surprised when it was heavier than I expected. Something inside shifted when I moved it.

I pulled off the lid and felt my stomach drop. It was filled with a collection of random stuff, but not just random knickknacks someone else might have in a shoebox. Hair ties in different colors, several tubes of lipstick and lip gloss, pieces from charm bracelets and necklaces, and, if that wasn't worrying enough, two small clumps of hair, clearly from different girls.

They didn't feel like mementos. They felt like trophies.

And then I noticed one of the pieces from a charm bracelet. It was a tiny silver megaphone, and I knew exactly where it came from. Melanie had complained about losing hers a few weeks ago. She hadn't specifically said she'd lost it here, since I think she didn't notice right away when it disappeared, but it was around the time she'd come over to study with me.

I was nearly certain these were all connected to different girls, and couldn't help but think of how he'd looked at Melanie that day.

I needed to show this to Dad. But even as I had that thought, I could predict how it would go. Mom would make excuses; he's just collecting things he finds, he doesn't mean anything by it. And Dad would defer to her like always, not wanting to upset her when she was already dealing with these headaches.

The sound of a car door slamming made me jump. I quickly shoved the drywall piece back into place, tucking the box under my arm. I needed time to think about how to handle this, but I wasn't going to let him keep his creepy ass trophies.

I ended up giving the box to Dad later that night, and he said he'd take care of it. I didn't hear anything else about it, but admittedly, I tried to stay away from the house as much as I could during the week. Mom was in a mood because of her headaches and when Josh was home, he was being a pain in the ass.

Since Dad had to work and wasn't around to mediate, I thought the best thing to do was to be gone. I hung out at Eduardo's a bunch, with Melanie several times, and even at Li's once, although her mom disapproved of us hanging out and watching TV, so we were put to work in the store instead. It was still fun. The more I hung out with her, the more her sense of humor emerged. She was slightly sarcastic, very dry, and could give burns with the best of them.

By Tuesday morning, it looked like Mom would feel good enough to cook Thanksgiving dinner, so Dad went and got all the stuff, including a big ham, which we always had instead of turkey. Thanksgiving morning, though, Mom had another of her headaches and couldn't get out of bed. Dad looked a little frazzled, so I volunteered to help him in the kitchen, not that I actually knew what I was doing.

"I think we need to cut it in half," Dad said, looking at the ham propped halfway in the pan, much too off-kilter to actually fit in our small oven.

"Mom never does," I pointed out.

"Yeah, but I have no idea how she makes it fit."

"Is there another pan?"

"I don't think so."

"Maybe once it cooks a bit, it'll shrink and fit in the pan."

"I'm not sure that's how this works," he said, crossing his arms and glaring at the offending meat as if it were a perp giving him trouble. "I'm hearing you don't think we should cut it in half."

"I mean, Mom likes the big presentation, and she'll definitely notice two halves of ham. Besides, I'm not sure we have enough glaze to do both parts."

"That's a good point. I guess we'll just do our best," he said, and grunted as he tried to force it in the pan, hitting it several times.

It did go into the pan more, although the meat kind of bowed at the bottom where he'd hit it.

"Wrap it in foil, and we'll see if it fits after it cooks for a bit," I suggested.

"Yeah, that's about all we can do."

After wrapping it up and getting it into the oven, I went back to mixing up the potatoes, double checking the instructions on the box, while he started looking at the package of stuffing.

"So," Dad said as he started pouring stuff into bowls. "Football season's over. What are your plans for spring semester?"

"I've been thinking about seven-on-seven. It'll help keep my passing skills sharp. Plus, by March, we should have enough saved from the betting to start with those trainers I was talking about."

"About that, you were right about the Vikings game."

"You're not still doubting me, are you?"

"No, no. I have faith. Even made a nice little bit on it myself. Just remarking on your track record."

"Good. I'm keeping notes on what's coming up next. I just want to do as much as we can the next few years because I don't know how long it will be until what I know isn't reliable anymore. Plus, once I hit college, I think we're going to have to stop the gambling completely because of NCAA rules."

"I hadn't thought about that part," Dad said, frowning.

"Yeah, I didn't at first, but it hit me the other day. They really frown on sports betting, especially on football. We might be able to get away with betting on other sports, but who knows? Also, like you said, the longer we gamble, the more likely someone notices how lucky we've been. There will come a point when we can put money into other things. I do know some stuff about companies, which ones get big, which ones crash in a few years, but nothing that's going to happen soon and the details are fuzzier there, too."

Again, I could kick myself for not really paying attention to those sorts of things. Still, the ones I did know about would be big, if I could figure out the best time to invest.

"We'll deal with that when we get there. Just make sure that as soon as you get a little unsure if something is worth betting on, we stop. The only reason I'm okay putting everything into every bet is because you're so sure. It becomes a lot more risky when you're not sure anymore."

"I know. I'll let you know when what I know starts feeling questionable. Promise."

"Good." Dad nodded. "Just keep showing that kind of judgment."

"Speaking of judgment, I think the stuffing's burning."

Dad rushed to pull the pan of Stove Top off the burner while I fought back a laugh. We spent the next hour cooking and just chatting. He even talked about his work, which he didn't do much. It was solid bonding time.

In the end, we managed to get the meal on the table. The instant mashed potatoes came out lumpy, the stuffing was a little crispy on the bottom, and the mac and cheese was definitely not traditional, but the ham at least looked decent.

I got everything set on the table while Dad got Mom and Josh. After a short grace, we all started to eat. To say things were tense would be an understatement.

Josh, naturally, didn't seem particularly bothered by anything, just focused on eating without giving a damn about anybody. Mom, still in the grips of her headache, barely looked up. She also didn't make herself a plate.

Instead, she poured herself some of the foul-smelling green liquid which she slowly sipped at. This seemed to set Dad off, who looked equally concerned and annoyed every time she picked up the glass of sludge.

We made it halfway through the meal without a sound beyond the clinking of silverware against the plates.

Josh was the first one to break the silence.

"I want a lock for my door."

"Why would you need that?" Dad asked.

"Blake's been going through my room!"

"I have not," I said.

While I had been, that once, I wasn't going to let him know that. I'd made sure to cover all of my tracks, even leaving my torn-up schedule under his bed. There was no way he could know I was in there.

"You were. You took my box of stuff."

"You mean the one that was hidden in the garage? With my missing headphones sitting on top of it? I didn't take it, I gave it to Dad."

I looked at Dad. Clearly, he hadn't talked to Josh or handled it like he promised he would. Instead of going at Josh myself, I'd done it the right way, letting him take care of it. So now would be a good time for him to back me up before Mom jumped all over my shit.

"What box?" Mom asked sharply.

"It's just some of my stuff. Things I found and collected."

"That's some BS. It's not just stuff he collected; it was full of stuff taken from girls at school. Hair ties, makeup, jewelry, including Melanie's bracelet charm that went missing the day she came over here to study with me."

"Joshua isn't a thief," Mom cut in. "Blake, stop making up stories about your brother. If Josh says it's just stuff he found, then that's all it is. To suggest he's doing something like that is hurtful, and I won't allow it."

"What! I'm not making anything up! Dad, tell her."

Dad cleared his throat, setting down his fork. "Heather, Blake did bring me a concerning collection of items."

"Tom, not you, too," Mom interrupted. "He's curious and likes to collect things. I won't sit here and listen to these horrible accusations. Joshua finds things people drop and keeps them because he's sentimental. To twist that into something else is cruel."

"Mom, he's dangerous!" I said. "These weren't just random items he found. They were personal things taken from specific girls. Trophies. He's been following them, watching them ..."

"I said enough!" Mom's face had gone flush.

Josh had gone very still during this exchange, his eyes fixed on his plate. But I caught the slight curl of his lip. This would just reinforce that Mom would defend him no matter what evidence we presented.

It was going to embolden him.

"Heather, we need to discuss this," Dad tried again. "The behavior indicated by these items suggests ..."

"It suggests nothing except that Blake is trying to hurt his brother again," Mom snapped. "And you're enabling him. Joshua, sweetheart, you don't have to sit here and listen to these awful accusations."

Josh's chair scraped back and he stood up, looking hurt and confused. He didn't fool me, though. I could see the triumph in his eyes, even if Mom and Dad were too focused on each other to see it.

"I can't believe you'd do this," Mom said, her voice trembling as she got up, wrapping an arm around Josh's shoulders. "On Thanksgiving of all days. Blake, go to your room. You're grounded until you apologize to your brother."

"I'm not apologizing for telling the truth," I said, standing as well. "Dad, please!"

"Tom, handle your son," Mom ordered as she directed Josh upstairs.

"Heather, I ..."

"No," she said, spinning to face him as Josh disappeared upstairs. "Why do you always take his side? Just because Blake plays football, just because he reminds you of yourself, you can't see anything else!"

"This has nothing to do with football. This is about Joshua's behavior."

"His behavior is normal! He's sensitive; he collects things that interest him. But you can't stand that, can you? You can't stand that he's not another dumb jock like you were!"

"Heather, that's enough." Dad's hands clenched on the table. "Joshua is sick. He needs help. It's not just him collecting things. His behavior is out of control. Hell, he even attacked you a few months ago. We can't keep ignoring this."

"He's not sick! You push and push him to be something he's not, and when he withdraws, you act like there's something wrong with him!"

"There is something wrong with him!" I shouted, unable to keep my mouth shut any longer.

"Don't you dare! You are just like your father; everything has to fit in your narrow little box of what's acceptable!"

"And you are just like your mother, refusing to see what's right in front of you!" Dad said. "Just like with these headaches. You won't listen to the doctors, you won't listen to reason, the only people you will listen to is that crazy friend of ..."

"Why would I listen to them?! They dismiss me, just like you do! Looking down their noses at my natural remedies while pushing their pills that don't work!"

"The pills would work if you actually took them."

"Don't you dare criticize my choices! I am the one suffering here, not you!"

"We are all suffering, Heather! The whole family is suffering while you pretend everything's fine!"

I just stood there frozen, watching them tear into each other. This had escalated a lot beyond the problem with Josh. They had both been piling up the resentment for months, and the floodgates had opened.

"Oh, now you care about the family? Where was that concern when Blake was struggling in school? When Joshua needed help with all the bullying he's gotten? You were too busy with work, with your precious overtime ..."

I couldn't take it anymore. The food on the table was completely forgotten as they laid into each other. They didn't even notice me as I left the room and went out the back door. I could still hear them screaming at each other, even as I walked down the driveway toward the street.

I had to do something about Josh, knowing what he was going to become, but I hadn't wanted it to turn out like this. For whatever reason, Mom had decided to put everything into defending him, no matter what, to an insane degree.

And I hadn't known Dad was holding in so much resentment over everything. I should have just tossed the box and pretended I didn't know what Josh was talking about. It wasn't like telling Dad had done anything other than making everything worse.

I had seen the look on Josh's face. He knew Mom was going to defend him to the end. It was going to have him behaving even worse.

No matter what I did.

Chapter 37

The rest of the holiday weekend was uncomfortable, with no one talking to anyone else and Josh strutting around when Mom wasn't looking, acting like he was untouchable.

Which he kind of was. When Mom was around, he went back to putting on the sad boy act, eating up the sympathy from her. Dad picked up some extra shifts, I think to try and avoid it all. I didn't blame him, but it left me outnumbered, with Mom glaring at me, pissed every time she saw me.

She refused to let me go out with Melanie on Friday, sticking with the bullshit grounding, and tried to keep me from going to the varsity game on Saturday. Thankfully, Dad was home for that and interceded, which started another shouting match, but Dad put his foot down.

Unfortunately, the game did not live up to the effort it took to get here. Like I remembered, Midland crushed us, winning 24-7. The team took it hard. They had somehow talked themselves into thinking they were going to win. Considering what they did to us during the regular season, it was a little far-fetched, but I guess it never hurt to have a positive attitude.

It officially ended our football for the year, but it didn't end sports. Wednesday was Li's first game, and I was excited to go and watch it. I wanted them to have good support for their first game, but it was like pulling teeth to get anyone to go with me. Eduardo had to do a thing with his mom and none of the guys on the team seemed interested. I finally managed to convince Melanie to come with me, but it had been a fight since she really hadn't wanted to come along, but agreed as long as I promised to take her out for dinner afterward.

I was a little annoyed with her, since she knew how important it was to me to support my friend, but it was also midweek after a holiday and she'd made a few comments about stuff going on at home, so I forgave her.

The gym was only half full on our side of the court, which was better than I'd feared it would be, but not as full as I'd wanted. To be fair, I don't think the games were ever well attended. We'd never made it past district in the history of our team, and that had been the boys' team. I don't think the girls' team ever even qualified for district playoffs, so it just wasn't a big sport for our school.

Melanie spotted Tammy and the other varsity cheerleaders setting up near the baseline as soon as we walked in and said, "Let's go say hi."

"Sure," I said.

We still had maybe five or so minutes until the game started. We made our way down the sidelines to where the varsity cheerleaders were set up. At first, Melanie just kind of stood a few feet back, waiting for them to see her.

When they did, I don't think it was everything Melanie had hoped for. Tammy looked over, saw her, and then started to turn away, like she hadn't even recognized Melanie. She only stopped when she saw me and something flashed across her face. I can only guess that Kenneth had talked to her and seeing me reminded her she was supposed to be nice or whatever to Melanie.

Tammy put a big smile on her face and pulled Melanie in for a hug.

"Hey, girl," Tammy said. "What are you doing here?"

"His friend is playing and he begged me to come," Melanie said, pointing her thumb at me.

I gave a small wave and Tammy gave me the same kind of fake smile she gave Melanie before pulling her into the group with the rest of the cheerleaders, who started talking excitedly about something.

I kind of waited on the outskirts, since I didn't really know any of the varsity girls very well and would have been really out of place in their huddle. It was a little awkward since, as soon as they started talking, Melanie all but forgot I existed, ignoring me completely, but whatever.

While they talked, I looked over to where the teams were warming up and spotted Li in her number twenty-two jersey. She caught my eye and gave a small wave before returning to the passing drills. The cheerleading huddle finally broke up when the refs started getting the teams set up for the jump-off.

Melanie gave them a wave, and we headed for a spot on the bleachers a few rows up from them.

"Did you see that?" Melanie said excitedly as the announcer began going through the starting lineups.

"I did. I guess your worry about Brandy getting to Tammy was all for nothing," I said, very specifically not mentioning I'd talked to Kenneth.

"Did you hear what they said about Casey and Jessica?"

"No."

I assumed Casey was Casey Jackson, the safety on the freshman football team, since he'd been seen, off and on again, with Jessica, one of the JV cheerleaders. Why the varsity squad would be talking about them, I didn't know, but I also stayed out of most of their drama.

"Well, Jessica told Sarah and Tammy that …" Melanie said, launching into the latest drama.

I was listening and making the right noises at the right time, but other than knowing Casey, I really had no connection to the story and didn't love this kind of gossip as much as Melanie did.

I knew she loved talking about it, though, and who was I to ruin her fun?

The teams were announced and they set up for tip-off. Li wasn't in the starting lineup, but I already knew she wasn't going to be. When I'd talked to her at lunch, she'd seemed okay with being a bench player for now. It was practically unheard of for a freshman to make the varsity team, so I think she was just reveling in that victory for now.

"Can you believe it?"

"Nope. I would have thought Casey was smarter than that."

"I know, right?"

The game started fast, both teams running their offenses at full speed. Amarillo's point guard was quick, but our defense stayed tight. We traded baskets back and forth, neither team able to build more than a four-point lead.

"I'm going to go talk to Katie for a second," Melanie said part-way through the first quarter.

"Do you want me to go with you?"

"No, I'll be right back."

I kept watching the game. Wheaton was actually doing okay and had it tied up at 18 when the second quarter started, and the coach finally sent Li to check in at the scorer's table.

"Let's go, Li!" I shouted, standing as she jogged onto the court.

Melanie, who had just returned, pulled at my arm. "Sit down."

"What? I'm supporting my friend."

Li took her position in the post as Amarillo brought up the ball. A guard drove in trying to get a layup, and Li put a hand up, not that it was necessary. She towered over the girl and made the shot all but impossible. After forcing a missed shot, she jumped up and grabbed the rebound. Instead of turning and dribbling it back downcourt, though, she rocketed the ball down to our point guard who'd just gotten to the top of the key on the other end of the court, hitting her in stride for a fast break.

It was an impressive pass, longer than a bunch of the ones I'd thrown this season.

I jumped to my feet again. "Yeah! That's what I'm talking about!"

"Blake!" Melanie hissed, yanking me back down. "People are staring."

They could stare all they wanted. Li was playing varsity basket-ball as a freshman, and she was killing it. Even as I thought that, she took a pass and made a clean layup, putting her first points on the board.

"No one's staring," I said. "Other people are cheering for their friends."

She made a face but didn't say anything else. Over the next few minutes, Li showed why she'd made varsity. She really did well controlling the paint-on defense and thwarting shots without fouling, although she did have one overly aggressive block called. On offense, she set a few solid screens and grabbed two offensive rebounds. When Amarillo tried doubling her in the post, she kicked it out to our shooting guard for an open three.

She was doing great, so I didn't understand why the coach pulled her after about three minutes, putting Taylor Stine back in. Even more perplexing was keeping Li on the bench the rest of the quarter.

The halftime buzzer sounded with Wheaton up 34-31.

"Do you mind if I go talk to Li for a second, I want to tell her how good they were?"

"Varsity's about to perform. Don't you want to stay and watch it?"

"I'll be fast, I promise."

"Fine," she said, almost pouting.

I gave her a peck on the cheek and hurried down the bleachers to Wheaton's side.

Li was seated at the far end of the bench, a towel draped around her shoulders as she sipped water. She looked up as I approached, her face lighting up with a big smile.

"Li! You're killing it out there," I said, stopping just shy of the sideline. "That pass was so good."

Her smile widened, and she ducked her head a little. "Thanks. I ..."

"Sims!" Coach Weyland yelled. "This isn't social hour. Back to your seat."

The fact that a coach I didn't play for knew my name probably wasn't a good thing. She'd decided I was a pest, and she was sticking with that.

Li gave me a quick, apologetic shrug before the coach turned her attention back to the clipboard in her hand. I raised my hands in surrender and backed away, shooting Li a thumbs-up before heading back up the bleachers.

Varsity had just started their routine as I got back to my seat, and Melanie jumped into explaining things they added late during the last practice, a section where they'd taken out a tumbling pass because one of the girls doing it couldn't land it reliably, and how much better it had gotten.

I didn't know much about cheerleading except for what I'd learned listening to Brady and now Melanie, but I had to give it to them, they were very good. Tammy did this series of back handsprings ending in some kind of flip that was impressive.

Definitely not something I could do.

"Did you see that?"

"Yeah. It was really good."

"No kidding. I've been trying that with my gymnastics coach, but I'm still having trouble nailing the back tuck on the dead floor."

"Dead floor?"

"It's like just regular floor. The rest of the gym the floor is on these springs, so it's a little easier to land tricks, but on the dead floor, you give up so much energy when you land, so it's harder."

"Ohh."

Amarillo must have gotten a talking-to at halftime because they came out on fire in the third quarter. The starters were all back in and Li was on the bench. For a few minutes, we kept within four points of them, and then Amarillo started to pull away. By the five-minute mark, our three-point lead had become trailing by eleven points.

Our biggest problem this quarter was turnovers. Bad passes, bad ball handling, and two steals gave them so many opportunities to run the score up on us.

Thankfully, Coach Weyland put Li back in and, from where I was sitting, it looked like she was having an immediate impact. On the first possession, she fought through a box-out to grab an offensive rebound and put it back up and in.

"That's what I'm talking about!" I jumped up, pumping my fist.

"If you're going to keep screaming, I'm going to go sit with the girls."

"Why does it bother you so much," I said, getting a little annoyed. "I'm not the only one cheering."

"Whatever, I'll be back," she said, and pushed past me.

Although she'd been kind of bored during most of the third quarter, she'd been in a good mood the rest of the night. Or at least until halftime. Maybe she didn't care much for basketball and once the cheer stuff was done at halftime, she didn't care.

It still didn't explain why she was so annoyed every time I cheered.

I wasn't going to chase after her, though. She knew where I was. If she wanted to come back and sit with me, she could.

Li was still playing great, picking off a lazy cross-court pass and hitting our point guard in stride with an outlet pass for an easy layup.

Which is why I was completely perplexed when Coach Weyland subbed her, sending Taylor back in.

"What are you doing?" I shouted, which must have been just loud enough to be heard at the bench because the coach actually turned around and looked up at me.

I looked right back at her. She was screwing up the chance to win. Li was absolutely playing better than Taylor. The coach frowned and went back to the game.

I thought maybe I should back off a little bit, since coaches could be as vindictive as any other teacher, and I didn't want her taking it out on Li.

The rest of the game was painful to watch. Taylor kept trying to force shots up over double teams instead of kicking it out. She was getting the rebound and putting it up again, but that was costing the team time, and she didn't get every ball back. Amarillo saw what she was doing and put more players in the paint to stop her, which meant she had guards on the outside who could have taken open shots if she was more of a team player.

Seeing how she was playing, I kept thinking Coach Weyland might put Li back in, but she didn't.

The final buzzer sounded with Amarillo up by eight. By my count, Li had put up eight points, had four rebounds, a block, and a steal in just five minutes. Taylor played thirty-two minutes to get fourteen points and ten rebounds.

A double-double on the sheet, but one that was mostly made up of her getting her own rebound from missed layups and putting it back in. I think the team as a whole played better when Li was in.

Melanie was still chatting with the cheerleaders.

"Hey, I thought we might go meet Li at the locker rooms and celebrate," I said when there was a break in the conversation.

"Why?"

"'Cause she's my friend and the reason we came to the game."

"Can't we just go get dinner ourselves? I'm starving."

"No. I mean, we can go eat, but I want to celebrate her first game with her. What if we took her out to eat so you could get some food and we could still celebrate?"

"I thought it would just be the two of us," she said, putting her hand on my chest, I guess thinking switching tactics from petulant to seductive would convince me.

I had no idea why she didn't want me to hang out with Li. She hadn't been really jealous before this, and when I'd asked her to come, I'd specifically mentioned it was to cheer on my friend.

"You and I are still going out on Friday and will have time for just the two of us, but we came to support Li, so we should do that. It's the whole reason we're here, right?"

"Fine," she said, reverting back to being annoyed. "But I'm not staying out late. I have a test tomorrow."

We made it to the locker room well before any of the girls came out. I was excited, looking forward to talking to Li about her first game and how she felt, even after having to sit on the bench for so much of it.

Melanie, on the other hand, practically radiated annoyance, arms crossed, not really looking at anyone, making it clear to everyone around that she didn't want to be there. I didn't bother asking her to lighten up. I liked Melanie and she had her good qualities, but the selfish part of her was starting to get on my nerves.

The door swung open, releasing a burst of laughter and chatter as a few players emerged. None of them were Li. One of the girls offered Melanie a distracted wave, and she returned it half-heartedly. I caught myself craning my neck toward the door, trying to catch a glimpse of Li's tall frame or hear her voice, but the next wave of girls didn't include her either.

"Are we really waiting out here?" Melanie finally asked, barely glancing in my direction.

"Yes. I want to congratulate her. She had a good game."

Melanie rolled her eyes, letting out a faint sigh. "She didn't even play half of it. Taylor was in most of the time."

At least, that was the first indication that she even noticed that a basketball game was going on. Speaking of her, Taylor Stine appeared next, giving me a curt nod as she walked past. I returned it. I didn't have any reason to dislike Taylor, except that she kept Li from playing.

The door opened another minute later, and finally, Li stepped out. She was smiling, her hair still damp from the shower, carrying her gym bag over one shoulder.

Her smile got even brighter when she spotted me.

"Li!" I called out, probably too loudly for the mostly empty hall. "You were incredible out there!"

"Really? Coach Weyland said …"

"Good job," Melanie cut in, her voice flat.

Li's smile faltered slightly. "Thanks. Coach Weyland actually told me I did great. Said my defensive positioning was really good."

"Coach knows talent when she sees it," I said. "We should celebrate! How about pizza at Napoli's?"

Li hesitated, glancing between Melanie and me. "I don't know."

"Come on, you deserve it. First varsity game, first points scored …"

"We could go to Silver Spoon instead," Melanie interrupted. "Most of the varsity squad will probably show up there."

"Yeah, I figured that, but we saw them earlier and I was hoping we could make tonight about celebrating Li's first game. I swear, Friday, we'll go wherever you want to go," I said, before turning to Li. "And I know for a fact you love Napoli's garlic knots."

"Yeah, pizza sounds good," Li said, going back to her quiet shy voice.

Melanie wasn't pleased with the decision, but didn't fight it. At least not directly.

The walk to Napoli's was short but tense. Melanie was mostly talking to me about cheer stuff and ignoring Li completely. When the conversation would lull and whatever thing Melanie wanted to talk about finished, I'd try to switch topics and bring Li into the conversation, but that seemed to prompt Melanie to realize there was something else she 'had to tell me about.'

It was hard not to see it as deliberate.

At least Napoli's made the walk worth it. The restaurant's familiar warmth hit us as we walked in, along with the smell of garlic and tomato sauce that always made my stomach growl. Business was kind of slow, midweek as it was, and one of the waitresses waved me to find a seat. I led them toward the back, picking a booth away from the entrance where we could actually talk.

I gestured for Melanie to get in on one side of the booth and then slid in next to her while Li settled across from us.

"Blake!" The waitress said as she came up to our table. "Happy the season's over?"

I kind of recognized her. She was in my science class, although she sat clear across the room from me, if she was who I thought she was. I hadn't even realized she knew my name.

"Yeah. Finally get some time to myself," I said as Melanie snaked her arm through mine.

"I hear ya," the girl said, clearly seeing Melanie staking her claim and her voice got more official. "What do you guys want?"

"Could we get some sodas to start?"

"Of course! What can I get everyone?"

"I'll have a Diet Coke and my *boyfriend* will have a Coke. Thanks," Melanie said dismissively.

Li ordered water. The waitress kept her smile firmly in place, but I caught her quick glance at Melanie before she headed off.

"So," I said, turning to Li. "That block in the third quarter was incredible."

"It wasn't that special," Li said, but I caught the hint of a smile.

"Are you kidding? You basically teleported into position. The look on that girl's face when you appeared out of nowhere ..."

"Did you see that new lift that Tammy did? It was great, right?"

"If you mean the one at the end, yeah, it was really good," I said, and then looked back to Li. "So what else did Coach Weyland say to you after the game?"

"Not much, really. Just the thing about defensive positioning."

"She should have said more. I was telling Melanie during the game that the team definitely played better when you were on the floor. Honestly, if they had played you more, I think we might have won."

"I don't know about that."

"You absolutely would have. Right, Melanie?"

"I guess," she said, clearly annoyed I hadn't stayed with the conversation about Tammy.

Li's face fell, and she started picking at the paper wrapper from her straw.

The waitress returned with our drinks and took our order. We ordered pizza with pepperoni, mushroom and sausage, which I knew was Li's favorite. Her mom didn't love her eating junk food, telling her it would make her fat, but we'd stopped here a few times after practicing before tryouts and it was clear she loved it.

"I'm serious," I said, getting the conversation back on track. "The defense really tightened up when you were in. Do you think Coach Weyland might give you more minutes next game?"

Before Li could answer, Melanie launched into a story about a college recruiter who'd been watching Kenneth at the playoff game. Li's responses dwindled to single words, her pizza barely touched.

I didn't shut her down right away, and we talked about Kenneth for a few minutes before I steered the conversation back to basketball, but every time Li started to say something, Melanie would interrupt with something she thought was clearly more important. Worse, she would say it directly to me each time, as if we were the only two people at the table. Li checked her watch so many times I lost count.

When we finished, Li started gathering her things before I could even offer to walk her home.

"I can walk with you," I said, but Li shook her head.

"It's fine. The store's only a block over," she said, standing and shouldering her bag. "Thanks for the pizza."

"You played great tonight, Li. Really."

"Thanks." She managed a small smile, then hurried toward the door.

I watched her go, frustrated at how the evening had turned out. We'd come here to celebrate her achievement and somehow ended up with her feeling bad.

Well, not somehow. I knew exactly how.

"Walk me home?" Melanie asked, pressing closer.

I paid and we walked out of the restaurant, Melanie still pressed against me, her arm looped through mine. All the babble about Kenneth and the varsity team stopped almost as soon as Li left, and now she was acting all content and happy, like she'd won a victory.

I managed to hold my tongue until we reached the corner, but my annoyance with her grew with each step.

"What the hell was that?"

"What?" She kept walking, not meeting my eyes.

"Back there. You were incredibly rude to my friend."

"I was polite. I said congratulations."

"No, you weren't polite. You were cold and dismissive. You kept interrupting her, changing the subject every time we started talking about basketball."

Melanie stopped and crossed her arms, tilting her head as if I was the unreasonable one. "I don't know why you're so worked up. It's not like she's the one you're dating."

I blinked, caught off guard. "What?"

"You heard me. You're always gushing about her, spending time with her, acting like she's some kind of hero. Honestly, Blake, it's weird. I should be the one that's pissed. How do I know you aren't with her behind my back?"

For a second, I just stood there, stunned. This wasn't the first time she'd pissed me off, but I'd been patient. I was trying to be a better person than I had been in the dream life.

But that patience had finally worn out.

"That's what you think? That I'm trying to get with Li because I support her? Because I want to see my friend succeed?"

"You don't see the way you talk about her, do you? You act like she's the most important person in the world. Meanwhile, I'm sitting there like an idiot, wondering why I even came tonight."

"You came because I asked you to come support my friend at her first game, and that was the one thing tonight you didn't want to do. And yet, I did everything you wanted to do except go to the Silver Spoon. You wanted to talk to the cheerleaders, and we did. Every time you interrupted her to talk about something, I didn't shut you down. We talked about it. Do you think it's fair to expect me to support your friends, but insane to think you should support mine?"

"That's not even the same thing. The team is important to me; she's just your tutor. Why would I need to be supportive of her?

She does nothing for us. Newsflash, Blake, I'm not on her team. I'm not the one trying to date her."

"Does nothing for us? What the hell is wrong with you? I'm not just friends with people because they can 'do something' for me! Is that how you really think of people? And I'm not trying to date Li. Do you really think the only reason I'd want to be nice to someone, or support someone, is because I want something from them? Is that all people are to you, a means to an end?"

"You're always so quick to defend her! Why can't you defend me like that?"

"Defend you?" I said, throwing up my hands. "Melanie, I've been defending you since the day we started dating. Why do you think Tammy's started talking to you all of a sudden? It's because I talked to Kenneth and some of the other guys, and made sure they put in a good word for you. And what do you do? You undermine my friend and flirt with Kenneth like it's your job."

Her face flushed. "I do not flirt with Kenneth. He's just … important, okay? If I want to make varsity next year, I need him on my side. You don't understand what it's like for me. Cheerleading is my life, Blake. It's not just some hobby."

"You think I don't get it? You think I don't know what it's like to have big goals? To want something so bad it feels like your whole life depends on it? Newsflash Melanie," I said, repeating her words back to her. "I'm busting my ass to make something happen too, but I don't tear down my friends to get there and I don't treat people like props to use and throw away. I don't … You know what! I'm done."

I turned to start walking away from her, but she ran around and got in front of me again.

"You're so insecure! You're going to break up with me over this? Because I was nice to another guy? I chose to date you, not Kenneth. Why can't you just accept that?"

"This has nothing to do with Kenneth. Have you not heard a word I've said? This is about you apparently only seeing people for what they can do for you. That's not how you treat anyone and it makes me think that maybe the only reason you're dating me is because I'm just another step on your social climbing ladder."

Melanie's face crumpled, tears welling in her eyes. "That's not true. I'm not using you."

"Then what is it? Because right now, that's exactly what this feels like."

"Everything's just ... complicated." Her voice caught. "You make everything look so easy. Making friends, getting people to like you. Even Li, who at the beginning of the year was a nobody. You turned her life around and she looks at you like you hung the moon. Everything you touch turns golden, and my life is fucked."

"Mel ..."

"No. It's, my family's ..." She broke off, wiping furiously at her eyes. "I'm so messed up. I don't know how to do relationships. I've screwed up every one I've ever had."

"I'm sorry things are hard for you, but that doesn't excuse how you treated my friend tonight or how you've treated me."

"I know. I'm just scared. All the time. Scared of being hurt again, scared of not being good enough. My family is such a disaster, I don't even know what normal looks like anymore." She was full-on sobbing now, shoulders shaking. "Please don't give up on me. I really like you, Blake. I want to make this work. I know I messed up, but please ..."

I wanted to still be pissed at her, but it was hard. This wasn't an act. I'd felt the tension in her house every time I'd been there lately and she'd canceled our date that one time, clearly after a big fight with her sister.

"Look, I appreciate you being honest with me," I said, my anger fading.

"I'll do better," she promised. "I'll apologize to Li. I'll work on my jealousy."

"Don't worry about it, I'll talk to her and smooth things over. Before we finish this conversation though, I want to make something clear," I said, lifting her chin so she could see how serious I was. "I don't like the way you treat people sometimes. I can't be with someone who sees people as tools. I won't be with someone like that."

"I understand."

"If you can't trust me, or if you keep putting your social climbing ahead of our relationship, we're done. I mean it."

"I know." She wiped her eyes. "I'll prove it to you. Just give me another chance."

I didn't answer her right away. I looked into her eyes, trying to read her. It seemed like she was being honest, like she really meant it. And, except for stuff like this, I really did like her.

Besides, I was getting a second chance. Why shouldn't I give the same to someone else.

"Okay," I said finally. "Let's get you home."

Chapter 38

"What if I say something stupid?" Eduardo said, not quite whining, but definitely heading that way.

We were sitting on the bleachers in the gym after school, watching Li and the rest of the team practice. Even though I'd celebrated being done with football just before Thanksgiving and having a much more open schedule, being able to just go home after school, Coach had cornered me and convinced me the day before, basically told me, that I was doing seven-on-seven and needed to start doing the practices after school.

While he was right that, after all the pushing I'd done about getting more training, I couldn't then turn around and skip opportunities to work on skills in a smaller, more focused environment. But I had really been looking forward to just relaxing for a while without the constant pressure of having things to do.

Still, sevens practice was a hell of a lot shorter than regular practice during the season, so it gave me a chance to stop and see Li's practice after I finished, and then walk at least halfway home with her before turning to go to my place.

There wasn't a lot of call for spectators at girls' varsity basketball practice, so I'd been by myself yesterday and was surprised when Eduardo showed up a few minutes after I sat down.

Or at least, I was until he jumped into his actual reason for coming to find me. He'd asked Sarah out yesterday and they'd set up their first real date for tonight, and he was freaking out.

"You talk to Sarah all the time. Hell, I think you two were the last ones to realize you were going to start dating. What's the difference between all the other times you two talked and tonight?"

"It's completely different. Here at school or when we talk on the phone, we're just hanging out. Tonight's like … for real."

"You're overthinking it. For real, it's just regular hanging out with the volume turned up. You already know her and are comfortable with her, and I've seen the two of you flirting. Yeah, it's official, but just do and say the kinds of things you usually say."

But what if …"

"No, you're going to freak yourself out with what-ifs. Just be you. You already know what she likes to talk about, what makes her laugh."

"Yeah, but before, if I said something dumb, it didn't matter as much."

"Ohh, it definitely mattered, trust me. She wouldn't have said yes if she didn't like you, and I know for a fact you've said some dumb shit."

Down on the court, Li stole the ball during the scrimmage they were playing and drove for a layup. Coach Weyland's whistle stopped the play before she could finish.

"Just be yourself," I continued. "That's who she wants to go out with."

"Easy for you to say. You're headed to be the star of the school. I'm nobody."

"First of all, you're not nobody. And think of it this way, a lot of people date someone because of the status it brings them. Look at Brandy, for Christ's sake. She's already dumped Mason to start dating one of the sophomores on varsity, and she's been flirting with Ben damn near constantly, since he's going to be quarterback and team captain next year. You know Sarah likes you for you."

"Because I'm a loser who has nothing to offer?"

"Exactly, because you're a loser," I said, laughing as he shoved me. "Where are you taking her?"

"Jimmy's, then maybe the bowling alley to play games."

"Jesus Christ," I said, dropping my head in my hands. "Have you ever known Sara to play video games?

"Uhh …"

"When we talked about it the other day, did she seem interested, or bored to tears?"

I already knew the answer because Melanie definitely was, and she and Sarah started making comments about not wanting to spend time with nerds. They were kidding, but even jokes have a core of truth to them.

"I didn't think of that."

"Okay, think about this. Still take her bowling, but just bowl. Don't go near the games."

"I suck at bowling."

"Even better. Something you two can laugh about. It's better than the movies because you can talk while you're doing it."

"That's a good idea," he said, but then got quiet again, clearly still fretting. "But, like, how do I make it feel different? Special and not just like we're hanging out."

"Little things. For one, dress nice, but not like ... church nice. Also, let her know the plans so she can dress accordingly. Compliment her when you pick her up. Notice something specific, her hair, outfit, whatever, and tell her you like it or it looks nice. And during the date, find excuses for small touches."

"Small touches?"

"Yeah, like putting your hand on her back when you're walking through a door. Or touching her arm while you're talking. Little stuff that shows you're interested."

"Won't that be weird?"

"Not if you're natural about it. She'll do the same thing back if she's into it."

"Okay, but at the end of the night, what about ... you know ..." he trailed off, face going red.

"Kissing her?"

He nodded.

"Unless the date goes horribly wrong, she will be interested. Just pay attention to her signals. If she's standing close to you, finding reasons to touch you back, that's a good sign."

"What if I mess it up?"

"Then you'll both laugh about it later and try again. Stop overthinking."

Eduardo took a deep breath. "Okay. Yeah. You're right."

We watched the team run drills for a few minutes. Li was getting a lot of time in the scrimmage; I just hoped it translated into time in the game itself.

"Hey," Eduardo said suddenly. "Speaking of trying things, I might throw a party."

I turned to look at him. "Really?"

"Yeah, my parents and Alex are going to my aunt's birthday party in a few weeks, just after we go on Christmas break. It's Rafe's mom, so I asked to stay behind cause I just can't deal with him. Dad was pissed but Mom talked him into letting me stay home. I think she was relieved, actually."

"She probably was. She is not his biggest fan."

"Ohh, I know that. But … I've never really thrown a party before, though. I don't know how to set it up, and I don't want it getting crazy."

"That's the easy part. Tell Sarah about it, I'll tell Melanie, and they'll handle everything."

Eduardo's eyebrows rose. "They will?"

"Trust me, cheerleaders live for planning parties. It's like their superpower. I'll make sure to let Melanie know to keep it from turning into a whole school thing and to not just go popular kid, although you want a little of that. It'll be good for your cred."

"That would be good. I don't want the house trashed."

"I'll talk to the guys at lunch about it, make sure Li knows. Between Melanie and Sarah, they'll keep it to the right size."

"Really? Just like that?"

"Just like that. Dating a cheerleader has its perks."

Eduardo smiled. "Thanks, man."

"Hey, that's what friends are for," I said, giving him a shove.

My legs felt like they were on fire, and the cool air was burning in my chest. I'd really enjoyed my two days of actual sleep after switching my workouts to the afternoon, and had cursed myself since Monday for having to be back at this early morning shit.

Not that I had anyone other than myself to blame. I'd been the one to ask for this, and even though Coach only required me three mornings a week, I'd been coming out the other two to practice on my own. It had seemed like a good idea at the time, and it wasn't so bad on those extra days, but I could kill dream me each time I got to the end of one of Coach Greer's sessions.

Or rather, I felt like past me had tried to kill current me, because I was hurting and I still had a full day of school to get through after this.

Not that I was going to stop.

I positioned myself between the cones for another round of sprint and cut drills, which was the thing Coach had focused on all this week. At least the kids walking in from the parking lot had grown used to it enough that they didn't really stop and stare at me practicing anymore.

I ignored them as Coach said go, focusing on pushing off and driving my legs forward the way he'd shown me. Even tired, I felt good about how I'd done as I rounded the last cone, pushing through the burn in my quads. I jogged it off for a second, letting my muscles cool down, before heading over to join Coach Greer.

"Good work," he said, handing me a water bottle. "Your cutting technique is improving, but you're still dropping your shoulder a bit on those sharp turns. Keep your upper body more upright."

I nodded, gulping down the water. "Got it. I'll watch it."

"Good. You know, I'm really impressed with your progress since we started training. You're noticeably faster and more agile now."

I couldn't help but grin. "Thanks. I've been feeling a difference during sevens practice, too. It's like I'm quicker on my feet, you know? More in control when I'm scrambling."

"That's exactly what we've been working towards. For a quarterback with your playing style, these skills are crucial. Or so I've been told. I'm not the only one who's noticed. I was talking to Coach Holloway the other day, and he mentioned seeing improvement in your performance as well."

"I appreciate that, Coach. I'm just trying to put in the work and get better every day."

That might have sounded a little too 'I'm gonna give a hundred and ten percent' cliché, but it was also true.

"That's the attitude I like to see," Coach Greer said. "Let's do one last run before calling it a day. I want you to put those improvements into action and run that zigzag pattern between the cones again, but this time, really focus on maintaining your upper body position through those cuts."

Damn, I didn't think he'd pull the 'one last run' routine today. I nodded, jogging back to the starting point. I ran the drill again, trying to keep my upper body in the right position.

It was hard for me to tell if I'd done it right, but when I jogged back to Coach, he said, "Much better. You're getting it. Your center of gravity is staying more consistent through the turns now."

"Thanks."

"Alright," Coach Greer said, glancing at his watch. "We're done with training for today."

He must have seen me looking over, eyeing my duffle bag and then the parking lot. I wasn't particularly subtle about it, since I was ready to be done.

"Before you head in, there's one last thing I'd like for you to do."

I resisted groaning. He'd already pulled his 'one last thing.' He was normally in a hurry in the morning when we finished training, I guess because he needed to get inside and set up for his first class. He doubled as our health teacher, and I think he had a first-period class for that.

"What's that, Coach?"

"I'd like you to run the 100 real quick."

I blinked, confused. "Really? We don't usually run that distance in football."

"I know, but I want to get a good measurement of how you've improved. We've been focusing on short bursts and agility, but I want to see your raw speed over a longer distance."

I frowned but said, "uhh, sure."

"I really want to see how much you've improved, so I want you to go all out. Full throttle. Run as hard as you possibly can."

"If you say so."

"And one more thing," Coach added as I walked towards the starting line. "I want you to run it the way I originally showed you, not the altered technique we've been using for football-specific movements."

Now I was really confused. Why go back to the old form after all the work we'd done? Even he'd said it wasn't what I'd use when actually playing. I guess years of being in organized sports took over, though, 'cause I didn't question him. Coaches usually had a reason for wanting things a certain way.

I got into position at the starting line, trying to recall the original form Coach had taught me more than a month ago. It felt a bit strange, completely different from how I'd do it on the field.

"Lower your hips a bit more," he said as I got down. "And keep your front foot a little further back from the line."

I made the corrections, feeling the stretch in my hamstrings as I settled into the proper starting position.

"Remember. I want to see everything you've got. Don't hold anything back."

I nodded, taking a deep breath.

"On your mark. Get set. Go!"

I exploded off the starting line, my legs pumping furiously as I accelerated down the straightaway. I could really feel the fatigue from earlier drills, but I pushed through it, focusing on maintaining the form he'd taught me. Arms tight, driving forward with my body straight so as not to waste energy with lateral movement.

My breath came in short, controlled bursts as I hit my stride.

It was a long run for me. Not even that big run I'd made during the mud bowl was this far. I couldn't remember the conversions, but it was almost as long as a whole football field.

Not a distance quarterbacks were asked to run much. As I entered the final stretch, my legs felt like they were on fire and every fiber in my body screamed at me to slow down. I ignored it and lengthened my stride, driving forward with everything I had left.

With a final burst of speed, I crossed the finish line and stumbled a few steps before managing to slow to a stop, bent over with my hands on my knees as I gasped for air. My lungs felt like they were on fire, and my legs trembled from the exertion.

"Good job!" Coach Greer called out.

I shook off the exhaustion and straightened up, still breathing heavily, and jogged over to where he stood, stopwatch in hand.

"How did you think that was? How fast?"

I shook my head. "No idea. Felt pretty good, I guess."

"Twelve point nine seconds, and that was after a full session."

I wasn't sure how to react. Was that good? Bad?

"Is that ... okay?"

"Okay? Blake, when you first came out here, you ran it in fourteen point two-one seconds, which is only okay for a runner, but pretty good for a football player."

"Well, we have a lot more things to worry about on the field."

"Oh, I know," Coach Greer said quickly. "I'm not criticizing you. The opposite, actually. But what I am really impressed by is how much you've improved."

"Thanks, Coach. I've been working hard."

"It shows. Do you know what kind of times top state-level sprinters run for the hundred meters?"

I shook my head. "No idea."

"The best high school sprinters in Texas are running it in about eleven point three seconds."

"Seriously? That fast?"

"Yep, but I think you're closer to that than you might think you are. If you were warmed up and fresh, I think you could have probably hit twelve point two or twelve point three. You're in striking distance of those winning times. Shaving off a second is hard, but it's achievable with the training you put in."

"I don't know what you're getting at, Coach."

He clapped a hand on my shoulder. "What I'm getting at is you're one of the fastest runners I've got at this school and the two guys faster than you are both juniors. I'd like you to consider trying out for the track team in the spring."

"Oh, uh ... I don't know, Coach. I've got seven-on-seven commitments, and ..."

"We can work around that," Coach Greer said quickly. "There isn't that much after-school football except for sevens and I can coordinate with Coach Holloway. We can make it work."

"I appreciate that, Coach, but I'm looking at getting some additional training in the spring with private trainers. I need time for that."

He looked surprised but actually pleased at the news.

"Really? I gotta say, you keep impressing me with your commitment to your future. But, I think we can make that work too. I'll coordinate to make sure you can do everything, *and* have time for your schoolwork. Look, Blake, I'll be honest, we need you. I've had my eye on the freshman class, and you're the best we've got. You're running faster forties than your running backs and none of the kids that have shown interest in track this spring have your speed either. And definitely not your work ethic. I want you to consider that being a dual-sport athlete has a lot of benefits. Both athletically and it can open up more college scholarship possibilities."

"Ohh," I said.

I hadn't thought about that.

"You've got natural talent, Blake. With some focused training, you could be a real contender in track events. That kind of versatility is very attractive to college recruiters, and it puts you into a category that colleges want to recruit, opening up the door to track scholarships. I know football is your thing and that's your focus, but you never know what's going to happen."

"I guess ..."

While options were always good, that wasn't what I wanted. I didn't want to settle for a different sport because college wasn't my goal.

The NFL was.

"I get it, and I'm not asking you to change your goals. But think about it, okay? Track could complement your football training; make you an even better all-around athlete."

"Sure."

Coach Greer grinned. "I've been a coach long enough to know that tone. I'll let you off the hook for now, but I'm not giving up that easy. I really want you on that track team, Blake."

I couldn't help but laugh. "Okay, okay. I promise I'll give it some serious thought."

"That's all I'm asking," he said, still grinning. "Now go hit the showers. You've earned it today."

I nodded, grabbing my water bottle and towel. It was an interesting option.

Chapter 39

The last week of school before break flew by. I had a bunch of tests to get ready for, and not just the regular end-of-semester tests everyone had to take. I guess Vice Principal Ford had been paying more attention to my extra work than I realized, because she'd arranged for all of the teachers who had me on plans to get on level to give me an additional test to see where I was to determine if I was doing the work to justify the teachers going to the effort.

While I appreciated that the school was really taking my request seriously, and were doing so much to help me, I did not love having double the tests of everyone else in school.

Thankfully, Li stepped in and helped me study. I'd had to cancel on helping out at Eduardo's on the weekend so we could fit the studying in. I also think Melanie was a little annoyed that I'd spent all weekend studying with Li, even after I'd explained why I was doing it.

She didn't say anything directly, and we didn't have another blowout, but I could tell she wasn't happy. I tried spending time with her each day and we went out Saturday night, but I really needed the help studying, and Li was really good at keeping me focused and on task.

By Friday, the last day of school before winter break, I was ready to just be done with it. My brain felt like it had melted. I think the teachers all knew that, because all of the tests were done the day before and today was essentially a goof-off day.

Well, except for conditioning. The coaches never let us skip that.

I got to my locker and started pulling out my gym clothes when Coach Holloway stuck his head through the door and said, "Sims, come here. I need to talk to you."

Oddly, it wasn't the normal "SIMS!" that I got. If anything, it was in a conversational tone.

To be honest, it kind of freaked me out. Coaches yelling at me I could deal with. When they got quiet and nice, I got suspicious. Not that there should be anything for him to be mad at me about. I'd been at all of the sevens practices and I thought I was doing really well at it. We were fielding two teams, and who was going to be on which team hadn't been decided yet, but I managed to beat Ben Harlan's team, even though he had mostly upperclassmen and I had some of my JV guys along with Miguel and Hunter, who was way, way less of a dick without Elijah around.

Elijah was apparently trying out for the baseball team, so he wouldn't be around for sevens, thank God. Mason and Jake were also not participating, although I didn't really know why and Aiden hadn't been paired up to play with me yet.

Which was good, because he was still a dick, even without Elijah around.

I dropped into the seat across from Coach without him asking. I guess he'd called me into his office enough that I was starting to get comfortable, although the frown he gave me when I did caused me to make a mental note to maybe not do that again.

"How're you doing, Blake?" he asked, again, way too casually.

"Good, Coach. Ready for winter break, that's for sure."

"I imagine. You had a hell of a season on JV."

"Thanks," I said, a little confused by the non sequitur and wondering where this was going.

"How'd you feel about the transition to JV? From your perspective, how has it been?"

"Good, I think. I'll admit, it was a little challenging at first, but the last few games of the season I felt really comfortable and I thought it went well."

Of course, what really mattered was if he thought so, too.

"I agree. You've adapted well to the new playbook and I think you have a bright future here, as long as you keep some of that enthusiasm on the field reined in."

I knew he was referring to all the scrambling and the demands for more passing. I would have liked to argue that everything I'd

435

done had worked out, but arguing with coaches rarely ended well for me.

"I'll try."

"Good, because we've got a bit of a situation on our hands. Ben Harlan is moving to Dallas."

I tried to look as surprised as I could. This had happened in my dream life, too, Ben leaving, making me the youngest starting QB in Wheaton history. In that life, I'd gone up to Varsity as Jorden's backup and he'd crashed and burned early in the season, so I was a little ahead of schedule, but Ben leaving was always going to happen.

"What does that mean for the team?"

"With Kenneth Ward graduating and Ben leaving, we've suddenly got an open spot for varsity quarterback," Coach said, watching me closely. "You're the most obvious choice to step up."

"I'm ready, Coach," I said, trying to sound nervous and excited.

Coach held up a hand. "Now, hold on, Blake. This isn't a done deal. Moving you to varsity would mean Jorden Kinsell becomes varsity backup, and Gabriel Neiva takes over as JV starter. It makes sense on paper, but I've got some concerns."

I hadn't gotten this speech the first time through, but then I'd only been the backup and, at the time, Jorden was a senior. Adding me had been a reaction, not a plan.

I just hoped that didn't make things change. Coach hadn't had time to consider the ramifications of putting a sophomore in as their starter after two huge losses in the dream life. Now that he had, I hoped he didn't second guess himself.

"Starting a sophomore on varsity is a big deal, Blake. The jump from JV to varsity is significant. We're talking about bigger, faster, more experienced opponents. You did well on JV, but that was only for half a season, and let's be honest, some of those teams weren't exactly powerhouses."

"I know it'll be tough, Coach, but I'm ready for the challenge. I've been working hard, and I know I can step up."

"It's not just about physical ability, Blake. To succeed at the varsity level, you'll need to develop your arm strength, improve the mental part of your game the most. I'm talking about your pocket awareness, being able to make faster decisions, and really honing your ability to read defenses. It's a whole different ballgame."

"I understand, Coach. I've actually been thinking about this a lot. You know I'm doing seven-on-seven, and I think that will help me improve over the spring, and I'm going to continue training with Coach Greer. Also, it has been a while since we talked about it, but I've been looking into additional coaching. I've talked to my dad and I think we've worked out a way to pay for it. We're hoping to get started in February or March, once we find the right coach."

"Really? That's good to hear. It shows you're taking this seriously."

"I am taking this seriously, Coach. I know it's a big step, but I really believe I can do this. I'm not just talking about playing varsity; I think I can lead this team to state."

We'd only made it to the semifinals in the dream life, but I hadn't been putting in serious work then. Plus, I didn't know everything I knew now, having already done it all once before. Maybe I was being overly optimistic, but I really believed we could do it.

Assuming Coach didn't revert back to his all-running playbook.

Coach Holloway's eyebrows shot up, and for a moment, I worried he'd think I was just blowing smoke, but then he chuckled. "I like the confidence, Sims."

"So I'm the new starter on varsity?"

"Nothing's official yet," Coach said firmly. "We'll evaluate your progress through the spring. If you do everything you just laid out and show the improvement we're looking for, then we'll talk about making it official."

"I'll be ready, Coach," I promised, and then remembered something else. "Oh, did Coach Greer talk to you about the track team?"

"He did mention it, yeah. What are you thinking about that?"

"I'm not sure. Football is my priority, and I told him that. He said he could work around my schedule, but I wanted to talk to you first."

Coach leaned back in his chair, considering. "Well, you'll certainly have a full plate if you do seven-on-seven, private coaching, *and* track. I talked to him and I think, just scheduling-wise, we can work around your school and seven-on-seven commitments at least. It'll be up to you for everything else."

"But should I do it?"

"I can't make the decision for you. I can say the speed training has definitely helped your game, and I think running track could further improve your speed. But it's up to you to decide if your schedule can handle it all."

I could only nod. Damn. It would have been easier if he had just said yes or no!

Walking through Eduardo's living room, I realized I might have made a mistake. Things had started off really well after we got everything set up, with a bunch of guys from the team showing up along with a bunch of the cheerleaders.

Sarah had come to help set up, so that part made sense and I'd invited guys from the team. Except the flow of new arrivals never stopped. By the time Miguel's older brother dropped off a keg, more than sixty kids had shown up. The entire football team was here, and not just JV, but the varsity and the freshman teams, too, along with both JV and varsity cheer squads and even a bunch of kids I didn't know.

The house was a wall of kids drinking and dancing; so many that they were spilling out and filling both the backyard and the front yard.

Any hope Eduardo might have had of keeping this small and manageable had gone out the window.

I couldn't help feeling bad. I told him I'd talk to Melanie and Sarah and make sure we kept this under control, and clearly we'd done a bad job of it.

I found Eduardo in the kitchen looking like a cornered animal.

"Hey, man," I said, clapping him on the shoulder. "How're you holding up?"

"This is insane. There's way more people than we planned for."

"Yeah, I'm really sorry about that, but don't worry. I've already talked to Mickey, Joe, and some of the other guys on the team. They've all agreed to help clean up afterward. We'll get this place back to normal so your parents won't know what hit it."

"I'm not sure that will save it. All the kids out in the yard ..."

"Yeah. Well, as long as no one breaks anything and we don't have big trouble, it should be okay."

"What if someone calls the cops?"

"Then we'll," I started to say, before a commotion at the front door caught my attention.

My stomach dropped as I saw Elijah and Mason swagger in. Worse, Elijah was already visibly drunk and very loud.

"What a dump! Who lives in this shithole?"

I felt Eduardo stiffen beside me. Elijah had the normal sneer on his face, which turned into a mean grin as his gaze landed on me and Eduardo, and he started pushing his way through the crowd.

"Well, well," Elijah slurred as he reached us. "If it isn't the big man and his new pet."

I stepped forward, putting myself between Elijah and Eduardo.

"Not tonight, Elijah. Just turn around and leave."

"Or what, Sims? You gonna make me?"

This wasn't school or practice. I didn't have to control myself to keep from getting kicked off the team or suspended, which meant I wasn't going to back down from him.

It was damn near time for Elijah to learn he wasn't as tough as he thought he was.

"Yeah, if I have to."

Elijah's grin grew bigger, as if he'd been waiting for this moment. He started to take a step toward me, his fists balling up, and then froze in place as Andre and Joe materialized on either side of me. Several other players closed ranks behind him, forming a wall between Elijah and the rest of the party and making it clear he and Mason were surrounded.

"Can't fight on your own, chicken shit? Gotta have your little fan club stand up for you?"

I opened my mouth to point out he had Mason right beside him, and we both knew that he wasn't going to stay out of it once I started to pound on him, when Kenneth showed up.

"Everything alright over here?"

"Just having a chat with the coach's new golden boy. Can you believe it, after you leave, they're putting him on varsity? Makes you wonder how long he spent on his knees in the coach's office to get that deal."

"Actually, Coach asked me who should be starting QB after I leave. I was the one who recommended Blake. I even hear Coach is thinking about making him team captain."

It was nice to hear Kenneth had suggested me, but we both knew Coach Holloway wasn't the sort to make decisions based on what other people suggested. Although, the captain thing was news to me.

I kept a straight face, though, not wanting to give Elijah the satisfaction of seeing my surprise.

Elijah's mouth opened and closed like a fish out of water. "You've gotta be kidding me. This team is gonna be a joke next year if that happens."

"I'd watch what you say, Elijah. Blake's got a lot of support, both on the team and with the coaches. You might want to think real hard about which side of this you want to be on," Kenneth said.

Elijah's eyes narrowed as he looked between Kenneth and me, the wheels visibly turning in his alcohol-addled brain. After a long moment, he spat on the floor and stormed off, Mason trailing behind him like a lost puppy.

As the tension dissipated, I turned to Kenneth. "Thanks for the backup. But ... captain? That's the first I'm hearing about that."

"Nothing's set in stone yet, but Coach has been talking you up. Says you've got real leadership potential. Between you and me, I think you'd be good for the team. But you know Coach. No one can tell him what he's gonna do."

"No kidding, although it kinda makes the 'I made the decision' speech a little bullshit, doesn't it."

"Ha, yeah, I guess it does. Still, he did ask me and I think it's the right call. Just don't screw up my legacy," he said with a laugh, slapping me on the arm.

As Kenneth moved off to rejoin the party, I turned back to Eduardo, who'd managed to get some of the color back in his face.

"Well, now that that's over, let's try to enjoy your party, yeah?"

Once he got out and started to talk to people, Eduardo calmed down. It might have been a little overwhelming at first, but I think it didn't take long for him to realize that he actually knew most of the people here. He'd been hanging out with us most of the semester, and they liked him. Especially once he started getting friendly with Sarah.

We started having a good time. I found Melanie a few times, but she was mostly hanging out with cheerleaders and I kept getting dragged off by the guys. She was having a good time, though.

I kept swinging by to check on her, both because I didn't want her to think I'd abandoned her and because she was steadily getting more drunk. I had nothing against drinking, really, and was drinking myself, but I'd kept it to a low level.

She didn't.

On my latest trip, I found her at the bottom of the steps, swaying and holding up a bottle of liquor that I hoped didn't belong to Eduardo's parents, since it looked practically empty.

Emily and Hanna were with her, both looking almost as unsteady. They were all giggling and passing the bottle from one to another.

"Whoops!" Melanie laughed as she stumbled, sloshing the liquor onto the floor. "I think we need a refill!"

I quickened my pace, reaching her just as she started to topple over, catching her arm and steadying her.

"Hey! Where've you been? You're missing all the fun!"

She was sweating heavily, her words were slurring together, and she could barely hold herself up.

"I think you've had enough fun for tonight," I said, gently prying the bottle from her fingers.

She pouted, reaching for the drink. "No fair! Give it back!"

"Come on, Mel. Let's get you somewhere to sit down for a bit."

"I don't need ... ohh, I don't feel so good," she said, looking a little green.

Eduardo and Sarah, both of whom were thankfully sober, showed up at that moment.

"Everything okay?"

"Yeah, she's just had a little too much to drink and I need to get her to lie down for a while. Mind if I use your room?"

"Of course not. Do you need help?"

"Nah, I've got her. Maybe you can check on those two," I said, pointing at Emily and Hanna, who looked equally green.

They went to help the other two drunk cheerleaders as I tried to guide Melanie up the stairs. She slipped on the very first one, her entire weight on me. Making a quick decision, I scooped her up in my arms. She squealed in delight, throwing her arms around my neck.

"Ooh, so strong!" she cooed, nuzzling against my chest. "My big, strong quarterback."

I just shook my head in amusement as I carried her up the stairs, careful not to bump her head on the wall. When we reached Eduardo's room, I shouldered the door open and gently laid her on the bed.

"There you go. Just rest here for a bit, okay?"

Melanie immediately tried to sit up. "No way! The party's just getting started!"

I put a hand on her shoulder, easing her back down. "Mel, you need to sleep this off. Another drink, and you're going to spend the night with your head in a toilet."

She giggled, grabbing my shirt and trying to pull me down beside her. "Only if you stay with me."

"Melanie, stop," I said firmly, extricating myself from her grip. "You're drunk. This isn't a good idea."

I'd had many fantasies, both in the dream life and since we'd started dating, of being with her. Melanie was maybe one of the most beautiful people I'd ever known, but I didn't want our first time together to be like this. Odds were, she wouldn't even remember it the next morning.

She did not take my hesitation the way I intended.

"Why not? Don't you want me?"

"Of course I do. But not like this. You're wasted."

"I knew it," she said angrily. "You'd rather be with Li, wouldn't you?"

"What? No. Come on, that's not fair. I just don't want to do this with you when you're this drunk."

Melanie's lower lip trembled, tears welling up in her eyes.

"I'm sorry. I didn't mean it. Please don't be mad at me."

I sat on the edge of the bed and said, "I'm not mad, Mel. I just want you to be safe."

"You're so good to me, Blake. I don't deserve you."

"No, I don't deserve you, which is why I want to wait until we're both going to remember being together."

Melanie's eyes were growing heavy, her words becoming more slurred. "You're right. You're always right. I'm just gonna ... rest my eyes for a minute ..."

Within moments, her breathing evened out as she drifted off to sleep. I carefully rolled her onto her side, making sure she wouldn't choke if she got sick. Then I grabbed the trash can from the corner and placed it next to the bed, just in case.

I stood there for a moment, watching her sleep and feeling a mix of emotions I couldn't quite sort out. Part of me wanted to stay, to make sure she was okay. But I knew that would only lead to more complications when she woke up.

With a heavy sigh, I turned and left the room, quietly shutting the door behind me.

I thought maybe it was my imagination as I turned back toward the stairs that the party seemed a lot quieter than it had when I'd gone upstairs. The music was just as loud as it had been, but something felt off.

I realized that the amount of chatter had dropped way off, and the music was the only real noise, which was what made it seem subdued.

I found the reason for it as soon as I hit the bottom of the stairs. Rafe was standing in the front doorway, blocking it, flanked by two guys I didn't recognize. I didn't have to know them to know how they knew Rafe, though. Smart money said they were guys from Rafe's gang.

"Where's my little cousin, huh? Too good for his own family now?"

Eduardo emerged from the kitchen, his face pale. "Rafe, what are you doing here?"

"What am I doing here?" Rafe's laugh was harsh. "Funny, I was gonna ask you the same thing. Why weren't you at your tía's birthday party, huh? But you can throw a party for all the white people?"

443

The way he spat out "people" made my blood boil. I started to move forward, but Joe caught my arm, shaking his head in warning.

"I called her and wished her happy birthday and explained it to her."

"Bullshit. You're forgetting where you come from, primo. Family comes first. Always. Which is why you're going to get rid of these people and come with us."

I couldn't stay quiet any longer. I didn't know what Eduardo was going to say to that, but this was the moment. I needed to break them apart once and for all if I was going to keep Eduardo from doing what he was destined to do.

I shook off Joe and pushed through the kids, stepping into the space that had opened up around Rafe, no one wanting to be near him.

"This is a private party. You weren't invited."

"Stay out of this, puta. This is family business."

Thankfully, I wasn't alone and several guys from the team backed me up. His guys might be tough, but Andre and Tyrell were huge. In a heartbeat, instead of facing me, he was facing ten guys whose body language said they were ready to back me up.

The almost sneers Rafe's guys had worn the whole time broke slightly as they started to do the math and realized they weren't in quite the position they thought they'd be in.

"Eddie's my friend. That makes it my business."

Rafe took a step towards me, his breath reeking of cheap beer. "You think you can come in here and play savior? You don't know shit about him or where he comes from."

"I know where he could go. What he could be capable of. And I know he'll never get there if he gets mixed up with you. Tell me again, how many of your 'friends' are in prison?"

Rafe's hand shot out, grabbing the front of my shirt. "You better watch your mouth, pendejo."

The room went dead silent. I could feel the tension. This was about to escalate, everyone on the verge of doing something really stupid.

"Get out, Rafe," Eduardo said, not shouting but loud and serious.

Rafe's head whipped around, his grip on my shirt loosening. "What did you say?"

"I said, get out. You and your friends. I don't want you here."

"You're going to pick this guy over family?"

"Family doesn't try to drag you down. Family supports you. These people," he gestured to the room, to me and the guys, "they're my friends. They support me. You? I have no interest in you or your ... friends."

To say Rafe was pissed was an understatement. He shoved me back, hard enough that I stumbled.

"You're gonna regret this, primo. Both of you."

With a jerk of his head, Rafe and his buddies stormed out, slamming the door behind them. Everyone at the party was frozen for a moment.

"Fuck them. This is a party, right?" Eduardo said, which may be the most unlike-him thing he'd ever said.

Which was something.

As everyone got back to partying, I put a hand on his shoulder and said, "You okay, man?"

He nodded, although his face made it clear how much the inter-action had shaken him up.

"Yeah, I think so. Thanks."

"Hey, that's what friends are for."

"No, I mean it. That's the second time you stood up to Rafe for me. It means a lot."

"Look, Eduardo, I'm just gonna be blunt here. I know what Rafe is trying to do, what he wants you to be a part of. You can't do it, man. You've got so much going for you. Getting mixed up in that, it would ruin everything. Not just your future, but your family's future, too. You've seen what's happened to everyone else who's gotten mixed up with him."

"I know, and you're right, and I wouldn't. I'm done with him, I swear. These last few months ... they've been the best of my life. For the first time, I feel like I belong somewhere. I didn't even feel like this when we were in Midland, and I lived there my whole life before moving here. I'm not going to throw this away. Not for Rafe, not for anyone."

Those were the words I'd been shooting for ever since I'd decided to try and change the future.

"Good. That's ... that's really good to hear, man."

The cops showed up and broke up the party about ten minutes later, which was probably for the best. Thankfully, no one went to jail for underage drinking.

One of the upsides of being a cop's kid, is that the police knew me and gave me some slack ... especially after we turned over the still half-full keg to them for 'evidence.'

They let us all scatter as long as no one who was drunk drove home, which wasn't a problem in a small town like this, where most of us lived within walking distance. Hanna and a couple of other cheerleaders were sober, or at least sober enough, and offered to get Meredith and the other drunk girls home safely, which was honestly a relief.

It saved me for being on the hook for Melanie's condition with her parents. Other girls bringing her home, it was a thing that happened. Her boyfriend bringing her home, it was me getting her drunk for nefarious reasons.

That only left Eduardo, me, and a few of the guys still sober enough to clean up the mess from the party. Except for a few moments, it had been fun. More importantly, Eduardo had publicly and very firmly separated himself from Rafe.

It felt good.

Chapter 40

The next week flew by and before I knew it, it was Christmas morning and I was waking up to the sound of muffled voices downstairs. I loved Christmas and was excited, although a lot of that was tempered by how things had been around the house since Thanksgiving.

Mom and Dad had started talking to each other again, but everything had been tense. The worst part was that there was nothing I could do about it. Except for that first night when Dad had slept in the guest room, they hadn't been sleeping in separate rooms, so I guess it could have been worse.

But it made everything at home a little more muted, made worse by the fact that Joshua acted like he'd won, instead of being the cause of all the strife in our family.

Still, it was Christmas, so hopefully today, everyone would decide to be on their best behavior and get along.

As I made my way downstairs, I could smell the canned cinnamon rolls Dad had bought a few days ago mixed with the scent of pine from the Christmas tree.

A big step up from our normal plastic Christmas tree that stayed in the attic for the first time in my life. Dad had gone all out with the decorations this year, probably trying to compensate for how everything else was going around the house.

When I got to the living room door, I paused, trying to just take in and enjoy the moment. The tree was lit up and there was a serious pile of presents under it.

Mom was curled up on the couch, clutching a steaming mug that gave off a pungent odor. One of her herbal concoctions that she'd been drinking more and more. She looked pale, squinting at the twinkling lights as if they hurt her eyes.

"Merry Christmas, Mom," I said as I walked into the room.

I had been overcompensating a little over the last month. Mom still sided with Josh way more than was fair, but I'd hoped that maybe I could do something to ease the tension around here.

It hadn't worked so far, but I kept trying.

"Merry Christmas," she said, her voice strained.

Dad emerged from the kitchen, carrying a tray of cinnamon rolls.

"Last one up as always."

"Not the last one. Josh isn't here."

"He went up to his room for a second."

Like the demon he was, Josh appeared, summoned by his name, bounding down the stairs, nearly knocking me over in his rush to get to the presents.

"See, he's up. Can we open them now? Please?"

"Hold your horses. Let's all get settled first."

Dad put the rolls on the coffee table and started handing out presents, one at a time, just like he always did while Josh and I ate our rolls. Once they were all handed out, we began to tear into them.

Josh was, for once, acting like a normal kid instead of a psychopath as he revealed a brand new Super Nintendo, along with some games, clothes, and a remote-controlled car from me.

"Heather, this one's for you," Dad said, handing Mom a small box after she had already opened some dresses, books, and perfume I'd picked out for her out of the small amount of gambling money I'd had Dad hold back for presents, but clearly this was a special present he'd saved for her.

She opened it slowly, revealing a delicate necklace. I didn't know much about jewelry, but it looked pretty expensive. For a moment, her face softened, and she looked up at Dad with a hint of a smile. But just as quickly, her expression soured again. She set the necklace box aside without a word.

Dad was clearly annoyed by her response, but he shifted back into happy Christmas mode, I guess not wanting to ruin it for us. He got golf clubs, a sweater, and a cookbook from me, part joke and part necessity since he'd been doing most of the cooking lately.

I was pretty happy with my presents. Some new running shoes, which would help with the running Coach Greer had me doing in my free time to build stamina, a pretty hefty gift certificate for clothes, and a Discman, which I'd asked for so that I would have something to listen to on long bus rides to games.

About when the last present was opened, Mom stood up shakily and said, "I think I need to lie down for a bit. Enjoy your presents."

Dad and I both looked at each other worried, but Josh seemed not to even notice.

"Can I hook up my Nintendo now?"

Dad frowned but said, "Sure. I'll help you set it up."

As they busied themselves with the new game system, I started gathering up the discarded wrapping paper and hauled it all to the outside garbage can before grabbing my stuff and taking it up to my room. I wanted it all locked away while Josh was excited and focused on his game rather than being a pain in the ass.

When I made it back downstairs, Dad was in the kitchen, cleaning up dishes while Josh was loudly playing his games in the other room. I leaned against the counter, watching him work.

"That was quite the Christmas haul this year," I said, trying to keep my tone casual. "You really went all out."

Dad glanced over his shoulder and said, "Well, we have you to thank for that. Your latest round of bets paid off big time."

"Yeah? How big are we talking?"

Dad dried his hands on a dishtowel and turned to face me. "Let's just say we did *extremely* well. Enough to pay some money back to you, put a chunk in savings, and still splurge on gifts."

"What about Mom's medical stuff? I thought that's what the money was for."

"That was the original plan, but ... things have changed. Your mother's decided to try other avenues."

"You mean her ..."

"So," Dad said, cutting me off abruptly, his tone making it clear he didn't want to discuss it further. "Even with placing some losing bets to keep under the radar, we both came out way ahead."

Part of me wanted to keep pressing, but it was Christmas. No reason to make everyone have a bad day.

"How much?"

"You ready for this?" He said dramatically. "You now have one hundred and ninety-seven thousand dollars. With the additional five thousand as pay back from me, that puts you just over two hundred grand."

My jaw dropped. "Two hundred thousand dollars? Are you serious?"

"Dead serious. It's a life-changing amount of money, son."

I let out a low whistle, considering the possibilities.

"I want to start looking for the trainers we talked about. I want to really capitalize on the off-season for football."

"I figured you might. We'll begin the search after the holidays, but even if we get everything you wanted, that's only going to be a part of what you earned so far. I really think you should consider investing a good chunk of this money instead of just continuing to gamble."

I shook my head. "I want to keep betting for a while longer. Long run, the trainers will eat up a lot, and I have college to think about afterward. I don't know how long I'll know what to bet on, but I want to ride it out as long as I do."

"I get that, and considering your track record, I'm not going to disagree on principle, but gambling with sums this large is going to attract unwanted attention, even if we keep putting in losers. I think it's best to keep your gambling threshold low. How about we invest half and continue betting with the rest?"

"Okay, that makes sense," I said, thinking hard.

I'd been thinking about what I wanted to put money into that wasn't gambling since Dad had brought it up last time. But I could only think of a few companies that would be worth a lot. Some didn't exist yet, or at least I didn't think they did, but I had gone by the library, looked at some newspapers, and found one that I knew was new and would be huge one day.

"Actually, I have a specific company in mind for investment."

"Oh?"

"Yeah, it's a small business out in California. I think now is the time to invest in it, but I'm not sure how to go about it. I was actually thinking about talking to Coach Plummer."

I'd spent some time thinking about this. I couldn't just show up money in hand and tell people I wanted to invest in their company. They'd definitely have questions I couldn't answer.

What I needed was someone who knew money and business, and Coach Plummer owned one of the largest businesses in town and knew about this stuff. If anyone knew what to do, it would be him.

"Are you sure about the company? How do you know about it, and how are you going to explain that to Mr. Plummer?"

"I'm not going to explain it. I'm just going to tell him I have the money and that I want to do this and try to convince him like I convinced you. And yes, I'm sure about the company. It won't take off right away, but in the next few years, it's going to become huge. I want to get in on the ground floor if the guy is still working out of his garage."

"How much are you thinking?"

"Maybe a hundred thousand? That leaves fifty for this year's coaches and fifty to keep betting, which is more than I started with, so I should be able to turn it into real money."

Dad mulled it over. "I'm not sure bringing someone else in on what you're able to do is a good idea."

"It's the only option. You and I don't know how to invest in things like this. We need someone who does."

"True. Still, it's a lot of money to risk on an unknown startup."

"Trust me, Dad, I know what I'm doing."

He studied me for a long moment, then nodded. "Alright, we'll talk to Mr. Plummer after the holidays. For now, how about we focus on lunch?"

"Sure."

As Dad started pulling ingredients from the fridge, I felt a wave of satisfaction wash over me. I couldn't believe it. I'd made this plan only a few months ago; I hadn't expected it to work out so well so fast.

True, not everything was great. I still had Joshua's increasingly disturbing behavior, Mom's illness, and Rafe's promise that he wasn't done with Eduardo and me to worry about.

Still, as I watched Dad trying to navigate the kitchen, I felt a surge of optimism. My prospects for varsity football and a future in the sport were better than ever. I had solid friendships, much better than the ones in the dream life, was well on the way to fixing my education, and a girlfriend who, despite our ups and downs, made me happy. Most importantly, Dad was safe. There was no way Eduardo would end up joining the gang and no way he'd end up killing my father.

No. On the whole, everything was working out great.

Dad glanced up from the cutting board, catching my eye. "What's that smile for?"

"I'm just happy."

To Be Continued ...

About the author

Travis writes science fiction, fantasy, and thriller novels (and the occasional coming-of-age story), with the hope of transporting and enthralling readers. Publishing novels since 2015, Travis's passion is creating worlds and characters that live and breathe, and experiencing the joy of those stories with his readers. When not writing, Travis enjoys connecting with readers and other writers, managing the popular Complete Marvel Reading Order website, where he works on his other passion for comics and graphic novels, and spending time with his family.
If you have enjoyed this book, please consider taking a moment to rate or review it wherever you found your copy, as it helps new readers find my works and ensures I can continue writing book into the future.

Find out more at:
amazon.com/TravisStarnes/e/B072YBDC3S/

Or visit
https://tstarnes.com

Maps available at
https://tstarnes.com/book-series/imperium/

Signup to get free previews and notifications of upcoming books
at
http://tstarnes.com/preview-notification-newsletter/

Also by

John Taylor Stories

Rebirth
False Signs
The Wrong Girl
Burying the Past
Family Ties
Election Day
Danger Close
Extraction
Designated Target
Border Crossed
Desperate Rendition

Country Roads Series

Playing by Ear
Fanfare
Dissonance
Elegy
From the Top
Center Stage

Imperium Series

Volume 1
The Sword of Jupiter
The Trumpets of Mars
The Sands of Saturn
The Depths of Neptune
The Fires of Vulcan
The Triumph of Venus
Volume 2
The Wings of Mercury
The Plains of Pluto

Shattered Lands Series

In the Shadow of Lions
An Ending of Oaths
The Barons' War

False Start Series

Second Down
Setback

The Veilguard Saga

Threads of Destiny
The Blackstar Legacy

Stand Alone

Going Home